THE SPIRIT-RAPPER

THE SPIRIT-RAPPER

AN AUTOBIOGRAPHY

O. A. BROWNSON

Published by Wildside Press, LLC.
Visit us online at wildsidepress.com

PREFACE.

If the critics undertake to determine, by any recognized rules of art, to what class of literary productions the following unpretending work belongs, I think they will be sorely puzzled. I am sure I am puzzled myself to say what it is. It is not a novel; it is not a romance; it is not a biography of a real individual; it is not a dissertation, an essay, or a regular treatise; and yet it perhaps has some elements of them all, thrown together in just such a way as best suited my convenience, or my purpose.

I wanted to write a book, easy to write and not precisely hard to read, on the new superstition, or old superstition under a new name, exciting just now no little attention at home and abroad; and I chose such a literary form as I—not, properly speaking, a literary man—could best manage, and which would afford me the most facilities for bringing distinctly before the reader the various points to which I wished to direct his attention. If the critics think that I have chosen badly, they are at liberty to bestow upon the author as much of the castigation which, in his capacity of Reviewer, he has for many years been in the habit of bestowing upon others, as they think proper. I have thought it but fair to give those whom I may have offended by my own criticisms in another place, an opportunity to pay their debts and wipe off old scores.

The book, though affecting some degree of levity, is serious in its aims, and truthful in its statements. There is no fiction in it, save its machinery. What is given as fact, is fact, or at least so regarded by the author. The facts narrated, or strictly analogous facts, I have either seen myself, or given on what I regard as ample evidence. The theory presented as their explanation, and the reasoning by which it is sustained, speak for themselves, and are left to the judgment of the reader.

The connection of spirit-rapping, or the spirit-manifestations, with modern philanthropy, visionary reforms, socialism, and revolutionism, is not an imagination of my own. It is historical, and asserted by the Spiritists, or Spiritualists themselves, as any one may satisfy himself who can have the patience to look through their Library. I have endeavored to be scrupulously exact in all my statements and representations in this respect. The shafts which the author shoots at random may perhaps hit some well-meaning persons who get crotchets in their heads, or astride of hobbies; but they are not poisoned with malice, and will titillate the skin, rather than penetrate the flesh.

I have not aimed at originality, or at displaying my erudition in the Black Art. I have certainly read some on the subject, and at one period of my life made myself acquainted with more "deviltry" than ever did or ever will do me any good. I have however drawn very little from "forbidden" sources. In writing, I have used freely a recent French work, from which I have taken the larger portion of my facts, and many of my arguments, although I had previously studied the subject for myself, had learned the same facts, with one or two exceptions, from other sources, and had adopted the same solution. The work I refer to is entitled, *Pneumatologie des Esprits et de leurs Manifestations fluidiques*. By the Marquis Etudes de M——. Paris, 1853. There are some views, not unimportant, in this work, which I am not prepared to accept; but, upon the whole, it is the only really sensible and scientific work I have seen on the subject, and I freely confess that I have done little more than transfer its substance to my pages.

The volume when it was begun was intended to be published anonymously, but my publishers have preferred to issue it with the name of the author. I think they have judged unwisely, but as they ought to know their own trade better than I, and as there is nothing in it that I am particularly ashamed of or unwilling to avow, I cheerfully comply with their request, and send it out with my name, to make or mar its fortune. If it tend in any degree to throw light on the dark facts of history, to check superstition, to rebuke unreasoning scepticism, and to recall the age to faith in the Gospel of our Lord, the purpose, the serious purpose, for which it was written will be answered, and I shall be content, whatever reception it may otherwise meet from the public.

THE AUTHOR.

Boston, August 11, 1854.

CHAPTER I.
THE FIRST LESSON.

My days are numbered; I am drawing near to the close of my earthly pilgrimage, and I must soon take my final departure,—whither, I dread to think. But before I go I would leave a brief record of some incidents in my worse than unprofitable life. A few who have known me, and will have the charity to breathe a prayer at my grave, may be glad to possess it; and others of my countrymen, who know not what to think of the marvellous phenomena daily and hourly exhibited in their midst, or are vainly striving to explain them on natural principles, may find it neither uninteresting nor uninstructive.

Of my exterior life I have not much to record, for though few have played a more active or important part in the great events of the past few years, my name has rarely been connected with them before the public. I was born in a small town in Western New York. My parents were honest agriculturists from Connecticut, and descended from ancestors who, with Hooker, founded the colony of Hartford. They were among the early settlers of what used to be called the "Holland Purchase," and, till emigrating to the new world west of the Genesee, were rigid Puritans. Like most emigrants from the land of "steady habits," they were intelligent, moral, industrious, and economical, and, as a matter of course, soon prospered in this world's goods, and became able to give their only son the best education the State could furnish, and to leave him a competent estate. I made my preparatory studies at Batavia, and entered, at seventeen, the Freshman class of Union College, Schenectady. I remained at college four years, a diligent, if not a brilliant student, and graduated at the close with the highest standing, and the general love and esteem of my classmates.

My early predilection was for the mathematical and physical sciences. The moral and intellectual sciences were not much to my taste. I took no great interest in them. They struck me as vague, uncertain, and unprofitable. I preferred what M. Comte has since called *Positive Philosophy*. I soon mastered mathematics, mechanics, and physics, as far as they were taught in our college, but I found my greatest delight in chemistry, which, by its subtle analyses, seemed to promise me an approach to the vital principle and to the essences of things.

On leaving college I studied—not very profoundly—medicine, and took my degree, less with a view to professional practice, in which I never engaged, than with a view to general science. After taking my degree as Doctor of Medicine, I resumed and extended my college studies, entered largely into the study of natural history, physical geography, zoölogy, geology, mineralogy, and indeed all the 'ologies, then so fashionable that one must have a smattering of them if he would woo successfully his sweetheart. I paid some attention to Gall and Spurzheim's new science of Phrenology, when Spurzheim visited this country, where he died, and was much interested in it till I had the misfortune to listen to a course of lectures in its exposition and defence, by George Combe, Esq., the great Scottish phrenologist. That course upset me, and I have since abandoned Phrenology, save so far as I find it taught by Plato in his Timæus, and only laughed at its pretensions and its adherents.

I was arrested, for a moment, by Boston Transcendentalism, but I could not make much of it. Its chiefs told me that I was not spiritual enough to appreciate it, and that I was too much under the despotism of the understanding to be able to rise to those empyrean regions where the soul asserts her freedom, and sports with infinite delight in all the luxury of the unintelligible. I thought they talked metaphysics, what neither their hearers nor themselves could understand; and finding myself very little enlightened by their intelligible unintelligibility, their dark utterances, and their Orphic sayings, I gave them up, and returned to my laboratory.

About 1836, I made the acquaintance of Dr. P——, or, as he claimed to be, the Marquis de P——, a native of one of the French West India Islands, but brought up and educated at Paris, where he had been a Saint-Simonian, and a chief of the *savans* of the new religion. The decision of the French courts in 1833, that Saint-Simonism was not a religion, and therefore that its chiefs were not priests, and entitled to a salary from the state, dispersed the new sect, and he soon after came to the United States, and commenced, though with a very imperfect knowledge of our language, and very little facility in speaking it, a course of lectures in several of our eastern cities, on Mesmerism, or, as he preferred to call it, Animal Magnetism. His appearance was by no means prepossessing, and his manners, though unpretending, were very far from indicating that exquisite grace and polish which are supposed, for what reason I know not, to be peculiar to the Frenchman; but he was a serious, earnest-minded man, who in several branches of science had made solid studies. I knew him well, and esteemed him much.

At that time I had paid not much attention to Mesmerism. I had heard of Mesmer indeed, of his extraordinary pretensions, and the wonderful phenomena which he professed to produce by his rod and tub; but I had supposed that the matter had been put at rest for all sensible persons by the famous report of the French Academy in 1784, signed, among others, by Bailly the astronomer, and our own Franklin. I supposed that every scientific man acquiesced in the conclusion of that report, that the extraordinary phenomena exhibited by magnetism were to be ascribed to the imagination, and that from the date of that report magnetism had ceased to occupy the attention of the scientific. I was therefore surprised, nay, scandalized, to find a man of real science, and, as I wished to believe, of real worth, professing faith in what I had been led to regard as an exploded humbug, and which, at the very best, could have no practical utility beyond illustrating the deceptive power of the imagination, and the sad consequences which might result to those weak-minded people who become dupes to their own disordered fancy.

Moreover, he assured me, that the report of the Academy had not settled the question, or seriously checked the cultivation or the progress of Animal Magnetism. It had at no moment ceased to be studied and practised, chiefly for its therapeutic effects, and, as he proved to me, was at the time firmly held and practised by large numbers of the most upright, benevolent, learned, and scientific members of the medical profession in France, Germany, and Great Britain. It had continued to make progress, and was now very generally held and respected on the continent of Europe. If I would not be behind my age, if I would not remain ignorant of a very curious and interesting class of phenomena, I must, he insisted, investigate and make myself acquainted with Animal Magnetism. I should do it as a lover of science; I should do it more especially as a lover of my race, as a friend of humanity; for I might rest assured that Animal Magnetism is the most facile and powerful means ever yet discovered of solacing, and to a great extent curing, a thousand ills that flesh is heir to.

My curiosity, I confess, was excited, and I resolved to investigate the subject. Dr. P—— had picked up, somewhere in Rhode Island, a somnambulist, an honest, simple-minded young woman, of no great strength of intellect, and very little education or knowledge. She was sickly, and suffering from some nervous affection. He had found her very susceptible to the mesmeric influence, and he made her the subject of numerous experiments. He had brought her, in the winter of 1836-7, to Boston, and there exhibited her to his class. Spending that winter in the same city, I consented one afternoon to be present at his experiments. There were some twenty or thirty gentlemen present on the occasion, mostly lawyers, physicians, ministers, and literary and scientific gentlemen of distinction, all disbelievers in Mesmerism, and on the alert to detect the least sign of deception or complicity.

The Doctor introduced his patient, who took her seat in an arm-chair placed in the centre of the room, and, without any visible sign from Dr. P——, was in a few minutes apparently fast asleep. Her breathing was regular, her pulse natural, and her sleep sound and tranquil. Was it sleep? It was, as far as we could ascertain, and sleep accompanied by complete insensibility. We resorted to every imaginable contrivance to awaken her. One tickled her nose with a feather, another shook her with all his might, another discharged a pistol close to her ear, another stuck pins and needles into her flesh,—all without the least effect. There was no quivering or shrinking, no muscular contraction, and to the rudest proofs she was as insensible as a corpse. We all exhausted our inventive powers in vain, and stood astounded, unwilling to trust our own senses, and yet unable to detect the least conceivable deception or collusion. We none of us knew what to think or say. We were taken all aback.

Various written questions, after we had given over trying to awaken her, were handed to Dr. P——, which he put to her mentally, without a word or sign that we could any of us discern, and to which she instantly answered. One question was, the time of the day; she answered, and answered correctly, much more so than most gentlemen's watches present. To every question put she answered, and so far as any of us knew, or could ascertain, with perfect accuracy. The Doctor at length told her he thought she had slept long enough, and would do well to wake up. Instantly she was wide awake, and apparently unconscious of all that had passed. She remained awake for some time, when Dr. P—— said to her, "I will you to go to sleep again for just fifteen minutes, and then to wake up." Instantly she dropped asleep. One or two of the company took the Doctor into a different part of the room, got him into an angry discussion, and made him forget the order he had given. I stood by the somnambulist holding my watch in my hand, and to my astonishment, precisely at the expiration of fifteen minutes, she awoke. Various other experiments were tried, various severe tests were put;—some of them with complete success, others, indeed, proved total failures; and after a session of about three hours the party broke up and went to their several homes, some two or three converted, the greater part satisfied that there was and could be no collusion or deception, and yet wholly sceptical as to the alleged magnetic power.

CHAPTER II.

GUESSES.

I do not give the results of my first experiments as any thing very wonderful. They would excite little attention now. Mesmerism is much more advanced than it was in the hands of my French friend. It is true, there were rumors even then of far more marvellous phenomena, strange stories of clairvoyance or second-sight were whispered, and strange revelations of an invisible world, not recognized by received science, were hinted; but my friend would not heed them. He was a rationalist, and would not hear of any thing not explicable on natural principles. But what I witnessed convinced me of the reality of the magnetic sleep, and of the subjection of the somnambulist to the will of the mesmerizer, or that one person can, under certain circumstances, exercise an absolute control over the organs of another, and render the somnambulist, during the magnetic sleep, absolutely insensible to all save the mesmerizer. Here was certainly a marvellous power; what was it? Was it, as Bailly and Franklin's Report of 1784 asserted, the imagination? Singular effect of imagination that would put a person asleep at another's will, render her completely insensible—dead to all the world but the mesmerizer; make her go to sleep and wake up at the time specified, answer questions only mentally put, and with a promptness and an accuracy wholly impossible in her normal state! A very inexplicable imagination that, and itself not less puzzling than the mesmeric phenomena themselves.

"No, it is not imagination," insisted Dr. P——, "any more than it is a magnetic fluid, as asserted by Mesmer. It is the will of the magnetizer operating immediately on the will of the somnambulist, and through that on her organs. Or rather, it is the spiritual being in me operating immediately on the spiritual being in her, and therefore these phenomena afford an excellent refutation of materialism, and reveal a great and glorious law of human nature, recognized, though misconceived, in all ages and nations; a mighty law, but hitherto denied to human nature, and supposed to be something lying out of our sphere, superhuman, and even supernatural. Modern science began by denying the mysterious facts recorded in history, but it is beginning to accept them, and to show that they are all explicable on the principles of human nature."

"What strikes me as most remarkable in the mesmeric phenomena," said Mr. Winslow, a rather grave minister of the extreme left of the Unitarian denomination, who had joined Dr. P—— and myself on our way to my lodgings, "what strikes me as most remarkable in the mesmeric phenomena is, not the kind of power they reveal, but the degree. Every man who has been accustomed to public speaking, if he has observed, is conscious of a kindred power."

"To put his audience asleep," interposed Jack Wheatley, a young lawyer, who was usually one of my companions while in the city, "but not always to make them submissive to his will."

"It is a mysterious power," continued Mr. Winslow, "which the orator seems to have over his audience, a power of which he is conscious, but which is wholly unintelligible to himself."

"But very intelligible to his hearers," interposed Jack.

"You are impertinent, sir," replied the minister, with offended dignity. Sometimes when I have attempted to preach, I have found myself, though perfectly familiar with my subject, hardly able to say a word. My ideas dance around and before my mind like summer insects, but at such a distance, and with such rapidity, that I strive in vain to seize them. If I do succeed in saying something, my words penetrate not my hearers; they as it were rebound, and affect only myself."

"Indeed!" interjected the incorrigible Jack.

"Other times," continued Mr. Winslow, not heeding Jack's exclamation, "my ideas seem to come of themselves, to flow without effort, and to clothe themselves, without any thought or intervention of mine, in the most fitting words. I find myself elevated above myself; I am in intimate relation with the minds of my hearers. It seems that an electric current passes from them to me and from me to them, making us as it were one man. I speak with their combined force added to my own, and each of them hears and takes in my words with the united understanding of all."

"There may be something in that," said Jack. "You know, Doctor," turning to me, "that I have no more religion than a horse, and am seldom serious for five consecutive minutes in my life. Well, being in the country the other evening, on a visit to a crotchety old aunt, whose very cat would not dare to purr or to wash her face on Sunday, and finding it exceedingly dull, I took it into my head to seek a little amusement or diversion by attending a Methodist prayer-meeting, or conference, held in a school-house close by. I seldom go to meeting, but once-and-awhile I like to attend a Methodist evening gathering. I sometimes find plenty of fun. The performances this evening had begun before my arrival, for, as usual, I was rather late. On entering I found the house crowded almost to suffocation. Ten or a dozen men, women, boys, and girls, were down on their knees, all screaming at once from the very top of their lungs, and the rest of the brethren and sisters were groaning, shouting, clapping their hands, in glorious confusion. I worked my way along to a vacant spot which I spied just before a blazing fire. Turning my back to the fire, and holding aside the skirts of my coat so that they should not get scorched, I stood and looked for some minutes on the scene before me. At first I was struck with its comical character, and was much amused; soon, however, I grew serious, became sad, and then indignant, that beings in human shape, and endowed, I presumed, with the faculty of reason, should make such fools of themselves. I inwardly resolved that for once I would "speak in meeting," and that as soon as there should be a pause or a lull, so that I could stand some chance of making myself heard, I would give them a piece of Jack Wheatley's mind. In a word, I resolved to give them a downright scolding, and to tell them plainly what fools they were to suppose that they could please God by acting like so many bedlamites or howling dervishes.

"Well, after some fifteen or twenty minutes, there came a slacking up, and I opened my mouth. I remembered what my old rhetoric master had taught me, though how I came to is a puzzle, and resolved to begin in a modest and conciliatory manner. It would not do to shock them in the outset. I must first gain their ears and their good-will. So I began with a grave face and a solemn tone, and made some commonplace remarks on religion, and the duty to love and worship God, meaning, (after my preliminary remarks, intended to gain the jury,) to bring in, with crushing effect, my rebukes. But the brethren did not wait. Mistaking me for a pious exhorter, they cried out almost at my first words, "Amen!" "Glory!" "Bless the Lord!" "Go on, brother!" Will you believe it? Instantly I caught the enthusiasm, became possessed by the **genius loci**, entered in spite of myself into the spirit of the meeting, and gave a most magnificent methodistical exhortation. The brethren and sisters were edified, were enraptured, and when the time came for the meeting to break up, the leader requested me to close the performances with prayer, which I did with great fervor and unction. The spell lasted till I got out of the house into the open air."

"So Saul was among the prophets," remarked Mr. Winslow, as Jack concluded. "I am not surprised, for something similar occurred to myself when I first began to preach. There is, I believe, something infectious in these Methodist gatherings, and a wise man often finds himself acting in them as a fool acteth."

"Few wise men, I should think, ever go near them," I remarked.

"I know not how that may be," replied Mr. Winslow, "but there are few men that are always wise, or who never find themselves doing a foolish action. Even the greatest and wisest of our race sometimes unbend, and prove that there are points in which they are united to ordinary humanity. There is in this secret and invisible influence, to which I refer, of one man over another that has long arrested my attention. Often have I known both speaker and hearers electrified by a few commonplace words, carried away, it would seem, by a force not their own; now melted into tears; now inflamed with a pure and unearthly love; now maddened with rage; now fired with a lofty enthusiasm, swelling with heroic emotions, and panting to do heroic deeds. In these moments man is more than man; a higher than man possesses him, and he becomes thaumaturgic, works miracles, removes mountains, stops the course of rivers, heals the sick, casts out devils, moves, speaks, and acts a god. I call it the demonic element of human nature, and I think, if these mesmeric phenomena turn out to be real, they will be found to have their explanation in this mysterious and even fearful element, which the older theologians called faith, and superstition looks upon as supernatural."

"That there is some analogy between Animal Magnetism and the class of facts to which you refer, or which you have in your mind," observed Dr. P——, "I do not deny. But, after all, what is the power which produces them? To resolve one class of facts into another, equally if not more mysterious, is not to explain them."

"In no case does it belong to man to answer similar questions," replied Dr. P——. "We in no case know the essences of things. All that men are able to do is to observe phenomena, and from them to infer or affirm that there is and must be an agent or power which produces them. Can you tell me what is gravitation? All you can tell me is, that bodies fall or tend to the centre of the earth, and what are the laws and conditions of that tendency. What is electricity? You cannot tell me. You can only tell me that there is a certain class of phenomena, which you can trace to a certain invisible and imponderable agent, and to that invisible and unknown agent, that 'occult power,' as an earlier philosophy would have called it, you give the name of electricity. All you can know of it is, its existence, the laws by which it operates, the means by which you can avail yourself of it, get power over it, avert it from your house or barn when it breaks forth in the thunder-gust, or use it to drive your machinery, to convey your messages, or to solace your pain. Science calls it a fluid, but what it is in itself science knows not, for it has seen it only in its operations or effects. So with this power, or law of human nature, to which I ascribe the magnetic phenomena. All I pretend to tell is, that the law is a reality, and all I pretend to demonstrate is, that we may avail ourselves of it, and use it for the most useful and noble purposes. This is enough. All we need to know is its existence, or the purposes to which it may be applied, and how we can apply it or render it serviceable. Let man know that he has it, and then let him learn how to use it."

"But after all, I am a little frightened at the supposition of this power," remarked Mr. Winslow. "There is something fearful in this complete subjection of one, soul and body, to the will of another. The somnambulist is, during the mesmeric trance, the slave of the mesmerizer, as much so as was the genie to the possessor of the wonderful lamp, and he may do with him or her what he pleases. Is there not danger here? May he not use his power in a base way, to gratify his passions, his lusts, his hatred, or his revenge, and with complete impunity, since the somnambulist retains no consciousness or recollection on returning to the normal state, of what passed during the magnetic slumber? Let Animal Magnetism become generally known and practised, and who could know when or where he was safe? Any one of us might at any moment fall a victim, or be made the blind instrument of the basest and most malignant passions of others."

"Those are idle fears," replied Dr. P——; "none but virtuous men can exercise the power, or if others can, they can exercise it only for honest and benevolent purposes."

"That, if true, would be reassuring," I observed; "but, for myself, I revolt at the bare idea of being so completely in the power of another, however honest or well-disposed he may be. I choose to be my own, and not another's."

CHAPTER III.

FURTHER EXPERIMENTS.

Dr. P—— continued his lectures, private instructions, and experiments for some months, and very soon they began to produce their natural effect. No people are more disposed to run after every novelty, or are naturally more fond of the marvellous than the Anglo-Americans. They live in a constant state of excitement, and are always craving some new stimulant. They have been transplanted from the old homestead, are without ancestors, traditions, old associations, or fixed habits transmitted from generation to generation through a long series of ages. They have descended, in great part, from the sects that separated in the seventeenth century from the Anglican Church, which had in the sixteenth century itself separated from the Church of Rome, and to a great extent broken with antiquity. They are a new people,—in many respects a child-people, with the simplicity, freshness, impressibility, unsteadiness, curiosity, caprice, and waywardness of children. They must have their playthings, and they no sooner obtain a new toy than they tire of it, throw it away, and seek another. Yet are they richly endowed, and they possess in the highest degree many of the nobler virtues of our nature. They are a poetical and imaginative, as well as a reasoning and practical people. They have a robust and not unkindly nature,—are susceptible of deep emotions, and capable of heroic deeds. They treat few subjects with absolute indifference, and seldom fail to give any one who has, or professes to have, something to say, a tolerably fair and patient hearing. Whoever is able to touch their fancy, stir their feelings, excite their curiosity, or their marvellousness, is pretty sure of having them run after him—for a time.

Animal Magnetism soon became the fashion, in the principal towns and villages of the Eastern and Middle States. Old men and women, young men and maidens, boys and girls, of all classes and sizes, were engaged in studying the mesmeric phenomena, and mesmerizing or being mesmerized,—some declaring themselves believers, some expressing modestly their doubts, the majority, while half believing, loudly declaring themselves inveterate sceptics. Jack Wheatley very soon became a famous mesmerizer—for sport. He laughed at the whole concern, and yet he was the most successful of the mesmerizers, and his *subjects* always behaved with great propriety, seldom, if ever, failing him, or disappointing the wondering spectators. Mr. Winslow, after hesitating a while, began to try experiments himself, and found that he had a wonderful magnetic power, especially over the young misses and spinsters of his congregation. He found by actual experiment, often repeated, and fully attested, that he could mesmerize without being in the same room with his subject, without any previous communication of his intent, and even persons with whom he had no acquaintance, and had never spoken. More than once he had thrown a young lady in an adjoining room into the magnetic slumber. Of this there could be no doubt. He knew well his own intention, and hundreds of witnesses were ready to depose to the fact of the slumber. At first he tried this experiment only upon those who had been previously mesmerized, but he afterwards tried it with brilliant success on others.

But the marvel did not stop here. Mr. Winslow soon found that he could magnetize material objects, which in turn would magnetize persons. He wished to mesmerize a young lady, without communicating to her his wish. He mesmerized a glass of water, which was handed her by a person ignorant of what he had done, and of his intention. She drank of it, and in a very few minutes sank into a profound magnetic slumber, and exhibited the phenomena usually exhibited in artificial somnambulism. When I first heard of this experiment I laughed at it, for it seemed to me a wholly inadmissible fact. I could conceive it possible for mind to act on mind; for the will of the magnetizer to affect the will of the magnetized; but it was repugnant to all received science to suppose that mind or spirit can, without some natural medium, operate on material objects. But from what I subsequently saw and did myself, and what I was assured of by others, both competent and credible, I became convinced that I must admit it, or reject all human testimony.

Mr. Winslow, once become a mesmerizer, very soon left Dr. P—— far behind. In pushing forward his investigations, he found that he could not only throw persons, not indeed every one, but one in twenty-five or thirty, into the mesmeric sleep, render them insensible, dead as it were to all the world except himself, but that he could develop in them, or superinduce upon them, a marvellous physical strength. I saw him place a weak and sickly boy in a chair on the platform of his lecture room, and so nerve his arm that not two of the strongest men could move it. He would, by his mental operation, so nail the chair to the floor that no force applied to it could raise it. He would throw the boy by the same operation upon the floor, render his whole body, neck, legs, arms, fingers, and toes, rigid, and stiff as a crowbar; then suddenly relax all his limbs, and render him as flexible as a reed—now fill him with rage, make him rave furiously, rush through the audience as one possessed, overthrowing every thing and every one in his way—now recall him, soothe his rage, make him cry and weep as if afflicted with the deepest and most inconsolable grief, and now dry at once his tears, and break forth into the wildest and maddest joy.

These were singular phenomena. Whence this apparently superhuman strength? That certainly was no effect of complicity, for the boy exhibited a physical strength far surpassing that of both mesmerizer and mesmerized in their normal state. It could not be the effect of imagination. "For how," said Mr. Winslow, "can you explain by imagination the effect produced on material objects? You see that I can magnetize a glass of water or a bunch of flowers. Do you pretend that these are endowed with imagination; are not only sensitive, but also intellectual, and even volitive? Have the most common material objects sense, intellect, and will? Imagination, highly excited, may indeed develop and concentrate the strength which one has, but how impart a strength which one has not?"

"I have been studying these wonderful phenomena," said Mr. Increase Mather Cotton, a rigid puritan minister of high standing, and who had accompanied me to see Mr. Winslow's experiments, "and I think I see in them the works of the devil."

"Why, sir," replied Mr. Winslow, "I do these things myself. My patients move and act, are paralyzed, laugh, cry, weep, rage, foam, run, fly, fight, or make love, at my will. Do you think I am the devil?"

"Be not too confident," replied Mr. Cotton. "You may yet find that, if not the devil yourself, that it is a devil, and a very base and wicked devil, that moves you, and uses you as the instrument of his malice."

"I have no belief," answered Mr. Winslow, "in devils or demons, as separate and intelligent beings."

"I know very well, sir, that you are a Sadducee, and believe in neither angel nor spirit, although you would fain pass for a Christian minister," replied, with a severe tone, the stanch puritan, whose great ancestor had taken so conspicuous a part in Salem witchcraft.

"You do me wrong, Mr. Cotton," replied Mr. Winslow. "I am a Christian, and no Sadducee. I believe in the Christian religion as firmly as you do. I do not deny angel or spirit. By *angel* I understand what the word itself imports, a messenger, and by *spirit*, a power, force, or energy. But I do not suppose that I am to understand by either an order of beings distinct and separate from man. I concede the spiritual power or energy, but it is the power or energy of the human being; I grant the demonic character of these phenomena, but the force that produces them is the demonic force of human nature itself. There are no personal angels, and no personal devils or demons."

"And no personal God, you will say next, I presume," replied Mr. Cotton with a sneer.

"God is personal in me, in the human personality," proudly answered Mr. Winslow. "Personality is a circumscription, a limitation; and God, since he is infinite, incapable of circumscription, cannot be personal in himself. He can be personal only in creatures, and consequently, only in such creatures as have personality, that is, men."

"Your notion of personality is of a piece with your whole miscalled theology," replied Mr. Cotton. "Personality is the last complement of rational nature. If the nature is rational, that is, capable of intelligent and voluntary activity, and complete, it is a person, and if infinite, an infinite person. Your argument is a mere sophism, founded on a false definition of personality. A little philosophy or common sense would be of great service to such *Christian* ministers as you are."

"Let us not," I interposed, "get involved in a theological discussion. We are to investigate this subject as men of science, not as theologians. We have here a scientific subject, and science leaves theologians to their speculations, without presuming to intervene in their interminable, useless, and wearisome disputes. If your theology is true, it can never be in conflict with science."

"If your science be true, or really be science," retorted Mr. Cotton, "it can never be in conflict with theology. I do not attempt to deduce my science from my theology, but I make my theology the mistress of my science. Whatever is inconsistent with it, I know beforehand cannot be genuine science, or true philosophy."

"That may or may not be so," I replied; "but I am no theologian. I am an humble cultivator of science, and I consider myself free to push my scientific investigations into all subjects independently, without restraint, without leave asked or obtained either from you or my friend Mr. Winslow. All history has its superstitious and marvellous side. Science has heretofore denied the reality of that side of history, and regarded the marvellous facts with which ancient and mediæval history is filled, as never having really taken place, or as the result of fraud, trickery, or imposture, exaggerated by the credulity, the ignorance, the wonder, and the disordered imaginations of the multitude. These mesmeric phenomena may throw a new light on that class of facts; they may even relieve history from the charges which have been brought against it, and rehabilitate the ages that we have condemned, so far at least as the facts themselves are concerned, though not necessarily as to the theories by which they were in past times generally explained. I am myself at present bewildered. I am not willing to admit the facts, but I am unable to deny them. If they must be accepted, I incline to the view of my friend Mr. Winslow, and am disposed to assume that there is in human nature a law not hitherto well understood, a mysterious power, what he here calls the demonic power of human nature, the limits and extent of which science has not as yet explored."

"There is something mysterious in man," remarked Mr. Sandborn, a Universalist minister present. "I remember, some years ago, that one summer I was very much out of health. I suffered much from a bowel complaint, which brought me very low. But my mind was exceedingly active, and I seemed to myself to have not only more than my ordinary intellectual power, but also at my command a mass of information on a great variety of subjects which I was sure I had never acquired in the course of my ordinary studies. I seemed familiar with several physical sciences which I had never studied, and with facts, real facts too, which I had never learned. While I was in this state, I was visited at my residence, in the village of Ithaca, New York, by a young friend, a brother minister, residing some eighteen or twenty miles distant. He saw my state, and urged me to go out and spend a few weeks with him at his boarding-house. The pure breezes, he said, from the hills would do me good, revive my languishing body, and restore me to health. I accepted my young friend's invitation, and the next morning we took the stage, and after some three hours' drive were set down at his lodgings. We were hardly seated in his library, when a servant brought him a letter which had been taken from the post-office during his absence. I saw a slight blush on his face as he took the letter, and instantly comprehended that it was from his 'ladye love,' although I was entirely ignorant that he was paying his attentions to any one, or that he had any matrimonial intentions. Asking my permission, he broke the seal, and read his letter in my presence. When he had done, I said to him,

"'You have there a letter from your sweetheart, the young lady to whom you are engaged to be married.'

"'How do you know that?' he asked in reply.

"'O that is evident,' I replied. 'I see it in your face. Let me see the letter, and I will tell you her character.'

"'I would rather not,' he answered.

"'I do not wish to read it,' said I, 'I only wish to look at the handwriting.'

"'But can you tell a person's character by seeing his handwriting.'

"'Certainly, nothing is easier,' I replied, although I had never tried, or even heard of such a thing before.

"He then handed me the letter. I fixed my eye on the writing for a moment without reading a word of the letter, and I saw, or seemed to see, standing before me, at some six or eight feet distant, a very good-looking young lady, a little below the medium size, with an agreeable expression of face, apparently about eighteen years of age, as plainly as I see any one of you now in this room. I proceeded quietly and at my ease to describe her to my friend. I told her age, described her size, her height, her complexion, the color and texture of her hair, the colors and quality of her dress, indeed her whole external appearance, even to a hardly perceptible mole on her right cheek. My friend, you may well suppose, listened to me with surprise, astonishment, and wonder, and several times interrupted me with the question 'Are you really the devil?' He agreed that my description was accurate, and far more so than he could himself have given.

"I then proceeded, to my friend's equal astonishment, to describe her moral and intellectual qualities, her disposition, her education, her tastes, her habits, &c., all of which he declared were correctly described, as far as he himself knew. I had never previously seen or heard of the young lady, who lived in another State, and was actually at the moment some hundred and fifty miles distant. But this was not all. My friend married the young lady in the course of two or three months, and two years afterwards I called at his house, and was introduced to a lady whom I instantly recognized as the one whose image I had previously seen before me.[1] There is something in all this, and analogous facts related and well attested by others, that I cannot explain."

We all agreed that the case was remarkable, and apparently inexplicable, on any known principles of received science.

[1] A literal fact, in the experience of the author.

CHAPTER IV.

AN EXPLOSION.

Dr. P—— having accomplished his object in visiting this country, and being invited home by his family, took his leave of us in the summer of 1840, and returned to the West Indies. I have not seen him since. But he left behind a large number of disciples, and we had no lack of mesmerizers, and mesmerizers to whom he was a mere child. Some of these made mesmerism a trade, and gave public lectures and experiments as a means of gaining notoriety and filling their pockets. Others made their experiments in private circles, and from curiosity, or in the interests of science, and not unfrequently by way of amusement. Mr. Winslow devoted much time to a series of experiments intended to prove the reality of what he called the demonic element of human nature. He wished to be able to accept and explain the miracles recorded in sacred and profane history on natural principles, without the recognition of the supernatural. Jack Wheatley continued his experiments, apparently more in jest than in earnest, and was remarkably successful. He had no theory on the subject, said nothing of the use to which mesmerism might be applied, and never speculated on the cause of the mesmeric phenomena. He contented himself with producing them, and leaving others to use or explain them as they saw proper.

A year had passed without my seeing Jack. In the winter of 1840-41, while on a visit to Boston, I met him one day accidentally in the street, and was startled at his altered appearance. His look was wild and oppressed, his face was pale and sallow, his youth and bloom were gone, and his body was wasted to a skeleton. He made as if he would avoid me, and with reluctance and a certain timidity replied to my greeting.

"Why, Jack, what is the matter?"

"Don't you see? I see her night and day," he replied with a shudder, as if he beheld some strange and horrible vision from which he would avert his looks, but could not.

"See what?" said I. "I see nothing."

He trembled all over, and seemed unable to speak. Seeing that he had either lost his wits, or was fast losing them, I took his arm in mine, and with gentle violence led him to my lodgings, at no great distance, conducted him to my room, and induced him to repose himself on the sofa. I closed the door, and seated myself by his side. I took his hand, and caressed his forehead and temples as if he had been a child. He seemed soothed. "Tell me, Jack," said I, in a voice almost as gentle and affectionate as that of a mother, "tell me what has happened."

"I am lost, I am damned."

"Say not that. As long as life lasts no one is lost, and nothing is irreparable."

"Life no longer lasts. I do not live. I killed her."

"No, no. But of whom do you speak?"

"You did not know. I never told you. You seemed to be a cast-iron man, as Miss Martineau says of Mr. Calhoun, and disposed to put every sentiment in your crucible, and subject it to your retorts and blowpipes."

"But Mr. Calhoun has a heart, as I have had ample occasion to prove."

"I was always light and trifling, careless, gay, and joyous, yet I truly and deeply loved."

"And none the less deeply and truly because gay and joyous."

"But you know nothing of love?"

"No man is always wise."

"But you will laugh at me."

"My dear Jack, there are few hearts without some little romance, in some hidden or unhidden corner. There are not many persons unwilling to listen to a story of true and genuine love."

"I was young and foolish, but I loved one, and one whom I thought every way worthy, a thousand times worthy, of my love. I felt myself infinitely her inferior, and unworthy even to kiss the ground on which she had trodden."

"That is easily comprehended."

"Now you are laughing at me."

"No, I am not. But you may leave something to my imagination, if not to my experience. I do not doubt that she whom you loved had all imaginable charms, all conceivable graces, and all possible and impossible perfections."

"But my Isabel *was* the most beautiful, sweet, amiable, and glorious creature that ever gladdened the earth with her presence."

"Unquestionably. He who doubts that his mistress is an angel, is divine, is a goddess, has his liver whole, and I will warrant him sound in wind and limb. The lover never finds his mistress mortal till after the wedding."

"You are incorrigible. You promised not to laugh at me. Indeed, indeed, Doctor, I do not deserve to be laughed at."

"I own it, my dear Jack, and nothing is farther from my heart than to laugh at you. But do tell me what has happened. I am really grieved to see you so afflicted."

"Well, I loved Isabel, and had the happiness of believing that she returned my love. I gained her consent, and that of her parents and my own, and we were only waiting till I was fairly established in my profession to be married. Notwithstanding Shakspeare's *dictum*, the course of our true love *did* run smooth. There never was a lover's quarrel between us, and there were no obstacles interposed by friends, enemies, or fortune. My acquaintance accidentally formed with you brought me into company with Dr. P——, and interested me in Animal Magnetism. In mere sport, as a pastime, I began trying my mesmeric powers on one and another of my young friends. Capital fun we found it. None of us dreamed of there being any harm in it, or that we might not sport with it as we pleased without any unpleasant consequences. I know not how it was, but I proved to be a powerful magnetizer, although I was said not to have the right sort of temperament for a mesmerizer. My experiments rarely failed, and were almost always unusually brilliant.

"One evening at a friend's house, where some ten or a dozen of my companions and acquaintances were assembled, I mesmerized a boy about twelve years old. I found him completely under my control, and perfectly docile to all my intentions. His behavior was admirable. I asked him mentally a large number of questions which it was certain that in his normal state he could not answer, and which he answered explicitly, with surprising accuracy. He had never been taught music, and in his normal state could not distinguish even one tune from another. I willed him to seat himself at the piano, and play for us a favorite waltz of Mozart. He obeyed, and performed it with accuracy, with spirit, a delicacy of touch, and brilliancy of effect, which none of us had ever heard equalled, or even approached. I then mentally ordered him to sing us, to his own accompaniment, one or two songs from Fra Diavolo, which were then in fashion. He obeyed. We were all surprised, and began talking among ourselves of the apparent miracle, when, to our still greater astonishment, he commenced playing of his own accord a strange piece, which none of us knew or had ever heard, and which, for its wild and unearthly character, for its brilliancy, depth, and pathos, surpassed all that we had ever conceived of music. We were all entranced. Here was some agency not the boy's, not mine, not that of any one present. Such strains had never had mortal composer.

"I knew not what to think, and so contrived not to think at all, but enjoyed the music, and looked no farther. *Carpe diem*, you know, was my philosophy. I saw I had a brilliant subject, and I resolved to make the most of him. I had heard of the marvellous powers of clairvoyance and second sight exhibited by some somnambulists. I blindfolded the boy, and gave him a letter. He read it with ease. I placed another at the back of his neck, he read that also; I placed another, folded up, on the back of his head. He told me who was the writer, described his appearance, his complexion, size, and character, with more accuracy than I could have done, although the writer was well known to me, and must have been a total stranger to the boy. I took the boy with me on a journey, that is, mentally. We stopped at Providence, went on to Stonington, took the steamer for New York, landed and went up Broadway, down the Bowery, and through several other streets. He named the hotels, churches, and other public buildings we passed, and read the signs over the shop doors. We went up the Hudson, to Albany, from there on to Utica, Rochester, Niagara Falls, and then returned, and on our way back stopped at your house in Genesee county, with which you know I am familiar. We went into the library, and the laboratory, in each of which he named and accurately described the principal objects. Having come back, we took an excursion into the other world, of which he told us strange things, which none of us believed, for we were all Unitarians, Universalists, or unbelievers, and his revelations seemed to favor what is called Orthodoxy.

"My betrothed was present at all these experiments. She was greatly excited. Time and again she wished that I would mesmerize her. She wished this much more after she had heard the boy describe what he saw in the other world. I know not why, but I shrunk from complying with her wish. I saw no harm in others being mesmerized, and I had, without any scruple, mesmerized young ladies by the dozen; but some how or other I could not bear to have my Isabel mesmerized, or even to mesmerize her myself. I instinctively felt that there would be something indelicate in it, something hardly modest, and that it would be a sort of desecration. She was modest, retiring, even timid, but her curiosity was excited, and she would brook no denial.

"A true daughter of Eve. Women are timid creatures, but will brave Satan himself to gratify their curiosity, or their passions."

"That now is malicious."

"Never mind; go on."

"I was at length obliged to consent, but only to magnetize her at her father's house, and at first only in presence of her mother or her sister. She yielded very readily to the mesmeric influence, and became a remarkable clairvoyant. She had, when in the magnetic slumber, not only a clear view of remote terrestrial things, of which she had no previous knowledge, and which were equally unknown to me, but also of heaven and hell, and revealed to me strange things of angels and spirits, of the state of departed souls, good and bad, and of their intercourse with the living. We both became deeply interested, and took every opportunity to make our investigations. We were left much alone, and she remained in the mesmeric state from one to two hours almost every day or evening. If I was unable to visit her, she would, though I knew it not, invite some female friend to mesmerize her, for gradually she seemed to wish to live only in the mesmeric state, and appeared restless and uneasy when out of it. Her physical system began to suffer. She complained, when awake, of a universal lassitude. The bloom faded from her cheek, her eye assumed a wild, lustreless glare, and her motions were heavy and languid. She was listless, absent, forgetful, taking little or no interest in anybody or any thing. I beheld her, as you may well believe, with great anxiety and alarm.

"One evening, about two months ago, I visited her. I found her alone, and in a few minutes threw her into the mesmeric sleep, for it was only in that state that her mind retained its strength and brilliancy. She was attacked with convulsions and spasms as I had never seen her before. I hastened to awake her. It was too late! I had killed her; and that countenance which had been so dear to me, which had so often beamed on me with the sweet smile of love, now bore only the expression of fear, horror, rage, and anguish. It was the face of a demon. It froze my blood to behold it.

"I had my own grief to bear, I had to endure the tortures of my own remorse and utter despair, and to face the grief, silent, but deep, of her father, and the rage of her mother, who cursed me, cursed me as only a mother in the violence of her wrath and grief can curse. How I lived through that dreadful night I know not. The relations agreed to conceal the circumstances of Isabel's death. I followed her to the tomb, and returned to my own home, blasted, withered, worse than dead.

"All this was bad enough, but worse followed. The day after the funeral, while sitting alone in my office, I saw, at a few feet from me, partly behind me, a grayish appearance, without any sharply defined outline. I looked at it for a moment, and it assumed then the well-known form of her I the day before followed to the grave, and, horror of horrors, with that fearful expression of face with which she had died. It came nearer to me, I receded; it followed, I rushed into the street; it pursued, I turned aside my face, it turned as I turned, so as to be always within my view. From that day to this has it haunted me; I have scarcely a moment's respite. Day or night, light or dark, with my eyes opened or closed, always does it stand before me, and glare on me with that terrible look. I cannot sleep; I cannot eat; I have no rest. The only few moments of quiet I have had are those since I have been with you in this room. I do not see it now. O, it was a sad day for me when I chose Animal Magnetism for a plaything!"

I was much affected by Jack's sufferings. I was not surprised at the fatal effects of mesmerism on the young lady; for death, I had been assured, is no unfrequent result of what the physicians who practise it call its injudicious use. The form which haunted him gave me no uneasiness, as it was, in my opinion, clearly a case of hallucination, a species of monomania, well known to the physicians of our lunatic hospitals, and our writers on mania or insanity. The shock my young friend had received had probably produced some slight lesion of the brain, and the imagination gave shape to the deceptive appearance, as in dreams we see often reproduced, following us, preceding us, or dancing around us, the shapes and images which had deeply impressed us when awake. But I was fond of poor Jack, and my great anxiety was to console him, and to prevent what might be only a temporary hallucination from becoming a confirmed insanity. Finding him better when with me, I persuaded him, with the consent of his family, who understood very little of his case, and feared for his reason, to accompany me to my home in Western New York, and to place himself under my care.

He remained very much depressed for several months, but gradually his appetite returned; he was able to get some sleep, and his health began to improve. The vision did not entirely leave him, especially when alone, or not with me, but its visits became less and less frequent, and less and less appalling. The expression of the face gradually became less horrible, and more human, but still indicated great suffering and profound grief. In the course of a year, however, he seemed to have recovered, and returned to Boston. But in proportion as he seemed to be regaining his health and peace of mind, as far as peace of mind he could hope to have, a very singular change began to come over me.

I had spent my time, since leaving college, in literary ease and scientific pursuits. I had had few strong or violent passions to trouble me, and few things had wounded me very deeply. I had had, it is true, my little romances, but not being of a sentimental turn, and having a strong constitution and most excellent health, they had hardly rippled the surface of the ordinarily smooth current of my life. I had pursued science as a pastime. I took an easy, pleasant interest in it, but had no passion for it. I had no enthusiasm, and found in the pursuit only a gentle excitement, as in reading one of James's novels, which, by the by, are the best of all novels, for you can take them up or lay them down when you please. Spare me, I always say, those much-be-praised works of fiction which deal with strong and violent passions, which produce in the reader a painfully intense interest, and which, when you once begin reading them, you cannot lay down till you have read to the end. I avoid reading such a novel, as I avoid a night's debauch.

But now a change came over me. I became restless, and had an intense longing to explore the secrets of things, and to look within the veil with which nature kindly shrouds her laboratory. I longed to make myself acquainted with the primal elements of being, and to be able to command them; I burned to enlarge not only my knowledge, but my forces. I would be able to raise the tempest on the deep, to fly through the air, to wield the lightning, to leave and enter my body at will, to succor my friends or overwhelm my enemies at a distance. I would read the stars, comprehend their influences, and command their courses. I envied the old Chaldean sages, the mighty magicians of the East, and the wizards and weird sisters of the North. Why should it not be literally true that mind is omnipotent over matter? Is not man called the lord of this lower creation? Why then should he fear, or not be able to exercise his lordship? Had we not seen the wonders of science? Had not man learned to make the lightnings his steeds, and flames of fire his ministers? What are the mighty forces of nature? May not man seize them, use them, and wield their might at his pleasure?

Such thoughts were new to me, still more new were those intense longings. The horizon of human power seemed to enlarge around me, and I seemed to rise in the majesty and might of my nature. I was becoming, as it were, a new man. The ethereal fire within had hitherto slumbered. It was now kindled, and its flames aspired to their native heaven. I would no longer be the puny thing I had been. Henceforth I would be a man; a man in the full and lofty sense of the word. Now suddenly my soul seemed to grow, and to become too large for my body, against which it beat as the prisoner beats his head against the walls of his prison-house. I knew not then the source or nature of these feelings, and I cherished them as precious intimations of my affinity with the Origin and Source of all things. At times I was elated; my eye glowed with an unwonted fire, and sparkled with an unearthly brilliancy; my step was elastic, and my whole frame seemed to have received new youth and buoyancy, and to be in some measure withdrawn from the ordinary laws of gravitation. It seemed as if all the great forces of nature flowed into me, and become subject to my will. Nothing was impossible to me.

CHAPTER V.

SOME PROGRESS.

Hitherto I had neither been magnetized myself nor magnetized others. I had read the principal works which had been written in French and English on the subject, and had witnessed and carefully analyzed the experiments made by my friends; but now I madly resolved to make experiments for myself.

A portion of the winter of 1841-2 I spent in Philadelphia, and as my acquaintance was principally with the Hicksite Quakers, Unitarians, Swedenborgians, Universalists, and open unbelievers in all religion, I was, as a matter of course, thrown into the very circles where Animal Magnetism, as well as all conceivable novelties and absurdities, were the order of the day. My friends and associates were nearly all philanthropists and world-reformers. There were among them seers and seeresses, enthusiasts and fanatics, socialists and communists, abolitionists and anti-hangmen, radicals and women's-rights men of both sexes; all professing the deepest and most disinterested love for mankind, and claiming to be moved by the single desire to do good to the race. All agreed that hitherto every thing had gone wrong; all agreed in denouncing all forms of religion and government that had hitherto obtained amongst men; all agreed in declaiming against the clergy of all denominations, in manifesting their indignation against all political and civil rule, and whatever tended in the least to restrain the passions of individuals or the multitude, in asserting the wonderful progress of the human race during the last hundred years, and in predicting that a new era was about to dawn for the world; but beyond this I could find scarcely a point on which any two of them were not at loggerheads.

I cannot say that the differences I found among these excellent people when it concerned their philanthropic projects or their various schemes of world-reform, edified me much, but I was charmed with their disinterestedness, with their zeal, and their superiority to the restraints of popular prejudice, and what they stigmatized as conventionalism. I was above all delighted to observe the new importance assumed in behalf of woman; and it was a real pleasure to hear a charming young lady, whose face a painter might have chosen for his model, in a sweet musical voice, and a gentle and loving look, which made you all unconsciously take her hand in yours, defend our great grandmother Eve, and maintain that her act, which an ungrateful world had held to have been the source of all the vice, the crime, the sin and misery of mankind, was an act of lofty heroism, of noble daring, of pure disinterested love for man. Adam, but for her, would have tamely submitted to the tyrannical order he had received, and the race would never have known how to distinguish between good and evil. How, with the sweet young lady—I see and hear her now—sitting on a stool near me, laying her hand in the fervor of her argument on mine, and looking up with all the witchery of her eyes into my face, how could I fail to be convinced that man is cold, calculating, selfish, and cowardly, and that the world cannot be reformed without the destruction of the male (it might be called the *mal*) organization of society, the elevation of woman to her proper sphere, and the infusion into the government and management of public and private affairs, some portion of the love, the daring, the enthusiasm, and disinterestedness of woman's heart? There was nothing to be said in reply.

But alas! unhappy Saint Simonians; you believed also that the evils endured by the race were owing, in great measure, to the fact that society had hitherto been organized and governed by men as distinguished from women, and therefore without the female element. You would in your reorganization of the world, avoid this sad mistake. You could not agree on the definitive organization of mankind till you had obtained the voice of woman. But how obtain that from woman, the slave of the old male organization? A *Père suprême* you had found, but a woman to sit by his side as *Mère suprême*, and to exercise with him equal authority, you found not, and could proceed no further. You selected twelve apostles, and sent them forth in search of a *Mère suprême*. They searched France, England, Germany, Italy, all Europe, even to the harem of the Grand Turk, but they found her not, and returned and reported their ill-success. Then fear and consternation seized you; then fell despair took possession of your souls; then you saw all your hopes blasted, and you separated and dissolved in thin air. Perhaps, if you had sent your apostles to the United States, to Philadelphia or Boston, you might have succeeded, and Père Enfantin not have vanished from Paris, the capital of the world, to waste himself as an engineer in the service of Mehemet Ali.

It was a real pleasure to find these men of advanced views, and these women of burning hearts and strong minds, who had outgrown the narrow prejudices of their sex, all substituting the love of mankind for the love of God. They all agreed that philanthropy was the highest virtue, and the only virtue. Charity was an obsolete virtue, no longer in use, and not suited to our advanced stage of human progress. That taught us to love man in God, but we have learned to love God in man; that is, man himself, without any reference to God. This was charming, and emancipated us from our thraldom to priests, and all old-fashioned religion. What was better still, I found that even this noble philanthropy received a very liberal interpretation, and did not interfere at all with those pleasant passions and vices, called anger, spite, envy, &c. It was only a love of man in the abstract, the love of mankind in general, which permitted the most sublime hatred or indifference to all men in particular. Wonderful nineteenth century! I exclaimed; wonderful seers and seeresses, and most delightful moralists are these modern world-reformers!

In this pleasant and delightful circle mesmerism attracted its full share of attention. I met it in almost every circle where I happened to be present. It seemed to take the place of cards, music, and dancing. One evening I was at a friend's house, where were collected some twenty-five or thirty gentlemen and ladies, or perhaps I should say, ladies and gentlemen, mainly on my account, for I was, in a small way, something of a lion, and our people are great in lionizing whenever they have an opportunity, as Dickens, Kossuth, Padre Gavazzi, and others hardly less worthy can abundantly testify. Indeed, our people are democrats only from envy and spite. In their souls they are the most aristocratic people in the world, and would be so avowedly, only they have no legitimate aristocracy. Democracy has its origin in the feeling,—since I am as good as you, and since I cannot be an aristocrat, you shall be a democrat with me.

In this private party there were two or three somnambulists, and twice that number of mesmerizers. My friend, Mr. Winslow, from Boston, was present, and also Mr. Cotton, who was in the city on some business pertaining to holding a world's convention in London for evangelizing France, Italy, and other benighted countries of Europe. Mr. Winslow was in high spirits. He was sure that he was making out his proofs that there is a demonic element in human nature, never once reflecting, that if demonic it is not human.

"I am," said he, "on the point of rehabilitating history. Miracles, divinations, sorceries, magic, the black arts, which surprise us in all history, sacred and profane, and which are either denied outright, or ascribed to supernatural agencies, I think I shall be able to accept, as facts, as real phenomena, and explain on natural principles. I think I have in mesmerism an explanation of them all."

"So you imagine that with mesmerism you may take your place with the magicians of Egypt, and enter into a successful contest with Moses," said Mr. Cotton. "You forget that those magicians were discomfited, and at the third trial were obliged to give up and acknowledge themselves beaten. 'The finger of God is here.'"

"Moses was a superior mesmerizer, and he mesmerized for a good, and they for a bad purpose, which makes all the difference in the world," replied Mr. Winslow.

"But these magicians, then, could exercise the mesmeric power up to a certain point, and for evil; I thought it was a doctrine of mesmerizers, that none but virtuous and honest men could mesmerize, and these only for a good and honest purpose," said Mr. Cotton.

"I am not," said I, "particularly interested in explaining what the Germans call the Night-Side of nature, or the marvellous deeds recorded in sacred and profane history; I would be able to do those deeds, reproduce those wonderful phenomena, and exert myself a power over the primordial elements or primitive forces of nature, be they spirits, be they what they will. I am tired of being pent up within this narrow cage, and of being the slave of every external influence. I would master nature; ride upon the whirlwind and direct the storm. There may, for aught I know, be an element of truth in the marvellous machinery of the Arabian Nights Entertainments, and something more than the extravagances of an Oriental imagination in those tales of magic, of good and evil Genii. What, if the tale of Aladdin's Lamp were true? Who dare say that the river and ocean gods, the Naiads, the Dryads, Hamadryads, Pan and his reed, Apollo and his lyre, Mercury and his wand, the supernal and infernal gods of classic poetry, were all mere creatures of the poetic imagination? Perhaps even the *diablerie* of modern German romance, of Hoffman, Baron de Fouquè, and others, has more of reality than most readers suspect."

"All the gods of the Gentiles were devils," replied Mr. Cotton, "and to a considerable extent I concede the reality you intimate. There are good angels and bad, and both have intercourse with mankind. The air swarms with evil spirits, with devils, fallen angels, endowed with a more than human intelligence, and a more than human power. These are under a chief called Lucifer, Beelzebub, Satan, who seeks to seduce men from their allegiance to God, to make them receive him for their master, to put him in the place of God, and to pay him divine honors. It was this fallen angel, the prince of this world as St. Paul calls him, and the prince of the powers of the air, who everywhere and unceasingly besieges the Christian, and against whom we have to be constantly on the guard, that the ancient Gentiles literally worshipped as God, and it is these evil spirits, these powers of the air, that swarm around us, and infest all nature, that ancient classic poetry celebrates, and that your modern philosophers would persuade us were mere poetic fancies."

"The powers or forces themselves, I concede," said Mr. Winslow, "but I do not recognize their personality, nor their superhuman character."

"Perhaps," said I, "Mr. Winslow is a little too hasty in supposing them to be the innate power or force of human nature. This power exerted by the mesmerizer may well be natural and yet not be human. It may be one of the mighty forces of universal nature, which the mesmerizer has the secret of using or bringing to bear in the accomplishment of his own purposes. In mesmerism, perhaps, we may find the key to the mysteries of nature, and the secret of rendering practically available all the great and mighty powers at work in nature's laboratory, so that a man may learn to strengthen himself with all the force of the entire universe."

"The power you speak of," said Mr. Wilson, an ex-Unitarian parson, and who passed for a Transcendentalist, "I believe to be very real. We sometimes ascribe it to the will, and it is true that under certain relations the will has great energy, and is well nigh invincible. Yet it is not, I apprehend, so much the energy of the will itself as of faith, which brings the will into harmony with the primordial laws of the universe, and strengthens it by all the forces of nature. 'If ye had faith as a grain of mustard seed,' said Jesus, 'ye could say to this mountain, be removed and planted in yonder sea, and it should obey you.' I am far from being able to prescribe the limits of full, undoubting, and unwavering faith. Faith is thaumaturgic, always a miracle-worker, and if we could only undertake with a calm and full confidence of success, I have little doubt but the meanest of us might work greater miracles than any recorded in history. 'If ye believe, ye shall do greater works than these.'"

"There is more in this power of faith than received philosophy has fathomed. By it one's eyes are opened, and he seems to penetrate the profoundest mysteries of the universe, even to the essence of the Godhead. We may mark it in all our undertakings. Whatever we attempt, nothing doubting, we are almost sure to accomplish. Let me, as a public speaker, desire to produce a certain effect, and let me have full confidence that I shall succeed, and I am sure not to fail. Let me utter a sentiment, with my whole soul absorbed in it, confident that it is going right to the hearts of my hearers, and it goes there. Whenever I am conscious in what I am saying, of this calm, undoubting faith, I am sure of my audience. I no sooner open my lips than I have them under my control, and I can do with them as I please. When I have felt this faith in what I was about to utter, I have felt before uttering it, its effect upon the assembly, and my whole frame has been sensible of something like an electric shock, and it seemed that my audience and I were connected by a magnetic chain. In conversing with a friend, in whom I have full faith, and to whom I can speak with full confidence, I have felt the same. Our souls seem to be melted into one, to move with one and the same will, and each to be exalted and strengthened by the combined power of both. Then rise we into the upper regions of truth, far above the unaided flight of either. Heaven opens to us, and we behold the hidden things of God. Something the same is felt also when one goes forth in love with nature, and yields to her gentle and hallowing influences. We inhale power with her fragrant odors, become conscious of purer, loftier and holier thoughts and feelings, and form stronger and nobler resolutions."

"All that," said Mr. Cotton, "is common enough, but it is easily explained by sympathy and imagination."

"But," Mr. Wilson replied, "what, then, is the power of sympathy or imagination? That is a question I cannot answer. I yield to the power, enjoy it, and question it not. Begin to question it, and it is gone. I know well that philosophers call the power I speak of under one aspect, love, under another, sympathy, under another, imagination, under still another, faith, but what it is in itself they cannot tell me. Be it what it will, it is demonic, supernatural, an element in human nature, of which men in all ages have had glimpses, but of which none of us have as yet had any thing more. The history of our race everywhere bristles with prodigies. These prodigies were once regarded as miracles, and supposed to be wrought by the finger of God; now an unbelieving age treats them as impostures, cheats, fabrications, proving only people's love of the marvellous, their natural proneness to superstition, and the ease with which they can be gulled by the crafty and the designing. I believe them, for the most part, real. I believe that there are times when man has a power over the elements, and can make the spirits obey him. Who knows but the time may come, perhaps is now near, when the law by which this power operates will be discovered, and this power, which has hitherto been irregular and transient in its manifestations, will became common and regular, and therefore bear the marks of a fixed and permanent law of nature?

"But, call it what you will, it is not identical with the human will, nor in my opinion is it, strictly speaking, a property of human nature. It is an overshadowing, an all-pervading power, identical, most likely, with that Power which creates and manifests itself in the universe. We can avail ourselves of it, not because it is ours, but by placing ourselves in harmony with it, within its focal range, and suffering its rays to be all concentred in us."

"That is substantially my own view," remarked Mr. Winslow, "and I regard mesmerism as revealing the regular and permanent means by which we can avail ourselves of that creative and miracle-working power. I do not pretend that man is thaumaturgic in himself, as distinguished from the Being from whom his life emanates, but by virtue of his union with the Fountain of All Force."

"I think," said Mr. Sowerby, an ex-Methodist elder, "that by magnetism, we shall be able to explain the operations of the Holy Ghost, and the mysteries of regeneration."

"More likely," interrupted Mr. Cotton, "the operations of Satan, and the Mystery of Iniquity."

"Yes, but in a sense thou dost not mean," interposed Obediah Mott, a Hicksite Quaker. "Thou knowest how difficult it is for thee to explain the Popish miracles, many of which thou knowest come exceedingly well attested. Mesmerism will show thee, that they were wrought by mesmeric influences."

"But I have no wish to explain Popish miracles on a principle that would take from Christian miracles all their value. I hate popery, but I love the Gospel more."

The conversation was continued for some time, in the small circle around me. In another part of the room they had got a somnambulist, and were making various experiments. When the larger part of the company had dispersed, I requested Mr. Winslow to try if he could not mesmerize me. He did not think he should succeed. He thought I had not the sort of temperament to be magnetized; that I had too strong a will, too robust a constitution, and quite too vigorous health. It would at any rate require far more mesmeric power than he had to subdue me. However, he would try, and do what he could.

I seated myself in an arm chair, with my feet to the south, and Mr. Winslow began with his passes. The first ten minutes he produced not the slightest effect, for I resisted him by the whole force of my will. At length I closed my eyes, and resigned myself to his influence. I now became aware of his passes, though they were made without actually touching me. It seemed as if slight electric sparks were emitted from the tips of his fingers, producing a slight, but agreeable, and as it were a cooling sensation. I felt slight spasmodic affections at the pit of my stomach, which gradually became violent. My arms made involuntary motions, and my legs and feet felt light and flew up as he extended his passes over them. I had not the least inclination to sleep, but found that he was actually exerting an influence over my body greater than at all pleased me. I tried, and found that I could arrest his influence if I willed, and that he had power over me only so long as I offered no voluntary opposition. I alternately yielded and resisted, and found that he had no power to overcome my own will. He operated for about an hour, with no other effects than those I have mentioned, and gave up the task of putting me to sleep as hopeless. The most remarkable thing about it, that I recollect, though it did not much strike me at the time, was, that although my eyes were closed, I saw or seemed to see distinctly, slight luminous appearances at the ends of his fingers as he made his passes. These luminous appearances were in rapid motion, and seemed of a bluish tinge edged with yellowish white.

There was nothing in the experiment that could establish the reality of the mesmeric influence to bystanders, but there was enough to satisfy me that it was neither jugglery nor imagination. I could easily see from the experiment, that upon persons differently constituted from myself, less accustomed to self-control, and to the quiet analysis of their own feelings, much greater and more striking effect must have been produced.

CHAPTER VI.

TABLE TURNING.

The point to which I at first directed my attention was to ascertain the power, which, by means of mesmerism, I might acquire over the elemental forces of nature. I found that with or without actual contact I could at will paralyze the whole body of another, subject it in great measure to my own will, and force it to obey my bidding. I could render it preternaturally weak and preternaturally strong. I found also that I could produce all these effects at a distance, by means of magnetized inanimate objects. For instance, I would magnetize a bunch of flowers, and a person knowing nothing of what I had done, who should take them up and smell of them, would exhibit all the usual phenomena of the mesmerized. Here it was evident that the mesmeric power, whatever it might be, could act directly on matter, and lodge itself in a material object. It was clear then that the mesmeric phenomena had a real objective cause, and therefore could not be the effects either of imagination or hallucination. Here was a most striking and important fact, and one which entirely refuted the ultra spiritualism of the majority of mesmerizers.

My experiments in clairvoyance and second sight were equally surprising in their results. The theory of those who conceded the facts was, that in some inexplicable way, the somnambulist uses the brain of him with whom he or she is *en rapport*, and therefore is restricted in the clairvoyant power to the images already in that brain. I mesmerize, say a young woman. In her mesmeric state she becomes clairvoyant. She can see with my organs of vision whatever I myself can see, or have seen, but nothing else. She can tell my most secret thoughts and intentions, or those of any one with whom she is *en rapport*, but nothing more. She can answer correctly any question the answer to which is known to the interrogator, but not questions the answer to which is unknown to him. But repeated and well-attested experiments prove to the contrary. Nothing is more common than for her to answer correctly questions equally unknown to herself and to those with whom she is placed in communication, and in cases where it is certain the answer could not be known by any human means to either. The magnetic power was, then, clearly a medium of knowledge distinct from the brain or mind of the magnetizer, or individual with whom the magnetized is *en rapport*.

What tends to confirm this is the surprising fact that persons mesmerized by a mesmerized glass of water, or bunch of flowers, manifest equally a superhuman knowledge. I passed one day by a boarding-school, and threw over the wall, unseen myself, a bunch of flowers which I had mesmerized. One of the young ladies saw it, picked it up, smelled it, and placed it in her bosom. Almost instantly she became strangely affected, seemed bewitched, acted as one possessed. But what it is important to note is, that she saw and described, as was clearly proved, things with perfect accuracy, which none of the inmates of the school, and neither she nor I, had any human means of knowing. She had learned no language but English, and yet could understand and answer readily in any language in which she was questioned, could and did foretell events, with all the particulars of time and place when they would happen. Moreover, the poor girl herself complained of feeling herself under a foreign power, and one which made her say and do things to which she felt, even at the moment, the greatest repugnance. It was clear, then, that the mesmeric power was not a mere blind force, but acted from intelligence and will, and an intelligence and will foreign to mine, for how could I lodge my intelligence and will in a bunch of flowers, and render them there more powerful than in myself? Clearly the force was not exclusively material, unless matter can be endowed with intelligence and will.

I was somewhat puzzled, it is true, but I was resolved to continue my experiments, and wrest from nature, if possible her last secret. I soon found that it was not necessary to operate with others; that I had the clairvoyant power myself. With a slight effort I could throw myself into the mesmeric state. As soon as I found myself in this state I seemed no longer master of myself. I suffered in entering into it, and on coming out of it, convulsions more or less violent. While in it, I felt oppressed at the pit of my stomach, and my organs of speech seemed to be used by another. When I spoke, it was clear to me that I heard a voice at the pit of my stomach, speaking the words, and I was perfectly conscious of struggling not to say things which, nevertheless, were uttered by my organs. If in this state I sat down to write, my arm and pen seemed seized upon by a foreign power, and moved and guided without any agency of mine. What I wrote I knew not, and had never had in my mind till it came off the end of my pen, and I read it as written down. Evidently the power was distinct from me, and operated by a will not my own.

But I was not at all pleased to find myself subject even momentarily to a foreign power. I did not choose to let another use my organs, and to suffer my own will to lie in abeyance. The question arose, whether the same power could not be made to operate without using my organs. If I could mesmerize a material object, and by that mesmerize persons, why might I not mesmerize by it other material objects, and make them serve as organs to this power? I tried the experiment. I mesmerized a bunch of flowers and laid them on a table in my room, with the will that they should communicate to the table their mesmeric virtue. Immediately the table began to move, and to dance round the room, to raise itself from the floor, to balance itself on two legs, then on one leg, to come to me or remove from me as I willed. I was delighted. I found the force could be communicated to the table. I wished to ascertain whether this power was intelligent or not. I required the table, if it could understand me, to give two raps with one of its feet. Immediately it did so. Then I required it, by the same sign, to tell me, whether it understood me by virtue of the mesmeric force. It gave the sign. Then I requested it to tell me, in the same way, whether this mesmeric force is one of the forces of nature, like electricity or magnetism, or whether it is a spirit. There was no answer. Is it, I asked, a spirit? No answer. If not a spirit, let the table, I said, strike with one foot. No movement. I went to the table, and found it, as it were, nailed to the floor. I could not move it. I am a strong man, of far more than ordinary physical strength, and was then in its full possession. The table was a light card-table, but with all my strength, repeatedly put forth, I could not so much as raise one end of it. This was extraordinary. I sat down on the sofa at a little distance. Immediately I began to hear slight raps, apparently under the table. Very soon they became louder, and seemed to be sometimes on the table, and sometimes under it; sometimes they seemed to come from a corner of the room, and sometimes from under the floor. I knew not what to make of them, but I felt no alarm, and remained calm and undisturbed, in the full possession of all my faculties. In some six or eight minutes they ceased, and then I saw the bunch of flowers which still lay on the table, taken up without visible agency, and carried and placed in a porcelain vase on the mantle shelf. I was sure I was surrounded by invisible and mysterious agencies, but I began to apprehend that I was in the condition of the Magician's apprentice, sung by Goethe, who had overheard the word by which the master evoked the spirits, but had forgotten or had not learned that by which he dismissed them. I however retained my equanimity, and felt that I had gained at least something.

The next day I tried my experiments anew. This time I merely mesmerized the table. It soon began to move, raising itself about six inches from the floor, and whirling round like a dancing dervish. It seemed animated by a capricious or rather a mocking spirit, and it was some time before I could make it behave with a little sobriety. But I had spent the greater part of the night in consulting an old work on magic, which some years before I picked up on one of the Quais of Paris. It was written chiefly in characters and hieroglyphics, which at first I could not decipher; but at length I stumbled upon what I found to be a key to their meaning, and which was scarcely any meaning at all. However, I obtained one or two significant hints, and I went armed with a new power. I held a long dialogue with the table, which, however, I shall not record. I ascertained the origin of the raps, how to produce them, and how to read them. But this was but a trifle. I would have the power visible to my eyes, submissive to my orders, and speak to me in plain and intelligible language, properly so called. I obtained a promise that this should come in due time, but that for the present I must suffer the force to remain invisible, and be content with a language of mere arbitrary signs.

I was informed that I was on the eve of gratifying my most secret and ardent wish, and that I should have, in full measure, the knowledge and power I craved. But I was not yet prepared, inasmuch as I craved them for an irreligious end. I was moved by no noble motive. I was moved by curiosity, and the love of power, for my own sake, not from love and sympathy with mankind. I was not in harmony with the great principles of nature, and did not seek the real end of the universe. I needed purification, a sublimation of my affections, and an elevation of my aims. I had devoted myself to the physical sciences, which was all very well, but I had neglected moral science, which was not well. I had only partially imbibed the spirit of the age, and took no part in the great movements of the day; felt no interest in the great questions of social amelioration and progress. I had no sympathy with the poorest and most numerous class, and made no efforts to emancipate the slave, or to elevate woman to her proper sphere in social and political life. I did not properly love my race, and had no due appreciation of humanity. I had great talents, great abilities, and might, if I would, make myself the Messiah of the nineteenth century.

But what had I done? What good cause could boast of having had me for its friend and advocate? Had I aided the Moral Reform Association? Had I raised my voice in behalf of the Abolitionists? Had Owen or Fourier found me a coadjutor in time of need? Had I risked my popularity in defending new and unpopular sects, those prophets of the future? Or had I given my sympathy to those noble spirits everywhere moving society, and risking their lives to overthrow the tyranny of church and state, to conquer liberty, and to raise up the down-trodden millions of mankind? No, no; I had done nothing of all this. I might have been kind and useful to this or that individual, and sympathized with suffering when immediately under my eyes, and removable or mitigable by my individual effort; but I had not sympathized with humanity, and labored to relieve the poor and destitute, to enlighten the ignorant and superstitious of remote and neglected regions. The age is philanthropic, and love is the great miracle-worker of our times. In love you place yourself in harmony with the source of all things, make yourself one with God, and possessor of his omnipotence. Learn to love, associate yourself heart and soul with the movement party of the times, and you will soon render yourself capable of receiving an answer to your questions and your wishes.

It must not be supposed that all this was told me at once, or in plain, direct terms. It was told me only a little at a time, and in a very indirect and cumbersome mode of communication. It required several weeks daily communing with my mesmerized table, and in spelling out the raps with which I was favored. But though it reproved me, I was still delighted. The power was good, and this accorded with my previous conviction. I regarded the power which, by mesmerism, was brought into play, as one of the primordial laws or elemental forces of nature, and as nature was good, as it worked always to a good end, of course I could hope to avail myself of it only in proportion as I myself became good and devoted to the end to which nature herself works. God will work with and for us, only as we work with and for him; that is, for the end for which he himself works. As to the intelligence apparently possessed by this force, that was in harmony with what of philosophy I had. Is not God infinite, universal intelligence? and is he not the original and similitude of the universe? What, then, is the universe itself but an emanation of infinite and universal intelligence. All creatures participate their creator, for they are nothing without him, and therefore all that exists must participate intelligence, or be a participated intelligence, and, of course, the higher the order of existence, the greater and more comprehensive its intelligence. All nature bears evidence that its laws are the laws of reason, and that its primitive forces are intelligent forces. How, then, should this force not be intelligent, and if intelligent, far more intelligent than I?

I resolved to prepare for placing myself in immediate relation with infinite power and intelligence. I thought I caught a glimpse of a deeper significance in the words, "ye shall be as gods," than had been generally suspected, and I began to think in real earnest that my sweet lady friend in Philadelphia, who had so eloquently and lovingly defended Eve in eating the forbidden fruit, was quite right, and that her disobedience was really a brave and heroic act. Man could really become as a god, but the priests had invented the prohibition to prevent him. The god of the priests, then, could not be the true God, and Satan, instead of being regarded as the enemy, should be, as the author of *Festus* seems to teach, loved and honored as the friend of man. A new light seemed to break in at once upon my mind. The world had hitherto worshipped a false god; it had called evil good, and good evil; it had enshrined in its temples the enemy of man, and chained to the Caucasian rock that god Prometheus, who was the true and noble friend and benefactor of the race.

CHAPTER VII.

A LESSON IN PHILANTHROPY.

Full of my new resolution, I immediately set myself at work to carry it into effect. The safest and most expeditious way of doing it, I thought, would be to place myself at once in communication with some prominent and well-instructed philanthropist. Accordingly, I started forthwith for Philadelphia, to consult the beautiful and fascinating young lady, who, in my previous visit, had so warmly and energetically defended the eating of the forbidden fruit at the suggestion of that first of philanthropists, as a brave, heroic, and disinterested act. She, of all my acquaintances and friends, was unquestionably the one best fitted to complete my initiation into the mysteries of philanthropy, and to inspire and direct me in my efforts at world-reform.

This lady, whom, out of respect to the great Montanus, who claimed to be the Paraclete or Comforter, and professed to have the power of working miracles very much of the character of those wrought by our modern mesmerizers and spiritualists, I must be permitted to call Priscilla, had some years before touched my fancy, and if the truth must be confessed, had made more than an ordinary impression on my heart. She had often visited me in my waking dreams, as a lovely, though flitting vision. She was at my last visit at least twenty-five years old, but as fresh and as blooming as at seventeen, when first I had the pleasure of meeting her. She was a sweet lady, with a lovely and graceful figure, exquisitely moulded, regular and expressive features, and as learned, as brilliant, as fascinating, and as enthusiastic as the celebrated Hypatia of Alexandria, who stirred up the zeal of the good monks of Nitria, gave so much trouble to Saint Cyrill, and spread such a halo around expiring paganism. She had been sent by the Abolition Society as a delegate to the great Anti-Slavery World's Convention at London, and being denied a seat in that illustrious body, because a woman, she had turned her attention to the question of woman's rights, and, after travelling a few months on the continent, had returned home well instructed in Godwin's Political Justice, and a devout believer in Mary Wolstonecroft. She was liberal in her views, and very far from being a "one-idea" woman. Her mind was large and comprehensive, and her heart was capacious and loving enough to embrace and warm all classes of reformers, white, red, black, religious, moral, political, social, and domestic.

The morning after my arrival in the City of Brotherly Love, I called on Priscilla at her residence in Arch Street, as I supposed with her mother.

I found her surrounded by some ten or a dozen reformers, variously dressed; some in petticoats, some in pantaloons: some with and some without beards; the majority appearing to be of what grammarians call the epicene gender. She greeted me kindly, and requested me to be seated; she would be disengaged in a few moments. I took a seat, and amused myself as well as I could in studying the interesting group before me, and considering the sort of materials that go to the making up of a world-reformer, and the charming associates I was likely to have in my new career. Having listened to their several reports, heard their suggestions, and given them her directions, Priscilla soon dismissed them with a sweet smile, and a graceful salute with her hand, that would have done credit to the grace and dignity of an empress. She then seated herself near me, and welcomed me most cordially and affectionately to Philadelphia. My visit was an unexpected pleasure, but all the more welcome. "But," she exclaimed, looking me more closely in the face, and struck with my changed and careworn expression, "what in the world, my friend, has happened to you?"

I was about to reply, when I observed that we were not alone. An exceedingly meek and submissive-looking man, if man he could be called, had just entered the room, and seemed to be hesitating whether to advance or retreat. I looked inquiringly at Priscilla.

"O, it is only my husband," she replied. Then turning, with her sweet face to him, with an indefinable charm in her soft musical tones, said, "You may leave us, dear James. This gentleman and I would be alone."

He quietly retreated through the door he had entered, gently closed it, and went away without speaking a word, or betraying the least sign of discontent.

"But, my dear madam," said I, "this takes me by surprise. I was not aware that you had a husband."

"Possibly not; yet I have been married these five years."

"What! you were married when I was in the city last year and had the pleasure of meeting you, and having that most pleasant and instructive conversation with you?"

"Most assuredly."

"This alters my plan. I had made up my mind,—"

"Not to marry me yourself?"

"Pardon me, my dear madam, but I own that I had dreamed of something of the sort."

"You might have done worse. I could have made you a good wife, but you would never have made me a good husband."

"Why not? I am not precisely a man to be slightly rejected."

"That may be; and had you proposed in season, I might not have rejected you. I am glad, however, that you did not, for I might have loved you, and you alone, and then I should never have become a philanthropist, and devoted all my sympathies and energies to the emancipation of my sex, and to the development and progress of my race. You would have engrossed all my thoughts and affections, and have been my tyrant."

"But if I had loved you in return, and laid my own heart at your feet?"

"That would have made the matter worse. In loving me you would only have loved yourself, and sought only your own pleasure. Men usually love only to sacrifice her they love to themselves; while woman, when she loves, is ready to sacrifice herself to her beloved. Man's love is selfish; woman's is disinterested."

"Women are disinterested creatures, and never exact any return for their love!"

"They are more disinterested than you believe. There is nothing that a true woman will not do for him she loves. She will abandon herself without reserve to his wishes, go through fire and water, nay, hell itself, for him, and take delight in damning her own soul, to please him."

"That is because her love is an instinct, a blind passion, a sort of madness or frenzy, not a sober, rational affection."

"Perhaps so; but it is rather because her love is love. Unhappily, woman feels, she does not reason, or if she reasons, it is only in the interest of her feeling. Reason is cold, calculating; love is warm and self-sacrificing. It is heedless of consequences."

"And therefore is the better for having reason or prudence for a companion."

"It is clear that you have never loved."

"Perhaps not; but at any rate I think I could have loved you very much in your own fashion."

"That is not improbable, at least, as far as it is in your calculating nature; for I have been thought to have my attractions, and it would not be difficult to make any man my slave—unless I loved him. Yet you would always have loved me as a master, and have always held me in subjection. There are natures born to command. You would never have loved me as my dear James loves me, and never have been the meek, submissive, quiet, dear good man that he is. His love is not tyrannical, and it imposes no burden on me. He interferes with none of my plans, restrains none of my movements, and is satisfied with feeling that he is my husband and belongs to me, without once presuming to think of me as his wife and as belonging to him."

"That is charming, and must, no doubt, entirely satisfy your heart."

"That is my own affair. But I will tell you that it does not, and that it does."

"But that is a riddle; pray rede it."

"It does not satisfy the deep want of the heart to love, for no woman can love, with all her heart, a man she can make her slave, or who does not maintain himself as her master. But as I would not become any one's slave, as I would not that any man should engross all my affections, and compel me to live all my life in love's delirium, it satisfies, and more than satisfies me. It leaves me free to be a philanthropist, and does not compel me to give up to one what was meant for mankind. If my husband engrossed all my affections I should be happy and contented at home, and should never seek relief in going abroad."

"And should it not be so?"

"Consult the parsons and old-fashioned moralists, and they will tell you that it should. But I am a philanthropist. My James loves me sincerely, warmly, disinterestedly, consults my wishes, does whatever I require of him, has full confidence in me, is proud of me, and never doubts that whatever I do is perfect. That is enough."

"But do you return his love with a disinterestedness and generosity equal to his own?"

"Why should I? It is enough for him that I permit him to love me, and to call himself my husband. For myself, I remain free to be a philanthropist. I cannot give my heart to any individual. I reserve its deepest and holiest affections for mankind."

"But mankind, without individuals, is an abstraction, a nullity; and to love the race, without loving individuals, is worse than loving a statue or a shadow."

"Ah! my dear friend, I see that you have not studied the profound philosophy of Plato, and are still a Nominalist, and therefore an egotist. You are still a psychologist, stuck fast in the slough of individualism."

"It may be so, my dear Priscilla, but I am willing and even anxious to be liberated and set right. I have resolved, let come what will, to be a philanthropist, and to become a world-reformer; and it is to solicit your instructions and assistance to this end that I have visited your city, and sought my interview with you this morning."

She shook her head and looked doubtingly.

"Do not doubt it," I said, "I am serious, never more serious in my life. I am on the verge of important discoveries, and perhaps well-nigh within reach of a more than human power. But it is necessary that I at first become a philanthropist, unite myself with the movement party of the age, and take a decided and an active part in the great philanthropic reforms now so widely agitated, and live henceforth for mankind, and not for myself alone."

"Is this true?"

"Most assuredly; as true as that I am here present."

Slowly conviction seemed to fasten on her mind as she saw my serious and earnest manner, and indeed my agitation, as I rose from my chair and stood before her. A brilliant joy suddenly sparkled from her large, liquid, deep blue eye, and radiated over her whole face. Springing from her seat, and seizing me by both my hands, "This is too much," she exclaimed. "This I had wished, had prayed for, but had not dared hope." Her eyes filled with sweet tears, and, as if overcome with her emotions, she sunk into my arms, and rested her head upon my shoulder. I pressed her to my breast. But she instantly recovered herself, and we both resumed our seats. After a few moments' silence, Priscilla, with an animated and contented look, exclaimed:—

"Now, my dear, dearest friend, I have hope. The good work will now go bravely on. Pure, noble, and strong-minded women to coöperate with me, I have found, but a man, a full-grown man, with a clear head, and a well-balanced mind, heretofore found I not. The men who have been ready to embark with me, are dwarfs, pigmies, simpletons, needy adventurers, cheats, knaves, or crack-brained enthusiasts, with but one idea in their heads, and that only half an idea. Drill them as I may, I can make nothing of them."

"But," said I, maliciously, "is not your dear James a philanthropist and reformer?"

"My dear James is my husband," she said, with dignity and spirit. "But you are slow to comprehend these things. The great and glorious work of regenerating man and society, cannot be carried on either by man alone or by woman alone. The two must be united and coöperate, or there can be no spiritual, as there can be no natural, offspring. But in regeneration, in the palingenesia, it is not at all necessary that they be husband and wife after the flesh. Married and made one in spirit they must be, but not married and made one flesh. Man and woman are each other's half, and they must be brought together to make a complete, active, and productive whole. But the relation of husband and wife is a purely domestic relation, and looks solely to a domestic end. If each finds the complementary half in the other, both are satisfied, contented, and neither has any wish or motive to look beyond the circle of the purely domestic affections."

"That is, they who find their bliss at home have no need and no temptation to go a-roaming."

"Precisely."

"Then it is unhappiness, discontent, uneasiness, want, at home, that makes men and women turn philanthropists, and take to world-reform?"

"Yes; and herein you learn the deep philosophy of life, and the significance of that Religion of Sorrow, of which Carlyle speaks so touchingly, and which the world has professed for two thousand years, but which it has never understood. Hear my favorite poet:—

'The Fiend that man harries
    Is love of the Best;
Yawns the pit of the Dragon
    Lit by rays from the Blest;
The Lethe of nature
    Can't trance him again,
Whose soul sees the Perfect,
    Which his eyes seek in vain.
'Profounder, profounder
    Man's spirit must dive;
To his aye-rolling orbit
    No goal will arrive;
The heavens that now draw him,
    With sweetness untold,
Once found,—for new heavens
    He spurneth the old.
'Pride ruined the angels,
    Their shame then restores;
And the joy that is sweetest
    Lurks in the stings of remorse.
Have I a lover
    Who is noble and free?
I would he were nobler
    Than to love me.
'Eterne alternation,
    Now follows, now flies,
Under pain, pleasure,
    Under pleasure, pain lies.
Love works at the centre,
    Heart-heaving alway,
Forth speed the strong pulses
    To the borders of day.'

"The 'love of the Best' is our innate and deathless desire of happiness, our being's end and aim. Happiness is ever the coy maiden, that still woos us onward, and flies ever as pursued,

'Man never is, but always to be blest.'

In this deep ever-recurring want of the soul for happiness, the source of all our pain and sorrow, is the spring and motive of all our activity, and in activity is all our life and joy. Hence, 'under pain pleasure, under pleasure pain lies.' All our life and joy have their root in pain and sorrow, in this eternal craving of the soul to be what we are not, and to have what we have not. The pain and sorrow spur us on, and lead us to acquire and possess. But no possession satisfies us. The most coveted is no sooner obtained than it is loathed and cast away.

> 'The heavens that now draw him,
>   With sweetness untold,
> Once found,—for new heavens
>   He spurneth the old.'

"Love dies in the wooing. The acquiring is more than the possessing. All possessing leaves the heart empty,—an aching void within, which nothing fills or can fill. This aching void will not let us rest, will not leave us in repose, which is only another name for inaction, death, but compels us to exert ourselves, to struggle with all our strength and energy to make new acquisitions. In this struggle, in these efforts, humanity is developed, and the progress of the race carried on."

"Carried on, my dear Priscilla, towards what? Sings not your poet,

> 'Profounder, profounder
>   Man's spirit must dive,
> To his aye-rolling orbit
>   No goal will arrive?'"

"That is the glorious secret, my dear friend. The end of man is not the possession, but the pursuit, of happiness, or rather eternal progress and growth. By the fact that the pain, the want, the aching void, remains eternally, there is and must be eternal activity, therefore eternal development and progress of humanity."

"But as that development and progress leave us as far as ever from happiness, or fixed and durable good, I see not in what consists their value."

"Their value is obvious. Good is relative to the end of a being, and consists in going to the end for which it exists. Progress being our end, of course our good must consist in making progress. This progress is the progress of the race, and is effected by the activity of individuals, and to it all the activity of individuals, whether what is called vicious or virtuous, alike contributes."

"If all our activity, our vices, and crimes, as well as our virtues, contribute to this progress, or to the realization of our destiny, I do not see any great call for us to be world reformers. Moreover, our destiny seems to be any thing but a cheering one. Your poet-philosophy is apparently very sad. If we are destined to chase forever a happiness that flies us, a good that recedes as we advance, all exertion seems to me as idle, as useless as that of the child striving to grasp the rainbow."

"So it may seem to you, for you are, as yet, not a philanthropist. You are still affected by your egotism, and unable to appreciate any activity that does not bring something solid and durable to the individual. Here is the rock on which all old-fashioned morality splits. Individuals are nothing in themselves; they are real, substantial, only in humanity. The race is every thing. Individuals die, the race survives. Men and women have no substantiality of their own. They are merely the bubbles that rise on the surface of the broad ocean of humanity, burst, disappear, and become as if they had not been. Foolish bubbles, ye forget your own nothingness, and would arrogate to yourselves all the rights and prerogatives, glory and happiness of humanity. The race is not for individuals; individuals are for the race. They are simply the sensations, sentiments, and cognitions of the race, in which it manifests its own inherent virtuality, and through which it is developed and carried forward in its endless career through the ages,—through which it grows and realizes its own eternal and glorious destiny. The progress you are to seek is not the progress of individuals, for individuals have, properly speaking, no progress; but the progress of the race, which is and can be effected only by the activity of individual men and women."

"Still, I do not comprehend the work there is for world-reformers."

"Why, you are stupid, Doctor. All activity, whether called vicious or criminal, is good, for it aids progress. But nothing is vicious, criminal, or sinful, except that which represses the free activity of individuals, and thus hinders the development and growth of the race. It was, therefore, not a friend, but an enemy, that imposed upon our first parents the prohibition to eat the fruit of the tree of the knowledge of good and evil. It was a friend, not an enemy, that inspired Eve with the thought and the courage to disregard that prohibition, to reach forth her hand and pluck the fruit, and having eaten thereof, to give it also unto her husband. The fable was invented by priests and governors as a means of imposing their system of restraints, of establishing their restrictive policy, to which they have adhered, as old fogie politicians adhere to protection. They have always had a horror of free trade, as incompatible with their monopoly, and have made it their study to repress our native activity, to keep us cabined, cribbed, and confined, within the narrow enclosure of their hidebound systems, of their immoral, contracted, galling, and senseless conventionalism. They will not allow nature, humanity, fair play. They brand, as from the enemy of souls, all free activity. The heart must move according to their rules, and love or hate as they bid; the mind must run only in the grooves which they have hollowed out, and never dare search beneath their solemn shams, or send sharp and piercing glances into the artificial world they have built up around us. We must repress our purest and noblest instincts, and crucify our sweetest and holiest affections. Everywhere restraint, repression, tyranny. The church tyrannizes over the state; the state tyrannizes over man and society; man and society tyrannize over woman, making her a puppet, a toy, or a drudge. Here, my dear, dear friend, behold your work, and that of your fellow-reformers. Go forth and break down this vast system of tyranny. Emancipate the state from the church, man and society from the state, and woman from man and society."

"But some government, some restraint is necessary to keep our appetites, passions, and lusts within bounds, and to maintain peace and order in the community."

"Alas! my friend, how hard it is for you to cease to be an egotist, and to learn to be a philanthropist. Know, that philanthropy seeks no individual, no exclusive good, and does not consist in loving and seeking the welfare of our fellow men and women. It is the love of man, not men, and seeks the welfare of the race, not of individuals. The welfare of the race consists in progress, which is effected only by free activity. All free activity is good, virtuous, right. Virtue is in action, not in non-action, which is death, the wages of sin. The only good is free activity, and every conceivable good is included in that one word, LIBERTY."

"But liberty, if not sustained and regulated by authority, may degenerate into license."

"Still, *mon pauvre ami*, in bondage to the law, and ignorant of the glorious liberty of the children of God. Away with your legal cant. By the deeds of the law no flesh ever was or ever will be justified. Long had the world groaned in this ignoble bondage, but know you not that it was to set them free that the Liberator came? O, liberty! sweet, sacred liberty! how I love thee! My heart and soul pant for thee as the thirsty hind pants for brooks of water. My flesh cries out for thee. Thou art my God, and to thee I consecrate my life, my love, and on thy altar I offer myself a living holocaust."

"Is there really no difference between liberty and license?"

"Be not the dupe of words. You seek to be a philanthropist. Philanthropy, I tell you again and again, is the love of man, mankind, humanity. Who that loves humanity would repress any thing human? If man is the supreme object of your love, how can you distrust any human tendency, or fear any human activity?"

"Suppose, my dear Priscilla, who speak to me as one inspired, I should forget myself so far as not to remember James, and proceed to make love to his wife?"

"She would say you have a very short memory, and no very great sagacity. She would most likely know how to oppose her activity to yours."

"And thus surrender her doctrine; for in such case her activity would overcome mine, or mine would overcome and restrain hers."

"Not necessarily. There would be a struggle of opposing forces, a free activity on both sides, and whatever the result, a development and progress of humanity. But all this is folly. There can be no love passages between us. We understand each other on such matters. United, married, if you will, in spirit, we are, or if not, must be, but we have no leisure or inclination for dalliance, which would be foreign to our mission. Our thoughts, I trust, yours as well as mine, rise higher, and move in a serener atmosphere. But be not disheartened. Our relation is, and must be, purely spiritual."

"I did but ask the question, my dear Priscilla, in order to see if you were prepared to carry out your doctrine to its legitimate conclusion."

"That was foolish. No true woman ever stops half way in her principles, or shrinks from carrying them out, by a cold and cowardly calculation of consequences. She leaves that to masculine virtue. When once women adopt a principle, they are prepared to follow it to its last results, without counting the sacrifice. You men cannot do this. You are always hesitating, deliberating, craving the end, but afraid to grasp it, compromising with your reason and your conscience. Recollect Macbeth, and Lady Macbeth, as painted by Shakspeare, who knew man's heart and woman's too. Here is the reason why you always stop half way in your reforms, or never do more than patch a piece of new cloth on to an old garment, which only makes the rent worse. Hence your need of woman's straightforward logic, her disinterestedness, her singleness of heart, her constancy of purpose, and her invincible courage."

"But perhaps, my dear lady, women are not seldom rash, and what you commend in them is the effect of narrowness of view, and not of that clear and enlarged comprehensiveness, that "many sidedness," to use a Germanism, which is desirable in a true and trustworthy reformer. Perhaps she lacks prudence, and may not use sufficient caution in adopting her principles, and thus may adopt false principles, and find ruin where she imagines she is to find only safety."

"It is safer to trust her instincts than man's reason. Yet I deny not the danger to which you allude, and therefore it is that it is never safe to trust her to act alone. Hence the necessity, in all our movements for reform, of the strict union of man and woman. She needs him as a drag on her too great rapidity of motion, and to temper her zeal with his prudence, and he needs her to inspire him with courage, energy, and love. Either is only a half without the other, and both must be united, as I have already told you, to form a complete and productive whole."

"I think I now understand what is meant by philanthropy. I have the idea, but as a pure idea it amounts to nothing. We must realize it, or reduce it to practice. Our great work is to remodel the world according to this idea. But how is this to be done?"

"That is undoubtedly the most difficult question, although our difficulties will not end even there. When we have ascertained what we are to do, and how it is to be done, we have still the difficult task to do it. But courage, *mon ami*. Once started, reforms are carried forward by their own momentum, and, like popular rumor, grow as they go onward. For myself, I am not exclusive, and have no special plan of my own. I listen to all sorts of plans, and countenance all sorts of reforms. None of them commend themselves in all respects to my understanding any more than to my taste. But all seem to me to be inspired by the same spirit, and in different ways to work to one and the same end. There is a diversity of gifts. All see not truth under the same aspect; none, perhaps, see it under all aspects at once, and each sees it under some special aspect. We must tolerate them all; for to attempt to bring them all into order, and to compel them all to think alike, and to work after one and the same manner, or in one and the same method, is absurd, and if successful, would only establish in another, and perhaps in an aggravated form, the very system of tyranny and repression we are laboring to demolish. You know something already of our reformers, and the most prominent are now in the city, holding conventions. We have representatives from all the Northern and Middle States, and several English and Continental philanthropists. Some of them, I cannot say how many, will meet at my house this evening, and you must meet with them. You will find their conversation interesting and instructive, and perhaps you will become acquainted with some who will give you valuable hints, although, to confess the truth, I have no very high opinion of any of them, taken individually. Be sure and not fail me; come early, at seven o'clock."

So saying, she rose, gave me her hand, *au revoir*, and I departed to my lodgings, charmed with the sweetness and fascinated by the manner of Priscilla, rather than enlightened by her philosophy or convinced by her reasons.

CHAPTER VIII.

A LESSON IN WORLD-REFORM.

When I returned in the evening, I found Priscilla in high spirits, more radiant and fascinating than ever. Her company were slowly assembling in her luxuriously, and even elegantly furnished rooms. Among the earlier arrivals were my friend, Mr. Winslow, and strange enough, my Puritan acquaintance, Mr. Cotton, who had recently become a resident of Philadelphia, and pastor of a Presbyterian church in that city. Others were announced, some whom I knew, but more whom I knew not. The majority were from the middle and upper classes, although all classes of society had their male or female representatives. The principle on which they came together was universal philanthropy, and whoever was a philanthropist, and had an idea, or the smallest fraction of an idea, had the *entrée*, unless he had African blood in his veins. All were of course abolitionists, or friends of the blacks, and therefore excluded studiously the negroes from their social gatherings. Generally speaking, all professed universal democracy, and hence were very exclusive in their feelings, and aristocratic in their tone and bearing; that is, so far as aristocracy consists in a consciousness, not of one's own worth, but of the worthlessness of his brother. The company was too large to have only one centre, and gradually separated into groups according to their special tastes and tendencies. In the centre of each group was some male or female reformer, distinguished from the rest by superior knowledge, volubility, or impudence, and regarded as the oracle of his or her own set, for however loud people's profession of democratic equality, nature will show itself, and every set of them will have its chief, honored as my Lord or my Lady.

Mr. Winslow had been dismissed from his parish, and having no other means of getting his living, he had followed the example of Mr. Sowerby, and devoted himself to lecturing and experimenting on mesmerism. He was urging upon Priscilla the importance of forming mesmeric circles in all the cities, towns, and villages, of the Union. The first thing to be done was to organize a philanthropic Ladies' Aid Society, for the purpose of supporting a mesmeric travelling agent or missionary, whose business should be to form these circles or associations, instruct some member of each in the art of mesmerizing, and serve as their common centre and bond of union. If no one more worthy were found he would himself consent to accept, for a moderate salary, such agency, or to be such missionary. These circles formed, and affiliated, visibly and invisibly to each other, would become a powerful body, and exert a moral influence which both the church and the state, politicians and clergymen, would be obliged to respect. In this way he was sure all the elementary forces of nature herself could be brought to bear on the great and glorious work of world-reform.

Mr. Edgerton, a New England Transcendentalist, a thin, spare man, with a large nose, and a cast of Yankee shrewdness in his not unhandsome face, was not favorable to this plan. "I dislike," he said, "associations. They absorb the individual, and establish social despotism. All set plans of world-reform are bad. Every one must have a theory, a plan, a Morrison's pill. No one trusts to nature. None are satisfied with wild flowers or native forests. All seek an artificial garden. They will not hear the robin sing unless it is shut up in a cage. The rich undress of nature is an offence, and she must be decked out in the latest fashion of Paris or London, and copy the grimaces of a French dancing-master, or lisp like an Andalusian beauty, before they will open their hearts to her magic power. Say to all this, Get behind me, Satan. Dare assert yourselves; plant yourselves on your imperishable instincts; sing your own song of joy, your own wail of grief; speak your own word; tell what your own soul seeth, and leave the effect to take care of itself. Eschew the crowd, eschew self-consciousness, form no plan, propose no end, seek no moral, but speak out from your own heart; build as builds the bee her cell, sing as sings the bird, the grasshopper, or the cricket."

"So," said Mr. Merton, a young man, with a fine classic head and face, who seemed to have been drawn hither by mere curiosity, "so you think the nearer men approach to birds and insects the better it will be for the world."

"I never dispute," replied Mr. Edgerton. "I utter the word given me to utter, and leave it as the ostrich leaveth her eggs. Men should be seers, not philosophers; prophets, not reasoners. I never offer proof of what I say. I could not prove it, if asked. If it is true, genuine, the fit word, opportunely spoken, it will prove itself. If it approves not itself to you, it is not for you. You are not prepared to receive it. It is not true for you. Be it so. It is true for me, and for those like me. Fash not yourself about it, but leave us to enjoy it in peace."

"But are we to understand," replied Mr. Merton, "that truth varies as vary individual minds?"

"Sir, you will excuse me. I am no logician, and eschew dialectics. Truth is one, it is the Whole, the All, the universal Being. It is a reality in, under, and over all, manifesting itself under an infinite variety of aspects. Every one beholds it under some one of its aspects, no one beholds it under all. Each mind in that it is real, is itself, is a manifestation of it, but no one is it in its integrity and universality, any more than the bubble on its surface is the whole ocean. Under each particular bubble lies, however, the whole ocean, and if it will speak not from its diversity, its bubbleosity, in which sense it is only an apparition, an appearance, a show, an unreality, but from what is real in it, from its real substantial self, it may truly call itself the whole ocean. So, under each individual mind lies all truth, all reality, all being; and hence, in so far as they are real, all minds are one and the same. Men are weak, are puny, differ from one another because they seek to live in their diversity, and to find their truth, their reality, in their individuality. Let them eschew their individuality, which is to their reality, their real self, only what the bubbleosity of the bubble is to the ocean, and fall back on their identity, on the universal truth which underlies them. If they will be men, real men, not make-believes, strong men, thinking men, let them be themselves, sink back into their underlying reality, on the One Man, and suffer the universal Over-Soul to flow into them, and speak through them without let or impediment."

"We must," said another Transcendentalist, sometimes called the American Orpheus, "return to the simplicity of childhood. 'Except ye be converted and become as a little child, ye shall in no wise enter into the kingdom of heaven.' The man who thinks, Rousseau has well said, is already a depraved animal. All learning is a forgetting; science and wisdom are gathered from babes and sucklings. We are not prepared as yet to talk of world-reform. We must *be* before we can *do*; be men before we can do men's work. All *being* is in *doing*; rather all *doing* is in *being*. Ideas are the essences, the realities of things. Seek ideas. They will take to themselves hands, build them a temple, and instaurate their worship. Seek not ideas from books; they are lies. Seek them not of the learned and grey-haired; they have lost them. Be docile and childlike; seat yourself by the cradle, at the feet of awful childhood, and look into babies' eyes."

"What we want to cure the evils of society," broke in Mr. Kerrison,—a tinker, I believe,—a small man in a snuff-colored frock coat, with sharp grey eyes, lank cheeks, a short nose, a pointed chin, and squeaking voice, "is a Children's Protection Society; a society that shall protect children from the indelicacy, the cruelty, and inhumanity of their brutal parents. There is nothing more shocking to our finer sensibilities, or more outrageous to true philanthropy, than to see a full-grown woman, tall and stout, with a red face, fiery eyes, and a harsh voice,—or a full-grown man, yet taller and stouter, stern and awful in his look, terrible in his anger tones,—seize a poor helpless little boy or girl,—yes, or girl,—not more than three or four years old it may be, and taking him or her across the knee, strike on the very seat of her or him, blow after blow, till the poor little thing screams with pain and agony. It is indelicate, cruel, barbarous. How would the father or mother like to be treated in the same way? It blunts the delicate sensibility of the child, sours his temper, hardens his heart, develops and strengthens all his harsh and angry feelings, and prepares him to be, when he grows up, as bad as was his father or his mother."

"Our friend," added Mr. Silliman, an amiable young minister, a Unitarian, I believe, or, as he said, a Preacher of the religion of Humanity, "has, I think, gone to the root of the matter. The evils of individuals and of society have their origin in the harsh, cruel, unfeeling, and indelicate manner in which parents bring up their children. Children should never be restrained, should never be crossed; they should always be caressed by the soft, delicate hand of love, be surrounded by sweet and smiling faces, by lovely and attractive images, live in communion with fresh and fragrant nature, and find life all one fairy day."

"Young America," interposed Mr. Merton, "will thank you both, I have no doubt. The abolition of corporal chastisement will meet the decided approval of our little folks, and perhaps of our patriots. It is questionable whether this flogging of children is not an infringement upon equal rights. I do not see what the father in my town, universal democrat as he was, had to reply to the question put to him the other day by Young America. A little rascal, some ten or twelve years old, had done some mischief, for which his father flogged him. Young America bore it with heroic fortitude, as if the honor of his country and of the race was at stake in his person, and when it was over, with the calm and dignified air of a man and a freeman, folded his arms across his breast, looked up to his father, and asked,—'Father, is not this a free country?' 'Yes.' 'By what right, then, do you flog me?'"

"Parents," said a cross-grained old maid, "are wholly incapable of bringing up their children. They have no judgment, no steadiness; at one moment whipping them without rhyme or reason, and the next soothing them with candy, and smothering them with caresses. They impart to them their own tempers, passions, weaknesses, and prejudices. There should be established infant schools at the public expense, where all the children, as soon as twelve months old, should be placed, and brought up by proper persons trained and prepared in normal schools for that purpose."

"You will have to go farther back than that, my good woman," said Mr. Long, an English gentleman just arrived in the country and announced as the Prophet of the Newness. "Children are born with an inclination to evil, and are hardly born before they manifest vicious tempers and a fondness for doing precisely what they ought not to do. If suffered to have their own way, they would never live to grow up. They must, as they are now born, be restrained and even whipped, for their own good. Here the sins of the parents are visited upon the children. We must begin with the parents. We live in a depraved state, and children inherit vitiated moral and physical constitutions from their fathers and mothers. We must look to this fact, and sternly prohibit all persons of obviously vitiated moral or physical constitutions from begetting or bearing children. After that we must turn our attention to improving the breed, as our English farmers have done in the case of their horses, oxen, cows, sheep, swine, dogs, and hens."

"That may be rather difficult to manage in a free country," said Dr. Muzzleton, a professor of Surgery in a Western medical college, "and can hardly be tried, except by the master with his negroes on our Southern plantations. The hopes of philanthropists must rest on something more practical, and less difficult to be accomplished. The philanthropist's dependence is on dietetic reform. The vitiated moral and physical constitution of parents, and which they impart to their children, comes unquestionably from the use of animal food. It is necessary, therefore, to abolish the use of animal food, and have people feed only on a vegetable diet. Nature shows this in the very construction of the human teeth, which are very different from those of the lion, the tiger, and other carniverous animals. Carnivorous animals have no grinders, and their teeth are fitted only for tearing. Man has incisors and molars, which shows that he was intended to cut and grind his food."

"But which serve him very well, since he does not usually eat flesh raw, but cooks it," remarked Mr. Merton. "But the antediluvians eat no flesh. They lived on a vegetable diet, were vegetarians, and yet they became so corrupt that the Almighty sent a flood and destroyed them all, with the exception of eight persons."

"Where do you learn that?" asked Dr. Muzzleton.

"From the Bible and tradition," replied Mr. Merton.

All stared, and many broke out into a loud laugh, at the joke of citing the Bible and tradition as authority in an assembly of philanthropists and reformers. Dr. Muzzleton looked round with great blandness, and said to Mr. Merton, "You see, my young friend, the majority is against you. I respect the Bible in matters pertaining to another world, but I am speaking now as a man of science, not as a theologian. I leave theology to the clergy," bowing on his right to Mr. Cotton, and on his left to Mr. Winslow.

"I respect the Bible in theology no more than I do in science," said Miss Rose Winter, a strong-minded woman, and a decided reformer, of Jewish descent. "The first thing for all reformers to do is to destroy the authority of the Bible and emancipate the Christian world from its morality. It is the great supporter of all abuses, and it and the church are almost our only obstacles to overcome. It sanctions the use of wine and animal food, slavery and the restitution of the fugitive slave, war and capital punishment. It asserts the divine right of government, and forbids resistance to power. It is the fountain of superstition, and the grand bulwark of priestcraft. It calls woman the weaker vessel, forbids her to speak in meeting, and commands her to be in subjection to her husband. We are fools and madmen to talk of our reforms as long as we regard the Bible as any thing more than a last year's almanac."

"In that I think you are right, my dear lady," said Mr. Cotton, dryly.

"I esteem the Bible a good book," said Mr. Winslow. "It contains more genuine and sublime poetry than any other book I am acquainted with, not even excepting Homer. But I do not accept its plenary inspiration, and I feel bound to believe only the truths I find in it."

"And these," remarked Mr. Merton, "I suppose are only what happens to accord with your own opinions for the time being."

"The Bible," interposed Priscilla, "is a genuine book, and faithfully records the real experience of prophets and seers of old times, and is of no value to us save as interpreted by the facts of each one's own inner life. Much of it is local, temporary, colored by the nation and age that produced it, and is no longer of any significance for us; but what there is in it universal, that is the genuine utterance of universal nature, and true for all persons, times, and places, should be accepted, as we accept every genuine word, by whomsoever uttered."

Mr. Merton shrugged his shoulders and said nothing; Mr. Cotton looked black, was scandalized, and muttered, "Rank infidelity." "And what else," said a very gentlemanly young man, who had been talking nonsense for an hour to a bevy of young ladies in a corner of the room, and apparently indifferent to the great matters under discussion, "and what else did his reverence expect in a company of reformers? Yet we are not really infidels. We have only thrown off the mask, and ceased to be hypocrites. Whatever man's profession, ever since it was said, 'It is not good for man to be alone,' and Eve was brought blushing to his bower, woman has been the real shrine at which he has worshipped. This is our ancestral religion, and true to the religion of my fathers, I make woman my Divinity, and lay my offering at Leila's feet."

"Do not believe him," said a saucy young thing, with a sparkling eye and pouting lips. "He worships only himself. Here I have been this half hour trying to convince him that there is something mystic in woman, and that science and religion, as now organized, are false and mischievous, because they are the product of man's genius alone. I have said all the flattering things I could to make him take up the cause of Woman's Rights, and he has only laughed at me."

"You wrong me, fair and adorable Leila; woman reigns supreme now, and we are slaves; what more can she ask?"

"She should be elevated to be the equal of man," said Leila.

"Lowered, my Leila would say," replied the young gentleman.

"And placed in the possession of the same political franchises, have the right to vote at all elections, and be declared eligible to any and every office political, civil, or military," continued Leila, without heeding the interruption.

"But that," said Mr. Merton, "would be hardly fair to us men, and would moreover be dangerous to republican liberty. Mademoiselle Leila would of course be a candidate for the Assembly. All the young men would vote for her, because they would secure her good graces, and all the old men would do the same, in order to prove that they are not old, and have not yet lost their sensibility to female loveliness and worth; she would be elected unanimously. In the Assembly she would rise to propose some measure, throw aside her veil, beam forth upon us with all her charms, and for the same reasons all would support her. She would reign as a despot, which, as a republican, I must protest against."

"She might have rivals; all men do not see with the same eyes," sagely remarked a venerable spinster, with a dried and withered form and face, puckering up her mouth, and endeavoring to look killing."

"That is well thought of," said Mr. Merton.

"Besides," added Mr. Winslow, "the votes of the women would be as numerous as those of the men, and might be thrown for a candidate of the other sex."

"And you may trust to the women themselves to see that no one of their own sex has a monopoly of power," added, caustically, Mr. Cotton.

"You are hard upon us women," pleaded Priscilla. "Women have their weaknesses as well as men theirs, but they can love and admire beauty in their own sex, as much as they do ugliness in men. I do not suppose that placing them on an equality in all respects with men will increase their power as women, but it will increase their power as reasonable human beings. I think woman would lose much of her peculiar power as woman over man, and this I should by no means regret. I would break down the tyranny of sex as I would that of caste or class. I would have men and women so trained, that they could meet, converse, or act together as simple human beings, without ever recurring, even in thought, to the difference of sex."

"That," said the young worshipper of woman, "would be cruel. It would be like spreading a pall over the sun, or extinguishing the lamp of life. Even the garden of Eden

—— was a wild,
And man the hermit sighed, till woman smil'd."

"As long as I remember my mother or my sister," said Mr. Merton, "I would never meet a woman, however high or however humble, without taking note of the fact that she is a woman."

"Things are best as God made them," added Mr. Cotton. "Men and women have each their peculiar character and sphere. Women would gain nothing by exchanging the petticoat for the breeches, or men by exchanging the breeches for the petticoat."

"But I wish," said Leila, poutingly, "to be treated as a reasonable being, and that the young gentlemen who do me the honor to address me would treat me as if I had common sense. I do not want compliments paid to my hands and feet, my face, lips, nose, eyes, and eyebrows."

"And yet," said I, "my sweet Leila, they are well worth complimenting."

She smiled, and seemed not displeased.

"I suspect," remarked Mr. Cotton, with his Puritan slyness, "that the young lady finds the affluence of such compliments more endurable than she would their absence."

"I do not deal much in compliments," said Mr. Merton, "but I do not much fancy persons who are always wise, and never open their mouths without giving utterance to some grave maxim for the conduct of life. There is a time to be silly as well as a time to be wise. Life is made up of little things, and he is a sad moralist who has no leniency for trifles. I love myself to look upon a pretty face, and find no great objection to those pleasant nothings which are the current coin of well-bred conversation between the sexes. Even a gallant speech, a happily-turned compliment, when it brings no blush to the cheek of modesty, is quite endurable."

"I thought you were a parson, Mr. Merton," said Priscilla, "and am surprised to find you so tolerant of what it is said your cloth generally condemns."

"The fair Priscilla may have mistaken my cloth. I am a man, and I hope a gentleman. I love society, and find an exquisite charm in the social intercourse of cultivated men and women. That charm would vanish were they to meet and converse, not as men and women, gentlemen and ladies, but as simple human beings. Could you carry out your doctrine, your sex would, I fear, be the first to suffer from it."

"Perhaps they would," said Priscilla; "but it is woman's lot to suffer, and she was born to redeem the race by her private sorrows. She will not shrink from the sacrifice. You need her at the polls, in the legislative halls, in the executive chair, on the judge's bench, as well as in the saloon, to give purity and elevation to your affections, disinterestedness and courage to your conduct."

"Rather let her be present to infuse noble qualities into our hearts in childhood, and to cherish and invigorate them in our manhood," added Mr. Merton. "Let her mission be by a sweet, quiet, and gentle influence to form us from our infancy for lofty and heroic deeds, and let it be ours to do them."

"I do not like this discussion at all," broke in Thomas Jefferson Andrew Jackson Hobbs, a thorough-going radical, with an unshaved and unwashen face, long, lank, uncombed hair, and a gray, patched frock coat, leather pantaloons, a red waistcoat, and a red bandanna handkerchief tied round his neck for a cravat. "The world can never be reformed by the instrumentality of government, whether in the hands of man or woman. The curse of the world is that it has been governed too much. That is the best government that governs least, and a better is that which governs none at all. We want no government, least of all a government made up of female politicians and intriguers. There never yet was a great crime or a great iniquity, but a woman had a hand in it. The devil, when he would ruin mankind, always begins by seducing woman, and making her his accomplice. We must get rid of all government, break down church and state, sweep away religion and politics, and exterminate all priests and politicians, whether in pantaloons or petticoats, in broadcloth or homespun, and bring back that state of things which was in Judea, 'when there was no king in Israel, and every man did what was right in his own eyes.'"

"Boldly said," remarked Signor Giovanni Urbini, a leader of young Italy, "but it is hardly wise. The people are not yet, especially in my country, prepared for it. They have so long been the slaves of power, and the tools of superstition, that they would be shocked at its bare announcement. They must have their Madonnas, their San Carlos, their San Felippos, and their capucin frati. But a thoroughgoing democratic revolution is no doubt needed, and such a revolution will necessarily result in a no less thorough and radical revolution in religion; but this last we had better leave to come of itself. You cannot work with purely negative ideas. You must have something positive, and that must be the positive idea of the age. Kings, princes, nobles, priests, religions in our times are at a discount, and the secret, silent, but irresistible tendency is to bring up the people. Assert, then, boldly everywhere people-king, people-pontiff, people-god. Fling out to the breeze the virgin banner of the people. Go forth to war in the name of the people, in the inspiration of the people, and always and everywhere shout THE PEOPLE, THE PEOPLE. Break the fetters which now bind the people, emancipate them from their present masters, assert their supremacy, and establish their power, which of course in the last analysis will be our power over them. They will then re-organize society, religion, and politics, and every thing else, after the best model, and in the way which will best meet our wishes."

"I am decidedly opposed to my friend Urbini's doctrine," frankly asserted M. Beaubien, from the sunny south of France, "I want no king-people, and if I must be tyrannized over, I prefer it should be by one man rather than the many-headed and capricious multitude. The evils under which society groans is individualism, which now exerts itself in universal competition, so highly prized by your foolish and stupid political economists. These evils can be removed by no political or religious revolution, neither by your Luthers nor your Robespierres. They can be removed only by the pacific organization of labor, and the arrangement of laborers in groups and series according to their special tastes and capacities, on the newly-discovered principle that 'attractions are proportional to destiny.'"

"A better plan," suggested M. Icarie, also from la belle France, "is to abolish all private property, all private households, industry, and economy, and have the whole community supported, lodged, fed, clothed, feasted or nursed, and transported from place to place, from house to house, at the public expense."

"Admirable," interposed Mr. Cotton, "but who will support the public, and whence will the public draw its funds?"

"Singular questions," replied M. Icarie. "The public will support itself, and draw the necessary funds from the public treasury, as a matter of course."

"And where does the treasury get them?" asked, with a sneer, M. Le Prohne, a native of the ancient Dauphiny, who towered head and shoulders above all the rest. "All your schemes are idle and absurd; property is robbery; abolish it, and all distinction between *thine* and *mine*, and establish a grand People's Bank, and give each one an equal credit on its books."

"And who," sarcastically remarked M. Icarie, "will take care of the Bank, and be responsible for its managers, or see that the drafts of individuals are duly honored?"

"Why not," I asked in my enthusiasm, "make an equal division of property among all the members of the community?"

"That would do very well for a start," suggested Mr. Cotton, "but he was afraid that come Saturday night, a good many would demand, like the sailor, that the property be divided again, as they no longer retained their proportion."

This produced a smile, and as it was late, the company broke up and departed. Those who had had an opportunity of bringing forward their views were very much edified; others who had been obliged to listen, or to keep back their own projects, thought the party exceedingly dull, and could not help thinking that the evening had been spent very unprofitably.

There were, indeed, persons there with plans of reform as wise, as deep, and as practicable as those I have taken notice of, and I owe an apology to their authors for my omissions. These omissions are the result of no ill feeling, and of no intentional neglect; and I certainly would repair them, but as I am pressed for time, and am not writing a history of reformers and projected reforms in a thousand volumes in-folio, the thing is absolutely out of the question. Let it suffice for me to say, that I have by me still some thousand and one of these projects, all of which their authors did me the honor to send me, with their respects, and all of which I examined with all the care and diligence they deserved.

I returned to my lodgings, not so much enlightened or edified by what I had heard as I might have desired, though not much disappointed or discouraged. No plan had been suggested that was not unsatisfactory, and, taken in itself alone, that was not obviously either mischievous or absurd. But under them all I saw one and the same spirit, the spirit of the age, and all were striking indications of a great and powerful movement in the direction of something different from what is now the established order. No one of them would be realized, but it was well to encourage this movement, to join with this free and powerful spirit. Something, as Mr. Micawber was wont to say, "might turn up," and out of the seeming darkness light might at length shine, and out of the apparent chaos order might finally spring forth. I would lend myself to the spirit working, and trust to future developments. With that I undressed, went to bed, and dreamed of Leila, no, Priscilla; no, yes,—it was Priscilla. I was the victorious champion of reform. She was binding my brow with the crown of laurel, when I awoke, and was sad that it was only a dream.

CHAPTER IX.

THE CONSPIRACY.

I slept late the next morning, and it was the middle of the forenoon before I awoke. I arose, made my toilette, drank a cup of coffee, and went to arrange my future plans with Priscilla. I found her sad and apprehensive. She was a true woman, and had no misgivings as to the excellence of the cause she had espoused, but she feared that the conversations of the previous evening might have disheartened me, and made me change my resolution. I set her mind at rest on this point, and assured her that, though I might often change my methods of effecting a resolution once taken, yet nothing could prevent my persistence in it but an absolute conviction of its wickedness, or its absolute impossibility. I had wedded myself to the spirit of the age for better or for worse, and would, if need be, devote myself body and soul to the cause of World-Reform.

On hearing me say this, her face brightened up, and shone with a radiance I had never seen it wear before. She seemed perfectly happy, and turned to me with a look of perfect satisfaction. I will not say that at that moment I had not forgotten the lady's husband, and I will not pretend to say what words of misplaced tenderness might have been uttered or responded to, if we had been left to ourselves. She was young, beautiful, fascinating, and I was a man in the prime of life. Happily, as the interview was becoming dangerous, Mr. Merton was announced. This young man, who seemed to have thought beyond his years, had deeply interested me the previous evening. I knew not who he was, whence he came, or why he associated with persons with whom he seemed to have very little sympathy. He was evidently a gentleman, and well educated. His dress was rich but plain, his manners were simple and unpretending. He was tall and well proportioned, with a classical head, a high, broad forehead, large, black eyes, and very thick, dark hair. His features were open and manly, and his voice low, rich, and musical. It was a pleasure to hear him speak. His name was English, but he seemed to be of foreign descent, although I afterwards learned that he was an American, and even a New Englander, but bred and educated abroad. He apologized for calling, but he could not refrain from paying his respects to his fair and amiable hostess of the evening. He hoped that she had enjoyed herself with her guests, and that she had suffered no inconvenience from the heat of the rooms occasioned by so great a crowd. He was most happy also to meet me. He had heard of me, knew and highly esteemed some of my friends, and regretted that he had not previously had the honor of making my acquaintance.

He was requested to be seated, and assured that his call was most agreeable, and that we both hoped to meet him often and cultivate a further acquaintance. The conversation ran on for some time in an easy natural way, on a variety of general topics, till Priscilla, whose soul was absorbed in her philanthropic projects, asked Mr. Merton how it happened that she had the pleasure of meeting him so often among reformers. "You evidently," said she, "are not of us. The quiet remarks, sometimes serious, sometimes sarcastic, which you every now-and-then make, prove that you have no sympathy with us."

"I am not surprised, my dear Madam, at your question," replied Mr. Merton, "yet I too am a reformer, in my way, perhaps not precisely in your way, nor on so large a scale as that on which you and your friends propose to carry on reform. I have not the talent, nor the disposition to engage in any thing so magnificent. I think reform, like charity, should begin at home."

"But not end there," said I.

"Certainly not," he replied; "certainly not with those who have leisure and means to carry it further. But I find that it is more than I can do, by my unassisted efforts, to reform myself, and if I can succeed in saving my own soul, I shall be quite contented. It is, I fear, more than I shall be able to do."

"I see, sir, you are no philanthropist," said Priscilla.

"Perhaps not, I am comparatively a young man, but am quite old-fashioned in many of my notions."

"One of those, I dare say, who have eyes only in the back side of their heads, and live only among tombs," said I, in a tone between jesting and earnest.

"I have not yet sufficiently mastered the wisdom of antiquity to be authorized to cry out against it," he replied. "I make no doubt, however, but you, dear lady, and you my learned friend, are quite competent to reject the old wisdom for the new."

"On the contrary, I am inclined to think that my present tendency is to reject the new for the old, the modern for the ancient. Or, rather, it seems to me that the progress of modern science is rapidly and surely leading us back to the ancient wisdom."

"There were in the old world, as there are in the modern, two wisdoms, the wisdom from above, and the wisdom from below. May I be permitted to ask to which of these you regard modern science as conducting?"

"There has been in regard to these ancient wisdoms," said Priscilla, "much misconception. The world in its nonage was imposed upon, and induced to call evil good and good evil. The wisdom I assume, and am laboring to diffuse, is that which the priests have branded as Satanic. Satan is my hero. He was a bold and daring rebel, and the first to set the example of resistance to despotism, and to assert unbounded freedom. For this all the priests, all rulers, despots, all who would hold their brethren in bondage, have cursed him. I take his part, and hope to live to see his memory vindicated, and amends made for the wrong which has been done him."

"That is a candid avowal, my fair lady, and one which we seldom, especially among your sex, hear made. I suspect, that Madame Priscilla has listened or will listen to the modern spiritualism, which seems to me to be a revival of demonic worship. May I entreat you, dear lady, to pause and reconsider the conclusion to which you have come? The ancient Gentiles deserted the true God, the Creator of heaven and earth, and all things visible and invisible, and followed strange gods, erected their temples and consecrated their altars to devils, to fallen spirits, and I need not tell you how their minds became darkened, and their hearts corrupted. Do not, I entreat you, seek to revive the gross, cruel, and obscene superstitions of the ancient Gentiles, and on which Christianity has made an unrelenting war from the first."

"I was sure, Mr. Merton, you were a parson. Will you deny it now?" said Priscilla.

"I am not aware that I have said any thing but what any honest Christian or fair-minded man, who really wishes well to his fellow beings, and who has read history, might not very well say. It is not necessary to be a parson, I should hope, in order to have good sense and good feeling."

"I do not see, Mr. Merton," said I, "any tendency to superstition in modern spiritualism. Superstition is in charging to supernatural intervention what is explicable on natural principles."

"That is one form of superstition," replied Mr. Merton, "but there is another, which consists in ascribing effects to inadequate causes, as where one augurs good luck from seeing the new moon over his right shoulder, or bad luck if on the day he sets out on his travels a red squirrel crosses his path. But I interrupt you."

"I believe the spirits which are evoked in our days are real, but that they are the primal forces of nature, and that it is on strictly natural principles that they are called to our aid," I resumed. "There is no superstition in this."

"It is not improbable that the ancient Gentiles thought as much. I am by no means disposed to ascribe all the phenomena of mesmerism, table-turning, and spiritual rapping to superhuman or preternatural agency. Satan can affect us only through the natural, but through that he may carry us beyond or drag us below nature. I believe mesmerism, strictly speaking, is natural, but I believe also that its practice is always dangerous, and that it throws its subjects under the power of Satan. In the so-called mesmeric phenomena there are those which are natural, and those which are Satanic, although in the present state of our science it may not be easy in all cases to distinguish between them."

Here the conversation, which was beginning to interest me, (for I had a lurking suspicion that Mr. Merton was right,) was interrupted by the entrance of Signor Urbini, who gave unequivocal signs that the presence of Mr. Merton was very disagreeable to him. Mr. Merton, probably not wishing to encounter young Italy, or to enter into a contest with him at that time, after a few commonplace remarks, took his leave. Young Italy was full of fire and enthusiasm, but at the same time, well informed, subtile, and clear-headed. He had been implicated in a conspiracy for overthrowing the Austrian government in Milan, and had escaped to England, where he had concerted with the friends of Italy a plan for revolutionizing the whole peninsula. He had come to the United States to enlist as large a portion of our own people as possible on his side, and to obtain pecuniary aid in carrying out his revolutionary projects. For himself be had no religion, and feared neither God nor the devil. At heart, as does every Italian liberal, he despised Protestantism, as a religion; but his chief reliance was on Protestant nations, and he made a skilful and adroit appeal to the Protestant hatred of Popery. Italy was the stronghold of Popery, and if Italy could be wrested from the Pope, the whole fabric of superstition and priestcraft would fall to the ground. But this could not be done by any direct attacks on the national religion, or any direct advocacy of the doctrines of the Reformation. Out of Italy the appeal might be made to the Protestant feeling, but in Italy, and by all the leaders of the Italian party it must be made solely to the national sentiment as against Austria, and to the love of liberty, the democratic sentiment, as against the Pope and the native princes. War must be made on the Pope indeed, but ostensibly on him only as temporal prince. Overthrown as temporal prince, and his States declared a Republic, and maintained as such, the church, as the upholder of tyranny on the Continent, would be annihilated, and universal democracy, and a purely democratic religion could be established throughout the world; and civilization, arrested by the Goths and Vandals, who overturned the old Roman Empire, might resume its triumphant march through the ages. Plans were forming to make the democratic revolution as nearly simultaneous as possible in France, Austria, Prussia, and Central Germany; at least to give these countries sufficient employment at home to render them unable to go to the assistance of the Pope.

Subsidiary to his purpose, he proposed a grand World's Convention, composed of delegates from the whole Protestant world, to be holden as soon as possible at London. It might be assembled ostensibly for the purpose of bringing about a better feeling and closer union of the various Protestant sects, and none but those who could be safely trusted should be initiated into its ulterior objects. Only the managers need know its real purpose, or *modus operandi*. It might form a Protestant Alliance, and recommend the formation of Protestant associations in all Protestant States for the protection of the Reformation against Popery, the conversion of the Pope and his Italian subjects. These associations would have nothing to do but to raise funds, and meet once a year, hear reports, and listen to flaming speeches in praise of the Bible and religious liberty, and against the tyranny, idolatry, and superstition of Popery. Thus they would, without knowing it, prepare the way and furnish the means of driving the foreigner out of Italy, dethroning the Pope, establishing the Roman Republic, and spreading liberty throughout the world, and in a way, too, not to alarm the religious sensibilities of the Italians, because those who showed themselves to Italians would have apparently no connection with the Protestant movement.[2]

The plan of Young Italy, communicated with further details, and which was substantially carried out from 1845 to 1849, when, contrary to all human foresight, Republican—not Imperial—France suppressed the Roman Republic, and restored the Pope, struck Priscilla and myself as admirable, and we resolved to give it our hearty support. I hoped, by the new power I had discovered, or was on the point of discovering, to bring an unexpected force to its aid. The Signor accepted our pledges, enrolled our names, administered to us the oath, and gave us the signs and passwords agreed upon by the government of Young Italy.

When Signor Urbini had taken his leave of us, we, that is, Priscilla and myself, came to a mutual understanding of the respective parts we were to perform. We agreed that it was useless for either to attempt any thing without the other. Our covenant was sealed. Poor Priscilla, little did she foresee what the future had in store for her! But let me not anticipate. We embraced, and I returned to my lodgings, intending to leave the next day for my home in western New York. Hardly had I regained my lodgings at the hotel, when I was called upon by the stanch old puritan, Mr. Cotton. I have departed far enough from the stand-point of my puritan ancestors, and have few traces in my moral constitution of my puritan descent; but, I care not who knows it, I am proud of these stern old men, the Bradfords, the Brewsters, the Hookers, the Davenports, and the stout Miles Standish, who came forth into a new world to battle with the wilderness, the savage, and the devil. Stern they were, stout-hearted, and strong of arm, yet not without a touch of human feeling. They had their loves, their affections, and their soft moments, when Jonathan or Ezekiel wooed his Beulah or his Keziah, who blushingly responded to his addresses, and the husband kissed his wife, the mother her boy, if it was not on the Sabbath. Honor to their memory! They did man's work, and earned man's wages, and as well might one of the modern Trasteverini blush for his old Roman progenitors, as I for my old puritan ancestors, who brought with them the bravest hearts and the best laws and the noblest institutions of old England, which they loved so tenderly, though she sent them forth as the Patriarch's wife did Hagar and the dear Ismael into the desert. I liked Mr. Cotton, too, for his great ancestor's sake, for great, O Cotton Mather, thou wast in thy day; hard service didst thou against fiends and witches, and powers invisible; and a noble epic hast thou left us in thy Magnalia. The college thou lovedst so well, and which thou didst cherish in thy heart of hearts, "*pro Christo et Ecclesia*," may have ceased to cherish thy memory, and the Second Church, over which thou wast pastor as colleague with thy father, has learned to blush at thy memory, and to imagine it shows its wisdom in calling thee a "learned fool." I, who have as little sympathy with them as with thee, honor thee as one of the worthies of my country, and as one who was not the least among the worthies of my native land in thy day and generation. Men look upon thee as antiquated, and fancy that they have become wiser than thou wast. Would to Heaven they had a little of thy good sense, and of the truth, which thou wast not ashamed to profess and defend!

But this is quite aside from my purpose, and is artistically considered a blemish in my narrative. But few are the writers who, if they speak out from warm hearts their true, deep, genuine feelings as they arise, but will violate some canon of art. I love art, but I love nature more. I love a smoothly shaven lawn; I say nothing against your artificial garden, trim and neat, where each plant and shrub grows and flowers according to rule; but the wild forest, with its irregularities, decaying logs, huge trees, fresh saplings, and tangled underbrush, was as a boy, when it was my home, and is now I am a man, much more my delight. By the same token, I love Boston, whose streets were laid out by the cows going through the brushwood to drink, where you cannot find a square corner, or a street a hundred yards in length without a curve, better than the city of Penn, laid out by a carpenter's line and chalk, and presenting only the dull monotony of the chess-board, without the excitement of the game. Yet the city of Penn has its merits. Many a pleasant hour have I spent there, and many a sweet association is entwined in my memory with its rectangles, and its plain, uniform, drab-colored costume. But I have left Mr. Cotton all this time standing. It was unintentional, for I was not displeased to see him.

He knew me as the son of an old friend, and he had, both as a friend and as a minister of religion, called to expostulate with me. He was sure that I was imperilling my soul, and he could not answer it to his conscience, if he did not solemnly and yet affectionately warn me of my danger.

I have been sadly remiss in my faith and in my conduct, yet never have I allowed myself to treat with scorn or contumely any professed minister of religion who addressed me in tones of sincerity and affectionate earnestness. Mr. Cotton, I was sure, meant well, although I knew his expostulations would avail nothing, and his warning be unheeded. I listened with respect, but untouched. At that time my heart was hard. I was laboring under a perfect delusion, and body and soul were under the power of the Evil One. "You may not believe it, Doctor," said Mr. Cotton, "but I tell you that you are forming a league with the devil. I know you have grown wiser than your fathers were; that you deny the existence of a devil or of evil spirits, but you are wise only in your own conceit, and you are now really dealing with the devil, are plotting to do the devil's work, under pretence of science and world-reform. I have watched you these many months, and I see where you are going. You are also permitting yourself to be seduced by a Moabitish woman, and allowing yourself to be cheated, with your eyes open, out of your five senses by the sparkle of her eye, and the ruby of her lip. Why have you suffered her to bewitch you? Leave her, never see her or speak to her again, or you are a lost man."

I am naturally a very mild-tempered man, and am not and never was very sensitive to wounds inflicted by the tongue; and Mr. Cotton might have abused me or said all manner of hard things against me till he was exhausted, and I could have remained unmoved; but when he alluded to my relation with another, especially since I could not defend it, and called the beautiful, the lovely, the philanthropic Priscilla a Moabitish woman, and attacked her honor, my blood was up, and I instantly resolved that he should suffer for it. I however kept this to myself, assured him that he was uncharitable, and judged an estimable lady rashly; that my relations with Priscilla were not precisely a matter for his cognizance, as we were neither of us under his parochial charge. I respected him as an old friend of my father's, and as a descendant of one of the greatest men of the early Massachusetts Colony. I had no doubt of his good intentions, and affectionate interest in me and my family; but I was of age, and competent to take care of myself. What I was doing I was doing with my eyes open, calmly, deliberately, and from what I held to be justifiable motives. I was prepared to take the responsibility. Warnings, expostulations, would avail nothing. I was resolved to push my scientific investigations to the furthest limits possible. I would, if I should be able, wrest from nature her last secret, and avail myself of all her mysterious forces. I did not pretend to say whether there were devils and evil spirits or not, although I believed God made all things good, very good; but if there were, I had nothing to do with them, for I invoked mysterious agencies only for a good end, in the cause of philanthropy and human progress. If they were spirits I was dealing with, they must be white spirits rather than black; and if I studied and even practised magic, I was sure it was not black magic, but white.

"All that is very well said," replied Mr. Cotton, "and yet you know that you are carried away by indiscreet curiosity, by an unholy ambition, and perhaps by lawless lust, and you dare not, alone in your closet, ask the blessing of God on your proceedings. Bear with me. I am an old man, and let my gray hairs plead with you, if not my sacred profession. I know that the young men of our time lose their reverence for religion, and turn up their noses in profound disgust when we speak to them of duty and the solemn responsibilities of life. I know they are impatient of restraint, and burning with a passion for liberty, as they call it. I know they deem it wisdom to depart from the old ways, to forsake the God of their fathers, and to hew out to themselves cisterns, alas, broken cisterns, which will hold no water. But let me tell you, my friend, that they are only sowing the seeds of future sorrow, and will reap only a too abundant harvest. No man in his old age ever regretted that he feared God and practised virtue in his youth."

"All that may be very true, Mr. Cotton, but much of it comes with no good grace from a Puritan who has allowed himself the freedom of his own judgment in religious matters. It is not long since your fathers forsook their fathers' God, and hewed out cisterns for themselves; whether broken cisterns or not, it is not for me to say; certainly they departed from the old ways, followed the new wisdom of their times, and you honor them for it. Perhaps posterity will in like manner honor me and my associates for daring to follow the new wisdom of our times, and to incur reproach for my adhesion to the work of human emancipation. I am enlarging the boundaries of human knowledge, laying open to view the invisible world, and proving that, under the old doctrine of the communion of saints, there is a great and glorious truth, cheering and consoling to us in this life of labor and sorrow. I am freeing the world from the monster, superstition, and delivering the people from their gloomy fears and terrible apprehensions. They shall no longer start and tremble at ghosts and hobgoblins, or be obliged, with the Papists, to cross themselves, or with our New England youth, to whistle Yankee Doodle to keep their courage up, when, after dark, they go by a graveyard. What torture did not my superstitious fears cause me in my childhood! I never have known what it was to fear any living thing. I have been tried, and have always found my courage and self-possession equal to the occasion, and I could alone face an armed host without trembling; but even now I cannot open the door into a dark room without trepidation, without starting back till reason comes to my aid. I never sit alone in my room reading till twelve o'clock at night, without having a mysterious awe creep over me. I am oppressed by the presence of the invisible, and my very lamp seems to burn blue. All is the sad effect of the frights I received in my childhood, occasioned by the ghost and witch stories which old people would meet together and tell of a long winter's evening. I, a lad, listened with ears erect, and hair standing on end. My blood seemed to freeze in my veins, and I dared not look around me lest I should see the invisible. I was ready to shriek with agony when sent to bed in the dark, and unless watched would throw myself into bed without taking off my clothes, and cover up my head and face in the bed blanket. How terrible was the dark! The impression wears not out with time, and will remain till death. Now I would free the mind from all these idle fears, and save the people, especially children, from these terrible sufferings. It is a good work, and none but white spirits will aid me in it."

So saying, he took up his hat and cane, and, slightly bowing, left my room without hearing a word in reply, or giving me a parting greeting. When he was gone, I laughed to myself at his solemn admonition, and renewed my resolution that he should suffer for the manner in which he alluded to my dear Priscilla. He should know whether she was a Moabitish woman or not. Warn me! Pray what had I done? Where was the harm? Was it wrong to investigate the principles of nature, to learn what nature really is, and to call her forces into play, providing they were not applied to a bad end? Could it be a good spirit that would debar us from acquiring science, or a bad spirit that would bid us inquire, to learn our strength, and to use it? Would it be no slight service to relieve the more mysterious parts of science from the reproaches cast upon them? Has it not been computed that more than a million of persons alone suffered as sorcerers and sorceresses, or for dealing with the devil, in the sixteenth century and seventeenth alone? What injury has not been done to genuine science by the absurd legislation against magic, sorcery, and the so called black arts generally. No man could rise above the vulgar herd, and produce some ingenious piece of mechanism, but the rabble accused him of magic, and it was lucky if he escaped a criminal prosecution and conviction before the courts of justice. Was not that noble heroine, Joan of Arc, who saved France from becoming an English province, burnt as a witch? Was not Friar Bacon, the father of modern science, and the forerunner of his namesake of Verulam, accused of magic, imprisoned, and thus scientific discoveries and useful inventions postponed for centuries? Had not hundreds of old women, who had nothing of sorcery about them but their poverty, weakness, and imbecility, been dragged before the courts, and hung or burnt as witches? What more lamentable page in our own American history than that of Salem witchcraft? Is it nothing to disabuse the world, to save so many innocent victims, remove so great a hinderance to science and heroic deeds, by bringing the class of facts, superstitiously interpreted, within the bounds of nature and legitimate science? Then, again, what may not be finally obtained for the human race? Are the resources of nature exhausted? They sought once the philosopher's stone, the elixir of life, the fountain of youth; who knows but these may one day, and that not far distant, be found, if not in the shape sought, in others, more simple and convenient?

Thus I resisted the admonitions of the good old man, and confirmed myself in my resolution. I meditated a long time as to my future procedure, and how I could bring my new science, which I trusted soon to complete, to bear on the great revolutionary movement which the active spirits of the day had concerted, and which must soon break out. I could discern my way only dimly, but I trusted the mist would soon clear away, and my method be no longer obscure or uncertain. Monarchy must be overthrown because it upholds religion, and religion because it upholds monarchy, and imposes vexatious restraints. So much was clear, and determined on. Time and events would reveal the rest.

Late in the evening I called at Priscilla's, saw her a moment, whispered a word in her ear, gave her one or two directions, pressed her hand, only as my accomplice, and henceforth my slave. The next morning I left Philadelphia, and returned home a much altered man. My body was light and buoyant, and I felt as if I was all spirit. I simply greeted my mother, but felt that the strong tie which bound me to her was broken; my sister, whom I had tenderly loved, was indifferent to me, and I hardly deigned to notice her. I went into my laboratory, saw that all was right there; from that I passed into my library to resume my experiments.

[2]This is in the main historical, and was communicated to the writer through a mutual friend, by a delegate from Connecticut to the World's Convention, alluded to in the text.

CHAPTER X.

MR. COTTON IS PUZZLED.

I proceeded to magnetize my table. It responded as usual. I put my former questions, but could get no answer to them, except that the time for the revelation I solicited was not yet come. I asked, if there was not a more direct mode of communication possible, and was told there was. By speech? Not yet. By writing? Yes. I took a slate and pencil, and placed my hand in the attitude to write. Immediately my hand was moved by an invisible force, and a communication was made in the handwriting and signed with the name of my father, who had been dead some eight or nine years. The purport of it was not much. I did not know but I unconsciously moved the pencil myself. I wished a better test. I placed the slate on the table, laid the pencil on it, and called up the power, whoever or what it might be, to write without my assistance. Very soon the pencil rose fully up, then fell back, then rose again, and after vacillating awhile, it became firm in its position and was moved regularly backwards and forwards, as if directed by the hand of a scribe. At length it flew up to the ceiling, whirled round there for a few seconds, and then placed itself quietly on the slate. I examined the slate, found a communication on it in the handwriting and signed with the name of Benjamin Franklin. The communication consisted of one or two proverbs from Poor Richard, and a commonplace remark about electricity. All this was marvellous enough, but very little to my purpose. It was not worth while taking so much trouble to get what was of no use when got.

I sat down in my great arm-chair a few feet from my table, and fell into a brown study. How long I remained so I do not know, when I was aroused by a great racket in my room. My table was cutting up capers, rising now to the ceiling and now frisking round the room, anon balancing itself on one leg, and then going off into a whirl, that would have broken the heart of the best waltzer, all to a tune which some invisible hand was playing upon my guitar,—tune I say, but it was rather a capriccio, and a medley of a dozen different melodies, thrown together in the wildest disorder. Very soon this stopped, and then came thundering raps all about my room, making every thing in it jar. I bid them be quiet, and not all speak at once, like a lot of old women at a tea-party. They partially obeyed me. One rapper however continued, but in a more gentle and polite manner. I was willing to have some conversation with him. I asked him who he was? He would not answer. What did he want? To communicate. Very well, I would listen; and he told me that I was not a good medium myself, for I held the spirits in awe. Ah, spirits, are you? said I. "Yes." Very well; I shall be very happy to make your acquaintance. "But you must find us other mediums; we cannot speak freely with you."

Close by me lived the Fox family. There were three sisters; one was married, and the other two were simple, honest-minded young girls, one fifteen, the other thirteen. As I passed by their house, I saw them in the yard. I greeted them, and offered them some flowers which I held in my hand. The youngest took them, thanked me with a smile, and I pursued my walk. These were the since world-renowned Misses Fox. In a short time afterwards they began to be startled by strange, mysterious knockings, which they could not account for, and which greatly annoyed them. It is not by any means my intention to follow these girls, in their course since, with whom I have had very little direct communication; but I owe it to them and to the public to say, that they were simple-minded, honest girls, utterly incapable of inventing any thing like these knockings, or of playing any trick upon the public. The knockings were and are as much a mystery for them as for others, and they honestly believe that through them actual communication is held with the spirits of the departed. They are in good faith, as they some time since evinced by their wish to become members of the Catholic Church, which certainly they would not have wished, in this country at least, if they looked upon themselves as impostors, and had only worldly and selfish ends in view. They are no doubt deceived, not as to the facts, as to the phenomena of spirit-rappings, but as to the explanation they give or attempt to give of them. They have not always been treated, I fear, with due tenderness, and sufficient pains has not been taken to enlighten them as to the real nature of these phenomena.

But who need be surprised at this? Received science rejects every thing of the sort, for it recognizes no invisible world, believes in neither angel nor spirit, and explains every thing on natural principles. Even theologians have to a great extent forgotten the terrible influence, in times past, of demonic agencies, and, if they do not absolutely reject the instances recorded in the Bible, they are disposed to treat all other cases as humbuggery, knavery, deception, or to class them with epilepsy, insanity, hallucination, and other diseases to which we are subject, and to dismiss them, when they cannot be denied, with the physicians, under the heads of mania, monomania, nymphomania, demonopathy, &c. I have before me the *Dictionaire Infernal* of M. Collin de Plancy, approved by the late Archbishop of Paris,—him who fell so gloriously on the barricades, June, 1848, whither he had gone as a minister of charity and peace,—in which, from beginning to end, there is a studied effort to represent all these dark and mysterious phenomena as explicable without any resort to superhuman or diabolical agency. The excellent author seems to write on the supposition that all the world, the physicians, the clergy, the magistrates, the civil and ecclesiastical courts during all past times were merely old grannies, and had no sound doctrine, and no capacity for investigating the truth of facts obvious to their senses. With his mode of reasoning, and with far less violence, I can explain away all the miraculous or mysterious relations in Biblical history. But so strong is the current against Satanic agency in the production of these phenomena, and such the prevailing and shortsighted incredulity of our times, that even those who suspect the true explanation are, for the most part, deterred from the ridicule which would be showered upon them from avowing it.

It is no wonder that no kind, considerate friend was found to take these poor Fox girls by the hand, and attempt to rescue them from their dangerous state. The great mass of those who could have done so, either paid no attention at all to the mysterious phenomena asserted, or looked upon the whole matter as mere humbug. It was easier to crack a joke at the expense of spirit-rappers, than it was to investigate the facts alleged, or to offer the true and proper explanation. I had foreseen that it would be so, or at least, had foreseen that they, whose duty it is to watch over the interests of religion and morals, were unprepared to meet the phenomena with success; that they would at first deny and laugh, and then vituperate and denounce, but would hardly understand and explain till too late, or till immense mischief had been done. Even now the first stage is hardly passed, and the movement I commenced by a present of flowers to these simple girls has extended over the whole Union, invaded Great Britain, penetrated France in all directions, carried captive all Scandinavia and a large part of Germany, and is finding its way into the Italian Peninsula. There are some three hundred circles or clubs in the city of Philadelphia alone, and the Spiritualists, as they call themselves, count nearly a million of believers in our own country. Table-turning, necromancy, divination becomes a religion with some, and an amusement with others. The infection seizes all classes, ministers of religion, lawyers, physicians, judges, comedians, rich and poor, learned and unlearned. The movement has its quarterly, monthly, and weekly journals, some of them conducted with great ability, and the spirits, through the writing mediums, have already furnished it a very considerable library,—yet hardly a serious effort has as yet been made in this country to comprehend or arrest it. It is making sad havoc with religion, breaking up churches, taking its victims from all denominations, with stern impartiality; and yet the great body of those not under its influence merely deny, laugh, or cry out, "humbug!" "delusion!" Delusion it is. I know it now, but not in their sense.

The public never suspected me of having had any hand in producing the Rappo-Mania; and the Fox girls, even to this day, suspect no connection between the flowers I gave them and the mysterious knockings which they heard; and nobody has supposed Andrew Jackson Davis, the most distinguished of the American *mediums*, of having any relations with me. He does not suspect it himself, yet he has been more than once magnetized by me, and it has been in obedience to my will that he has made his revelations. The public have never connected my name with the movement, and even Priscilla has never known my full share in it. I have had my instruments, blind instruments, in all civilized countries, with whom I have worked, and yet but few of them have known me, or seen me.

My readers may indeed be incredulous as to the influence conveyed by flowers; but I shall satisfy them on that score before completing my Confessions. While the Fox girls were annoyed by these mysterious knockings, and were beginning to draw on them the attention of the curious and the credulous, and while Andrew Jackson Davis, as yet only a somnambulist, was dictating his wonderful revelations, and learned doctors were disputing whether he received them from a white or a black spirit, whether he really saw what he professed to see in his clairvoyant state, or only reported to the scribe the lesson which some cunning scamps had previously taught him, and made him commit to memory; my old friend Mr. Cotton was made to suffer a severe penalty for the slighting manner in which he had spoken of Priscilla. Contrary to her usual custom, Priscilla went one Sunday evening to his evening service. On leaving the meeting-house, she mingled in the crowd, and so contrived it as to rub against a granddaughter of Mr. Cotton, an interesting child of some twelve or thirteen years of age, and without anybody observing it. She then turned a little aside, got into her carriage, which was waiting, and drove home. The next day, the young girl, Clara Starkweather, was singularly affected. Every thing she touched seemed to stick fast to her fingers. All the dresses, cloaks, shawls, in the house seemed to have an irresistible propensity to fly to her, and arrange themselves on her back. She went into the kitchen; the poker, shovel, and tongs, pots, kettles, pails, basins, all set to dancing towards and around her, and the frying-pan fastened itself on her head as a cap. Her mother scolded her, and she, poor thing, began to cry, and declared that she did not do it, but that it was done by a strange woman, very beautiful, but very wicked, whom she did not know. The family were all in consternation. Mr. Cotton was called upon to interpose. He concluded that it was a case of witchcraft, or of diabolical obsession. He summoned all the inmates of his family to his study. He was a brave man, and nothing at all loath to come to hand-grip with the devil, for whom, with his orthodoxy, he fancied himself more than a match. "We must," he said, "resist the evil one; we must wrestle in prayer." With that he seated himself before his table, on which lay a splendid edition of the Bible. He opened the book, intending to read a chapter, before making his prayer. But he had hardly opened it before it was violently closed, and rising, seemingly of itself, hit him a heavy blow in his face, which knocked him from his chair, and nearly stunned him, and then rested itself on the top of Clara's head. Mr. Cotton soon recovered from the blow, and stood up, after the manner of his sect, to pray. He had hardly opened his mouth, before there was heard such a knocking behind the walls, against the doors, and under the floor, that every word he attempted to utter was completely drowned. It was impossible to proceed amid such a thundering din and racket, which threatened to pull the house down about their ears. Forthwith out marched from the library shelves a complete edition of Scott's Family Bible. The several volumes drew themselves up on the floor, and proceeded, with great skill and even science, to knock one another down, while various sounds, as of mockery and laughter, were heard from various quarters. The brave old man was fain to resume his chair, when lo! he found himself seated on the heated gridiron. He started up very quick, as may be imagined, but happily received no serious injury.

For attraction now succeeded repulsion. All the objects near Clara, instead of being drawn towards her, were repelled, and moved away from her. Soon one article of her dress after another flew off, and it was with the utmost difficulty that they could keep enough on her to hide her nakedness. This lasted an hour it may be, when all was quiet, and every thing was found restored to its place, and Mr. Cotton himself began to think that all was some optical illusion, and to think that he might have been too hasty in concluding that the devil was engaged in it.

However the annoyances were only suspended, they were not removed. During the following night all in the house were awakened by tremendous knockings heard on the walls and under the floor of the apartment where Clara slept. All rose, and in their night-clothes rushed to her room, and found her lying on her bed sobbing, and apparently in the greatest agony. The bedclothes and her own dresses were scattered all about the room, cut into narrow strips and entirely ruined. The rappings then were heard in the library. Mr. Cotton took a light, and went into the room, and was not a little surprised to find it occupied with some half a dozen figures of men and women fantastically dressed, all seated, and listening with grave faces to an inaudible discourse from another figure in Genevan gown and band, standing before the table on which Mr. Cotton's great Bible lay open. Mr. Cotton was a little startled at first, but he summoned up his courage and advanced. He went straight up to the figure in gown and band, who seemed to have usurped his functions, and boldly laid his hand upon his shoulder. Immediately his candle was extinguished, and he received a blow which felled him to the floor. In a moment he recovered, passed into another room, obtained another light, and returned. The phantoms were still there, but he now saw what they were. The seeming minister was a huge folio of theology, moulded into a human shape by pieces of carpet, a coat and trousers of his own, and dressed in his own gown and band. The other figures were volumes from his library, elongated and stuffed out in a similar way, and dressed in clothes belonging to different members of the family. They were stripped, replaced on the book-shelves, and the dresses returned to the several wardrobes where they belonged. There was no more disturbance that night.

The next day, when the family were all at dinner, the table, with every thing on it, suddenly rose to the ceiling, and then suddenly dropped upon the floor with a noise that shook the whole house, but without any other injury, or any thing on it being displaced. In the evening, while they were all seated around the table, listening to a chapter which Mr. Cotton was reading from the Bible, terrible knockings were again heard all through the room, and Clara was seen to be raised as it were by some invisible hand towards the ceiling, and to be borne with great force through the room, and set down standing on her head. Then, after a moment, she rose again and hung suspended to the ceiling by her feet and her head downwards. After an hour the annoyances ceased, and the family were left quiet. The annoyances continued, varying in their character from day to day, for three weeks.

Priscilla sent me an account of them, and I thought my old friend had been sufficiently punished. Moreover, I did not wish too much eclat to be given at that time to the fantastic tricks I was playing. Mr. Cotton was sure that it was the work of the devil, that it was witchcraft, and he did not hesitate to accuse Priscilla. He had tried to get the authorities to arrest her as a witch, but in this he had failed; for, although the laws of Pennsylvania, at that time, if not now, recognized witchcraft as a punishable offence, no magistrate in the city could be found who did not look upon witchcraft as imaginary, and suspect the good minister of being in need of physic and good regimen for entertaining a belief in its reality. I however did not wish Priscilla's name to become associated in the gossip of the day with reported phenomena of the sort, and I sent her an order to discontinue the annoyances, and to restore every thing which had been injured to its previous condition. The night she received my order, the noises ceased, Clara rested quietly, and the family were undisturbed. On rising and going through the house in the morning, no trace of the previous disorder was discovered, every thing was in its place, and the clothing and bedding which had been cut into ribbons, were all restored, and not a mark of injury was to be found on them. Clara was well, and retained no recollection of any thing that had happened to her or to the family during the period she had been so grievously afflicted. Even the family, Mr. Cotton among the rest, began to doubt, if they had not been the sport of some strange hallucination, and almost to persuade themselves that the annoyances had had no objective character.

All this may strike many as wholly incredible, but a thousand instances, as well attested as any facts can be, of a similar character, can be adduced. Let me be permitted to relate an instance still more marvellous, which occurred in 1849, at the presbytery or parsonage of Cideville, France, in the Department of the Lower Seine, and which became indirectly the subject of a judicial investigation. The curé of Cideville encountered at the house of one of his sick parishioners, an individual, a Mr. G——, who had the reputation of curing diseases in a mysterious manner. He reproved him severely, and sent him away. Shortly after, Mr. G—— was arrested and condemned for his malpractices in other cases, to two years' imprisonment. The wretched man, recollecting the reproof he had received from the curé, believed that it was owing to him that he had been arrested and sent to prison, and, it is said, he threw out threats of vengeance. One Thorel, a shepherd, a friend and disciple of the Mr. G——, was also heard to say, that the curé would be made to repent of what he had done, and that he (Thorel) would himself see that his master was avenged, and his orders executed.

Two boys, one twelve, the other fourteen, were boarded and educated in the parsonage by the curé. They were sons of honest, pious, and much esteemed schoolmasters of the district, and appeared to have inherited the good qualities of their parents. They were both intended for the priesthood, and were a great comfort to the good curé, who loved, cherished, and instructed them, and perhaps obtained something for their board and tuition to eke out his scanty means of living.

One day there was a public auction, where a great crowd were collected, and these boys were present among the rest. The shepherd, Thorel, was there, and seen to approach the younger of the two, but nothing more was observed. Immediately on the return to the parsonage, a violent hurricane struck it, followed by blows as from a hammer in every part of the house, under the floors, above the ceiling, and behind the wainscoting. Sometimes these blows were weak, short, abrupt, sometimes so violent as to shake the house, and to threaten to demolish it, as Thorel, in a moment of rashness had foretold. The blows were heard at the distance of two kilometres, and a large portion of the inhabitants of Cideville, a hundred and fifty at a time, it is said, surrounded the parsonage for hours, examining it in all directions, and seeking in vain to discover whence the blows proceeded.

This was not all. Whilst these mysterious knockings continued, and made themselves heard on every point indicated, they reproduced the exact rhythm of whatever air was demanded of them; the glass in the windows were broken, and rattled in every direction; the tables were overturned, or were seen walking about; the chairs were grouped together and suspended in the air; the dogs were thrown crosswise over one another or were hung by their tails to the ceiling; knives, brushes, breviaries, flew out by one window and back through another on the opposite side; the shovel and tongs quit of themselves the fire-place and walked alone into the room; the andirons, followed by the fire, recoiled from the chimney even to the middle of the floor; hammers flew in the air, and dropped as slowly and as softly as a feather on the floor; the utensils of the toilet suddenly quitted the chambranle on which they were placed, and as suddenly returned of their own accord; enormous desks rushed one against another and were broken, and one loaded with books approached rapidly and horizontally close to the forehead of Mr. R. de Saint V——, and, without touching him, dropped perpendicularly upon its feet.

Madame de Saint V——, whose chateau was near to the parsonage, whose testimony cannot be questioned, and who had witnessed a score of similar experiments, felt herself drawn one day by the corner of her mantle, without perceiving the invisible hand that drew it. The Mayor of Cideville received a violent blow on his thigh, and at the cry forced from him by this violence, he received a gentle caress, which instantly relieved him from the pain.

A proprietor, residing fourteen leagues distant, and from whom I hold this relation, came unexpectedly to Cideville, wholly ignorant of the mysterious events which were taking place. After a night spent in the chamber of the boys, he questioned the mysterious knocking, made it strike in different corners of the room, and established with it the conditions of a dialogue. One blow, for example, would say yes, two blows, no; then the number of blows would indicate the number of the letter in the alphabet, &c. This settled, the witness caused to be rapped out his surname and Christian name, and those of his children, his age and theirs, to the year, month, and day,—the name of his commune, &c. All this was done with such rapidity that he was obliged to conjure the rapper to proceed more slowly, that he might have more leisure to verify the answers, all of which he found perfectly exact. What is more striking is, that this gentleman knew nothing at the time of spirit-rapping, then beginning to excite attention in the United States, and it was not till several weeks after that he heard of it.

All this, the sceptics will allege, may be attributed to jugglery, to the cunning and craft of the juggler, divining the thoughts of the interrogator before he had detected them himself. But there was something more still; something which the sceptics will hardly be able to explain. A priest, a vicar of St. Roch, the Abbé L——, came accidentally, and wholly unlooked for, to Cideville. To similar questions he received apparently through his brother, like himself wholly unknown in the place, answers equally prompt and exact, but with this singular difference: In one instance the questioner himself was ignorant, and unable to verify the details of the answer obtained. He was, indeed, told the age and Christian name of his mother and his brother, but he had either never known them or had forgotten them. He however took a note of the answers, and, on his return to Paris, consulted the registers, and found them literally exact. What now becomes of the objection against the previous witness, or the explanation insisted on, that the answer is given by the brain of the interrogator?

Two landholders from the town of Eu came all express to Cideville. They were told their names, Christian names, the number of their dogs, their horses, &c. But still more astonishing were the phenomena that accompanied the boy believed to have been touched by the shepherd Thorel. He perceived continually near him the *shade*, or appearance of a man, in a blouse, whom he did not know, but whom he identified with Thorel, the first time he was confronted with that person. Even one of the ecclesiastics present, when the boy said he saw the phantom, perceived distinctly behind the lad a sort of grayish column or fluidic vapor, a phenomenon often observed on similar occasions. One day the boy fell into convulsions, then into a sort of ecstatic syncope, from which for several hours nothing could rouse him, and which caused a fear that he was dead. Another time he said that he saw a black hand descending the chimney, and he cried out that it struck him. Nobody could see the hand, but those present heard the blow, and saw its mark on the face of the child, who in his simplicity ran out doors, thinking to see this hand come out the top of the chimney.

At length several ecclesiastics united at the parsonage, and consulted how they might be disembarrassed of the annoyance. One proposed one thing, another proposed another, and a third remarked that he had heard it said that those mysterious *shades* feared the point of a sword. At the risk of a little superstition, they armed themselves with swords, and stabbed with them wherever the noises were heard. But it is difficult to hit an agent in constant and rapid motion, and they were about to desist, when one of them, having more skilfully pursued one of the noises than the others, all at once a flame flashed forth, followed by a smoke so dense that they were obliged to open all the windows to escape immediate suffocation. The smoke dissipated, and calm succeeding to so terrible an emotion, they resumed their stabbing, and soon they heard a groan; they continued, the groaning redoubled, and at length they distinctly heard pronounced the word "pardon." "Pardon! yes, certainly, we will forgive you; and more than that, we will pass all the night in praying for you; but on condition that you come to-morrow, in person, and beg pardon of this boy." "Will you forgive us all?" "How many are you?" "We are five, including the shepherd." "We will forgive you all." All then became quiet in the parsonage; and the rest of that terrible night was spent calmly in prayer.

The next day, in the afternoon, Thorel presented himself at the parsonage. His attitude was humble, his language embarrassed, and he attempted to conceal with his hat certain bloody excoriations on his face. The boy, as soon as he perceived him, exclaimed, "That is the man, that is the man who has followed me this fortnight." He pretended, when questioned, that he came to get a small organ for his master. "Not so, Thorel; you know it is not for that that you have come," he was answered. "But whence those wounds on your face? who has given them?"

"That is no business of yours; I will not tell."

"Tell us, then, what you want. Be frank. Have you not come to beg this boy's pardon? Do it, then. Down on your knees."

"Well, be it so; pardon then," said Thorel, falling upon his knees, and even while begging the lad's pardon, drew himself along, and tried to seize him by his blouse. He succeeded; and from that moment the sufferings of the boy, and the mysterious noises in the parsonage, redoubled. The curé, however, persuaded him to go to the mayor's office. He went, and as soon as he entered it, he fell three times on his knees, without being required, and before all the witnesses, begged pardon; but, at the same time, he drew himself along on his knees, and endeavored to touch the curé, as he had touched the boy. The curé, after retreating to a corner of the room, had, in self-defence, to beat him off with his cane. He avowed that all was to be referred to M. G——, whom the curé had prevented from earning his bread, and that he could easily disembarrass the parsonage of the annoyances that were passing there, if made worth his while.

The curé, in consequence of what had occurred, said, or was reported to have said, that Thorel was a sorcerer, and had practised sorcery on the boy at the parsonage. Thorel brought, in consequence, an action against him for slander. The cause came to trial; the curé pleaded the truth in justification, and was acquitted. On the trial, the facts I have stated, as well as many others of no less importance, were testified to under oath, by a large number of highly intelligent and respectable witnesses, and not one of them can be denied, if human testimony is in any case to be taken as conclusive.

Persons of sceptical and critical disposition may imagine that Thorel was concealed behind the wainscot, but the persons who used their swords had sense enough to ascertain whether that was so or not; besides, to suppose it, were wholly inconsistent with other well-established facts in the case. An hypothesis, to be acceptable, must meet and explain all the facts, not merely a portion of them. It will not do to adopt a theory, and then, after the manner of learned academicians and *philosophical* historians, reject as inadmissible all the details of the case not compatible with that theory. But I have introduced this narrative to prove the credibility of some of my own doings, not to prove that there is such a thing as is commonly called sorcery—to prove the validity of an alleged class of phenomena, not their proper explanation. To this latter point I shall have occasion, before I close, to speak at full length.

The annoyances, I may add, continued at the parsonage for some time, in fine till the bishop removed the boys, and the malice of the persecutors had completed the ruin of the curé. They then ceased, when the original reason for producing them had been answered.[3]

---

[3]Pneumatologie des Esprits, par le Marquis Eudes de M——.

CHAPTER XI.

WORTH CONSIDERING.

I failed for a long time yet to get any new light on the essential nature of the agent with which I was operating, and remained still undecided in my own mind whether it was a spiritual person, superhuman and invisible, or a simple elemental force of nature, placed at the command of every man who knows how to use his own powers. The answers I obtained to my questions were vague, contradictory, and unsatisfactory. I had no doubt that I was doing what in the eyes of ignorance and superstition was called dealing with the devil, and practising what had been denounced, and in former times punished, by the civil law as sorcery or witchcraft. So much was clear and undeniable. But had not all the world misunderstood the real nature of what it had condemned as witchcraft, sorcery, maleficia, and magic? Had they not assumed unnecessarily a preternatural agency, and an evil agent, where there was really only a natural, a good, and a benevolent agent?

The bearing of this question on the Christian religion was very obvious, and I well understood the significance of what Voltaire said, one day, to a theologian, "*Sathan! c'est le Christianisme tout entier*; PAS DE SATHAN, PAS DE SAUVEUR," and I felt that there was truth in what Bayle, the ablest and acutest of all modern authors opposed to Christianity, had said: "Prove to unbelievers the existence of evil spirits, and you will by that alone force them to concede all your dogmas." In any point of view, Christianity was pledged to assert the existence of Satan and his intervention in human affairs, for according to it, Christ was revealed from heaven and came into the world that he might destroy the devil and his works. If there was no devil, the mission of Christ had no motive, no object, and Christianity is a fable.

Moreover, all Christians, whether Catholics asserting the infallibility and authority of the Church, or Protestants asserting simply the infallibility and authority of the Bible, were bound to assert the existence of evil spirits, and the reality of demonic obsession and possession, of witchcraft, sorcery, and magic, in the common and opprobrious sense of the terms. As to Catholics, there could be no question. The Church plainly and unequivocally recognizes the existence of Satan, as may be gathered from the prayers and ceremonies of Baptism, as well as from the significance of the Sacrament itself; and not only his existence, but his power over the natural man, and even material objects. Thus when the priest, in administering the Sacrament, breathes gently three times in the face of the child, he exclaims, "Exi ab eo, immunde spiritus, et da locum Spiritui Sancto Paraclito:" Go out of him, impure spirit, and give place to the Holy Ghost, the Paraclete; and also after the prayer *Deus patrum nostrorum*: "Exorcizo te, immunde spiritus, in nomine Patris et Filii, et Spiritus Sancti, ut exeas, et recedas ab hoc famulo Dei. Ipse enim tibi imperat, maledicte damnate qui pedibus super mare ambulavit, et Petro mergenti dextram porrexit. Ergo, maledicte diabole, recognosce sententiam tuam, et da honorem Deo vivo et vero, da honorem Jesu Christo Filio ejus, et Spiritui Sancto; et recede ab hoc famulo Dei, quia istum sibi Deus et Dominus noster Jesus Christus ad suam sanctam gratiam, et benedictionem, fontemque, Baptismatis vocari dignatus est." The candidate, before receiving baptism, is asked, "Dost thou renounce Satan?" and answers, "I renounce him." "And all his works?" "I renounce them." "And all his pomps?" "I renounce them." So, in blessing the salt which is used in administering the Sacrament, the priest says, "Exorcizo te, creatura salis, in nomine Dei Patris omnipotentis, et in charitate Domini nostri Jesu Christi, et in virtute Spiritus Sancti, exorcizo te per Deum vivum, per Deum verum, per Deum sanctum," &c. The whole proceeds on the supposition that Satan is to be expelled, dislodged, and the Holy Ghost to be placed, so to speak, in possession, or the grace of Jesus Christ is to be infused, so that the Holy Ghost shall henceforth dwell in the heart of the baptized, instead of Satan, who previously held dominion over it. The Church has also her exorcists, and her forms of exorcising of evil spirits.

The Bible is no less clear and explicit on the subject than the Church. It teaches that Satan, in the form of a serpent, seduced Eve to eat of the forbidden fruit; it relates the doings of the Egyptian magicians; it forbids necromancy and evocation of the dead, and commands the Jews not to suffer a witch to live; declares that all the gods of the Gentiles are devils; tells us that the devil is the prince of this world, that he goeth about like a roaring lion, seeking whom he may devour; bids us resist the devil and he will flee from us. St. Paul speaks of the prince and the powers of the air that besiege us, and against whom we must put on the whole armor of God, and do valiant battle. Moreover it speaks of demoniacs, or persons possessed with devils; and among the marvellous works ascribed to Jesus Christ, is that of expelling demons, or casting out devils. All Christians, then, must admit that there is a devil, and that there are evil spirits, who may, and who do, interfere with men, harass them, and sometimes take literal possession of them. A recent French author, a sincere Christian believer, has felt this. "The question," he says, "at the Christian point of view, is by no means indifferent, but is, as it were, the mother question, the question of questions. It is no less than to determine whether the Bible and the Church have or have not been really mistaken in one of their fundamental principles. For a man filled with Christian desires, and cherishing at the same time a respect for evidence, the question is most grave. It touches the whole of faith, neither more nor less; and as it will not do to admit in the sacred Scriptures, whose language is assumed to be inspired, what is called *manners of speaking*, or *complaisances* for the age, or *remains of ignorance*, we must be permitted to say, that if it were proved that the Bible in the time of Pharaoh mistook simple and miserable jugglers for real *magicians*, poor charlatans for *enchanters*, a few knavish and lying priests for the false gods of the Gentiles, simple mummeries for real *evocations*, delirious cataleptics for spirits of Python, &c.; if it were proved that Jesus Christ, in granting to his disciples the gift, and prescribing to them the rules, of expelling demons, mistook a fact of pure physiology; if it were proved that the Church, in instituting exorcism, and prescribing for it precise and learned formulas, and, moreover, practising it for eighteen centuries, has been deceived during all that period,—we should feel that it is all over with Christianity; we should regard it as condemned, and hasten to renounce an authority so little judicious, and so little to be depended upon." Christians may, undoubtedly, dispute as to this or that particular case, and say that the evidence of demonic intervention, in this or that particular instance, is not conclusive; but they cannot, without renouncing their faith, and becoming Sadducees, deny that such intervention is possible, or assert that it is improbable. They must concede its possibility, its probability, and its susceptibility of proof; and therefore when the evidence in any particular instance is sufficient to establish the reality of any other class of facts, they are bound, as reasonable beings, to admit it. To them there is, and can be no *à priori* difficulty, for they already believe in the reality of demonic agents adequate to produce the mysterious phenomena that they are called upon to accept. Hence, in those ages and countries in which nobody doubted Christianity, all men of science, physicians, magistrates, as well as the clergy and the people, readily admitted the demonic character of the phenomena like those produced in our day by mesmerism.

But, if the belief in the reality of demonic intervention is integral in Christianity, the most obvious way of getting rid of Christianity and its restraints would be to deny that reality, and to explain the phenomena commonly held as evidence of such intervention, on physiological and other natural principles. This has been the aim of science, especially medical science, during the last two hundred years. This aim was adopted by the so-called wits and philosophers of the last century, and during this it has begun to be adopted by jurisprudence, and even to be acquiesced in by a large portion of professed Christian ministers. Literary men, like Sir

Walter Scott; founders of new sects, like the late Hosea Ballou, of Boston; neologist theologians everywhere; and that "fourth estate,"—journalism, have all combined to reason, explain, or laugh away, every thing pertaining to demonology, and to make the world believe that there is no devil, that evil spirits are only the creatures of a disordered brain, that apparitions or ghosts are only hallucinations, possession a peculiar kind of madness or insanity, and magic mere charlatanry or sleight-of-hand. All this, for an anti-Christian purpose, was admirable, since even the conservative portion of the clergy seemed to acquiesce in it.

Nevertheless, this could suffice only to a certain extent. It might serve to emancipate the intelligent classes, but could not emancipate the people. The latter half of the eighteenth century—a century of anti-Christian light, philosophy, physical science, and materialism—was more distinguished for the mysterious phenomena, usually called demoniacal, than any other period since the Christianizing of the Roman Empire, with the single exception of the sixteenth century. Weishaupt, Mesmer, Saint-Martin, and Cagliostro, did far more to produce the revolutions and convulsions of European society at the close of that century, than was done by Voltaire, Rousseau, D'Alembert, Diderot, Mirabeau, and their associates. These men had no doubt a bad influence, but it was limited and feeble. It was not they who stirred up all classes, produced that revolutionary madness, that wild ungovernable fury of the people which we everywhere witnessed, and nowhere more than in Paris, the politest and most humane city in the world. The masses were possessed, they were whirled aloft, were driven hither and thither, and onward in the terrible work of demolition, by a mysterious power they did not comprehend, and by a force they were unable, having once yielded to it, to resist.

You feel this in reading the history of those terrible events. It seems to you that Satan was unbound, and hell let loose. The historians of that old French Revolution, such as Mignet, Thiers, Lamartine, Carlyle, all feel that there was something *fatal* in it, and have been led, at least all except the last, to defend it on the ground of fatalism. The Royalist and Catholic historians, who oppose it, seem never to seize its spirit. They declaim, denounce, find fault here, find fault there, now with this action and now with that, but they never explain any thing, solve any problem which comes up, and they leave the whole a mystery, or an enigma.

The same phenomena, only on a reduced scale, were observable in the revolutions of 1848. Everywhere there seemed to be an invisible power at work. Good, honest Father Bresciani, would explain all this by the Secret Societies. It is in vain. They did much, those secret societies; but how explain the existence of those societies themselves, their horrible principles, and the fidelity of their members in submitting to what they must know is a thousand times more oppressive than the institutions they are opposing? Tell me not that all these revolutionists were incarnate devils; that they cooly, and deliberately, from ordinary human motives and influences, planned and carried out their revolutionary enterprise. There were in their ranks men of the highest intelligence, the purest virtue, and the humanest feelings; men, all of whose antecedents, whose tendencies, whose studies, professions, interests, and, I may say, convictions, placed them in the ranks of the conservatives, were carried away by an invisible force, and shouted out, Liberty, Equality, Fraternity, and hurled the brand of the incendiary at temple, palace, and castle, which sheltered them, as if it was not they who did it, but a spirit that possessed them. Men caught the infection, they knew not how, they knew not when, they knew not where. The revolutionary spirit seemed to float in the air, as it undoubtedly did.

Without Weishaupt, Mesmer, Saint-Martin, Cagliostro, you can never explain the revolution of 1789, and without me and my accomplices you can just as little explain those of 1848. There was at work in the former a power that the wits ridiculed, that science denied, philosophy disproved, and the clergy hardly dared assert. There was there the mighty power, whatever it be, which it is said once dared dispute the empire of heaven with the Omnipotent, and which all ages have called Satan, whether it is to be called evil with the Christian, or good with the philanthropist, a person with the believer, or a primitive and elemental force with the mesmerist. France, Europe was mesmerized. So was it again in 1848, though with less terrible external convulsions.

It is impossible to bring the great body of the people of any age to agree with our Voltarian philosophers—to be genuine Sadducees. In the first place, the writings of the philosophers and academicians do not reach the mass; and, in the second place, there are constantly occurring phenomena which, in their apprehension, give the lie to Sadduceism. At the very time when the philosophers of pagan Rome were losing all faith in their national religion, doubting almost the existence of the Divinity and the immortality of the soul, and laughing at augurs and soothsayers, the people were more superstitious than ever. It was then that magicians from Asia and Africa flocked to the Eternal City, and that Isiac, Bacchic, and other Eastern superstitions, with all their impurities and wild fanaticism, in comparison with which the national religion was pure, reasonable, and moral, were introduced, and spread as an epidemic; and the laws of the earlier emperors show how hard and how ineffectually authority labored to suppress them.

The enemies of Christianity may accept the mysterious phenomena, commonly regarded as diabolical, and explain them and the miracles of the Bible and the alleged miracles of the Church on natural principles, and if they cannot explain them on any known natural principles, they may make them the basis of an induction of a new natural principle; or, in other words, invent a natural principle to explain them, as Baron Reichenbach has done—a principle, element, substance, or force, which he calls *od*. They may do this, or they may recognize their real spiritual and superhuman origin, but ascribe them to good, not to evil spirits, or what is the same thing, maintain that what the world has hitherto worshipped as good is evil, and what it has been taught to avoid as evil is good. That is, that Satan is God, and God is Satan.

Swedenborg, in founding his New Jerusalem, or New Church, and Joe Smith, in founding the Church of the Latter Day Saints, as Mahomet in the seventh century, virtually adopted the latter course. Swedenborg became, in the later years of his life, a somnambulist, and could throw himself into the state which some mesmerists call sleep-waking, in which he was a clairvoyant, and had the power of second sight. He fancied himself a prophet, and capable of teaching angels as well as men. But he held the power he found himself able to exercise, to be good as well as supernatural.

The same was the case with Joe Smith, an idle, shiftless lad, utterly incapable of conceiving, far less of executing the project of founding a new church. He was ignorant, illiterate, and weak, and of bad reputation. I knew his family, and even him also, in my boyhood, before he became a prophet. He was one of those persons in whose hand the divining-rod will operate, and he and others of his family spent much time in searching with the rod for watercourses, minerals, and hidden treasures. Every mesmerizer would at once have recognized him as an impressible subject. He also could throw himself, by artificial means, that of a peculiar kind of stone, which he called his Urim and Thummim, into the sleep-waking state, in which only would he or could he prophesy. In that state he seemed another man. Ordinarily his look was dull, and heavy, almost stupid; his eye had an inexpressive glare, and he was rough, and rather profane. But the moment he consulted his Urim and Thummim, and the spirit was upon him, his face brightened up, his eye shone and sparkled as living fire, and he seemed instinct with a life and energy not his own. He was in those times, as one of his apostles assured me, "awful to behold."

Much nonsense has been vented by the press about the origin of his Bible, or the Book of Mormon. The most ridiculous as well as the most current version of the affair is, that the book was originally written as a novel, by one Spalding, a Presbyterian minister in Pennsylvania, and that Joe got hold of the manuscript and published it as a new Bible. This version is refuted by a simple perusal of the book itself, which is too much and too little to have had such an origin. In his normal state, Joe

Smith could never have written the more striking passages of the Book of Mormon; and any man capable of doing it, could never have written any thing so weak, silly, utterly unmeaning as the rest. No man ever dreamed of writing it as a novel, and whoever had produced it in his normal state, would have made it either better in its feebler parts, or worse in its stronger passages.

The origin of the book was explained to me by one of Joe's own elders, on the authority of the person who, as Joe's amanuensis, wrote it. From beginning to end, it was dictated by Joe himself, not translated from plates, as was generally alleged, but apparently from a peculiar stone, which he subsequently called his Urim and Thummim, and used in his divination. He placed the stone in his hat, which stood upon a table, and then taking a seat, he concealed his face in his hat above it, and commenced dictating in a sleep-waking state, under the influence of the mysterious power that used or assisted him. I lived near the place where the book was produced. I had subsequently ample means of investigating the whole case, and I availed myself of them to the fullest extent. For a considerable time the Mormon prophets and elders were in the habit of visiting my house. They hoped to make me a convert, and they spoke to me with the utmost frankness and unreserve.

Numerous miracles, or what seemed to be miracles—such miracles as evil spirits have power to perform—and certain marvellous cures were alleged to be wrought by the prayers and laying on of the hands of the Mormon elders. Some of these were wrought on persons closely related and well known to me personally; and I have heard others confirmed by persons of known intelligence and veracity, whose testimony was as conclusive for me as would have been my own personal observation. That there was a superhuman power employed in founding the Mormon church, cannot easily be doubted by any scientific and philosophic mind that has investigated the subject; and just as little can a sober man doubt that the power employed was not Divine, and that Mormonism is literally the Synagogue of Satan.

It matters little to the enemies of Christianity, whether the public deny altogether the marvellous phenomena heretofore regarded as diabolical, whether they accept and explain them by means of a primitive force or primordial law of nature, or simply ascribe them to Satanic invasion, provided it be held that Satan is a philanthropist, the friend and benefactor of the race, not the enemy; for in any case, Christianity is denied or undermined. But the purely sceptical theory answers only for the few, who, it is to be remarked, never see any of these marvellous phenomena, and who, if they did see them, might be led to embrace Christianity; but it will never suffice for the many, and can never subserve the views of reformers who would operate upon the masses.

It however makes no practical difference which of the other two hypotheses is adopted. For myself, I in some sense adopted both, though, as I have said, I inclined to the naturalistic theory. But even then I had begun to contemplate an ulterior object, which might make it more convenient to adopt the latter hypothesis, for it might become necessary to overthrow Christianity by the introduction, apparently by supernatural means, of another religion—a religion in harmony with the wants of the flesh. It is impossible to overthrow a positive religion by a pure negation, or to get rid of Christianity without substituting something positive in its place; for it is to be remarked, that sceptical ages are the most credulous, and that as Christian faith recedes, superstition advances. Hence we see in Scandinavia unmistakable evidences of a revival of the worship of Odin; and only a short time since, the government had to adopt measures to repress it in the north of Norway. In many parts of Germany we see a decided tendency to revive the superstition which Christianity supplanted. When men have no longer religion, they take refuge in superstition; and when they cease to worship God, they begin to worship the devil. The most interesting people to the Englishman Layard that he found in the East, were the devil-worshippers.

But all this is premature. World-Reform, as I had sketched it to myself, had for its object unbounded liberty, and was to be accomplished, on the one hand, by the overthrow of all existing governments, and the complete disruption of all political and civil society; and on the other, by the total demolition of the Christian Church, and extirpation of the Christian religion. Of course it would not do to avow all this, for if I did, I should defeat my own purposes. Faith still lurked in many a heart; and the persuasion was very general, that some kind of government, some kind of political, civil, and even moral restraint was very generally entertained, even by those whom I must make my accomplices, and use as my tools. It was necessary to keep one's own counsel, or to confide it to the smallest number possible. To the world it would do to avow only the design of divorcing religion from politics, and of democratizing the church and society. This might be avowed without shocking the public at large. For this the public mind was in a measure prepared. A pious priest could be persuaded to advocate ecclesiastical democracy, as we have seen in the work of the excellent Rosmini, in the Five Wounds of the Church.

A popularizing tendency among Catholics had been much encouraged by that powerful priest, the Abbé de La Mennais, and his enthusiastic associates. It is true, he had fallen under censure, and had been excommunicated, *eo nomine*, by Rome; but the party he formed, though disavowing him, still retained somewhat of his spirit, and followed his tendency. There was a growing party in France, even among the clergy, who wished to divorce the church from the state, and induce her to abandon the courts, and cement an intimate alliance with the people, and lend her powerful influence to the democratic movements of the day. They had much that was plausible in their favor. The royal and nobiliaire governments of Europe had always labored to convert the dignitaries of the church into courtiers, and to make her their tool for enslaving and fleecing the people. The greatest injury religion had ever received, it had received from courtier bishops, and the tyranny of the state over the church, equally fatal to her and to the people. The real interests of the church would therefore seem to demand of her to make common cause with the people against kings and aristocrats, and in favor of democratic institutions. This conviction was becoming very general among the more earnest and influential Catholic laymen. A corresponding conviction was also becoming general among the great mass of the Protestant populations. It was possible, then, to labor to democratize society without alarming religious convictions; nay, it was possible to enlist them to a great extent in the same work. Nobody, it is well known, helped us on more effectually in Europe than many of the most distinguished among the Catholic clergy and laity. I need only mention Ventura and Gioberti in Italy, Montalembert, Lacordaire, Cormenin, Maret, and Archbishop Affre, in France.

But, after all, great movements are never carried on by simple human means alone, and never get beyond brilliant theories unless inspired and sustained by a superhuman power, either from heaven or from hell. Christianity had taught us the weakness of human nature, and I found that weakness confirmed by experience. Between the power to conceive and to execute there is a distance. Men might form the most brilliant ideals, bring out the soundest, most attractive and perfect theories of reform, but it would avail nothing unless endued with a power not their own, to realize them in practice. Here was the defect in the plan of Signor Urbini and Young Italy. It was skilfully devised, it had all of human wisdom on its side, but it was ideal, and had no power or energy to realize itself. No man lifteth himself by his own waistbands. Without the Whereon to stand, Archimedes, with all his mechanical contrivances, cannot move the world. It is necessary to have a support outside of man; a source of power which is not human, and as the world would say, either Divine or Satanic, to be able to accomplish any thing.

But had I not this very power in the agent I had been experimenting with? What else was this mesmeric agent, whether a primitive, an elemental force of nature, or indeed a superhuman spirit endowed with intelligence and will? Mr. Winslow was, in the main, right. Mesmeric clubs or circles must be formed on all points on which it is necessary to operate, and batteries be erected everywhere, so that anywhere, and at any moment, a mesmeric current may be sent instantaneously through the masses, infusing into them a superhuman resolution and energy, and making them stand up and march as one man. This, then, was the first thing to be done. I would erect my mesmeric batteries in every country in Europe, all connected by an invisible, but unbroken magnetic chain.

This plan, as far as I thought it prudent, I forthwith communicated to Priscilla, without whose coöperation I could not carry it into effect. She approved it, and was ready to coöperate in any way I wished. The poor lady, I may remark, had no longer any will of her own. She had craved liberty, and had induced me to aid her in establishing it, and was now only my slave, bound to me in chains, which, struggle as she might, she could not, of herself alone, break or unfasten.

CHAPTER XII.

A MISSIONARY TOUR.

The civil and political revolution I wished to effect, had apparently, to a considerable extent, been already effected in my own country, and the principal theatre of my operations must be in the Old World. There is no doubt, that, at bottom, the American system does not differ from the European. It is the same system of repression, and, though it dispenses with kings and nobles, it asserts, with equal emphasis, the necessity of government, of law, and morals. The American, in making his revolution, had no socialistic dreams, no thought of resolving society into its original elements, denying all authority, rejecting all government, abolishing all religion and morality, and leaving every man to do freely whatever seems right in his own eyes, however wrong it may seem in those of his neighbor. The authors of the American Revolution, and founders of the American States and the American Union, were any thing but democrats in the present prevailing sense of the word.

But the progress of ideas and events has so modified the American system, and done so much towards restoring a perfect democracy, where the demagogues have every thing their own way, that the chance of getting up any considerable revolutionary party, except to operate abroad, is not worth counting. Indeed, it is not necessary to hasten the march of things here, which is sufficiently rapid towards that point where democracy resolves itself either into complete individualism or into an absolute social despotism. I saw and felt this, and looked upon my own country as more ready to assist me in my philanthropic or Satanic efforts to revolutionize foreign countries than in need of similar efforts on its own account.

Let me not, however, be misunderstood. Let me speak as I think and feel as I lie here confined to my room, from which I am to be removed only to my grave. I love not democracy, which I regard as from below, not from above; but I love as little, perhaps much less, absolute or unlimited monarchy,—your Czarism, Cæsarism, or Imperialism. I may think it unwise, wrong, wicked even, to attempt to overthrow by revolutionary violence, an absolute government, where it exists, and is not intolerable in practice, for the sake of introducing a republic, or even a constitutional monarchy; but I hold no government a good one, where one man alone represents the will and the majesty of the nation. I demand a government of estates, whenever that is practicable, but always a representative body, with real legislative power, capable of imposing real and effective restraints on the administration. I demand for the nation the means of making known freely and effectively, within the limits of the moral law, its will. I demand freedom of discussion, deliberation, and decision. I demand the freedom of the press, temperately, and answerable for its abuse, (which, however, must be a real abuse;) to criticize publicly the acts of political authority, to point out the defects of its policy, and to suggest measures for the public good. I demand a political constitution in which the nation governs through a king or president, and parliament or legislative body or bodies. I am, what is sneered at by your imperialists, a parliamentarian, a constitutionalist, and have no sympathy at all with the Cæsarism of either France or Russia. I am no radical, no revolutionist, no friend of sedition, but I love a wise, prudent, well-regulated liberty, which leaves me all my power to do good, and therefore, necessarily, to some extent, even to do evil; for if you so bind me by the civil power that I can do no evil, you take from me my manhood, make me an automaton, and deprive me of all power to do good and to acquire merit. Such is my political creed, and therefore let no man dare, because I favor not now the wild radical movements of the age, accuse me of being an enemy to liberty, or a worshipper of Cæsarism, or what is called absolutism.

Not seeing much to be done in my own country, I resolved to go abroad. I required Priscilla to make herself ready to accompany me, and to take her husband along with her. I know not whether this latter request pleased her or not. Woman is woman even when under the power of the Evil One; and that Priscilla loved me, and loved me madly, she hardly pretended to conceal. I had, perhaps, loved her, too, for a moment, when I might do so innocently, and I loved her still as much as remained in me the power to love. But love or lust was not precisely my ruling passion, and I would as soon have taken another with me as Priscilla, could she have served my purpose as well. Even in my worst days I was as much repelled as attracted by a woman who could betray her husband's honor, and I always found a woman, mastered by her passion, and ready to give up all for love, as it is called, a troublesome rather than an agreeable companion. A man wishes to find in the woman of his affections a free soul, moral dignity,—a tender, loving heart, indeed, but with sufficient strength to stand alone. Lads and lasses in their teens have very false notions of love, and this is why love so seldom survives the honeymoon, and why so many complain of unrequited affection and broken hearts.

But I could not do without Priscilla, and I wished her husband to accompany her to avoid scandal, and also to serve as manager, to take charge of all the arrangements in travelling, residing in one place, or in going from that to another, for which he was admirably adapted. I found him far more intelligent, far more of a man than I had been led to suspect from his ready submission to petticoat government. Priscilla had entirely mistaken him, and might one day find him more than her master.

In a couple of months our arrangements were made for the voyage to Europe, and for a longer or shorter residence abroad, as we should find it convenient. We embarked from Boston in one of the Cunard steamers for Liverpool, in May, 1843. We arrived at Liverpool after a pleasant passage of thirteen days, and as soon as we could land, and get our baggage through the custom-house, we departed for London, where we proposed stopping for some weeks. Let not the reader fear that I am about to inflict on him a journal of my travels in England and on the Continent. I did not go abroad as a curious traveller, to see other lands, and study the ways, manners, customs, institutions, laws, politics, or religion of other nations. I went for a special object, and to that I confined myself. I could, if I would, tell very little more than I might have learned at home. My mission was not to observe and learn, but to do, and to prepare, and hasten on the grand movement I contemplated.

I did not find in England much remaining to be done, or that I needed to do. I saw very few of her nobility, and I was not even once invited to dine with the Queen. The middle classes I found very much like my own countrymen, with very much the same culture, ideas, habits, and pursuits. I found, as at home, a large number of philanthropists, though less thoroughgoing than ours, and narrower, and less comprehensive in their views. The common Englishman is a little insular in his notions, and looks with disdain or pity on all who do not happen to be natives of his own island world. The American is broad and expanded in his views, like his extended prairies and boundless forests. No pent up Utica confines him; the globe is too small for him; and he seriously contemplates forming a joint-stock company for the construction of a railroad to the moon. He thinks it will prove a good speculation. They are both proud, equally proud; but with the Englishman, pride assumes the form of haughtiness, or a low estimate of others; while with the American, it assumes that of a conscious superiority to all the rest of creation.

I did not see much chance of a reform or a democratic revolution in England at present. True, she had at that time a very considerable body of Chartists, and a numerous *canaille*, but these I counted for nothing. No revolution is ever made by the proletarian classes. Wat Tyler, Jack Cade, and the Jacquerie of France have proved that. No people can ever overthrow a government till the government betrays itself. In 1789, and in 1848, in every instance the government, with a few whiffs of grape-shot, might have dispersed the mob and suppressed the revolution. *Quem Deus vult perdere, prius dementat.* I placed no reliance on the democracy of England, yet I did not at all despair of her. She had her

Reform Bill of 1832, which in due time would be followed by another, and another, till her House of Commons would come to be regarded as representing population, not an estate. The extension of her commerce and manufactures was compelling Sir Robert Peel, an able man, but a short-sighted statesman, to break up the protective system, establish free trade, and throw the power into the hands of the urban class. I did not need to mesmerize him; he was doing my work as fast as it could be done with safety. Lord John Russell, Lord Palmerston, and their friends, I found had been visited before me. Mr. Gladstone needed a slight manipulation; but I saw that he was an impressible subject, and I foresaw that, when he became Chancellor of the Exchequer, I should have every reason to be satisfied with him. Lord Shaftesbury, then Lord Ashley, I found amply mesmerized by nature and inheritance.

As to aid from England, in carrying on democratic revolutions on the Continent, especially in Italy, if not in France, I might count on it with entire confidence, so far as beginning the movements and getting into trouble were concerned. But I thought possibly I might find her aid like the devil's, which suffices to help one into a scrape, but leaves him to get out the best way he can. She had no interest in helping the reformers to establish democracy, but she was ready enough to throw the Continental states into confusion and anarchy. Hers has of late years been only a half-way genius. Nevertheless, I found in her a few choice spirits, and erected a mesmeric battery, which has since done some service to the cause I had at heart. Priscilla was still more successful among the philanthropic ladies and women with whom she was able to communicate. We made sure, without much difficulty, of Exeter Hall. It was a battery already charged, and served, with skill and ability.

We prepared an agent to visit Liverpool, Manchester, Birmingham, and other considerable English towns, and, upon the whole, were very well satisfied with our mother country, and in good spirits left England for Dublin. We were received there with true Irish hospitality. The Liberator was then in his glory, and filled a large space in the eyes of the world. He had obtained the Catholic Relief Bill, and opened to his co-religionists of Great Britain and Ireland a political arena, and was now agitating for the legislative independence of his native country. A few months after he was arrested, and sentenced to a fine and a year's imprisonment, which virtually put an end to his movement. It broke his heart both as a patriot and as a lawyer. He received us very coolly at first, because we were Americans, and the Americans held negro slaves; but on learning that we were abolitionists and philanthropists, he opened his large heart to us, and bid us a hundred thousand welcomes. We could not, however, make much of O'Connell. He was an admirable type of the general Irish character, and not easily understood. He struck us as a bundle of opposing qualities, not usually thrown together in the same individual. A pious Catholic, he was surrounded by unbelievers, and the patron of the whole herd of philanthropists, whose chief aim was to rid the world of his religion; a man of impulse, as capricious as a child, wily as a village attorney, and subtle as the most crafty lawyer, and acting always upon calculation; a warm-hearted patriot, a genuine lover of his country, yet with a sharp eye to the "rint," and leaving it doubtful to many minds whether he had any higher motives in what he did than to gain personal distinction, and to elevate his family. He however interested us as the inventor of a "peaceful agitation," an invention which could have been made only by an Irish lawyer, and it was as a "peaceful agitator" that we chose to think of him. We found his "peaceful agitation" might be turned to good account in the constitutional states of the Continent, and we took care to introduce it into France, when we visited that country, with what effect those who remember the "Reform Banquets" which preceded the Revolution of February, 1848, need not to be informed.

From the Liberator, or, as we chose to call him, the Agitator, we went to meet the chiefs of the Young Ireland party, still apparently acting in harmony with him. We formed no great expectations of them. They talked too much, and made too much noise and bluster. We found them in excellent dispositions, but too unsubstantial for our purpose. They were all blaze, and no heat. The devil, having no creative power, could not himself make much of them, and gave them up in despair. Hence their miserable failure four years later at Slievnamon. Indeed, Ireland was a country by no means to our philanthropic and reforming purpose, and we made no account of her in preparing our revolutionary movements. We however erected a small battery in the west, with a view to some ulterior operations, and which we left in charge of Exeter Hall. It has produced some temporary effect; but inasmuch as it has served to arouse the Popish bishops and clergy to a more diligent discharge of their duties, in regard to the religious and moral instruction of the people in that hitherto somewhat neglected district, it is not certain but it will, in the long run, produce an effect the reverse of that intended. Rome, too, has sent a man after her own heart to look after the Irish Church, the present Archbishop of Dublin and Primate of Ireland; so the philanthropists have not much to hope from Ireland. Pat will sometimes live and talk as an unbeliever, but he has a singular propensity to die a Christian.

From Ireland we visited Edinburgh, Glasgow, the Highlands, and the Hebrides—the Highlands and the Hebrides, for the purpose of making observations on the "second sight" of the natives. We were much pleased with Scotland. The Scottish character has many admirable features, and there is not upon the whole a finer race in Europe than the Scotch, when unperverted. We found nothing to do among them. There was no need of mesmerizing them. Their own *"ingenuum fervidum,"* a sort of permanent mesmerization, was amply sufficient for all our purposes. Besides, there seemed to be a natural and ample supply of the odic fluid in her own mountains and glens, which were still peopled by brownies and fairies.

CHAPTER XIII.

THE TOUR CONTINUED.

Finding all right in Scotland, we visited Norway, Sweden, and Denmark, the ancient Scandinavia, the land of Odin, and home of the most strongly-marked devil-worship to be found in history. With all my study and experiments, I was far below many mesmerizers I found among the natives of these countries. I found operative the spirit of the old Vikings, the Berserkirs, and the Sagas, which had made the Norsemen the nobility of Europe, and the plunderers of every maritime district, which had precipitated Gustavus Adolphus upon the Empire to perish at Lützen, and Charles the Twelfth upon Russian Peter, to meet his fate at Pultowa. It still survives, hardly restrained by the Christian profession, and capable of being kindled up anew, and set to work in all its pristine vigor. Of these northern countries I felt sure, and that I might safely leave them to themselves.

We passed on to St. Petersburg, and had an interview with the Czar of all the Russias. We found him one of the noblest-looking men in Europe, simple, affable, intellectual, and well-informed. He treated us with distinction on account of our country, with which he said he and his predecessors had always been on friendly terms, and whose unexampled prosperity he saw with pleasure. He could understand our politics, and respected them, for they were based on a principle—a wrong principle he believed—nevertheless a principle, consistently carried out. He believed the Russian system, under which one man governs, is far preferable to ours, under which all govern. However, we might honestly disagree with him. Apparently he was the most bitter as well as the most powerful enemy of our revolutionary plans; but we did not despair of him. He seemed wedded to the *status quo*; but we felt that when once we had destroyed that, we could make him and his legions do our work, for we found him a sort of Pope in his own dominions, and not indisposed to supplant the Pope of Rome. He was, if a friend to Papacy, the enemy of the real Pope, and that was enough for us.

The Czar, foreseeing the revolutionary movements which would be attempted in Western Europe, had for the moment ceased to favor the Panslavic movement which he previously set on foot; but we saw that the impulse had been given, and that ultimately he must return to it, go on with it, or be swept away by it. This Panslavic movement to unite the whole Slavic race, numbering upwards of seventy millions, and holding a territory capable of supporting twice, if not three times that number of inhabitants, under one Slavic government, imperial or republican, would operate, we thought, altogether in our favor; for it would ruin Austria, the chief support of the Papacy, and give a decided predominance to the anti-Catholic powers throughout all Europe. We therefore favored it, and took care to form various circles in support of it, as we traversed the Empire from St. Petersburg to Moscow, Ninjï Novogorod, Little Russia, to the Black Sea; and also, among the Serbs of Bulgaria, Servia, Bosnia, in European Turkey; Transylvania, the Banat, Croatia, Slavonia, and Bohemia, in the Austrian Empire.

We visited, on leaving Russia and Slavic Turkey, the kingdom of Hungary. There we found Kossuth, and he answered our purpose. Priscilla formed a circle among the Magyar ladies, but it was quite unnecessary. I initiated Kossuth into my plan, and laid my hand on his head, and breathed into his mouth, and left him to take care of the Magyar race. Highly delighted, we passed from Presburg to Vienna, where we stayed some weeks. The Imperial family and high aristocracy were proof against our arts, but we found the burghers, the *employés* of the government, and especially the students of the University, quite impressible, and we charged them for a revolution.

From Vienna we passed through Cracow to Warsaw, and from Warsaw we went to Berlin. In all these places we found every thing favorable. We passed through the capitals of several of the smaller German States and principalities, stopped a few days in the Grand Duchy of Baden, and then hastened to take up our residence at Geneva, in Switzerland. We did not visit Munich, but sent Lola Montes there, whom Priscilla, at my order, had prepared. She did very well, but not so well as I expected. She used her extraordinary powers too much for her own aggrandizement. She should never have suffered King Louis to have made her a countess. She was too vain and ostentatious.

We arrived in Geneva, late in the autumn of 1844, and made it our principal residence till the spring of 1846. We had made no prolonged stay in Poland, for we found the Poles already mesmerized. Cold and callous as I had become, I yet had a tear for poor Poland, and, let my conservative brethren say what they will, I still weep her fate. I am not affected by the prevailing Russo-phobia, and in the contest now raging between Russia and the Western powers, I believe that she has the advantage on the score of justice, though now that they have been mad and foolish enough to wage war against her, the interests of Europe perhaps demand their success; for if they fail, she becomes quite too powerful. There are traits in the Russian character I like, but I can never forgive the murder of Poland. Catherine, Frederic, and Maria Theresa, in that crime opened the way to modern revolutions, and deprived crowned heads, to a powerful extent, of the sympathy of the friends of justice and order. The Poles had their faults, great and grievous, but the partition of their kingdom by the three powers of Russia, Prussia, and Austria, was a crime that no faults could justify, and, what some would say is worse, a political blunder. Since then, the Polish nobles have been, and will long continue to be, their evil genius.

We did not remain long in Germany, for we found most of the German states already prepared, and already in close communication, after the German fashion, with the powers of the air. The German genius is mystic, and plunges either into the profoundest depths of Christian mysticism, which unites the soul with God, or into the demoniacal mysticism, which unites it in strictest union with Satan. The German, whatever his efforts, can never make himself a pure rationalist. He has too much religiosity for that. He must worship, and when he worships not God, he worships the devil, and either through the elevating power of the Holy Ghost rises to heaven, or, through the depressing power of Satan, sinks to hell. You never find him standing on the simple plane of human nature, and he is always either superhumanly good or superhumanly wicked. For an Englishman, an American, an Irishman, there is a medium, a possibility of compromise, a sort of split-the-difference character—now saying, good Lord, and now saying, "good devil,"—a *via media* genius, which offends both extremes, and satisfies nobody. I like the German genius better. If the Lord be God, then serve him, if Baal be God, then in Satan's name serve Baal. Be either cold or hot, not lukewarm. *Ernst ist das Leben* is the German's motto, and whatever he proposes to do, whether good or evil, he sets about it in downright earnest. There is more to hope, and more to fear from the German or Teutonic race than any other in Europe, for it has very little of the Italian and French, or the English and American *frivolezza*, that curse of modern society.

At Geneva we met Mazzini, a remarkable man, in his way, the very genius of intrigue, and wholly sold to the devil. We also met there the Abbate Gioberti, a Piedmontese, who had been exiled as a liberal by the government of Carlo Alberto, the *cidevant* Carbonaro. He was a Catholic priest, and though under the censure of the government, and distrusted by the Jesuits, nay, violently opposed by them, he had not at that time, so far as I could learn, fallen under the censure of his church. He was one of the ablest men we met in our European travels, and a fine specimen of the higher order of Italian genius. Though comparatively young, not much over forty, he was deeply and solidly learned, and as a writer on political and philosophical subjects, had, saying nothing of his peculiar views, no superior, and hardly an equal in all Italy, if indeed in all Europe.

Gioberti affected to be an Ultramontane, a rigid Catholic, a thoroughgoing Papist; yet his sympathies were with the liberal or revolutionary party. He was, first of all, an Italian, and held that the moral, civil, and political primacy of the world belonged to Italy, and it was because God had, from remote ages, given to her this primacy, that the Papal chair was established at Rome. The primacy belonged to the successors of St. Peter in their quality of *Roman* pontiffs, who, as such, were heritors of the Italian *primato*. The Papal authority was founded in divine right, but mediately through the divine right of the Italians as heritors of the old Roman sacerdocy, and Italo-Greek civilization. According to him, the Papacy did not so much continue the synagogue, as the old Roman priesthood, or rather, the Jewish and Pagan priesthoods both meet and become one in the Papacy—the summit and representative of the Christian priesthood.

His plan, therefore, was, first of all, Italian unity, not the republican or democratic unity of Mazzini and Young Italy, nor yet a monarchical unity, under a purely secular prince; but a federative union under the moderatorship of the Pope, made one in the Papacy. The Romans, he held, at least from the time of Numa, had been an armed priesthood, and should now resume, under the Pope, their old character and mission. Italy thus united, thus organized, under the moderatorship of the Pope, could reassert her primacy, and carry on the work of civilization. With her twenty-five millions of inhabitants, the natural superiority of her genius, the moral weight of the Papacy, her peculiar geographical position, and the productiveness of her soil, she would be impregnable to attack, and more than able to cope single-handed with any one of the great European powers. In other words, he sought for the Pope and the Italians what Nicholas is supposed to seek for the Czar and the Russians.

The rock on which he split, and I told him so at the time, was in assuming the intrinsic compatibility of Gentilism and Christianity. He wished to combine the antique pagan and the modern Christian spirit, and to train youth to be devout Catholics, and yet, at the same time, proud, daring, and energetic Gentiles. He did not agree at all with the Abbé Gaume and the party laboring to exclude the Greek and Roman classics from our colleges and universities; he had no very high opinion of the fathers of the Church, with the exception of St. Augustine, and no patience with the mediæval knights and doctors. He waged unrelenting war on the philosophy taught by the Jesuits, and, indeed, upon the whole system of education pursued by those renowned religious religions, which, he contended, had practically emasculated the European mind, deprived it of all depth and originality, and of all free and vigorous activity. Its effect had been to produce, in nearly all Europe, a universal *frivolezza*, or frivolity of thought and action.

But he forgot to note, that Gentilism and Christianity are directly opposed one to the other. Christianity educates for heaven, Gentilism for earth; the former is based on pride, the latter on humility; the one exalts God, the other exalts man. The Gospel teaches us to despise what Gentilism honors, and to honor what Gentilism despises, and to possess the world by rising above it, and trampling it under our feet. A Christian discipline has for its end, to mortify the flesh, and to make men live as if dead to the world, and to overcome the world by dying, not by slaying, by relying on the wisdom and power of God, not on their own. Gentile discipline trains men primarily for the world, develops the nobility of pride, not the higher nobility of humility—trains men to act, by their own wisdom and sagacity, on men, to be artful and overreaching statesmen, intrepid soldiers, able and invincible commanders. It is obvious to every one that these two systems can never be combined, and made to work harmoniously together. Ye cannot serve God and Mammon.

Taking the Gentile standard, taking a Fabricius, a Scipio, a Cato, a Cæsar, instead of a St. Bruno or a St. Francis, of Assisium, as a model man; or a Cornelia instead of Santa Clara or a Santa Theresa, for a model woman, there can be no doubt of the vast superiority of ancient Gentilism over modern Catholicity, or even Christianity itself, and, in this sense, the devout Irishman was right when he said, "Religion has been the ruin of us," and more especially as it regards Catholics. Non-Catholics, as to the empire of this world, display a wisdom, an energy, and a decision, which you seldom find in strictly Catholic states, and the only cases in which so-called Catholic states approach them, is when they put their religion in their pocket, war on the Pope, or for purely secular ends, on purely earthly principles. The French Republic, in putting an end to the Mazzinian Reign of Terror, and restoring Pius the Ninth to his temporal estates, professed no religious motives, and would have failed if it had. It acted from worldly policy, and avowedly for the purpose of watching Austria and maintaining French influence in the Peninsula.

The question is not as Gioberti conceives it; it is not a question of the fusion of Christian and Gentile virtues, but a question between Gentilism and Christianity itself. It is not how to train our youth to be great, noble, energetic, according to the Italo-Greek standard, but whether we are or are not to be Christians. If Christianity be true, there can be no question that our youth should be trained for heaven and not for the world, and taught to be meek, humble, self-denying, unworldly—to die to the world, and live only to God—to prepare themselves for dying and living eternally hereafter in heaven. If so trained, they will not exhibit those traits of character which you so much admire in the great men of pagan antiquity; they will meditate when you will think they should act, pray when you would have them fight, and run to the church when you would have them run against the enemy. But, at the same time, if Christianity be true, there can be no question that the management of earthly affairs on Christian principles and for a Christian end, would be decidedly for the interests of society as well as for the salvation of the soul. "Seek first the kingdom of God and his justice, and all these things shall be added unto you."

There is an innate and irreconcilable antagonism between Italo-Greek Gentilism and Christianity. According to Christianity, the world by wisdom knows not God; and the whole economy of the Gospel is undeniably to discard the wisdom of this world, and to rely solely on the wisdom from above, to trust not ourselves, but God alone. The Gospel reverses all the maxims of Gentile wisdom, and blesses what it curses, and curses what it blesses. Gentilism had said, Blessed are the proud, the distinguished, they who are honored and abound in this world's goods; the Gospel says, Blessed are the poor in spirit, that is, they who are humble, lowly-minded, and despise riches and honors. Gentilism had said, Blessed are they who are quick to resent and avenge their real or imaginary wrongs; the Gospel says, Blessed are the meek, for they shall inherit the land. The former had said, Blessed are they that rejoice; the latter says, Blessed are they that mourn. Gentilism had said, Blessed are they who thirst for fame, for honor, power, and who live in luxury, who eat, drink, and are merry; the Gospel says, Blessed are they who hunger and thirst after justice, Blessed are the merciful, and Blessed are the clean of heart. Gentilism had said, Blessed is the man who delights in arms, whom no one dares attack, whom none slander, revile, or persecute, and who, by his force, craft, or wisdom, has triumphed over all his enemies, and subjugated them to his will; the Gospel says, Blessed are the peacemakers, Blessed are they that suffer persecution for justice' sake, Blessed are ye when men shall revile you, and persecute you, and say all manner of evil against you falsely for my sake: rejoice and be exceeding glad, for great is your reward in heaven.

The principle of Christianity is humility, meekness, gentleness, forgiveness of injuries, love of enemies, self-denial, detachment from the world, and a delight in living, suffering, and dying for the glory of the cross. In every respect, the principle of Gentilism is the direct contradictory. Look at the Gospel as you will, and its direct denial of heathenism everywhere strikes you. Its Author came into the world not in the pride, pomp, and power of an earthborn majesty. He came in the form of a servant, a slave, the reputed son of a poor carpenter, at whose craft he worked with his own hands. The foxes of the earth have holes, and the fowls of the air have nests, but poorer than they, he had not where to lay his head. Of the rich, the proud, the great, and honored, none were with him. His disciples were poor fishermen and publicans. He sought and accepted no earthly honors; and when the people, in a fit of momentary enthusiasm, would make him perforce their king, he withdrew, retired into the mountains, concealed himself, and prayed to his Father. When betrayed by one of his followers, and delivered into the hands of his enemies, he made no resistance, and permitted none to be made. He patiently endures insults, mockeries, and revilings, and opens not his mouth in his defence, when confronted with his accusers before the bar of Pilate, but meekly submits to the unjust sentence pronounced against him, suffers himself to be led unresistingly, bearing his cross, to the place of execution, and to be crucified between two thieves.

Here is the whole spirit, the whole economy of Christianity. If Christianity be from God, this means something, and proves that if Christians are sincere and in earnest, they cannot adopt or even value the wisdom of the world; and it must always be true, that the children of this world are wiser in their generation than the children of light. Concede the Gospel to be true, and you must own that Christian asceticism is the highest wisdom, and Gentile wisdom, or the wisdom of this world, the sublimest foolishness. This St. Paul well understood, and hence he says, "We preach Christ crucified, to the Jews a stumbling-block, and to the Greeks foolishness; but to them that are called, Jews and Greeks, Christ the power of God, and the wisdom of God. The foolish things of the world hath God chosen to confound the wise, and the weak things of the world hath God chosen that he may confound the strong; and base things of the world, and things contemptible hath God chosen, and the things that are not, that he might bring to nought the things which are."

There is no denying this, and hence the error of Gioberti. He would be both a Christian priest and a Gentile philosopher, at once a disciple of the Gospel and of the Portico, and he labored with an ability and a subtlety to demonstrate by means of a philosophy, considered apart from the use he made of it, worthy of profound esteem, that this was not only possible, but demanded by the deepest and truest principles of ontological science. I do not think that he was at that time an unbeliever, or that he entertained any doubts of the religion he professed. But he had little of the sacerdotal character or the Christian spirit, and I think he was disgusted with what he considered the weakness, tameness, abjectness, the *frivolezza* of the Catholic populations of France and Italy, and out of patience with seeing them crouching before the haughty infidel, and the domineering heretic or schismatic. He wished to see them men, men of lofty and daring souls, scorning to be trampled on, and indignantly hurling back the invading hosts of barbarians, and boldly and triumphantly asserting the proud prerogatives which belong to them as possessors and guardians of the truth of God. He was right after the wisdom of men, but wrong after the wisdom of God, if Christianity is our standard, and was animated by the spirit of Gentilism, not by the spirit of the Gospel. He failed, for he was too pagan for a Christian, and too Christian for a pagan.

The remedy, if remedy is needed, is the return of modern society to real, earnest, living faith in the Gospel. The age is frivolous, because it is educated to be Christian, and is at heart unbelieving. It is not heresy or schism that needs now to be attacked, but unbelief—a moral and intellectual scepticism, which books and schools do not teach us to attack successfully. Here schoolmen, men of routine, with their *probos*, *respondeos*, and *objectiones solvunturs*, stand us in poor stead. Exquisite polish, gracefully-turned periods, charming pleasantries, pretty conceits, and soft, sweet sentimentality for boys and girls in their teens, will stand us in just as little. It is necessary to abandon routine, the easy habit of speaking *memoriter*, and learn to think, to master, not merely repeat, what others have said, but to master for ourselves the principles involved, and to speak out in a tone of strong, impassioned reasoning, in free, bold, and energetic language, in defence of the Gospel itself.

CHAPTER XIV.

ROME AND THE REVOLUTION.

In June, 1846, the death of Gregory the Sixteenth, and the election of Cardinal Mastai and his elevation to the Papacy, under the name of Pius the Ninth, summoned us to Rome, the Eternal city. I felt a momentary grief, as I saw the mouldering ruins of pagan Rome, the ancient capital of Gentilism, and felt indignation at beholding the diminutive Rome that had supplanted it; but I felt sure that the old gods lingered still in those ruins of the Capitoline and Palatine hills, and that the time was drawing near when we might evoke Jupiter Tonans and the fiery Mars, and the Goddess of Victory, from their slumber of centuries; revive the old Roman spirit, and reëstablish the old Republic, so long triumphed over by the barbarism of the cross. Never before had I felt how thoroughly alienated from the Christian world, and assimilated in my feelings to the old Gentile world I had become. I was in the capital of the Christian world, the centre of Christian art, and of the most glorious Christian associations for two thousand years, and my heart was touched only at sight of the monuments of pagan antiquity, which time and the still more destructive hand of man had spared.

But we had no leisure for sight-seeing, and still less for sentimentalizing over the ruins of that stupendous superstition of which Rome was the capital, and which had gradually supplanted the patriarchal Christianity, only slightly corrupted, of the primitive Romans. The superficial politicians, Catholic and non-Catholic, regard the Papacy as comparatively of little political or social significancy in our times; but whoever looks a little below the surface of things, knows very well that the Pope, though weak as to his temporal states, is not only the oldest but the most influential sovereign in Europe. The death of one Pope and the accession of another, is an event which reverberates through the whole civilized world; and the policy of the sovereign pontiff, the feeble old man of the Vatican, with hardly a regiment of guards, has not seldom the preponderating weight in the councils of princes, although unseen, unrecognized—so much the more inexplicable, as there no longer remains a truly Catholic government on the globe, and not a Catholic nation in whose heart lives and breathes the old Catholic faith. Not a nation in Europe would, to-day, for the sake of religion alone, rush to the assistance of the Pope; yet the Papacy is everywhere, and not a court in Europe but trembles when it thinks of the Pope, even weak and unsupported as he is.

All the Liberals throughout the world held a jubilee as soon as they heard of the death of the old Pope, who had, no one could tell how, held them in check. The whole world seemed to have been suddenly relieved of an invisible burden, and bounded with a wild and frantic joy. The good time that had been a-coming, now could come. This joy grew wilder and more frantic still, when it was known that Cardinal Mastai was the new Pope. He was known to be gentle and humane, kind-hearted and pious, and suspected of leaning to liberal views, and of being a Giobertian; and nobody doubted that he would attempt a policy the reverse of Gregory's. We, who were in the secret, knew that he was not the choice of Austria, and had no doubt that he would incline to France, and follow, to no inconsiderable extent, the advice of Count Rossi, the French Ambassador, and one of our friends.

At that time Guizot was at the head of the government of France under Louis Philippe, a Protestant and a quasi-conservative statesman, but with many sympathies with the European Liberals. He believed, or professed to believe, that a change in the institutions of the monarchical states in Europe, giving the people a moderate share in the government, was demanded by the exigencies of European society, and if freely offered by authority, and not given as a concession to the people in arms to effect it, would be a wise and beneficial public measure, and in an eminent degree politic too, as it would tend to extract the point from the declamations of the radicals, and prevent, or at least indefinitely postpone, the revolution with which all Western and Central Europe was threatened. He had urged this policy upon Prussia, perhaps upon Austria, certainly upon the smaller German states which had not yet adopted the constitutional *régime*, and upon the Pope and the other Italian princes.

We were perfectly well aware of Guizot's policy, and knew equally well how to turn it to our account. Your *doctrinaire*, *juste-milieu*, or *via-media* statesmen, who follow expediency, and govern without principle, are generally regarded as wise, prudent, and eminently practical, but they are among the shortest-sighted mortals to be encountered, and are as miserable humbugs as the Genevan banker, M. Necker, who could never understand that government was any thing more than a question of finance, or its administration any thing more than the administration of a joint-stock bank. When there is no serious discontent on the part of subjects, and not the least danger of revolution or insurrection, authority may modify without danger, immediate danger at least, the constitution, in favor of popular power, as the English government did in 1832; but when there is grave discontent, with or without just cause, and a secret conspiracy is forming in behalf of liberal or popular institutions, nothing is less wise or statesmanlike than for authority to make popular concessions with a view of forestalling and disarming it. The disaffected attribute such concessions solely to the weakness and fears of the government, and only rise in their demands, and conspire with the more energy and courage.

The government, in times of general discontent, as was the case in Europe from 1839 to 1848, should either concede all and abdicate itself, or concede nothing, because, if it is to defend itself it needs all its prerogatives and the concentration of all its powers. The advice of Guizot was fitted only to weaken the powers that entertained it, and to render them, in the hour of trial, timid and undecided; and it is only where authority is timid, hesitating, and undecided, that a popular revolution can ever succeed. The only wise and even merciful way in such times is, to make, on the first outbreak, a free use of grapeshot and the bayonet. There will be no second outbreak, however powerful or well concerted the conspiracy may have been. Napoleon understood this, and his nephew understands it, also, tolerably well. No man understands it better than Nicholas, Autocrat of all the Russias, although his single unarmed presence is ordinarily all that is necessary to quell an insurrection in his capital.

There is no doubt that Pius the Ninth, during the first days of his pontificate, followed, in temporal matters, the advice of the French government, which, as far as I have been able to learn, never, since Philip the Fair, has been guilty of giving the Pontiff advice not to his own hurt. France advised the fatal amnesty and some sort of quasi-popular institutions. The former was granted, the latter were promised, and the world was made to believe that for once it had a liberal Pope. There was nothing heard but *Evviva Pio Nono!* throughout Rome, Italy, France, England, and the United States. Radicals, Infidels, Protestants, and even the Grand Turk, united in one grand chorus of loud and prolonged exultation. It seemed, to those who saw only the external manifestation, that all hostility to the Papacy had ceased, and that all the world were on the eve of becoming Papists. Rome became one perpetual festival. Songs, hymns, processions, benedictions, speeches, addresses, congratulations, became the regular order of the day. Multitudes of Catholics, honest, simple souls, really felt that the day of heresy and schism, of conflict and trial, for the Church, was over. Some shrewd old cardinals at Rome took their pinch of snuff, shrugged their shoulders, and retired to their palaces. We, who knew what agencies were at work, laughed in our sleeve, and, with all the chiefs of the liberal party, called upon all the powers which we had prepared, visible and invisible, to aid in increasing the general intoxication, not doubting but the Papacy was at its last gasp. For we felt sure that if, by flattery, by enthusiasm, by loud, long, and reiterated shouts of *Evviva Pio Nono!* we could get the Pope fairly to enter the path of reform, or what was, we supposed, the same thing for us, make the Catholic world believe he had entered it, it was all over with the Papacy, therefore with Christianity, law, and social order.

No doubt some of the enthusiasm manifested was real, but a great deal of it was feigned, for the precise purpose of imposing upon the public. We were not ourselves for a moment deceived. We felt sure that Mastai was a genuine Pope, that he could hardly be deceived by the demonstrations which must have been painful to him; which, in fact, gave him no rest, and which, under pretence of unbounded devotion to him, were becoming unmanageable, secretly undermining his throne, and growing into a real conspiracy against his freedom of action. We knew well there must come a point beyond which he could make no further concession, and our plan was to get the Catholic populations of Europe so committed to the cause we pretended he favored, that when that point was reached, we could turn the popular enthusiasm against him, and he find himself disarmed and powerless to resist it. In this it is well known that we fully succeeded.

We should not have gone so far, and succeeded so rapidly, perhaps, had we not been aided by English politics. Lord John Russell and Lord Palmerston did not disappoint my expectations. At the time of our visit to Rome, the government of Louis Philippe was in the zenith of its glory. The wily monarch seemed to have fully confirmed his throne, and his prime minister was successful in urging upon a large number of princes constitutional reforms, and it seemed likely, for a moment, that the revolutionary party would spend its fury harmlessly under the lead of the sovereigns themselves. But he deeply offended England by the Spanish match, the marriage of the Duc de Montpensier with an Infanta of Spain. By this marriage, he seemed to have completed his circle of alliances, and to have made himself too powerful for English politics, and was rendering himself still more so by the constitutional reforms he was urging upon German and Italian princes. It was necessary to thwart him, and put an end to his illegitimate reign. Lord Minto was despatched, and other agents instructed to confer with the chiefs of the revolutionary party in Italy, and also in France, and encourage them to insist on reforms effected by the people from below, and to refuse to be satisfied with reforms effected from above by the princes. These chiefs were assured of the sympathy, perhaps they were promised the assistance, of the English government, which makes it a point to support a revolutionary party in every foreign state.

In the mean time, all the batteries we had erected were opened. Exeter Hall, and the Protestant Alliance were in full operation, and I thought it quite certain that a force was accumulated and brought to bear on the

Rock of Peter that would shiver it into ten thousand atoms. Our presence was no longer necessary at Rome, and after Easter of 1847, we went to Paris, to fire a train in that city of combustibles. We were not needed there, for having had interviews with the chiefs of the revolutionary party in Geneva, we had already prepared them. They had more than profited by our instructions; they had even improved on them, and stood in closer relation to the Unknown Force than we did ourselves. All we could do to aid on the revolution which broke out the following February, was to persuade some of the leading Liberals to introduce the "peaceful agitation," reduced to so perfect a system by O'Connell in Ireland, which was done in what were called the "Reform Banquets."

All France at that moment was, in some sense, revolutionary. Guizot, at the head of the government, was a reformer, as I have shown, but only on condition that authority took the initiative. But, to admit the necessity or propriety of any reforms or changes was a tacit concession altogether to the prejudice of the existing order. After Guizot and his party, came the dynastique reformers, such as Thiers and Odillon-Barrot, who wished the Orleans family to possess the throne, but to deprive the throne of all effective power, and to establish a parliamentary despotism. The watchword of these at that moment was, the extension of the electoral franchise. There were at that time, out of a population of thirty-six millions, only about two hundred thousand electors. After the dynastique reformers, came the Catholic party, led on by the noble, learned, eloquent, and singularly pure-minded Montalembert, a man of principle, of faith and conscience, with whom religion was a living and all-pervading principle. This party consulted, first of all, the freedom and independence of the church, and was comparatively indifferent to the dynastique question. Its drapeau was neither that of Henri Cinque nor that of the House of Orleans, but religion and social order. The watchword at that time was, Freedom of Education, denied by the monopoly secured to the University, which educated in a pantheistic, Voltarian, or an irreligious sense. As the government sustained the University, and denied freedom of Education guarantied by the constitution, they opposed the government.

Behind these came the Legitimists, the adherents of the elder branch of the Bourbons, filled with old Gallican reminiscences, and whose watchword was Henri Cinque. They were opposed to the existing government, ready to take active measures to overthrow it, and were ready to support the church, in so far as she demanded nothing for herself, and would lend all her resources to uphold and decorate the throne. They were a set of superannuated old gentlemen, with polished manners and courtly address, decorated with some very respectable prejudices, but wholly ignorant of their times, and incapable of learning. They were a clog on the Catholic party, and were chiefly answerable for the reëstablishment of the Bonapartists and the present Napoleonic Cæsarism in their beautiful country. However, they were opposed to Louis Philippe, and ready to effect a change.

After the Legitimists, who were royalists and opposed to the existing government, came the Republicans, moderate and immoderate; the moderates having for their organ *Le National*, the immoderates *La Réforme*. These, however, were all opposed to monarchy, whether in the elder or younger branch of the Bourbons, and wished the *république*,—some, as Lamartine, Arago, with the Girondins, those phrase-mongers of the old revolution, the république of the respectables, of the Bourgeoisie, attorneys, professors, and hommes de lettres; others, such as Ledru-Rollin, and the Montagnards, a république démocratique, une et indivisible, with Robespierre, Couthon, Saint-Just, Danton, and Marat; while others still, too numerous to mention, wished, with Barbeuf, La République démocratique et sociale; and not a few wished no government, no political or social order at all. These were the Subterraneans, reformers after our own hearts, and on whom we chiefly operated, and through whom we brought the odic force to bear on the revolutionary movement.

Aside from all these, but ready to coöperate, for the moment, with any or all of them, as would best serve their purposes, were the Imperialists, the Bonapartists. After the fall of Napoleon, and the Restoration of the Bourbons, the Bonapartists had affected liberal, I may say, democratic ideas, and had lent their powerful influence throughout Europe to democratize the public mind; and at the time of which I speak, the chief of the family was very nearly an avowed socialist, and was hand-and-glove with the Subterraneans. They knew well that they could be healed only when the waters should be troubled; and, whether they were troubled by an angel of light or an angel of darkness, was a matter of perfect indifference, unless, indeed, they had more confidence in the latter than in the former.

Add to these parties the intrigues of England, who could not forgive the Spanish match, that crowning act of the Philippine policy, also the illusions we were able to keep up as to the views and intentions of Pius the Ninth, and it required no messenger from another world to announce that France was on the eve of a tremendous convulsion; that the days of the King of the Barricades were numbered; and that, whatever might be the afterclap, the reigning dynasty must fall, with a crash that would be reverberated throughout all Europe. The only care of our party was to push forward in front the more moderate reformers, more especially the dynastique reformers, while we organized a Subterranean force that would drive them, in the moment of their success, beyond the point at which they aimed, and compel them to accept the République, which, if proclaimed at Paris, we felt certain that we could, during the panic which would succeed, fasten upon the nation.

The history of the events that followed is well known, and need not be repeated. The old king, in the moment of peril, proved that he was a true Bourbon, incapable of a wise decision or an energetic act. All at once he had a horror of bloodshed, sacrificed his ministry, called to his council Thiers, Odillon-Barrot, and other dynastiques, who, vainly imagining that their bare names would allay the storm which they still more vainly imagined that they had conjured up, ordered the troops back to their barracks, and gave up the king and his dynasty to the armed and infuriated mob. The king abdicated; the Regency, under the Duchess of Orleans, was scouted; the royal family scampered for their lives towards England, that *refugium peccatorum*; monarchy was abolished; the République was proclaimed; a provisional government was organized impromptu, and a convention of delegates, to be chosen by universal suffrage, was ordered to meet and give France a regular political organization.

But a few days elapsed before the movement in Paris was followed by insurrections in Berlin, Vienna, and a large number of the smaller German states. The Italian peninsula was all in a blaze; democracy was in the ascendant in all Europe, except Russia, Spain, Belgium, and Holland. Hungary demanded independence of Austria; the Slavic populations of the Austrian Empire at Prague and Agram were preparing to join in a panslavic movement; Pius the Ninth was deprived of all freedom of action, and held virtually imprisoned; Naples and Sicily were in full revolt, and the king ready to concede every thing, and, Bourbon-like thwarting every effort of his loyal subjects to protect him; Charles Albert declared himself the sword of the Holy See; the Lombardo-Venetian kingdom rejected Austrian supremacy, and chose him for king. He marched at the head of his troops, swelled by contingents from all Italy, to drive the barbarians back over the mountains, and to clear the peninsula of every vestige of foreign dominion.

We were elated; we felt that success was sure, and that our grand philanthropic World-Reform was on the point of being completely realized. But alas! *homo proponit, Deus disponit*. The spirits had deceived us. Pius the Ninth displayed a passive courage that we had not counted on, and nothing could induce him to sanction the war against Austria; and in spite of all we could do, it finally leaked out, that he had not sanctioned it, and that the revolutionists had belied him, and entirely misrepresented his principles, conduct, and wishes. Old Radetzky, after retreating before Charles Albert till he had obtained reënforcements, turned upon his pursuer, defeated him, and drove him, with shame and loss, out of Lombardy. Prince Windishgrätz beat the rebels in Prague; the lazzaroni flogged the republican heroes in Naples, and the people seized the throne, in spite of its weak and pusillanimous occupant. In fine, Cavaignac, after four days of hard fighting, prostrated the Subterraneans of Paris, and became Dictator of the Republic. We were no longer in the years of grace '91, '92, or '93. The age was not as far gone in unbelief as we had reckoned, and the friends of religion and society were more numerous and more energetic than we had believed.

Our hopes were damped, but not extinguished. We had thus far used the Pope, but we could use him no longer, and we must get rid of him, and completely secularize the Roman government. We had used the Italian princes; we must now reject them, and abandon Gioberti for Mazzini. We succeeded in wresting the government entirely from the Pope, but he himself escaped us, and fled to Gaëta, which was a serious injury to our cause. The Pope in exile is more powerful than in the Vatican. We meant to have confined him in his palace, and held him as a puppet in our hands, and still for a time continued the use of his name; but in this his flight defeated us. We were obliged to proclaim the Roman Republic, and the temporal deposition of the Pope, prematurely; but still we hoped, as we took care not to touch his person or his spiritual prerogatives, that we should not lose the sympathy of the Catholic public.

But it was all in vain. Our magic failed us; a more powerful magician than we intervened, and everywhere the reaction gained ground against us. Austria, whom we thought we had disposed of, rose Antæus-like from the ground; the Giobertians, predominant in the Subalpine kingdom, would not own us. Florence was deserting us; Venice held out, indeed, but Lombardy was chained by old Radetzky. Great Britain wished us well, gave us good advice, but came not to our aid; and Spain and Portugal, that we thought dead, suddenly started into life against us. Russia, though she loved not the Papacy, detested us, and was ready to interpose to bring Prussia to her senses, and to assist Austria. And last of all, the French Republic, which we had been the principal agents in creating, fearing the preponderance of Austria, and anxious to have an outpost in the Eternal City, sent her troops against us.

It was in vain to struggle. I saw clearly that the battle was against us, and that we should never succeed, by political and social revolutions, in effecting our purpose; and I made up my mind at once to have nothing more to do with them. I resolved to return home, and fall back on what I have hinted as an ulterior project. It was in the Autumn of 1849. The abortive attempt to reorganize the German Empire had failed, and not to our regret, since we saw, if reorganized at all, it would not be on democratic principles; the authority of St. Peter was reëstablished at Rome; the Magyars were forever prostrated in Hungary, and our friend Kossuth had taken refuge with his friends the Mussulmans, and France was becoming an orderly government under the Presidency of Louis Napoleon and the conservative majority of the Legislative Assembly. There was nothing more that we could do.

It is true, that many of our friends thought differently from me, and wished to continue the struggle; but I told them that, if they did, they must do so without my active coöperation; that I should leave them to their simple human strength, and they would find all their plans miscarry. The time is not opportune. Christianity has yet a stronger hold on the European populations than you or I had calculated, and the Christian party can no longer be duped and made to fight for us. They thrill with horror now to hear us say, "Christianity is democracy, and Jesus Christ was the first democrat." They are beginning to see, as clearly as we do, that all this is at best absurd, and that our movement is essentially anti-Christian. They see, they admit, they deplore a certain number of political and social abuses; but they believe these abuses more tolerable than the reforms we would effect.

We have given the bishops, the clergy, and the pious laity a horrid fright; and you will see them, almost to a man, before three years expire, exultingly consenting to the reëstablishment of pure Cæsarism, in order to be relieved of their fears of us. Louis Napoleon will succeed in making himself, almost with the unanimous voice of France, proclaimed Emperor, with absolute, or virtually absolute power, with no effective check on his arbitrary will; parliamentary government will be scouted, as hardly a step removed from Subterranean democracy; free discussion of public affairs will be closed; the press will be muzzled, and no voice will be heard throughout the empire, save a voice in praise or flattery of the new Emperor.

But herein is our consolation and our hope for the future. The new Emperor will have to deal with Frenchmen; and he counts without his host, if he thinks he can, for any great length of time, silence thirty-six millions of French voices, or make them all speak one way. Mortal man cannot do it. Satan himself could not do it; and only One, whom we name not here, could do it. Now they are afraid of us, and have had even an excess of talk. They will consent for a time, even as a novelty, to be silent, or shout, as an admirable change, *Vive l' Empereur*, instead of *Vive la République démocratique et sociale,—à bas les Démocrates*, instead of *à bas l' Aristocrates*, or *l' Aristocrates à la lantern*, and *à bas les socialistes*, instead of *à bas les Rois*. But rely upon it, that after a brief repose, these same Frenchmen will be desirous of *mouvement*, and will by no means be pleased to find themselves doomed to the silence and stillness of death. Then will be our time once more, and perhaps then we may be more successful. Till then I engage no more in political and social reforms. I shall take myself to that which underlies all political and social ideas, and slowly, perhaps, but surely, prepare a glorious future. You will hear from me again, or if not, you will feel the influence of what I shall do.

With remarks like these, I took my leave of my European revolutionary friends. I communicated to Priscilla, who had faithfully served me throughout the time I had been abroad, and powerfully contributed to such successes as we had had, my design of returning home. We were in Paris. She would, perhaps, have rather returned to Rome. She had, in fact, began to droop, and to be weary of the part I had forced her to play. She had, during our stay in Rome, become a mother, and new feelings and affections had been awakened in her heart. Her husband had treated her kindly, forbearingly, but he had much changed, and no longer favored philanthropy or reform, and it was rumored that he had become devout. Priscilla evidently began to turn to him with something approaching the love and esteem she owed him, and would gladly have broken her *liaison* with me. But I would not hear of it; she must return with me.

CHAPTER XV.

THE ULTERIOR PROJECT.

It may be asked why I wished Priscilla to return with me, against her will, since I had no passion for her, and respected the honor of her husband. I wished it partly from spite, and partly because it was necessary to my purpose. She had induced me, or had had more influence to induce me than any one else, to embark in a cause which I loathed, and which at the same time I felt myself totally unable to abandon, and I wished to make her suffer with me. Then, again, I could do nothing without an accomplice, and that accomplice a woman. I travelled abroad in the character of a simple American gentleman, not as a mesmerizer, a magician, or one who commands invisible powers. Nobody abroad, or even at home, ever suspected me, unless it was good old Mr. Cotton, of any thing of the sort. In all cases when the mysterious force was to be exerted, as long as she was connected with me, I employed Priscilla as my agent. I gave her my orders, which she, without exciting any suspicion against her or myself, seldom failed to execute to the letter.

Even after her own views and feelings began to change, and she felt the slavery and degradation of her position, she dared not disobey me. She stood in awe of my power, and knew well the merciless punishment that awaited her. Often, often has she begged me, with tears and in the deepest agony, to undo my spell over her, and to let her go free. I would not. Had she not declared her spirit eternally wedded to mine? The truth is, I was half afraid to undo the spell, and emancipate her. She knew too many of my secrets, might expose me, and defeat all my plans; and once freed from me, once restored to the empire of reason, she would feel herself bound in conscience to do so; and when a woman once takes it into her head to act from conscience, she is, whether she have a good or a false conscience, as unmanageable as if she were in love. She is as headstrong under conscience as under passion, and of course absolutely uncontrollable, because in either case she uses her reason simply in the service of her feelings. Then, again, I did not like accepting a new accomplice.

Priscilla, not daring to resist, finally persuaded her husband to consent to return home. We crossed the Channel to England, and hastened to embark at Liverpool on board a steamer for New York. We had a stormy passage, and came near being cast away; but at length arrived in port, and soon found ourselves in Philadelphia, after an absence of six years and six months amidst scenes and events of the most exciting character. We were all changed in looks, but still more in feelings. The fire of our enthusiasm was extinct, the freshness and sanguine hopes of youth had fled forever; our labor had been in vain, and there was no bright or cheering prospect before us. I took my leave of Priscilla at the public-house where we stopped. When I saw her faded cheek, her sunken eye and withered form, the wrinkles gathering on her brow, and heard her, in a broken voice, renew her oft-repeated request, and remembered what she was some ten or twelve years before, and thought of what I was too at that time, and what I was now, I had a touch of human feeling, and pressing her hand to my lips—I had not the heart to refuse—I told her I would consider it, perhaps I would, and hurried out of the room, to conceal my emotion, not sorry, after all, to find that I had not wholly ceased to be human.

The next day, I started for my home in Western New York. Home, alas! no longer. The house was desolate. During my prolonged absence, my mother and my only sister had died, and all my family were gone. My library and my laboratory remained as I had left them. They had no charms for me now. I looked out upon the familiar scenes of my childhood; they seemed changed all, and were tame and listless. I met some companions of my earlier life; there was nothing in common between them and me. Their voices sounded strange, and grated on my ears. The sad conviction, for the first time in my life, forced itself upon me, that I was alone, and deeply I felt my loneness. I had lost my childhood's faith, which, though meagre and but a shadow, yet was something. I had no Father in heaven, no brother or sister on earth. I believed in neither angel nor spirit. All existence, all being, had dwindled into one invisible, elemental, impersonal Force, which indeed I could wield, but to what end?

In my loneness, I felt that the vulgar belief in the devil, in ghosts, and goblins damned, would be a solace. They would be something, and any thing is better than nothing. Better is a living dog than a dead lion. Alas, I had sold myself, and my redemption was far off. Strange enough, I felt something like passion revive in my guilty breast. I felt, I even regretted Priscilla's absence; and it seemed that she was dear to me, and that I could not endure life without her. I pictured her to myself as I had first known her, and I wept as I remembered how for long years I had enslaved her. A voice whispered in my heart, emancipate her. A momentary feeling of generosity possessed me. I summoned her, as I knew how, to my presence. She appeared, instantaneously.

"Priscilla," said I, "I am sad and weary. Life has lost its charms for me, and I care not how soon I die. I have nothing to live for. You are a wife and a mother. I absolve you from your pact; be free; return, and devote yourself to your husband, who is worthy of you, and to your boy. I have, and will no longer have, power over you."

A gleam of joy spread over her face, a smile of gratitude played on her lips, and a look of love shot from her eyes, and the place where she stood was vacant. She had vanished; but a chattering, as of a thousand mocking voices, filled my room, and then impish, mocking faces were seen all around, making mouths at me. I cared not for these. I silenced the former, and sent away the latter with a word. I retained my magic force still. But there was joy as well as sorrow in that house in Arch street, Philadelphia. Priscilla, the day of returning to her own house, had been taken ill; her husband was alarmed, and called a physician, who could understand nothing of her case. She grew worse and worse; and during the time I had summoned her to me, she fell into a sort of stupor, a complete trance, and to all except her husband, who had seen her in that state before, and knew that she was subject to trances, she seemed to be dead. The moment I had absolved her, she came to herself, a sweet smile on her face, with the hue of perfect health. She arose in bed, embraced her husband with a warmth and sincerity of affection which he had never before known, and for the first time since his birth looked upon her boy with the glad joy of a mother's heart. But at this moment her husband was more to her than her babe. She hung on his neck, she pressed him to her heart, she half-smothered him with kisses, spoke in the terms and tones of the tenderest and sweetest affection, and it seemed as if she would pour out upon him, in a single moment, the loaded affections of a lifetime. "My dear husband, you must forget and forgive the past. I am yours, yours now, yours alone; heart, soul, and body, forever. The spell is broken. The delusion is gone; take me, take me, dear James, to your heart."

James was a man. He had been dazzled by the beauty and accomplishments of Priscilla, and thought it enough to be accepted as her husband, without much scrutiny into the state of her affections. She had, for a moment, imposed upon him, and he had accepted her notions of woman's rights, philanthropy, and world reform. But he did not lack good sense; he had even a strong mind, firm principles at bottom, and all the elements of an upright, manly character. A few months' practical experience served to cure him of a good deal of his philanthropy, and to damp the ardor of his zeal for reform. He was, of course, displeased with my intimacy with Priscilla, and he owed me, it must be owned, no good will. But his observation pretty soon satisfied him, that whatever the bond of that intimacy, it was not what directly affected his honor as a husband, and he resolved that he would seem not to regard it. It was a bitter trial to him.

His tour abroad, his observation, and his conversations with gentlemen and ladies, not always of our clique, had opened his eyes to many things, and made him a stanch conservative. He abandoned all the loose notions he had previously entertained, renounced his Quaker quietism, and had become sincerely converted to a real objective Christian faith. His first thought and care were to reclaim his wife, and, if possible, to release her from the mysterious power which I seemed to have over her. He found her as anxious to be released as he was to release her, and he thought he discovered in her, at times, a growing affection for himself. It was a difficult case to manage, but he thought it best to be prudent and discreet, and to avoid every thing that could excite remark, or that he himself might afterwards regret.

Feeling now that he had himself not been entirely free from blame, that he was bound to be forgiving, that Priscilla was really his wife, the mother of his child, and that she probably was freed, though he knew not how, and did now really love him, he responded with a warmth nearly equal to her own, to her strong expressions of love, frankly forgave her all, and pressed her to his heart as his own, his truly beloved wife. It was for both the happiest moment they had ever known, and in that one moment James seemed to have been compensated for his patience, forbearance, and suffering, for so many years.

Priscilla immediately regained her health and cheerfulness, and resolved, if possible, to recover me from the bondage in which she knew I was held. How she sped in this, and what new trials, if any, awaited her, will appear as I proceed in my narrative.

My own feeling of loneness, of desolation, was not relieved by my release of the woman I had so long held spell-bound, but was aggravated by the constant annoyance of a passion which I had seldom before experienced, or which, without much trouble, I had always been able to subdue. As Priscilla became purified and less unworthy of her husband, and as she seemed the more completely to have escaped me and to be lost to me forever, the more did I feel that I could not live without her, and the more impossible did I find it quietly to endure her absence. I was mad. I called her. The charm was broken, and she came not; I saw only a vague, undefined form, flit before my eyes, and heard only a wild mocking laugh.

Weeks passed, but they seemed ages. Priscilla, in all her loveliness, in all her gracefulness and dignity, in all the brilliancy of youth and beauty, was constantly present to my morbid fancy by day, and to my dreams at night. I was completely unmanned,—wept now as a child over a lost toy, or now raved as a madman. I could not eat, I could not sleep. I could endure it no longer. I sold my house and furniture, disposed of my laboratory and scientific apparatus, packed up my library, and resolved that henceforth I would take up my residence in Philadelphia.

I had no sooner established myself in my new home, than I called in Arch street to see Priscilla. Instead of her I found James. He received me civilly, even kindly, conversed with me of what we had seen abroad, but Priscilla did not appear. No matter, I would call again. Did so; saw Priscilla only in presence of her husband. She was looking well, was affectionate in her tone and manner, but offered me not her hand, and seemed to take care that I should not so much as touch her dress. Well, said I to myself, be it so. The weakness shall last no longer. I will be myself again, and resume the project I had contemplated. I went home, not cured, but resolved, and immediately commenced my evocation, and communicated my orders to all the circles I had established throughout Europe.

I have already hinted what this new project was. It was clear to me, from my historical reading and my personal observations amid the exciting scenes of the more recent European revolutions, that the grand support of social order, and what I have somewhere called the system of restraint and repression, is Christianity, and that the political and social reformers can never fully carry out their reforms till they have totally rooted out from modern society all belief in the Gospel, and all peculiar reverence for its Author. This is more than hinted by Mazzini and Kossuth, although the latter is a vice-president of the American Bible Society, boldly avowed by M. Proudhon, and stoutly contended for by the German Turnverein and Freimänner. If you concede the Christian idea of God, says Proudhon, you must at once and forever abandon your idea of liberty.

It was equally clear to me, that the attempt, by means of political organizations, and revolutions directed against the papacy, or any church organization, Catholic or Protestant, to root out Christianity from the hearts of the people, must at last prove a failure. After all, there is a natural religiosity in man, and though he will often restrain and mortify it, and act only in view of purely secular ends,—practically live as if there were no God, and no hereafter,—he will almost always return to the order of religious ideas, and adopt or institute some kind of religious worship to which he will subordinate his political ideas, and his secular ends. An Epicurus may deny Providence, a Lucretius may sing, in no mean poetry, that it is impossible, "*revocare defunctos*," and even Cicero may laugh at augurs and aruspices, and doubt the immortality of the soul, yet the sentiment of an invisible Force, of a mysterious Power that overshadows us, is universal, and the sceptical philosopher feels an indefinable shudder of awe, perhaps of fear, whenever he finds himself alone in the dark. Everywhere the shades of Acheron wander or flit around and before him.

Even in the midst of our pleasures the thought of the invisible and the supernal intrude unbidden to mar our festivities, and to dash our joy with an indefinable sadness, shame, and remorse. Even a Voltaire trembles and blasphemes in dying, at the thought of being denied Christian burial, and a Volney, who resolves God into blind Nature, and Christianity into astrology or astronomy, prays lustily to the God he disowns, in a storm on Lake Erie. Do what we will, we cannot divest ourselves of the belief or apprehension of invisible powers, who hold our destiny in their hands; and a people absolutely without any religion, or at least superstition, is never to be found.

Never had unbelievers a fairer chance for rooting out Christianity by political and social revolutions, than in the eighteenth century. The laugh was everywhere against religion and the clergy, a decided materialistic and infidel philosophy pervaded literature, possessed the schools, ruled in the courts, and domineered over thought and intellect. There was lukewarmness in the religious, there were scandals among the clergy, there were abuses in the state, and therefore an imperious call for reform. The reformers directed all their movements against religion, and their means were democratic and social revolution. They were strong, they were overwhelming in their power. At their bidding, down went throne and altar, and in ten years the religion they had abolished was reëstablished, the churches they had closed were reopened at the order of the soldier they had made their chief, and for democracy in the state they had an incipient Cæsarism, which, two years later, became a fully developed and perfect Cæsarism. The same result had followed our own movement. In January, 1850, religion was far more vigorous in Europe, than in January, 1840, and democracy at a far greater discount.

It was idle, then, to hope either to destroy political and social authority in the name of absolute unbelief and irreligion, or to root out Christianity by political and social movements. Christianity could be eradicated only by means of a rival religion, and a religion which could appeal to a supernatural origin, and sustain itself by prodigies, or what the vulgar would regard as miracles. I had suspected this from the beginning, and resolved now, that instead of working with the purely secular passions of men, I would make my appeal to their religiosity. Mahomet, in the seventh century, had done this admirably for his time and the East, but had incautiously fixed his superstition in the Koran, and made it unalterable, and therefore incapable of adapting itself to the new face which things might assume in the vicissitude of events, the development of society, and the progress of the race.

Swedenborg had done better, and so had Joe Smith, but neither had sufficiently provided for the progressiveness of the race, or with sufficient explicitness consecrated the principle of innovation and change, and both had retained too many conceptions taken from the old religion. Yet Swedenborg was to be taken as our starting point, and we were only to avoid his mistakes, the principal of which was a too strict and rigid church organization.

When I returned from Europe, I found the directions I had given, before going abroad, had been pretty faithfully followed; and mesmeric revelations, through Andrew Jackson Davis, and spiritual communications, through the Foxes, were beginning to attract public attention. The spirits were becoming exceedingly anxious to communicate, and made, as it was supposed, many important revelations. In a few months, spiritual knockings were becoming quite common, and mediums were found in all parts of the country. At first, intercourse with the spirits was obtained only in the somnambulic state, or through the slow and toilsome medium of raps, but at the same time intimations and assurances were given that before a great while a more easy and direct method of communication would be vouchsafed; but, as yet, the public and individuals were not prepared for that more direct method. The spirits were willing, but the mediums were not sufficiently advanced, nor sufficiently spiritualized; and the public was too gross, too materialistic, and too sceptical. As soon as minds should become more refined, spiritual, and believing, open vision would be permitted them, and easy and regular communication would be established, and whoever wished would have as free and familiar intercourse with the spirit-world as with the world of the flesh.

At first the great object was to establish the reality of the spiritual communications. This was to be done by the communication of secrets, either known only to the interrogator, or incapable of being known to the medium in any ordinary human or natural way. Sometimes the spirits played the part of fortune-tellers; sometimes they assumed to be prophets, and ventured to predict future events, but always events which either depended on them, or lay in the natural order, and which a knowledge of natural causes and effects could easily enable them to foresee.

As the spiritual intercourse extended, and believers multiplied, the somnambulic and rapping mediums ceased to be the only mediums. The artificial somnambulic mediums, or mesmerized mediums, disappeared almost wholly, and to the rapping mediums were added writing mediums and speaking mediums, and in some instances the spirits became actually visible to the seers, and telegraphed their messages by visible symbols, and occasionally in words. Spiritual telegraphing, in some one or all these ways, became, in a few months, common in all parts of the country; and, at the expiration of two years, there were three hundred spiritual circles or clubs in the single city of Philadelphia, and more than half a million of believers in the United States. The epidemic had broken out in the North of England and Wales, had spread all over Norway, Denmark, and Sweden, and Northern and Central Germany, penetrated France in all directions, and made its appearance even at Rome. In France and Italy, where the population is either profoundly Christian or profoundly infidel, the spiritual manifestation had to adopt more discreet and less startling forms than in our own and some other countries, and to give place at first to doubt whether it was not mere trickery, or explicable on recognized scientific principles; and confined itself, to a great extent, to the phenomena of table-turning, which excited curiosity without alarming conscience. In France, in the most polished, fashionable, and, I may almost say, most Catholic society, table-turning became an amusement.

The next point to be attended to, was the doctrines, the philosophy or religion, that the spirits were to teach. It would not do to attack the Gospel too openly, and it was necessary to undermine, rather than to bombard it. In some respects even, it was advisable to seem to confirm, as it were by one rising from the dead, some portions of Christian belief,—such as the immortality of the soul, and the reality of an invisible spirit-world. The latter was doubted by the free-thinkers; but it was essential to my project that the free-thinkers, in this respect, should be converted, for their conversion and acknowledgment of belief in God and a spirit-world would do much to commend our spiritualism to a large body of silly and ill-informed Christian believers, who, seeing such apparently good effects resulting from it, would conclude that there could be nothing bad in it. By their fruits shall ye know them.

In the American community, to a very great extent, the belief in the immortality of the soul is supposed to be identical with the belief in the resurrection of the dead, taught by Christianity; and our Unitarians, with their rationalistic erudition, very generally hold that the peculiar and distinctive doctrine taught by our Lord was the immortality of the soul. But the immortality of the soul was believed by the whole ancient world, Gentile as well as Jewish; and, though questioned by some ancient and modern sophists, there never has been found a people who, as a body, were ignorant of it, or that denied it. All the ancient, as all modern superstitions recognize it. All believe the soul is imperishable, though many suppose it will be absorbed in the Great Fountain of Life, as a drop in the ocean—a misinterpretation of the Christian doctrine of union with God in the Light of Glory, as the ultimate end or final beatitude of the just. The doubt was as to the body, or the *umbra*, the material envelope and companion and external medium of the soul in this life. The gross outward body they believed returned to dust, and mingled with its kindred elements; but this *umbra*, shade, the manes of the dead, which all antiquity carefully distinguished from the soul, was also, for the most part, believed to be imperishable; but its reunion with the soul, I do not find the heathen world ever clearly asserting. In other words, the ancient heathen world, though it retained the primitive belief in the immortality of the soul, had lost belief in the resurrection of the body, and the reunion of soul and body, or at least only retained some traces of it in their doctrine of metempsychosis, or transmigration of souls.

The peculiar Christian doctrine, or the doctrine so insisted on by the Apostles, was not the immortality of the soul, which was always presupposed, but the resurrection of the dead, the return to life, not of that which had not ceased to live, but of that which had died, to wit, the body. Hence the article in the Apostles' Creed is not, I believe the immortality of the soul, but, I believe the resurrection of the body, *resurrectionem carnis*, the resurrection of the flesh; and to this belief, it must be remarked, that the spirit-manifestations afford no confirmation, and indeed they virtually contradict it.

The distinguishing trait of Christian morality is charity, which is distinguished from philanthropy or benevolence, as a supernaturally infused virtue is distinguished from a mere human sentiment, but, in the minds of but too many of those who call themselves Christians, really confounded with it. The spirits were then, under the name of charity, to teach a philanthropic, sentimental, and purely human morality, for in doing so, they would seem to the mass of superficial Christians to be confirming the distinctive trait of Christian morality, and at the same time appealing to the morbid spirit of the age.

Bald, naked Universalism is not popular; but there is a very general disbelief, among the leading men of the times, in the old orthodox doctrines of heaven and hell, of the last judgment, the everlasting punishment of the wicked, or that our eternal state is fixed by that in which we die. Swedenborg had greatly modified these doctrines, and taught that the punishment of the wicked is purely negative; that men are in hell only inasmuch as they are not in harmony with God; and not to be in harmony with God, that is, good, is to be out of the Divine protection, and exposed to all the sufferings incident to our abandonment to the natural order of things. He had also recognized different heavens, rising one above another, and different hells, one below another; and had hinted or asserted the possibility of the inhabitants of each improving, and advancing in wisdom and virtue, by their intercourse with the inhabitants of this world. He had himself even instructed angels, and assisted feeble and undeveloped souls. Here were the germs of all that was required. The spirits were to teach that there are different circles in the other world, into which souls are admitted according to their respective tastes and degrees of development, with the chance to rise in due time, if faithful, from the lowest to the highest. In the lower circles, they are improved by intercourse with us, as we are ourselves improved by intercourse with spirits of the higher circle.

The dominant doctrine of our age is that of progress; that the universe started from certain rude and imperfect beginnings, and, by a continued series of developments and transformations, is eternally advancing towards perfection, without however reaching it; and that man, beginning, if not in the oyster or the tadpole, at least in a feeble and helpless infancy, develops and advances towards perfect manhood. This doctrine, which a few facts in natural history, in geology, and anthropology, at first sight seem to favor, is at bottom wholly repugnant to the Christian doctrine of a fixed creed, of final repose or beatitude in God, of final causes, and the final consummation of all things. So the spirits are to accept it, systematize it, and propose, as the highest reward of virtue, to be placed on the plane of eternal progression.

The age is indifferent, syncretic, and disposed to accept all religions and superstitions as true under certain aspects, and as false under others, and to pronounce one about as good and about as bad as another. The spirits, therefore, make no direct war on any of them. In some places they teach that the Catholic Church is the truest and best of prevailing religions, but that Protestantism is nevertheless a safe way of salvation, and that the spirits do not, in the other world, think so much about differences of churches and creeds, as they did when in this world. In other places they teach that the Catholic Church is false; that it is wicked, the enemy of moral and social progress, and that effectual means should be taken to prevent its extension in the United States. They do not deny the Bible, nor affirm its inspiration, but take, to a great extent, the neological view of it, conceding it to be truthful in many respects, but maintaining it to be unreliable in others. It was very well when men had nothing better, and no surer means of information in regard to the spirit-world.

Such is a brief outline of the new religion, which was intended to supplant Christianity, and to open the way for that "good time a coming," for which all our philanthropists and reformers are looking, as any one may satisfy himself by reading the *Shekinah*, the *Spiritual Telegraph*, or Judge Edmands's work, from the prolific press of Partridge & Brittan, New York. This new religion, which, indeed, contains nothing new, and which it certainly needed no ghost from the other world to teach or to suggest, would amount to very little if promulgated on mere human authority, unsupported by any prodigies, mysterious or marvellous facts; but, communicated mysteriously from alleged denizens of another world, bearing the imposing names of William Penn, George Washington, Benjamin Franklin, Thomas Jefferson, and Thomas Paine, assumes in the minds of the vulgar a high importance, and can hardly fail to be regarded as overriding Moses and the prophets, our Lord and his Apostles. It strikes at the foundation of Christianity itself, and once accepted, it will seem to have a directness and a completeness of evidence that will entirely set aside, in the minds of the spiritualists, that in favor of the Gospel. This is what I intended, and what I hoped.

Having set the so-called spirits in motion, and through them set afloat a system which I fancied would supplant Christianity, whether in its Catholic or its sounder Protestant forms, my work seemed done, and I could retire from my labors. My superintendence was no longer necessary, and whether the agents I employed were really the spirits or souls of the dead, as they themselves asserted, or mere elemental forces of nature, as I was inclined to believe or had wished to persuade myself, became to me a question of no interest. The work would go on of itself now, and in a few years Christianity and the Church would be undermined and fall of themselves. Then monarchy, aristocracy, republicanism, all forms of civil government, would crumble to pieces, and universal freedom, leaving every one to believe and do what seems right in his own eyes, will be realized, and all here, as well as those not here, will be placed on the plane of eternal progression—progression towards—what?

CHAPTER XVI.

A REBUFF.

I asked not the question, for in fact it did not occur to me; but I asked another question, What shall I do with myself? A grave question this. Do what I would, turn the matter over as I might, there was, now the novelty of the idea had worn off, nothing inspiring in this idea of eternal progression;—this ever learning, and never coming to the knowledge of the truth—this everlasting chase after good, and never coming up with it. Why continue a pursuit which you know beforehand will bring you never any nearer the object than you are, for as you pursue, it flies. Is not this evil rather than good, hell rather than heaven? Is not this the punishment of Ixion?—That war of the Titans upon the gods, has it not a deep significance? The Titans, the Giants, the Earthborn, *Terræ filii*, would dethrone the gods, the heaven-born, the divine, and were defeated and doomed to punishment, to turn forever a wheel, to roll a huge stone up the steep hill, and just as it is about to reach the summit, have it slip from the hands and roll down with a thundering sound; to a task never completed, and always to be renewed, or to hunger, with food ever in sight, and always just beyond reach; to thirst, standing to the neck in water, and have it recede always as approached with the lips. Is not, after all, this the doom that they bring on themselves who reject the wisdom from above and follow what my friend Mr. Merton calls the wisdom from below?

I can very well understand progress towards an end, towards a goal that is fixed and permanent, but a progress towards nothing, or towards a movable goal, a goal that recedes as approached, is to me quite unintelligible, and, when I think of it, it seems as absurd as the supposition of an infinite series. Infinite progression is, in reality, an infinite absurdity. The origin and end of all things must be perfect, fixed, and immovable. Every mechanic knows that he cannot generate motion without a something which is at rest, which can cause or produce motion without moving itself. Without the immovable, there is and can be no movable. In like manner, no motion towards what is not immovable, for if the two bodies remain in the same position relative to each other, neither, in relation to the other, has moved.

Progress is morally motion towards an end, and if there is no approximation to the end, there is no progress. As progress is inconceivable without some end, so it is equally inconceivable without a shortening of the distance between the progressing agent and the end. If this distance can be shortened, however little, if not more than a line in a million of ages, it is not infinite, and the progress cannot be eternal. This infinite or eternal progression is, then, only a lying dream.

At the bottom of this idea of progress, which our modern reformers prate about, is the foolish notion that man is born an inchoate, an incipient God, and that his destiny is to grow into or become the infinite God; that he is to grow or develop into the Almighty; that, to be God, is his ultimate destiny; and, as God is infinite, he is to be eternally developing and realizing more and more of God, without ever realizing him in his infinity. The bubble does not burst and lose itself in the ocean, but by virtue of its bubbleosity it grows and absorbs more and more of the ocean into itself.

I cannot understand this eternal absorbing process, which, though always absorbing or assimilating, leaves always the same quantity, physical or moral, to be absorbed or assimilated. It is impossible to be satisfied with such a destiny. To be always seeking and never finding, to be always desiring, craving, and never filled, is not heaven, it is hell, and the severest hell, in comparison with which the pain of sense, or natural fire and brimstone were a solace. Man is not moved to act by desire. His desire to attain must become hope of attaining, before it can move him, and when you deprive him of that hope, you take from him all courage, all energy, and all motive to act. Desire to possess the beloved, may remain and torment the lover, but it can never suffice to make him continue his pursuit when all hope of success has been extinguished. I do not say love cannot survive hope, but I do say that love's efforts cannot, and it is seldom that even love itself does.

The Christian is stimulated to constant activity, not by charity or love of God alone, but by hope; and the hope of possessing God, of being filled with his love, of reposing in the arms of all-sufficing charity, stimulates onward from grace to grace, and from one degree of perfection to another. Though he finds not yet perfect repose, though he is not yet filled, though he has not yet attained, yet he is upheld, buoyed up and onward by the sure promise, the steadfast hope of attaining, of at last finding repose, rest in the bosom of his love and his God. He may feel the clogs of flesh, he may feel that he is absent from his love, and sigh to reach his home and embrace the spouse of his soul, but he grows not weary, faints not, and knows nothing of the *ennui*, that listlessness of spirit, that disgust of life, and disrelish for every pursuit, which he feels who has no object, no hope, and sees not even in the most distant future any chance of finding that fulness and repose which his soul never ceases in this life to crave. In losing sight of God as final cause, in losing the hope of possessing God as the supreme good, in substituting endless progression for endless beatitude, full and complete, I had lost all stimulus to exertion, all motive to exert myself for any thing.

Why should I act? What had I to gain? Money I did not want; I had more than I could use. Fame I despised. It was a mere word, born and dying in the very sound that made it. Power, I had it. If I had more, it could procure me nothing more than I already possessed. Pleasures? The richest dishes and the most precious wines palled upon my taste. There remained another kind of pleasure; but we can even grow weary of women, and loathe what the morbid senses continue to crave. Still nothing else remained for me. Yet I had outlived love in any virtuous or innocent sense of the word, and early training, and some remains of self-respect, made any other love far more of a torment than a pleasure.

The simple truth was, that I could reconcile myself neither to the philosophy of the Portico nor the philosophy of the Garden, and was alike disgusted with the Cynics and the Academicians. I was a man, and could not live on air, or feed on garbage; I had a soul, and could not satisfy it by living for the body alone, and having no God, no heaven, no hope of beatitude, and no fear of hell, I saw nothing to seek, nothing to gain, and I could only exclaim, *Vanitas vanitatum, et omnia vanitas*. I could not say, with young and thoughtless sinners, in the heyday of their youth, and the full flow of their animal spirits,—"Come on, therefore, and let us enjoy the good things that are present, let us use the creatures as in youth. Let us fill ourselves with costly wine and ointments, and let not the flower of the spring pass by us. Let us crown ourselves with roses before they be withered, and let no meadow escape our riot. Let none of us go without his part in voluptuousness, and let us leave tokens of our joy in every place, for this is our portion and our lot." For of all vanities I had learned that this was the most empty. Even the devil himself is said to loathe the sensualist, and to find his stench intolerable. Still Priscilla—I had lost her perhaps. That touched my pride. We often grieve that lost, which possessed, was not valued.

CHAPTER XVII.

A GLEAM OF HOPE.

I had not seen Priscilla for over a year, and had struggled hard against the madness that possessed me. Finding myself out of work, having completed what I had undertaken, as far as depended on me, I felt that passion, which I even loathed, reviving within me. Nothing would do but I must see my former accomplice again. I called as an old friend, and this time found her alone. She received me with ease, grace, and cordiality.

There are those who believe that a woman who has once lost even the modesty and chastity of thought, can never regain them, and become a truly modest and pure-minded woman. They are greatly mistaken. The Magdalene had fallen lower than that, and yet those were pure tears with which she washed our Lord's feet, and but one purer heart than hers beat in the breasts of those holy women who stood near the cross, and heard the loud cry of the God-Man, as he bowed his head and consummated the world's redemption. The Fountain, which that rude soldier opened with his spear that day, suffices to cleanse from the deepest filth, to wash away the foulest stains, and to make clean and fragrant the most polluted soul. O ye fallen ones, whether women or men, bathe in that fountain! and if your sins be as scarlet, they shall be as white as snow, and if they be red as crimson, they shall be white as wool.

I had never seen Priscilla more beautiful. The bloom had returned to her cheek; her form had regained its roundness, and her complexion its richness. Her eyes were serene and tranquil, and her countenance wore a sweet, pure, and peaceful expression. She had no need to fear me at that moment, for I stood, not repelled, but awed, and felt myself in the presence of virtue, not haughty, austere, and repellant, but lovely, chaste, and affectionate; natural, easy, and wholly unconscious of itself.

"I am glad to see you, Doctor," said she, with a sweet smile. "Sit down. I have been hoping that you would call, but I was afraid that you had entirely deserted us."

"You are changed, Priscilla, since I last saw you; and I should think my presence would now be even more disagreeable than then."

"Not at all. I was never more glad to see you in my life, and I never met you with kinder or more pleasant feelings."

I did not understand this speech, and began to draw, in my own mind, certain very foolish conclusions.

"Yes," she resumed, "I wished to see you, and to see you as I now do, alone. It is of no use referring to what we were for so many years to each other; but I wanted to tell you that I did you no little wrong. You were not innocent, but I was the most guilty. We were both miserable; and you, you, my dear friend, are unhappy still."

"I make no complaint. Nobody has heard me whine or whimper over my own lot. If I have suffered, I have done so in silence."

"That may be. But you have not forgotten our sojourn at Rome in the winter of 1848-49?"

"Forgotten it? no, and shall not, as long as I live."

"Do you remember an old Franciscan monk, that my husband concealed in our house for some weeks?"

"I do."

"He was an old man, nearly fourscore. His head was almost perfectly bald, only a few gray hairs escaped from beneath his *calotte*, and partially shaded his temples; his form, which had been tall and manly, was now bent with years, labors, and mortifications; but his feelings seemed as fresh and playful as those of a child; and the expression of his face was calm, sweet, and affectionate. It was a peculiar expression, not often met with, but like that which, you may remember, we one day remarked in the face of Pius the Ninth. It was an expression of exceeding peace and celestial love, of a pure and holy soul shining through a pure and chaste body. The expression is indescribable, but once seen, can never be forgotten, and seems to be that which Italian painters seek to give to their saints, especially to the Madonna.

"This venerable old man had, as you may recollect, been denounced, by the Circulo del Populo, as an obscurantist, an enemy to the republic, and an adherent to the Pontifical authority. It was intended to include him in the number of priests and religious massacred at San Callisto. My husband had formed an acquaintance with him, and, having learned his danger, smuggled him into our house, where it was presumed nobody would think of looking for a proscribed priest."

"I remember him; I did not at all like him, and, had I cared much about him, would have betrayed him to the Club; for I had the wish of Voltaire in my heart, that 'the last king might be strangled with the guts of the last priest.' But, as he seemed old and harmless, and generally kept out of my way, I let him pass."

"He was a quiet, inoffensive man, and I own I was not sorry that he should escape the cruel death to which philanthropists and sworn friends of liberty doomed so many of his brethren. I was not cruel by nature, and my soul recoiled from the part I was often compelled to take. I thought it was hardly consistent for us, who advocated unbounded freedom of thought and action, to send the dagger to the heart, or coolly sever the carotid artery in the neck of those who chose to think and act differently from us; but I was held then by a force I could not resist."

"You mean, Priscilla, now to reproach me."

"No, my friend, no; I reproach only myself. Had I not originally consented, no power could have held me in that terrible thraldom. The agents you employed have no such power over us against our will; though, when we have once assented to their dominion, it is not always in our own power alone to reassert our liberty. My husband grew very fond of the venerable old man, and they spent hours, and even days, together. What was the subject of their conversation, I knew not, and did not inquire.

"You returned to Paris, to prevent, if possible, the French from interfering to suppress the Roman Republic, by organizing a new insurrection of the Subterraneans, and by reminding the Prince-President of his previous republican and socialistic professions, and making it evident to him that the reëstablishment of the Pope would be fatal to the supremacy of the state, whether republican or imperial. During your absence you left me tranquil, and I began, for the first time since my marriage, to enjoy the sweets and tranquillity of domestic life. The good Franciscan would sometimes spend an evening with me and my husband. He was of a childlike simplicity, and of most winning manners, but a man of a cultivated mind, extensive information, and various and profound erudition. He discoursed much on the old Roman Republic and Empire, on the grasping ambition and tyranny of the government, the hollowness of the Roman virtues and the old Roman people, the cruel and impure nature of their religion, and the looseness and profligacy of their manners.

"He sketched then the introduction of Christianity, showed what enemies it had to encounter, why it was opposed, the change it introduced into the moral and social life of the people, its triumphs over paganism, its conversion and civilization of the northern barbarians, and the chastity, peace, and happiness it had introduced into the cottage of the peasant, the castle of the noble, and even the palace of the monarch. His views seemed clear and precise, and his mind seemed to be enlightened, and singularly free from the cant of his profession, and from that credulity, ignorance, and superstition which you and I had been accustomed to associate with the name of monk. To every question I asked, he had a clear and intelligent answer; and he was always able to give a reason, and what appeared a good reason, for whatever judgment he hazarded. He was evidently a man of an order of intellect, ideas, and culture entirely different from any that had fallen under my observation; and I must own that when I listened to him, I was charmed. I seemed to be under the gentle but superior influence of a good spirit. I felt calm and tranquil, and I wished that I too might believe, be pure, holy, a Christian like him.

"Weeks passed on. At length we had a chance to send him in safety to Portici, where the Holy Father then held his court. The evening before he was to leave us, he came into the sitting-room, and sat down by me. 'My dear lady,' said he, 'I leave you to-morrow, and I shall not see you after to-night. You must permit me to thank you for your kindness to the poor old proscribed monk, and your evident desire to procure him comfort; all so much the more commendable in you, since you are a stranger, and not of my religion. I give you my thanks and my blessing; they are all I have to give; and I shall not cease to pray the good God, who is no respecter of persons, to reward you for your goodness, and to grant you his grace.

"'But, my dear lady, I am a priest; I am also an old man, and have not many days to tarry here. Let me speak to you in all sincerity and freedom.'

"Do so, my father, said I, as my eyes filled with tears.

"'You are still young and beautiful,' said he; 'you have naturally a kind and warm heart, an enthusiastic disposition, and a sincere love of truth and justice. But, my dear child, your education has been sadly neglected, and you have been trained to walk in a path that leadeth where you would not go. You have fallen among evil counsellors and evil doers, and you are entangled in the meshes of the adversary of souls. This cause, to which you give your heart, soul, and body, is not what you think it. You sought liberty, you have found slavery; you sought love, and you have found only hatred; you sought virtue, disinterestedness, fidelity,—you have found only vice, selfishness, and treachery; you sought peace and social regeneration,—you have found only strife, war, murder, assassination, confusion, anarchy, and oppression. For yourself personally, the only peaceful days you have known for years have been during the last few weeks; and your present peace is disturbed by a mysterious dread, that I need not name or explain to you.

"'Ask yourself, my child, and answer to yourself, honestly, if you have not been deceived, and been acting under a fatal delusion. Ask yourself if it was not a terrible mistake you committed, when you took Satan for the principle of good, and the Christian's God for the principle of evil.'

"But, *padre mio*, what shall I do? I have a suspicion that what you say is true. I have been a proud, vain, rash, wicked woman. But what shall I do? I am bound in chains; I am damned.

"'Damned, not yet, my child. As long as there is life, there is hope. Those chains must be broken.'

"But they are too strong for me.

"'True, true, my child, but not too strong for the Lion of the tribe of Judah. You must be assisted——'

"At that moment the door was burst open; a gang of ruffians rushed in, and fell upon the aged monk. The old man gave me one look, made rapidly the sign of the cross over my head, as I had dropped on my knees to implore them not to harm him. I might as well have pleaded to my marble jambs. They threw him down. He rose upon his knees, folded his hands across his breast, and with a bright, celestial expression, exclaimed, O God, pardon them, and lay not this sin to their charge, for they know not what they do,—when the leader of the gang plunged a dagger to his heart. His blood flowed out into my face, and over my dress. After a minute, they took up the body, and removed it and themselves from my house. Though protected, to some extent, by our American character, we did not think it prudent to remain longer in Rome, under the Republic; and the next day we started for Paris, where we rejoined you."

"But you never told me of the fate of that old monk before."

"True, why should I? I could not, before we had separated, have spoken of him to you without arousing your indignation, and inducing you to send me again on some of those terrible secret missions on which you had so often sent me, and which I so abhorred. But I can speak calmly now, and without fear; and let me beg you to ask yourself the question the old monk urged me to ask myself. Truth is truth, let it be spoken by whom it may; and there is no reason why we should not follow good advice, because given by a monk, even if monks have been all our lifetime the object of our wrath, or of our derision."

"Priscilla, I have asked myself that question; but it is of no use. I have pledged myself, body and soul, and sworn that, come what might, I would never repent."

"But that oath was unlawful, and cannot bind. He who has your pledge is a deceiver, had no right to ask it, has no right to hold it."

"But I cannot free myself from these chains of death and hell which bind me."

"Such as you have been, such as I fear you are, I am told seldom find mercy; but the deliverance is not impossible. I, worse than you, have found it."

"That is not so certain. You are free, only because I, in a sudden fit of despair, freed you. But I have but to will, and you are as completely in my power as ever."

"That I doubt. Except when you called me to emancipate me, you have exerted no power over me, since the good old priest was received into our house in Rome."

"That is owing to my forbearance."

"Will you swear that? Will you swear that, within twenty-four hours after you had declared me free, you did not use all your art to enthrall me again? Did you not call again and again, within a month, at my house, for that very purpose?"

"But you avoided me, and I could not so much as touch the hem of your robe."

"Very true, for I feared you, and I dare not defy you even now; but I feel very certain that, under the protection of a name at which even devils must bow, I am safe from all your arts."

As she said that I rose, walked once or twice across the room, came up before her, took her hand unresistingly, and placed my hand on her head. I trembled. I was struck dumb, for I perceived at once that I had no power there; and, though I evoked them, no spirits came to my aid. But before I had let go her hand, her husband came into the room, saw us, feared what I might do, drew his dagger, and before Priscilla could stop him, or offer a word of explanation, aimed a blow at my heart. Priscilla attempted to avert it, and so far succeeded, as to change somewhat its direction. It penetrated, however, the chest, reached the lungs, and inflicted a wound which, though it is apparently healed, and I seem to myself to be suffering only from pulmonary consumption, which wastes me away slowly but surely, my surgeon tells me will yet prove the occasion of my death.

The moment James, a man of peace, and not at all given to striking, had struck the blow, he was filled with terror at what he had done. I assured him, for I retained my presence of mind, which I never yet lost in any case in my life, that so far as I was concerned, he need not blame himself, for I deserved the blow, and had long foreseen that sooner or later his hand must deal it; but, had he delayed a moment, he would have found it unnecessary, that his wife was safe from my annoyances, and proof against any art I possessed. Priscilla, as soon as she recovered from her fright, rather than swoon, told him as much; and we both did all in our power to reassure and console him. But the matter must not be bruited abroad, and he must conceal it for his and Priscilla's sake. It was concluded that I must remain for the present in their house. James did what he could to stanch my wound, aided me to remove to another room, and sent immediately for a surgeon whom we both knew and could trust. For several weeks I lay at their house, nursed with great care and tenderness, till I was able to be removed to my own house. It was rumored that I had been stabbed in the street, but such things not being rare in our cities, it excited very little remark; and suspicion, though it fell on the secret societies known to exist, fell upon no individual in particular, and no pains were taken to ferret out the supposed assassin. The fact was noted in the journals, and was instantly forgotten.

CHAPTER XVIII.

RELIGIOUS MONOMANIA.

I had no sooner been removed to my own house, than my old acquaintances and friends came to see me. Mr. Cotton, the stern but well-meaning old Puritan, who had infinitely more mind and heart than Young America, that has learned to laugh at him, had indeed died during my absence abroad. Mr. Winslow and the others whom I have already introduced, remained. Poor Jack had recovered, not his former gayety, but his health and tranquillity, and was entirely freed from the vision which had haunted him, and which I have no reason to believe was any thing more than a simple hallucination, occasioned by a powerful shock to his nerves, producing a diseased state of the imagination. He had returned to Boston, given up mesmerism, confined himself to the law, and had prospered in his profession. When he heard of the accident which had befallen me, he came immediately to see me, and to render me such assistance as his warm heart prompted. He is still my chief nurse, and declares that he will not leave me as long as my life lasts. I have remembered him in my will, and bequeathed him the bulk of my estate, though he knows it not,—a poor compensation for the blight I brought upon his early hopes.

Mr. Merton, returning to the city about the time of my being wounded, lost no time, after my removal to my own house, in renewing our former acquaintance. Mr. Winslow, and Mr. Sowerby, and Leila and her admirer, who had become husband and wife, and a sober and sensible couple, were frequently in the sick man's room. Nobody deserted me; and never in my life have I had occasion to complain of ingratitude, or the loss of a friend. The world is bad enough, but after all not so bad as sometimes represented. I have always been treated infinitely better than my deserts; and I have found good sense, warm hearts, and noble virtues, where least I expected them. I have reproaches only for myself. I have done a world of wrong, and no good; and yet I have found myself, from my childhood, surrounded by generous and disinterested affection. People, speaking generally, are far better individually than they are collectively; and many private virtues may be found, even in bands of revolutionists, robbers, and assassins,—virtues which do not rise above the natural order indeed, and have no promise of reward in heaven, but which nevertheless are virtues. My observation has taught me to distrust the censorious, those who rail in good set terms at all mankind or womankind, although no man living was ever further than I am from believing in the sinlessness of the race, or from joining in the modern worship of woman, prompted too often by an innate pruriency unconscious of itself.

As I became able to bear conversation, and to take part in it occasionally, mesmerism and the Spirit-Manifestations were a frequent topic of discourse. Jack sturdily maintained that it was all humbug. There were indeed strange things, some phenomena which he could not explain, but he set his face against the whole movement, had no belief in it, and would have nothing to do with it. There was, though he might be unable to detect it, some cheat or trickery at the bottom.

Mr. Winslow held fast to his belief in the connection between mesmerism and all the marvellous, prodigious, or miraculous facts recorded in history. He accepted those facts substantially as related, but did not accept their usual explanation. The miracles of sacred history, and the marvellous facts of profane history, were to be explained on natural principles, by the mesmeric agent, or by whatever other name we might call it.

Mr. Merton argued that, if the phenomena usually called Satanic, obsession, possession, witchcraft, black magic, ghosts or apparitions, clairvoyance and second sight, could be explained without resort to the supernatural, the other class of facts, the miracles of sacred history, could be also explained without the supposition of the special intervention of Divine power. He thought, if we could account for the former without Satan, we could for the latter without the supernatural intervention of God.

Mr. Sowerby held with Mr. Winslow as to the reality of the phenomena, and their natural explanation, but thought they should be divided into two classes, one good and the other bad, as produced for a good or a bad purpose. When produced in a good cause, for a good end, they might be called Divine; when in a bad cause, for a bad purpose, they might be called Satanic or diabolical. The agent is in both cases the same, and the difference is in the mind or will that employs it.

Dr. Corning, my physician, who was a distinguished manigraph, and had written a work, highly esteemed by the profession, on Insanity, was quite ready to concede the phenomena called spiritual, or rather demoniacal, and thought we were bound to do so, or to give up all human testimony. He also conceded the connection contended for by mesmerists between mesmerism and so-called demonic phenomena,—a connection, in his judgment, very evident, and wholly undeniable; but he contended, with the most eminent manigraphs of France, and indeed with the members of the profession generally, that the marvellous phenomena recorded were those of mania, monomania, theosophania, nymphomania, demonopathy, and all to be explained pathologically. He included them all under the general head of insanity, and regarded their variety only as so many different sorts of madness. He had himself witnessed the greater part of them in his practice, and treated them as symptoms of mania.

"That," said Mr. Merton, "would be very satisfactory, if the limits of madness or insanity were well defined, and if physicians could never mistake, and treat as insane one who is only possessed or obsessed by the devil. To include the marvellous facts of history under the head of insanity, without having first established their pathological character, and settled it that there is no generic or specific difference between them and acknowledged pathological symptoms, is not to explain them. How do you prove that a person, otherwise in perfect health, with no disturbance of the pulse, of the digestive, or any other organs to be detected, who on all subjects speaks rationally, but who tells you that a spirit has possession of him, speaks through his organs, throws him down, and otherwise maltreats him, is insane? I do not say that such a man is not insane, but how do you prove him insane?

"Why, he exhibits the symptoms of insanity, for none but an insane man would utter such nonsense."

"Perhaps so, and perhaps not so. He exhibits symptoms of what you are pleased to *call* insanity; but how do you know that you have not called insanity what you ought to call by another name, possession, for instance?"

"I do not believe in possession."

"Precisely, and therefore when you meet what is called possession or obsession, you call it insanity. That is a convenient way of reasoning, and not uncommon with learned physicians and physicists; but it is a begging of the question, not its solution. You reason from a foregone conclusion. As you yourself and all the profession treat insanity as a disease, as symptomatic of some lesion or alteration of the physical system, or of the organs on which the manifestations of the mind depend, I should suppose it necessary to establish the fact of such lesion or alteration, before concluding the presence of actual insanity."

"Insanity, in such case, would be found to be very rare."

"Very possibly, and perhaps it is much rarer than is commonly supposed. It is not impossible that a large proportion of those you call insane, and treat as lunatics, are as sound of body or mind as you or I. Where we find, physically considered, all the symptoms of health, we cannot, from purely mental phenomena, infer disease. That the vulgar have often regarded as under the influence of Satan persons who were merely epileptic, cataleptic, or insane, is no doubt very true; but it is not impossible that the learned and scientific have committed not unfrequently a contrary mistake, and regarded as insane, cataleptics, or epileptics, persons who were totally free from all pathological symptoms.

How will you, dear Doctor, explain by insanity a case taken from a thousand similar ones, which I chanced to be reading this morning, and which is well attested. Allow me to relate it as given by Dr. Calmeil, one of your own profession, a learned and highly esteemed manigraph, author of a work, *De la Folie*,[4] and who entertains the same views that you do. Missionaries who now, says M. Calmeil,[5] cross the seas to shed the light of faith in the New World, are frequently surprised to meet energumenes among their neophytes, whilst they acknowledge that it is seldom that the devil takes possession of the faithful in the mother country. The letter which I am about to report, addressed to Winslow, a celebrated physician, in 1738, by a *worthy* missionary, proves that the delirium of demonopathy may everywhere become the lot of feeble and timorous souls.

"I cannot refuse, at your earnest request," writes the missionary Lecour, to write you a detailed account of what took place in the case of the Cochin-chinese who was possessed, and of whom I had the honor to speak to you. In May or June, 1733, being in the province of Cham, in the kingdom of Cochin China, in the church of a burgh called Cheta, about half a league distant from the capital of the province, there was brought to me a young man from eighteen to nineteen years of age, and who was a Christian. His parents told me that he was possessed by a demon. A little incredulous, I might say to my confusion, quite too much so, in consequence of my little experience at that time in such things, of which I had never seen an example, although I had often heard other Christians speak of them, I examined them to ascertain if there were not simplicity or malice in their statement. The substance of what was gathered from them was, that the young man had made an unworthy communion, and after that had disappeared from the village, had retired to the mountains, and called himself only the traitor Judas."

"On this statement, and after some difficulties," resumes the missionary, "I went to the hospital where the young man was detained, fully resolved to believe nothing, unless I saw marks of something superhuman. I began by questioning him in Latin, a language of which I knew he had not the least tincture. Extended as he was on the ground, frothing at his mouth, and violently shaken, he rose immediately on his seat, and answered me very distinctly, *Ego nescio loqui latine*. I was so astonished and frightened that I withdrew, with no courage to question him any further....

"However, some days after, I recommenced with some probationary commands, taking care to speak always in Latin, of which the young man was ignorant. Among other commands, I ordered the demon to throw him forthwith upon the floor. I was instantly obeyed, but he was thrown down with so much violence, all his limbs being stretched out and rigid as a crowbar, that the noise was rather that of a falling beam than of a man. Wearied and exhausted, I thought I would follow the example of the Bishop of Tilopolis on a similar occasion. In the exorcism, I commanded the demon, in Latin, to bear him to the ceiling of the church, feet up and head down. Forthwith his body became stiff, he was drawn into the church to a column, his feet joined together, his back set against the column, and, without the aid of his hands, he was run up to the ceiling in a twinkling, as if drawn up by a pulley, without any act or motion of his own, suspended with his feet glued to the ceiling, and his head hanging downwards. I made the demon confess, as I intended to confound and humble him, and to compel him to quit his hold, the falsity of the pagan religion. I made him confess that he was a deceiver, and at the same time compelled him to acknowledge the sanctity of our religion. I held him suspended in the air, his feet adhering to the ceiling and his head down, for more than half an hour, but not having sufficient constancy, so much was I frightened at what I saw, to continue him there for a longer time, I ordered the demon to place him at my feet without harming him. He forthwith cast him down, as a bundle of dirty linen, but without his receiving the least injury. From that day the young man, though not entirely delivered, was much relieved, and his vexations daily diminished, especially when I was in the house, and after about five months he was wholly released, and is now perhaps the best Christian in Cochin China."

"Pass over the effect of the exorcism, if you please," resumed Mr. Merton, "and tell me what you think, Doctor, of the facts in this case, which Dr. Calmeil concedes, and which, if he did not, it would not amount to any thing, for this is only one case out of a thousand."

"I will say," replied the Doctor, "with M. Calmeil, that I am very much obliged to the good missionary for not withholding his account, for he has described, without knowing it, the phenomena of religious monomania."

"It strikes me," replied Mr. Merton, "that Dr. Corning has not well examined the case. That some of the phenomena may be regarded as symptoms of insanity, I do not question, but if I understand insanity, it is a derangement, an access of what properly belongs to one in his normal state, but not the accession of something preternatural. It may, in some respects, sharpen the senses, revive the memory, and render the faculties, or at least some of them, morbidly active; but I have never understood that it could enable a man to understand and speak a language which he had never learned, and of which, in the full possession of all his faculties, he knew not a word. I can easily understand that in delirium a man may fancy that he is possessed, and act on the conviction that he is, but I do not understand how delirium alone can enable a man, however agile, to climb to the ceiling of a church, his back against a column, with his feet fastened together, and without using his hands or arms, and to remain by the simple application of his feet to the ceiling for one half an hour with his head down, carrying on all the time a close controversy in this very inconvenient position, and finally dropping upon the pavement without the least injury. Such a delirium would, to say the least, be very extraordinary, and I suspect the Doctor has never found a similar delirium amongst any of his numerous patients who were unquestionably insane. I will venture to say that however striking the delirium, the thing is absolutely impossible without superhuman aid."

"Part of it is hallucination," replied the Doctor.

"Whose hallucination? The young man's, or the missionary's?" asked Mr. Merton. "Not the missionary's, for there is no pretence that he was insane; and not the young man's, because the question turns not on what he saw, or fancied, or imagined, but on what another person, the missionary, saw."

"Probably the facts are much exaggerated," replied Dr. Corning. "The missionary confesses that he was greatly frightened, and being so, he may, without impeachment of his honesty, have failed to be strictly accurate as to the details."

"Then you question the relation. That alters the case. Let us take, then, the case, also well attested, of the nuns of Uvertet, which, about 1550, caused for a long time so much astonishment in Brandenburg, Holland, Italy, and especially in Germany. The nuns were at first awakened and startled by plaintive moanings.... Sometimes they were dragged from their beds, and along the floor, as if drawn by their legs.... Their arms and lower extremities were twisted in every direction.... Sometimes they bounded in the air and fell with violence upon the ground.... In moments in which they appeared to enjoy a perfect calm, they would suddenly fall backwards and be deprived of speech.... Some of them, on the contrary, would amuse themselves in climbing to the tops of trees, when they would descend, their feet in the air and their heads down. These attacks began to lose their violence after a duration of three years. A very singular madness this, which, as the *Dictionnaire des Sciences Médicales* says, 'extended over *all* the convents of women in Germany, particularly in Saxony and Brandenburg, and gained even Holland,' and it might have added, also, Italy. 'All the miracles,' it continues, 'of the Convulsionaires, or of Animal Magnetism, were familiar to these nonnains, who were regarded as possessed. They all foretold future events, leaped and capered, ran up the sides of walls, spoke foreign languages, &c.' You may read the fourteen well authenticated cases recorded by Cotton Mather in his Magnalia, and you will find that all these, and similar phenomena, were exhibited by the bewitched or possessed in Massachusetts near the close of the seventeenth century, and known under the name of 'Salem witchcraft,' though only a portion of them occurred in that famous town. Do you include all these under the head of insanity?"

"Cotton Mather was a pedant, vain, arrogant, and ambitious of power, and I did not expect to hear him cited as an authority," replied the Doctor, in evident vexation.

"Cotton Mather," Mr. Merton replied, "was one of the most learned and distinguished men in New England in his time, and, though I am of another parish, I respect his memory. I do not cite his opinions; I merely cite him as the recorder of facts which either he himself had witnessed with his own eyes, or which had been confessed or proved before the courts of the colony, and thus far at least his authority is sufficient. But I will ask you to explain on your hypothesis the phenomena exhibited by the Ursuline Nuns of Loudun, France, in the seventeenth century, and the authenticity of which both Bertrand and Calmeil, as well as others, admit were triumphantly vindicated."

"I know the case to which you refer," answered Dr. Corning. "It is the case of a certain number of nuns who took it into their heads that they were bewitched by one Urban Grandier, whom they had refused to accept as their director,—a man of a scandalous life, a great criminal, who deserved to be executed as he was, if not for sorcery, at least for his crimes. I see nothing in this case but the usual symptoms of demonopathy, or religious monomania."

"The physicians of the time thought differently, and there were then and there physicians of great eminence who were consulted, and required to make to the authorities twenty-five or thirty elaborate reports on the case. But let us recall some of the facts.

"Shortly after, Grandier, a bad priest, was refused by these ladies as their director; he passed by the convent, and threw a bouquet of flowers over the wall, which was taken up and smelt of by several of the nuns. From that moment the disorder commenced. Up to that moment all these ladies were in the enjoyment of the most perfect health, and strictly correct in their deportment. They were all connected with families of distinction and of high birth, and had been carefully brought up, and yielded to none in their education, their intelligence, their piety, their virtues, and their accomplishments.

"After some weeks of silence, in which they had sought relief from their vexations by religious exercises, prayers, fasts, and macerations, without avail, recourse was had to exorcism. The phenomena then assumed gigantic proportions. One religious, lying stretched out on her belly, and her arms twisted over her back, defied the priest who pursued her with the Holy Sacrament; another doubled over backwards, contrived to walk with the nape of her neck resting on her heels; another still, shook her head in the most singular and violent manner. The exorcist says he had *frequently* seen them bent over backwards, with the nape of their neck resting on their heels, walk with surprising swiftness. He saw one of them, rising from that posture, strike rapidly her shoulders and breast with her head. They cried out as the howlings of the damned, as enraged wolves, as terrible beasts, with a force that exceeds the power of imagination. Their tongues hung out black, swollen, dry, and hard, and became soft and natural the moment they were drawn back into the mouth.

"During the intervals of repose, the afflicted ladies sought to return to their religious exercises, to resume their industry and the deportment proper to their rank and their state. But on the arrival of the exorcist nothing was any longer heard but blasphemies and imprecations. Then the nuns would rise, pass their feet over their heads, throw their legs apart, with entire forgetfulness of modesty. Then came what Dr. Calmeil calls hallucinations, which made them attribute their state to the presence and obsession of evil spirits. The Abbess, Madame Belfiel, while replying to the questions of the exorcist, heard a living being speaking in her own body, as it were a foreign voice emanating from her pharynx. They all heard a voice distinctly articulated, proceeding from within them, stating that evil angels had taken possession of their person, and indicating the names, the number, and the residences of the demons.

"In the month of August, 1635, Gaston, Duke of Orleans, brother of Louis the Thirteenth, wishing to judge for himself of the state of the Ursulines, went to Loudun, and was present at several sessions of the exorcists. The Superioress at first worshipped the Holy Sacrament, giving all the signs of a violent despair. The Abbé Surin, the exorcist, repeated the command he had given her, and forthwith her body was thrown into convulsions, running out a tongue horribly deformed, black, and granulated as morocco, and without being pressed at all by the teeth. Among other postures they remarked an extension of the legs, so great that there were seven feet from one foot to the other. The Superioress remained in this position a very long time, with strange trembling, touching the ground only with her belly. Having risen from this position, the demon was commanded again to approach the Holy Sacrament, when she became more furious than ever, biting her arms, &c. Then, after a little time, the agitation ceased, and she returned to herself, with her pulse as tranquil as if nothing extraordinary had happened.

"The Abbé Surin himself, while he was speaking to the Duke, and about to make the exorcism, was attacked and twice thrown upon his back, and when he had risen and proceeded anew to the combat, Père Tranquille demanded of the supposed demon wherefore he had dared attack Père

Surin. He answered with the organs of the latter, and as if addressing him: 'I have done so to avenge myself on you.' Was the Abbé Surin insane? or did he simulate delirium?

"The Superioress, at the end of the exorcism, executed an order which the Duke had just communicated secretly to the exorcist. In a hundred instances it appeared that the energumenes read the thoughts of the priest charged with the exorcism. They answered in whatever language they were addressed, in Greek, Latin, Spanish, Italian, and Turkish. They even answered M. de Launay de Razelly in the dialects of several tribes of American savages, very pertinently, and revealed to him things that had passed in America. Urban Grandier, when commanded by his bishop to take the stole and exorcise the Mother Superior, who he said knew Latin, refused, although challenged to do it, to question her in Greek, and remained quite confused. Also, the Mother Superior remained for some considerable time suspended in the air, at an elevation of about two feet above the ground. In about three months of exorcism the trouble ceased, and the Ursulines were restored, and resumed in peace their pious exercises and their usual labors."

"I see no reason to change my opinion," remarked the Doctor, at the conclusion of this recital. "It was a case of monomania, if the facts were as stated."

"The facts," replied Mr. Merton, "are unquestionable. They have all the authenticity that facts can have, and there is not the least ground for suspecting the good faith of the parties. They were all in perfect health, with no symptoms of any disease about them. Now, as insanity, of whatever variety, cannot render a man more than human, I demand, if these facts can all be brought within the humanly possible? Does insanity enable one to assume such difficult postures as are described? Does it enable one to bend over backwards and walk rapidly with the nape of the neck resting on his heels; to have the extraordinary extension of legs mentioned; to read the thoughts of others not expressed; to tell what is passing fifteen hundred leagues off; to understand and speak languages never learned or before heard; and to remain for some time suspended unsupported in the air? And, above all, is insanity or madness cured by exorcisms? No, no, Doctor. The facts in the case, that is, if you take not one or two, but *all* of them, are certainly inexplicable without the presence of a superhuman power."

The Doctor was not at all pleased with this conclusion, which he would by no means admit. He said the conversation, if continued, might injure his patient, and giving me a few directions, took his hat and cane and departed, apparently in a very unpleasant humor, and muttering something about superstition, Salem witchcraft, and the absurdity of educated men in the nineteenth century believing in such nonsense.

[4]Paris, Chez Balliere, 1845. 2 vol. gr. in-8vo. .

[5]T. 2, p. 417.

CHAPTER XIX.

MESMERISM INSUFFICIENT.

Insanity explains abnormal, but not superhuman phenomena. It is a disease of the body, not of the mind itself. The mind, being a simple spiritual or immaterial substance, is not susceptible of physical derangement, and mental alienation proceeds from the lesion or alteration of the bodily organs or conditions on which the mind is dependent in its manifestations. It is cured, when curable, by medical, not by purely spiritual treatment; by physic and good regimen, not by exorcisms.

A few days after the conversation I have detailed, my friends being again present, the subject was resumed. Dr. Corning sustained his hypothesis triumphantly by selecting such facts in the cases brought forward as it would explain, and by denying all the rest,—a very convenient and common practice of theorizers,—even out of the medical profession.

Mr. Sowerby, who had made a fortune by mesmerism and spirit-rapping, thought that only a monomaniac would attempt to explain the mysterious phenomena in question by insanity. There was in the cases not a symptom of mania, and the persons affected, in their moments of repose, and even while the affection lasted, were in the normal exercise of their faculties, and indicated no signs of mental alienation, answering always, when answering at all, pertinently, never at random, consecutively, never incoherently, as is the case with the insane. He explained them, not by mental alienation, but by the accumulation or increased activity of a great and all pervading principle, perhaps the vital principle itself, called the mesmeric or odic principle. He had himself produced phenomena analogous to the most extraordinary recorded in history.

Mr. Sowerby would not listen to him, and there was almost a quarrel between the two ex-ministers. But their rage being finally mollified by a witticism from Jack, the conversation resumed its pacific character.

"You say, Mr. Sowerby," said Dr. Corning, "that you have produced phenomena analogous to those recorded in history?"

"Certainly," answered Mr. Sowerby.

"And by the mesmeric or odic principle?"

"Undoubtedly."

"What is your evidence of the existence of such a principle? or your proof that such a principle exists?"

"The phenomena I produce or find produced by it."

"So, you take the phenomena to prove the principle, and the principle to explain the phenomena," said Dr. Corning, who could reason as well as anybody when it concerned the refutation of a theory not his own.

"I am not disposed to question the existence of such a principle," said Mr. Merton, "except in the form asserted by Mr. Dodson, or when it is explained as the immediate action of the mind or will of the mesmerizer upon the mesmerized. The fluid asserted by Mesmer, after the animal magnetists of the sixteenth and seventeenth centuries, as Wirdig, Fludd, Maxwell, Kircher, Van Helmont, simply revised by Baron Reichenbach with a great show of demonstration, though denied by Deleuze and some other mesmerists, I have no good reason for doubting. I am willing to concede the fact, that this fluid or agent exists and is employed by Mr. Sowerby in his experiments. I am willing to concede that there is a fluid or agent, not electricity, not magnetism, but analogous to them, contended for by Baron Reichenbach, that pervades a numerous class of bodies, and may be artificially accumulated, or stimulated to increased activity. But suppose this; suppose the mesmerizer, wizard, sorcerer, witch, magician, actually uses it, I must still ask Mr. Sowerby to tell me how he proves it to be the sole principle of the phenomena produced? That in most of the cases recorded, if not in all, there are proper mesmeric or odic phenomena, naturally or artificially produced, is, I think, undeniable. The flowers used by Grandier, in the case of the nuns of Loudun, and the fumigations and sufflations of the old magicians, all prove the resort to magnetism. The rod and tub of Mesmer, and the cumbrous machinery he used, though not indispensable, every magnetizer knows are a useful mean. But as these are only subsidiary, how is it to be demonstrated that mesmerism itself is the sole efficient cause, not merely of some of the accessory phenomena, but of them all? In the phenomena of table-turning, so extensively witnessed, magnetism is not absolutely essential. They began, as all the recent spirit-manifestations, in mesmerism, and at first the table was mesmerized by a circle formed round it, joining their hands and resting them on it."

"The tables are turned," said Dr. Corning, "by the involuntary and unconscious muscular contraction of the hands pressing upon it. This has been proved."

"So says a French Academician, and so also says Professor Farraday, and tables, very likely, may be turned in some such way; but the table is frequently known to turn and cut up its capers without any circle being formed, without any person being near it, or visible hand touching it."

"That is true," said I, "for I have myself seen the most extraordinary phenomena of table-turning when it was certain no pressure, voluntary or involuntary, had been applied to it by any person visible in the room. I have seen a table turn in spite of the efforts of four strong men to hold it still, rise up without any visible agency, fly over the heads of the company, rush with violence from one end of the room to the other, spin round like a top, balance itself on one leg and then on another,—in fine, move along some inches on the floor with the weight of a dozen men resting on it, raise itself from the floor with them, and remain suspended a foot above it, for some minutes."

"There can be no doubt of that," said Mr. Merton. "In Cochin China, we are told on good authority, that in the time of the predecessors of Gia-long, it was a custom in the province of Xu-Ngué, on certain solemnities, to invite the most celebrated tutelar genii of the towns and villages of the kingdom to games and a public trial of their strength. A long and heavy bark, with eight benches of oars, was placed dry in the centre of a large hall, and the trial consisted in seeing which of these could move it farthest or with the greatest ease. The judges and spectators took their stand at a little distance, and saw, as they called the names and titles of the genii placed on the bark, the huge machine tip one side and then the other, and finally advance and then recede. Some of the genii would push it forward several feet, others only a few inches. But one who made it come and go with the greatest facility, was the tutelar genius of the maritime village of Ke-Chan, worshipped under the name of Hon-Leo-Hanh, whose temple was in consequence thronged with pilgrims, and enriched with votive offerings."

"But conceding," continued Mr. Merton, "that mesmerism plays its part, I wish to know how Mr. Sowerby proves that it alone suffices for the production of the phenomena? Is it not possible that another power steps in, and, either alone or in concurrence, produces them? May it not be that mesmerism only facilitates or prepares the way for the demonic action, produces the state or condition of the human subject favorable to Satanic invasion, and therefore is to be regarded rather as the occasion than as the efficient cause of the phenomena?"

"But I admit no devil; I do not believe that there are any demons," said Mr. Sowerby.

"I am aware of that," said Mr. Merton, "but I suppose that, notwithstanding your disbelief, there may be a devil, the prince of this world, as the Scriptures plainly teach. It is possible that there are whole legions of devils, that the air swarms with them, and that they have power to tempt and to vex and harass those they would seduce from allegiance to the Most High. Their non-existence, at least their non-intervention, must be proved before you are entitled to conclude that your mesmeric or odic agent is the sole efficient cause of the phenomena."

"But that," said Mr. Dodson, "would overthrow all the so-called inductive sciences."

"If so, I cannot help it," replied Mr. Merton. "The inductive philosophers have accumulated a mass of rich and valuable facts by their observations and experiments, for which I am grateful to them; but I set no great store by the ever-changing theories which they imagine or invent to explain these facts. But let this pass. If Mr. Sowerby's mesmeric or odic force does not explain all the phenomena in the case, I presume that he will concede that it is not the sole principle of their production."

"Certainly," replied Mr. Sowerby.

"This odic agent, is it not a simple natural principle or force, and without reason or intelligence?"

"It is in itself unintelligent, I admit."

"But in the phenomena there are evident marks of intelligence, which proceed neither from the mesmerizer nor the mesmerized. How do you explain that?"

"The intelligence is the instinctive or involuntary intelligence proceeding from the back part of the brain," answered Mr. Dodson.

"Back part of whose brain?" asked Mr. Merton.

"The mesmerized or psychologized," replied that philosophic gentleman.

"But there cannot proceed, voluntarily or involuntarily, instinctively or rationally, from the back brain or the front brain, what is not in it, or an intelligence which its owner does not possess. I do not now speak of the intelligence of either the operator or the one operated upon, but of an intelligence of a third party. In the recorded and undeniable phenomena to be explained there appears a third party, which acts intelligently, and gives information unknown to either of the other parties. Take the case of the spectre that appeared to Brutus before the battle of Pharsalia, or that which appeared to Julian on the eve of the battle in which he fell mortally wounded, and hundreds of similar cases."

"They are mere hallucinations," interposed Dr. Corning.

"What proves the contrary," replied Mr. Merton, "is the fact that they had accurate knowledge of future events, which hallucinations have not. I place no stress on the fact that a prediction was uttered, or seemingly uttered, for that might be a hallucination; the point to be attended to is its literal fulfilment, showing a knowledge of the future not possessed by the individual to whom the prediction was made, nor, supposing mesmerism employed, by the mesmerizer. Here was an intelligent third party.

"There is a very well authenticated case of a domestic in the German village of Kleische, who, returning one evening from a place near by, where she had been sent of an errand, saw a little gray man, not larger than an infant, who, because she would neither go with him nor answer him, threatened her, and told her, as she reached the threshold of her master's house, that she should be blind and dumb for four days. The prediction was exactly fulfilled. Instances enough are on record of persons afflicted, as they supposed, by evil spirits, who have foretold the day and hour when they would be delivered. In the case of the parsonage of Cideville, which in 1849 made so much noise in France, the agent that rapped was intelligent, for the raps gave distinct and intelligent answers to the questions addressed to it, and communicated facts unknown to the questioner and to all the persons present.

"The ancient pagan oracles may be cited. They did not, I concede, foretell what belongs exclusively to the supernatural providence of God, but they did foretell, clearly and distinctly, events belonging to the natural order, beyond the reach of ordinary human foresight. That many of the responses were false, that many of them were ambiguous and suited to the event, let it turn out which way it might, I by no means deny, but this cannot be said of all of them. The contrary is evident from the great reputation they enjoyed, and the long ages that they were consulted, not by the vulgar only, but by kings, princes, nobles, and philosophers, of the most learned and polite nations of Gentile antiquity. Men are deceived, deluded, but never by pure falsehood. It is the truth mingled with the falsehood that deceives or misleads them."

"But the whole," said Jack, "was a system of jugglery, cheatery, and knavery, of the heathen priests."

"I do not defend," replied Mr. Merton, "the ancient pagan superstitions, nor the strict honesty, any more than the immaculate purity, of the ancient priesthoods; but I have learned not to explain great effects by petty causes, like the shallow-pated philosophers of the last century, and the historians of the school of Voltaire, Hume, and Robertson, who had no more comprehension of the real causes and concatenation of events than a respectable goose. All heathenism was founded on delusion, but not a delusion originating with, and kept up by, the trickery and jugglery of priests, who were often greater dupes than any others. No art, craft, jugglery, or fraud, could be carried on for three thousand years in the bosom of cultivated nations without detection. There were men in ancient heathendom as able and as willing to detect human imposture, as are our modern philosophers, who tell us so gravely in their elaborate works how the priests contrived to work their miracles, and to keep the people in subjection. The only sound philosophy proceeds on the assumption of the general good faith of mankind, or that they dupe and are duped, save in individual cases, without malice prepense.

"In these oracles there was a superhuman intelligence, and an intelligence which was neither that of those who consulted nor that of those who gave the response, and it tells you itself why the oracles after the birth of our Saviour and the spread of Christianity, became mute.

> Me puer Hebræus, divos Deus ipse gubernans,
> Cedere sede jubet, tristemque redire sub Orcum;
> Aris ergo dehinc tacitus abscedito nostris.

The Hebrew youth, himself God and master of the gods, had reduced them to silence. Whence this third intelligence? It cannot come from the odic agent, for that is unintelligent."

"I do not agree with Mr. Sowerby," said Mr. Winslow. "I believe all existence is intelligent, and all forces intelligent forces. God is infinite intelligence. He is the principle and similitude of all things, and therefore every thing must, like him, be intelligent."

"That was my view," said I, "or else I should have had no hesitation in explaining a large portion of the mysterious phenomena by the old notion of demonic invasion."

"Yet this view," replied Mr. Merton, "is decidedly untenable. God, in the sense of creator, is the principle of all things, and in the sense that the ideas or types after which he creates them are in his eternal reason, he is their similitude; but it is not necessary to suppose that every creature imitates him in all his attributes, which would suppose that a cabbage has intellect and will, and a granite block is endowed with charity. The infinite intelligence of God supposes that all are created, ordered, and governed by, and according to, intelligence, but not that every creature is intelligent, or an intelligence. We might as well say that every creature is infinite, for God is infinity, as well as intelligence.

"In the phenomena of demonopathy the patient is distinctly conscious of an intelligence not his own. The Mother Superior in the convent of Loudun was distinctly conscious that the words spoken by her organs did not proceed from her intelligence, and that they were uttered, not by her will, but against it. There is a thousand times more evidence of this third intelligence, and that it is personal, than Baron Reichenbach has adduced in proof of his odic agent. The nuns of Loudun knew what they did, and they struggled with all their might against the power that afflicted them. They knew as well that their words and actions proceeded from a foreign personality, and not from themselves, as you know that my words and actions do not proceed from you. They held in the greatest horror the blasphemous words their organs were made to utter, and the indecent postures they were made to assume, and sought deliverance by prayer and pious practices. That does not proceed from one's own will, which he holds in horror, and struggles against."

"The will and intelligence was that of Grandier, who mesmerized them. He, by the mesmeric agent, had placed himself in relation with them, and he moved them as a mesmerizer does his somnambulist," said Mr. Sowerby.

"That Grandier persecuted them, and was in some sense near them, is what they uniformly asserted, and what I am not disposed to deny, but that it was he who possessed them, and used their organs, is not to be supposed; because one human being cannot thus possess another, and because the intelligence and will displayed surpassed his own. Grandier, if he afflicted them, did it only by means of a foreign power, foreign both to his personality and theirs, as even Mr. Sowerby contends; but this foreign power must have had, as is evident from the recorded phenomena, intelligence and will of its own."

After a long discussion on this point, which I had hardly for a moment questioned, for I had proved it by my experiments with Priscilla, and with tables and inanimate objects, time and again, though I saw not all that it involved, all except the Doctor and Jack agreed that it must be so. The Doctor would not make an admission that required him to modify what he had written and published on insanity, and Jack would not hear a word on the subject. His experience was explicable on the assumption of hallucination, and he would not believe anybody had had a more marvellous experience than his own.

"But," said Mr. Merton, "this wonder-working power, if it have intelligence and will, must be a spirit, good or bad, and, also a superhuman spirit, since the phenomena are superhuman."

"So," said Dr. Corning, "here we are in the middle of the nineteenth century, in this age of science, after so much has been said and written against the folly, ignorance, barbarism, and superstition of past ages, back in the old superstitious belief in demons, good and bad angels, ghosts and hobgoblins, fairies and ghouls, witches and witchcraft, sorcery and magic. Well, gentlemen, I have done. I am inclined to believe there must be a devil, for if there were no devil we could hardly have such poor success in bringing the world to reason, and curing it of superstition."

"There may be more truth in what you say than you suspect," said Mr. Merton. "The devil is the father of ignorance, credulity, and superstition, no less than of false science, infidelity, and irreligion."

CHAPTER XX.

SHEER DEVILTRY.

A few days after this last conversation, I was visited by Judge Preston, whom I had slightly known in former years,—a man of very respectable gifts and attainments, and of high standing in the community. He had been a politician, lawyer, legislator, and was now a Justice of the Supreme Court of his native State. He was moral, upright, candid, and sincere, but like too many of his class, as well as of mine, had grown up and lived without any fixed or determinate views of religion. To say he had rejected Christianity, would be hardly just; but he had only vague notions of what is Christianity, and if he did not absolutely disbelieve a future state, he had no firm belief in the immortality of the soul. He rather wished than hoped to live again. He had not long before lost his wife, whom he tenderly loved, and her death had plunged him into an inconsolable grief. He wept, and refused to be comforted. A friend drew him one evening into a circle of Spiritualists or Spiritists, and after much persuasion, induced him to seek through a medium an interview with his deceased wife. What he saw and heard convinced him, and he soon found that he was himself a medium—a writing medium, I believe.

Judge Preston, in connection with a physician of some eminence, and his friend Van Schaick, formerly a member of the United States Senate, a prominent politician a few years since, and in religion a Swedenborgian, had just published a work, of large dimensions as well as pretensions, on Spiritualism and Spirit-manifestations, very well written, and not without interest to those who would investigate the subject of demonic invasion.

He said that he had called to see me in obedience to an order given him by Benjamin Franklin, who assured him that I could, if I chose, give him some information on the subject of the spirit-manifestations, for I had had more to do with them than any man living.

I replied that I was very glad to see him; but, as to the conversation on spirit-manifestations, I must decline taking part in it myself. I was very weak, and I did not think I could give him any information of importance. He could probably learn much more from the shades of Franklin, William Penn, or George Washington, than from me. George Fox and Oliver Cromwell could tell him many things; Swedenborg and Joe Smith more yet. I advised him to call up the Mormon prophet, who could probably give him more light on the subject than any one who had gone to the spirit-world since Mahomet. I should, however, be most happy to hear him and my highly esteemed friend Mr. Merton, who was present, converse on the subject.

"Mr. Merton," said the Judge, "I perceive is not a believer, and I am not fond of conversing with sceptics."

"Judge Preston," said Mr. Merton, "can hardly call me a sceptic, and I think, were we to compare notes, he would find me believing too much rather than too little."

"It may be so," said the Judge, "but I feel as if I was in the presence of an unbeliever, and an enemy of the spirits."

"We must not place too much reliance on our feelings; and the habit of carefully noting them, and taking them as our guides, is not to be encouraged," answered Mr. Merton. "Our feelings become warped, obscure our perceptions, and mislead our judgment. I certainly do not deny the facts, or the phenomena which you call spirit-manifestations, although I may not, and probably do not, admit your explanation of them, nor the doctrines concerning God, the universe, and man and his destiny, which I find in your book."

"But do you believe that spirits from the other world do really communicate with the living?"

"That there is in many of the phenomena, I say not in all, which you call spirit-manifestations, a real spiritual invasion, I do not doubt; but whether the spirits are the souls of the departed, or really demons or devils personating them, is a question to which you do not seem to me, from your book, to have paid sufficient attention. You are necromancers, diviners with the spirits of the dead. Necromancers are almost as old as history. We find them alluded to in Genesis. Moses forbids necromancy, or the evocation of the dead, and commands that necromancers shall be put to death. In all ancient and modern pagan nations, necromancy is found to be a very common species of divination. The African magicians found at Cairo practise it even at the present time, as we find testified to by an English nobleman and a French academician, though by a seeing medium, not, as is the case with you, by rapping, talking, and writing mediums. The famous Count de Cagliostro, or rather Giuseppo Balsamo, at the close of the last century, professed to enable persons of distinction to converse with the spirits of eminent individuals, long since dead; and evocation of the dead has long been practised at Paris by students of the University. You are real diviners, attempting, by means of evoking the dead, to divine secrets, whether of the past or the future, unknown to the living. You practise what the world has always called divination, and that species of divination called necromancy. Thus far, all is plain, certain, undeniable, and therefore you do that which the Christian world has always held to be unlawful, and a dealing with the devils. This, however, is nothing to you, for you place the authority of the spirits above that of Jesus Christ, and do not hesitate to make Christianity give place to spiritism. But what I wish you to tell me is, the evidence on which you assert that the invading or communicating spirits are really the souls of men and women who once lived in the flesh?"

"They themselves expressly affirm it, and prove it by proving that they have the knowledge of the earthly lives of the persons they say they are, which we should expect them to have in case they were those very persons."

"The question, you will perceive, my dear Judge, is one of identity—a question with which, as a lawyer and a judge, you must have often had occasion to deal. Is the evidence you assign sufficient?"

"On my professional honor and reputation, I say it is."

"Do you find the spirits always tell the truth?"

"No. I have said in my book they frequently lie."

"Then the simple fact that a spirit says he is Franklin, Adams, Jefferson, Washington, George Fox, William Penn, or Martin Luther, is not a sufficient proof that he is."

"I concede it. But I do not rely on his word alone. I examine the spirit, and I conclude he is identically Franklin only when I find that he has that intimate acquaintance with the earthly life of Franklin which I should expect to find in case he really were Franklin."

"But that intimate acquaintance does not establish the identity, unless you know beforehand that the spirit could not have it, unless he were Franklin. The spirits, I find by consulting your book, have told you the most secret things of your own past life, and secrets which could by no human means be known to any one but yourself. Yet the spirit who knew these secrets was not yourself, but an intelligence distinct from you. Now, if the spirit could show himself thus intimately acquainted with your earthly life without being you, why might he not be intimately acquainted with Franklin's earthly life without being Franklin?"

"That is a point of view under which I have not considered the question. But, nevertheless, I have subjected the spirits to severe tests, and compelled them to confirm what they say by extraordinary visible manifestations."

"But the difficulty I find is, that there is nothing in those manifestations that necessarily establishes the identity pretended; for they do not necessarily establish the credibility of the power exhibiting them, as you yourself allow, when you acknowledge that the spirits are untruthful, and not unfrequently lie to you. Miracles accredit the miracle-worker, establish his credibility, only when they are such as can be performed only by the finger of God. If they are such as can be performed by a created power, without special Divine intervention, or such as might be performed by a lying spirit, they prove nothing as to the credibility of their author. A messenger, or a person claiming to be a messenger from God, performs a miracle which can be performed only by the hand of God, and thus establishes his credibility, because he proves by the miracle that God is with him, vouches for what he says; and God, we know, can neither deceive nor be deceived, and therefore will not endorse a deceiver. But prodigies, though superhuman, which do not transcend the powers of created intelligence, do not accredit the agent who performs them, certainly not when it is conceded the agent can, and in many cases does, lie and deceive. I must think, my dear Judge, that you have been hasty in concluding the identity pretended. All you can conclude, from the phenomena in the case, is, that there is present a superhuman spirit, personating or pretending to be Bacon, Franklin, Penn, Swedenborg, or some other well known person who has lived in the flesh, and is able to speak and act in the character assumed."

"My attention, I grant, has not been so specially turned to the question of identity of the spirit with the individual personated, as it has been to establishing the reality of the spiritual presence," said the Judge.

"And you have been mainly intent on and carried away, I presume, by the revelations you have received, or doctrines on the greatest of all topics taught you by the spirits."

"That is true. I have been much more impressed and confirmed by them than by the visible or physical manifestations which I have witnessed. The sublime doctrines and pure morality which the spirits teach have chiefly won my conviction."

"But these, however much they may seem to you, are very little to the Christian believer. In their most favorable light, they do not approach in sublimity and purity, human reason alone being judge, the Gospel of our Lord. There is nothing new in your spiritual philosophy, and your morality merely travesties a few principles of Christian morality. You assert the immortality of the soul, never, in ancient or modern times, denied by the heathen world; but the peculiar Christian doctrine of the resurrection of the dead, and of future rewards and punishments, you do not recognize. You hardly stand on a level with Cicero or Seneca. You travestie the Christian doctrine of charity, or substitute for it a watery philanthropy, or a sickly sentimentality. There is in your system some subtilty, some cunning, chicanery, and ingenuity, but no deep philosophy, no lofty wisdom, no broad, comprehensive principles, no robust, manly virtue. The point on which you place the most importance is that of infinite progression, which is an infinite absurdity; and inasmuch as it denies the doctrine of final causes, denies God himself, and is, in the last analysis, pure atheism.

"That some true and good things are said by the spirits, I do not deny. The devil can disguise himself and appear as an angel of light. He is a great fool, no doubt, but not fool enough to attempt to seduce men by evil as evil. He must present falsehood in the guise of truth, and evil in the guise of good, if he would do evil. It is not likely that he would begin by shocking the moral sense of the community, and we should expect him to recognize and appeal to the moral sentiments and dominant beliefs of the men of the age; and this is all that you can say of the teachings of the spirits. But, except the confirmation of the fact taught by religion in all ages, that there are spiritual beings, superior to man, who surround us and may invade us, nothing they teach can be relied on, because their veracity is not established, and their unveracious and lying character is conceded."

"There are lying spirits, I concede, but all are not," interposed the Judge.

"Be that as it may, in what transcends your own knowledge, or is verifiable by your own natural powers, you have no means of distinguishing them, or of determining when the communication is true, or when it is false. When a spirit unfolds to you a system of the universe,—a system which comes not within the range of scientific investigation,—you cannot say that he is not deluding you, and giving you fairy gold, which will turn out to be chips or vile stubble."

"You think us deluded, then?"

"That this is the fact," said I, "I am quite sure. If any proof of it were wanting, it might be found in the fact that these spirit-manifestations are even by Judge Preston himself identified with those which have always been opposed to Christianity, and by it pronounced Satanic; and by the further fact, that they teach as truth the principal doctrines which the movement party of the day oppose to the Gospel. Take the doctrines set forth by the Seer Davis, those which you find in the *Shekinah*, and even in Judge Preston's own book, and you find them in substance the prevailing infidelity of the times, dressed out in a spiritual garb. I have very good reasons for knowing that these spirit-manifestations have been started for the very purpose of overthrowing Christianity by means of an infidel superstition. The prime mover had precisely this object, and no other."

"We have," said the Judge, "only your word for that. I regard these phenomena from God."

"So the devil wishes you to regard them, for he seeks, by means of them, to carry on his war against the Christian's God, and to get himself worshipped as God," said I.

154

"The devil," said Mr. Merton, "can go only the length of his chain, and that chain is much shorter than it was in old heathen times. He can do only what he is permitted, and it is very possible that what he is now doing will turn out to his signal discomfiture. It will give a serious blow to the materialism and Sadducism of the age, lead men to believe in the reality of the spirit-world, and when that is done, they will have made one step towards believing in Christ. The age is so infirm as to deny the existence of the devil; and even becoming able to believe once more in the reality of his Satanic majesty, will be a symptom, slight though it may be, of convalescence."

"We," remarked the Judge, "are no Sadducees. We believe in both angel and spirit, in good angels and bad angels."

"That is something," said Mr. Merton; "and, if you open your hearts, and keep them open to the light, you may in time believe more, and escape the meshes in which Satan has now entangled you. Your great mistake is in supposing that these good and bad angels are departed souls. I do not say that departed souls may not revisit the earth; they have done so, and they may continue to do so, but the human soul never becomes an angel or a demon. It is all very well to say of a departed dear one, he or she is an angel in heaven, but taken literally, it is never true. In the resurrection, our Lord says the just are like the angels of God, in the respect that they are neither male nor female, and neither marry nor are given in marriage, but he does not say that they are angels; and the Scriptures distinguish between the company of the angels and the spirits of just men made perfect. Men were created a little lower than the angels, and they are of a different order. The demons or devils are not wicked souls separated from their bodies, and wandering on this or the other side of the dark-flowing Acheron, but the angels who kept not their first estate, and were cast out of heaven.

"These fallen angels, under their chief, Lucifer or Satan, carry on their rebellion against God by seeking to seduce men from their allegiance to their rightful sovereign. They can and do invade men, because they are superior to men, and are malicious enough to do it. But the good angels never do it, for they work not by violence, but by moral, persuasive, peaceful, and gentle influences; and human souls cannot do it, for the *strong* keepeth the house till a *stronger* comes and binds him. Nothing remains then, my dear Judge, but to regard these spirit-manifestations, in so far as real, as the invasions of Satan, as produced, not by good angels or departed souls, but by the fallen angels, called demons by the Gentiles, and therefore, all these mysterious phenomena, in so far as they are not produced by natural agencies, as sheer deviltry. This is the only conclusion to which I, as a Christian philosopher, can come respecting them."

CHAPTER XXI.

SPIRIT-MANIFESTATIONS.

Mr. Merton's conclusion did not precisely please me, although I had suspected it from the first. Yet it troubled me, and I would gladly have escaped it. The next day, when Mr. Merton called to see me, as he did every day, I told him that I did not like his conclusion, and I wished he would give me his real thoughts on the subject.

"I am unwilling to suppose the supernatural, and will not, where I cannot satisfactorily demonstrate the insufficiency of the natural. The whole history of our race bristles with prodigies, with marvellous facts, clearly divisible into two distinct and even opposite orders. The one seem to have for their object to draw men towards God, and assist them in ascending to him as their last end and supreme good; the other seem to have for their object to draw men away from God, and to aid men in descending into the depths of night and darkness. Man has a double nature, is composed of body and soul, and on the one side has a natural aspiration to God, and on the other a natural tendency from God, towards the creature, and thence towards night and chaos. A supernatural power assists him to rise; a preternatural power assists him, so to speak, to descend. But whether in the ascending or in the descending scale, it is not easy to say where the natural ends and the supernatural begins, for in both cases the foreign power presupposes the natural, and blends in with it, and simply transforms the action.

"There is, no doubt, much in either order set down by the vulgar to foreign intervention, that is really explicable on natural principles. Good, pious people cry out 'a miracle,' not seldom where no miracle is; and I should be sorry to be obliged to make an act of faith in all the miracles recorded in the legends of the saints. I should be equally sorry to be obliged to believe every tale that is told of Satanic invasion. I have a deep and settled horror of scepticism, but also a horror no less of superstition. I would no more be credulous than incredulous. I do not like to undertake the refutation of those who explain the facts of the night-side of nature on natural principles, for it is hard to do it, without giving more or less occasion in many minds to superstition. It is only in cases, like the present, where the disease is an epidemic, more destructive than the cholera or the plague, that I am willing to do what I can to draw attention to their real character.

"In regard to the dark prodigies, if I may so call them, I think not a few included by the vulgar under this head should be dismissed as mere jugglery; others may be explained by animal magnetism, and imply neither fraud nor dealing with devils, but are not innocent, because produced not by a justifiable motive, and are in all cases to be discountenanced because of dangerous tendency; others still may, perhaps, be explicable by natural causes, which science has not yet investigated, and of which we are ignorant.

"But a residuum remains which it is impossible to explain without the assumption of Satanic intervention. Such are some of the cases which you have heard me relate. Such are many of the phenomena which you yourself must have witnessed, and perhaps been instrumental in producing. Such, too, is the inspiration of Mahomet, if we may rely on the account given us by his friends, as well as the demon of Socrates, and such are evidently the well known cases of the Camisards or Tremblers of the Cevennes in 1688, George Fox and the early Quakers, Swedenborg, and the trance or ectasy of the Methodists, and finally Joe Smith and the Mormon prophets. In all these cases there are evident marks of superhuman intervention, and which no man in his sober senses, and instructed in the Christian religion, can pretend is the intervention of the Holy Ghost, or of good angels. The perturbation, the disorder, the trembling, the falling backwards, the foaming at the mouth, the violence which always in these cases accompany the presence of the spirit, are so many sure indications that it is an evil, not a good spirit. The Lord was not in the strong wind that rent the mountain; he was not in the fire that wrapt it in flames; but in the still small voice that made the prophet step forth from his cave to listen. When the Lord comes in his gracious visitations all is sweetness and peace. No disturbance of the physical system, no whirling and howling, no storm or tempest, no wringing and twisting of the arms and legs, no violent or indecent postures, no abnormal development or exercise of the faculties, mark the incoming of the Holy Ghost. All is calm and serene; the understanding is illuminated, the heart is warmed, the will is strengthened, and the whole soul is elevated by the infusion of a supernatural grace. There is no crisis, no forgetfulness on awaking from a trance. But whenever it is the reverse, wherever there is violence, distortion, quaking, trembling, and disturbance, we know that if any spirit is present it is an evil spirit, which delights in violence and disorder, and displays power without love, force without goodness, knowledge without gentleness.

"Everybody has heard, I suppose, of the prodigies wrought by touching the tomb of the Deacon Paris, the famous Jansenist saint, and the violent controversy they occasioned between the Jansenists and the Jesuits, the former trying to magnify them into miracles to the honor of their sect, and the Jesuits very unnecessarily and very unwisely, in my judgment, laboring to disprove or discredit them as facts. The prodigies are well authenticated, and I see no way of denying them without throwing doubt on all human testimony. Among them I select those which indicate, on the part of the affected, a surprising power of physical resistance, and among these I select only one, that of Jeanne Moulu, a young woman, from twenty-two to twenty-three years of age, given by the *Dictionnaire des Sciences Médicales*. This young woman, in her convulsions, was placed with her back against a wall, and a man of great strength took an andiron weighing some twenty-five pounds, and struck her on her stomach several blows in succession with all his strength, sometimes to the number of one hundred blows and over. A brother gave her sixty blows, and afterwards, trying his blows against the wall, it gave way at the twenty-fifth blow. It was in vain, says Carré de Montgeron, a grave magistrate, that I struck with all my force, the convulsionary complained that my blows brought her no relief, and obliged me to place the andiron in the hands of a large and very strong man found among the spectators. He spared nothing, but put forth all his strength, and dealt such terrible blows on the pit of her stomach that they shook the wall against which she was supported. She made him give her the hundred blows which she had demanded at first, counting for nothing the sixty she had received from me. When the andiron sunk so deep into the pit of her stomach as to seem to reach her back, the young woman would exclaim, 'That relieves me. Courage, my brother; strike harder, if you can.' The blows were struck on the naked skin, but without bruising or breaking it in the least. The convulsionary, after this, lay on the floor, and there was placed upon her a heavy plank on which stood a score or more of persons, weighing all together at least four thousand pounds. Then a flint stone, weighing twenty-two pounds, was hurled with full force a hundred times in succession upon her bosom. At each blow, the whole room shook, the floor trembled, and the spectators shuddered at the sound of the frightful blows.

"There were other phenomena of a character no less extraordinary, but I pass them over, all of which were notorious, and witnessed by half, one writer says, all Paris. Hume says that they have all the authenticity that human testimony can give, and that we can deny them only on the ground that such things are absolutely impossible. Humanly impossible I concede, but, as they are not of a character to come from God, I must believe them to be Satanic, and that the persons were really possessed and sustained by evil spirits.

"The case of frequent occurrence among the lower class of the Lamas, related by M. Huc in his travels in Mongolia, Thibet, and China, is one that cannot be explained save on the ground of Satanic intervention,—that of a Lama, a sort of Boudhist monk, who opens his belly, takes out his entrails, and places them before him, and then returns immediately to his former state.

"'When the appointed hour has arrived,' says M. Huc, 'the whole multitude of pilgrims repair to the great court of the Lama convent, where an altar is erected. At length the Bokte makes his appearance; he advances gravely amid the acclamations of the crowd, seats himself on the altar, and taking a cutlass from his girdle, places it between his knees, while the crowd of Lamas, ranged in a circle at his feet, commence the terrible invocations that prelude this frightful ceremony. By degrees, as they proceed in their recital, the Bokte seems to tremble in every limb, and gradually fall into strong convulsions. Then the song of the Lamas becomes wilder and more animated, and the recitation is changed for cries and howlings. Suddenly the Bokte flings away the scarf which he has worn, snatches off his girdle, and with the sacred cutlass rips himself entirely open. As the blood gushes out, the multitude prostrate themselves before the horrid spectacle, and the sufferer is immediately interrogated concerning future events and things concealed from human knowledge. His answers to these questions are regarded as oracles.

"'As soon as the devout curiosity of the pilgrims is satisfied, the Lamas resume their recitations and prayers; and the Bokte, taking up in his right hand a quantity of his blood, carries it to his mouth, blows three times on it, and casts it, with a loud cry, into the air. He then passes his hand rapidly over his stomach, and it becomes whole as it was before, without the slightest trace being left of the diabolical operation, with the exception of an extreme lassitude.'

"Occurrences like these are not rare, and I could fill volumes with phenomena equally extraordinary, which I cannot deny, and which cannot be explained without the assumption of a superhuman agent, and I may add, a diabolical agent. Dupotet exhibits, by means of his magic ring, almost daily in Paris, the most extraordinary magic wonders, and he confesses that he does it by means of a mental evocation, and by virtue of a PACT.

"Now these, and facts like these, instructed as I am in the Christian faith, and holding it without any doubt, prove to me that the Satanic invasion, demonic possession, and obsession, are no fables, but facts not to be denied, though each particular case must stand on its own merits, and be received or rejected according to the evidence. In general I am slow to believe this or that particular case is diabolic, and I require clear and irrefragable proof, strong and perfectly reliable testimony.

"The criteria of demonic invasion or obsession, as laid down by the Christian church, for the guidance of exorcists, are seven:

1. Power of knowing the unexpressed thoughts of others.

2. Understanding of unknown languages.

3. Power of speaking unknown or foreign languages.

4. Knowledge of future events.

5. Knowledge of things passing in distant places.

6. Exhibition of superior physical strength.

7. Suspension of the body in the air during a considerable time.

"Now I find all these in the recent spirit-manifestations, clearly and distinctly testified to by such occular witnesses as Dr. Dexter, Judge Edmands, and the Hon. N. P. Talmadge, not to mention any others. The Spiritualists or Spiritists do not deny, they assert that the manifestations they witness are strictly analogous to the class of facts which have been always regarded as Satanic. At first, the spirits communicated by rapping and moving furniture. But now, besides rapping mediums, there are writing mediums, seeing mediums, and speaking mediums. In these last three cases they admit the fact of spiritual invasion, and even call it possession. In the case of the speaking medium particularly, I find it contended that the spirit takes possession of the medium, generally a woman, maltreats her at times, throws her down, gives her convulsions, and forces her to do things which she is unwilling to do, and compels her organs to utter words to which she has the greatest repugnance.

"Hear Judge Edmands. 'I have frequently known mental questions answered, that is, questions merely framed in the mind of the interrogator, and not revealed by him or known to others. Preparatory to meeting a circle, I have sat down alone in my room, and carefully prepared a series of questions to be propounded, and I have been surprised to find my questions answered, and in the precise order in which I wrote them, without my even taking my memorandum out of my pocket, and when I knew not a person present even knew that I had prepared questions, much less what they were. My most secret thoughts, those which I never uttered to mortal man or woman, have been freely spoken to, as if I had uttered them. Purposes which I have privately entertained have been publicly revealed, and I have once and again been admonished that my every thought was known to, and could be disclosed by, the intelligence which was thus manifesting itself.

"'I have heard the mediums use Greek, Latin, Spanish, and French, when I knew that they had no knowledge of any language but their own; and it is a fact that can be attested by many, that often there has been speaking and writing in foreign languages and unknown tongues by those who were unacquainted with either.'

"Dr. Dexter is explicit to the same purpose. I need not multiply citations. The books of the spiritualists are full of instances in point. And as it is clear, from the phenomena presented, that the superhuman intelligence and power manifested are not Divine, I can, as a rational man, only conclude that they are Satanic. I believe the persons engaged in the unhallowed intercourse are, to a great extent, in good faith, and have no suspicion that they are really dealing with devils."

"I believe you are right," said I. "One thing is certain, that even in mesmerizing, there is always an implicit mental evocation, and without it, I venture to say, no one was ever able to exhibit the mesmeric phenomena. The effort of the will which the mesmerizer makes, whether he uses passes or not, is at bottom an evocation, a calling up of the mesmeric spirit; and he who set the spirits a rapping, you may be sure, had made a virtual, if not an explicit, a tacit, if not an express compact with the devil. But there is one thing farther I would have you explain, that is, the connection of spirit-manifestations with so-called animal magnetism."

"That is a great subject, and would lead me too far for my time and for your strength. There are different spirits that besiege us or invade us, but those that usually do so probably, after the language of St. Paul, swarm in the air, and inhabit what the ancients called Ether. Many of the fathers, and some later doctors of the Church have believed that they are created with and inhabit fine ethereal bodies. However this may be, they no doubt, in their operation, assume such bodies, and consequently find their operations facilitated by a subtile material medium, such as the mesmeric fluid. Hence I do not regard mesmerism itself as Satanic, but as facilitating demonic invasion.

"There is also in man what the ancients called the *umbra*, the shade, which is not the soul, nor the body in its mere outward sense. It is, as it were, the interior lining of the body, capable, to a certain extent, of being detached from it, without however losing its relation to it. Hence the phenomena of bi-location, so frequently noticed in the annals of sorcery or witchcraft, can be conceived as possible. The body lies in a trance, and the soul with its *umbra* is able to carry on, by the assistance of the demon, its deviltry, even at a distance; and the wounds given to the shade will reappear on the body, as has been often observed.

"But you must excuse me from entering further into this intricate and mysterious subject. Many ingenious theories have been devised, but I wish to deal as little with them as possible. There is a laudable curiosity, there is also an unlawful curiosity, and there is a science which is not desirable. I have been obliged, in the way of my calling, to study it; but I never touch it, without regretting its necessity. Spare me. The knowledge that cannot enlighten, that cannot aid virtue, and only leads astray, should never be sought."

CHAPTER XXII.

SUPERSTITION.

I had, almost from the first, suspected Mr. Merton's conclusion, and should never for a moment have doubted it, had I not grown up in the disbelief of evil spirits. Science, or what passes for science, had long denied all supernatural and all superhuman intervention in the affairs of mankind; and I, like the majority of my contemporaries, had grown up a complete Epicurean. There was, perhaps, a God who had created the world, but having created it, and impressed upon it certain fixed and invariable laws, he left it to take care of itself. I denied his providence, or, what is the same thing, resolved it into the uniform and inflexible laws of nature, and like my friends of the French Eclectic school, saw the Divine intervention only in the necessary and immutable elements of human history. God was for me simply Fate, Invincible Necessity, and therefore no free person, no object of reverence, love, or worship.

Having excluded Providence, I necessarily rejected the ministry of angels. I resolved all nature into a collection of forces operative by intrinsic and necessary laws. Man is one of these forces, neither the strongest nor the weakest. In his own intrinsic strength he is not much, but by placing himself in a right position with regard to the other forces of nature, he may make them work in him and for him, and thus increase his strength by the whole of theirs, as the millwright makes use of the force of the stream to turn his mill, the inventor of the magnetic telegraph of the lightning to convey his messages, or as the sailor avails himself of the wind to propel his ship.

Belief in the free or voluntary intervention of the Divinity in human affairs, I had been taught by received science to regard as superstition. Religion, Christian or Mahometan, Jewish or Pagan, inasmuch as it always presupposes the supernatural, or the intervention of God *extra naturam*, or otherwise than in and through the laws of nature, was superstition. The ministry of angels was superstition. The assertion of Satanic interposition was, beyond all doubt, superstition. The facts which had led to the supposition of Divine providence, and of the ministry of good and evil angels, were, no doubt, real; but ignorant of the laws of nature, men had misinterpreted them, and assigned them causes which are unreal. All religion has, I said, its origin in ignorance, and necessarily recedes as science advances. Hence I felt that it would be only a proof of my ignorance and superstition to ascribe the mysterious phenomena to any spiritual or supernatural agency.

Even after the explanations of Mr. Merton, and after my reason was silenced, I was unwilling to abandon my prejudices, and accept his conclusion. What, should I, in this nineteenth century, in this age of genuine science, which has done so much to roll back the clouds and dissipate the darkness which enveloped past ages, consent to adopt the vulgar belief of the sixteenth century, when men were but just escaping from the thraldom of Romanism—of the thirteenth century, when they were but just beginning to emerge from barbarism—of the first century, when still buried in the night of heathenism? My pride of science, my pride of intellect, revolted at the thought. What ridicule would not be showered upon me by the wits and free-thinkers of the age, should it be known, or even suspected!

I hesitated long, for I saw at once, that if I admitted the existence and influence of Satan, I must go farther, and concede the Christian mysteries. I must abandon liberal Christianity, deny the supposed progress of recent times in religious notions, and return to old-fashioned orthodoxy. Perhaps I should find it necessary to go even further back than the orthodoxy of my own country. This was no pleasant thought. To unlearn all I had learned, to regard all my most cherished convictions as so many delusions, to become in reality as a little child, and to commence life anew, as Jesus Christ taught we must do, if we would enter into the kingdom of heaven, was too humiliating to be contemplated with pleasure even on my dying bed, and when the world was fast disappearing from my view. What would have been the result of my internal struggle, if I had been left wholly to myself, I will not pretend to say. But I was not so left. Mr. Merton was with me almost daily, and seemed always to read my thoughts before I expressed them, and to comprehend my difficulties.

"Your great mistake," said he to me one day, when the subject came up, "is in supposing that religion is the offspring of ignorance, and stands opposed to science. Your assumption that man began in ignorance, and has attained to science only by long and patient research and laborious experiment, is at best gratuitous. Some things, of course, have been acquired only in process of time. Man has made progress in the knowledge of all that which he himself has done, or has suffered; but nothing requires you to assume that his progress in knowledge is any thing more than progress in the knowledge of his own doing and suffering. It is not likely that Adam knew the history of the battle of Pharsalia, of Hastings, Bovines, or Waterloo; it is not probable that he was acquainted with the steam-engine, the cotton-gin, the spinning-jenny, the power-loom, or the lightning telegraph. But he may have received from his Maker, as religion teaches, a knowledge of the nature and causes of things, and of his moral relations and duties, equal to that possessed by the most enlightened of his posterity.

"Historically considered," proceeded Mr. Merton, "the earliest belief of mankind was the existence, unity, and free providence of God—a belief in strict accordance with the deductions of genuine science in every age. Every language under heaven bears indelible traces of that belief, and would be unintelligible, absolutely insignificant, if it were denied. Yet all languages are radically one and the same, and must, in some form, have been given supernaturally to man, for man speaks only as he has learned to speak; and it would have required language to invent language."

"But if all languages are radically the same, how do you explain their manifest differences?" I asked.

"That is a question which I leave to the philologists; but they, I believe, very easily prove that these differences are not radical, and that they are due principally to the differences of pursuits, of circumstances, temperaments, and pronunciation of different tribes having little or no intercourse with one another. However great or small they may be, or whatever their causes, it has been proved that they are only modifications of one and the same original tongue."

"But you know," said I, "that religion is progressive, and that the earliest religion of mankind was a gross fetichism, a worship of animals and inanimate things. From that gross superstition we can trace its gradual purification and progress towards the sublime monotheism of Moses, Socrates, Plato, and Jesus, moulded by the Church fathers into Christian theology."

"I know no such thing," replied Mr. Merton, "and St. Paul, who was a good philosopher as well as an inspired apostle, tells us that men left the true God to worship creeping things and four-footed beasts. The monotheism you speak of is historically older than the fetichism of which you would make it a development. What you are pleased to call the monotheism of Moses, was older than that lawgiver. Moses, under Divine inspiration and direction, founded the Jewish state, or commonwealth, and instituted the Jewish worship, but he did not introduce a new faith or theology. The faith or doctrine he taught concerning God and moral duty, was that of the old patriarchs, and the same which had been held from Adam. Christian faith and theology have come down to us through the line of the patriarchs and the Jews, not through that of the Gentiles, and, if a development at all, is not a development of heathenism, but of the earlier patriarchal religion preserved in the synagogue. Hence St. Augustine says, that faith has not changed; as believed the fathers, so we believe—only they believed in a Christ who was to come, and we believe in a Christ who has come.

"Then, again, the monotheism, if monotheism it was, of Socrates and Plato, was not a development or gradual purification of fetichism or of the gross forms of nature-worship. They themselves tell you as much, and always claim to be restorers, not innovators. In asserting the unity of God, they profess always to revive the belief or the wisdom of the ancients. No one can have studied the various forms of heathenism without finding in them ample evidence that they are not primitive formations. They all bear witness to a type which is not in themselves—a type from which they have departed, not a type which they are approaching or realizing. They bear the deep traces of corruption, and are evidently travesties of the old patriarchal or primitive religion, without a knowledge of which they are absolutely inexplicable. The memory of the loss of its primitive perfection, all heathenism retains in its heart. All heathenism is imprinted with profound grief for a lost good, and never does it show signs of a true joy. There is sadness in all its rites, gay and joyous as it tries to make them. Its joy is a drunken joy, and its boisterous mirth is the wild laugh of the maniac. But over the whole of heathenism, even in its grossest forms, there hovers always the primitive monotheism. It retains always some reminiscence of the belief in one supreme God, Father of gods and men. Anaxagoras, Socrates, Plato, and others, acquainted with the Jewish belief, and meditating on this reminiscence, undoubtedly rose to sublimer and more rational views of the Divinity than those which were entertained by the vulgar; but this says nothing in favor of that gradual development and purification of heathenism, which you and a well known modern school assert, and assert without one single fact to support you.

"You must rely on history," continued Mr. Merton, "for your theory professes to be historical, and to sustain itself by facts. But history has been tolerably authentic for some thousands of years. How happens it, if your theory be correct, that we find no instance of this gradual development and purification of heathenism? In all the cases where the history can be traced, it is undeniable that the purest or the least deformed state of any heathen superstition is its earliest; and the grossest, the most corrupt and revolting, is always its latest. Nothing in this world ever reforms itself, and the inevitable tendency of all error, as of all vice, is from bad to worse. Compare the popular religion of Rome under the kings, with the popular religion under the pagan emperors, and you will find this proved.

"Indeed, my friend, your whole theory is false. Never yet has religion receded before the advance of true science, and religion, as you well say, has always asserted the supernatural, the interposition of God in human affairs, *extra naturam*. Always, too, has it asserted the existence of good and bad angels, and their intervention on the one hand by Divine command, and on the other by Divine permission, in the affairs of mankind. This belief of all ages is itself a phenomenon to be explained, accounted for; and you will find it impossible to explain it, or account for it, without admitting its substantial truth. Men may err in supposing a supernatural or superhuman intervention where none takes place, and undoubtedly they have so erred time and again; but they could not have so erred if they had not already had the idea or belief of such interposition. Whence comes that idea or belief? If that is false, explain whence comes the general error before the particular? A general *à priori* error is impossible. All error is in the misapplication of truth. A general error is nothing but a generalization by way of induction of particular errors, or misapplications of truth to particulars, and is therefore necessarily subsequent to them. If there were in reality no true religion, there could be no false religion, as if there were no genuine, there could be no counterfeit coin. Always is the true prior to the false; and how then could mankind come to assert a false supernatural interposition, if they had no prior belief in a true supernatural interposition, or believe in such an interposition, if no such interposition had ever taken place?"

"But how will you clear this belief in Satanic interposition from the charge of superstition?" I asked.

"There are two opposite errors," concluded Mr. Merton, "both equally hostile to religion and to good sense,—superstition and irreligion. Each is an abuse, as the schoolmen say, an *excess* in a contrary direction; and unhappily, the tendency of most men is to one or the other. Nothing is more certain than that in every age much superstition has been connected with the doctrine I have contended for."

"That," said I, "is what makes me dread and hesitate to accept it."

"I know," Mr. Merton replied, "all that you would say on that score. I have myself read history, and, no less than you, been shocked by its abuses. But there is no truth that cannot be or that has not been abused. I am as much opposed to these abuses as you are. It will not do to suppose that every event a little out of the range of our ordinary experience, is a miracle, or effected, if good, by Angelic, if bad, by Satanic agency. Every time a murrain prevails among the cattle, it will not do to ascribe it to sorcery, or when the butter will not come, to lay the blame upon Robin Goodfellow. The tendency to do so is undoubtedly a superstitious tendency. But the contrary, or Sadducean tendency, to believe in neither angel nor spirit, is even more dangerous. I do not believe every tale of witchcraft I hear, and I am slow to believe in actual Satanic invasion in any particular case that may be alleged. The Church has always asserted the possibility of such invasion, but she does not permit a resort to exorcism on every apparent instance of it. She demands previous consultation, long examination, and the judgment of the most rigid science. While the greatest caution should be exercised as to every case of supposed actual Satanic invasion, we should guard equally against running into the contrary error of denying that such invasion ever takes place. An unreasonable scepticism is as far removed from true wisdom and virtue, as an unreasonable belief. Modern science is sceptical; and it is more important just now to guard against scepticism and its irreligion, than it is to guard against superstition.

"Yet we deceive ourselves, if we suppose that the scepticism of science has penetrated far into the popular mind, even in our own country. Science can never root out popular superstitions. While the few laugh at the superstition of the vulgar, that superstition, though modified perhaps as to its forms, continues to thrive, and attains, not unfrequently, even a more vigorous growth. The old popular superstitions, brought hither by our ancestors, still live in the heart of the people, and in forms as gross and as revolting as in the seventeenth century. Superstition is cured, not by a sceptical science, denying altogether the spirit-world, but by religion, which, while it recognizes that world, teaches us to draw accurately the line of demarcation between genuine and counterfeit spirit-manifestations. The people cannot live in absolute irreligion; and where they have not religion, they will have superstition. The tendency of modern science is to destroy all religious faith, and therefore to promote, indirectly, the very evil it proposes to cure,—the common effect of all unbaptized science, as of all unbaptized philanthropy."

"There is some truth in that, I must own," I remarked. "I know not why it is so, but every effort made, although with the purest and best intentions in the world, outside of Christianity, seem always to fail, or to end only in aggravating the very evils they were intended to cure. There is less real liberty in France to-day than there was before the meeting of the States-General in May, 1789. The revolutions which, during the last sixty or seventy years, have so terribly raged on European soil, though made in behalf of liberty or of popular representation, have resulted only in depriving each nation in which they have taken place of its former too feeble checks on power, and in rendering the monarchy more absolute. The same may be said in principle of all our efforts at philanthropic reform on a smaller scale."

"Undoubtedly," replied Mr. Merton; "and the reason is, that the glory of whatever is good is due to God, and he will suffer no plans to succeed that would rob him of his due. He has himself given us his law, and provided us the means of salvation, temporal and eternal; and whosoever seeks salvation by any other means, or in contempt of that law, must fail, and shamefully fail."

CHAPTER XXIII.

DIFFICULTIES.

"What you say, Mr. Merton," said Jack, "may be very plausible, but you will never convince me that Almighty God, the loving Father of us all, would ever permit his children to be exposed to Satanic invasion. It would impeach either his wisdom and love, or his power."

"I do not pretend to be able to say how that is," replied Jack, "but I will never believe that God will allow the devil, or any other being subject to his power, to have such influence over the children he loves. It is contrary to common sense. It is nonsense, absurdity, blasphemy."

"I am very much of Jack's opinion," interposed Dr. Corning, who had for a long time ceased to take any part in our conversations. "If there is a God, a God who is Lord Omnipotent, the devil, if devil there be, must be subject to him, and unable to do any thing without his permission. Can any reasonable man believe that God would permit the devil to harass and afflict, besiege and possess his children? Would a human father permit, if he could help it, an enemy to exercise a corresponding power over his own offspring? God is love, and love worketh no ill, and, as far as in its power to prevent, suffers no ill to be worked to any one."

"All that," replied Mr. Merton, "would be very conclusive, if the facts or phenomena did not exist to give it a flat denial. Here are the facts, and whatever origin you assign them, they remain, in themselves considered, the same. You assign insanity as their origin. Be it so. But would a God who is love, who is wisdom, who is omnipotence, suffer his children to be afflicted with so grievous a disease as insanity, one so terrible and so humiliating in its effects? Insanity must be subject to his dominion; and why then does he suffer any one to become insane?"

"Many of these facts, as you call them, are the result of mere jugglery and sheer imposture," answered the Doctor, "and do not deserve a moment's consideration."

"Be it so," replied Mr. Merton. "But how can God permit such jugglery and imposture?"

"They are the works of man, and the results of evil passions," promptly replied Dr. Corning.

"But that," said Dr. Corning, "is a question for you to answer, as well as for me."

"Not in the case before us," rejoined Mr. Merton, "because your objection concedes the existence of evil, and only denies it as the work of a particular agent. But let that pass. I can answer the question only in the light of Christian theology. According to that theology, there is no real evil but sin; and sin is always voluntary on the part of the sinner. God chose to create men and angels free moral agents, that they might be capable of virtue, and of meriting the rewards of obedience. He could not so create us without making us capable of abusing our freedom, for obedience is not and cannot be meritorious where there is no power of disobedience, as disobedience is not culpable where there is no power of obedience. Hence the saints in heaven, having no longer the power of disobedience, do not merit by their obedience, and simply enjoy the rewards of their obedience in their state of probation on earth. If any do not obtain the rewards of obedience, the fault is their own, and they have no one to blame but themselves. Their failure is voluntary; they fail only because they choose to fail.

"In regard to the Satanic vexations," continued Mr. Merton, "we must bear in mind that Satan has no power to harm us—not even a hair of our head—against our free will or deliberate assent. It is always in our power to resist him, and even to turn his machinations and vexations against him, and to make them occasions of merit. 'Count it all joy, my brethren,' says the blessed Apostle St. James, 'when ye fall into divers temptations,' that is, trials and afflictions. The evil is not in the temptation even to sin, but in the free, voluntary assent; it is not in the vexations and afflictions, obsessions and possessions, but in our voluntary abuse of them, or failure to turn them to a good account. God suffers no one to be tempted or tried or harassed beyond what he can bear. Always is his grace sufficient for all straits. Always stands firm his promise, 'My grace is sufficient for thee;' and this sustains and consoles us in the midst of our greatest distress, our severest trials, and our most perfect abandonment. We may always, if we will, come forth from the furnace of affliction purified as gold tried in the fire. It depends on our own free will whether the vexations of Satan shall do us good or harm. If we choose, we can always prevent his wiles from doing us evil, and derive profit from his malice. This is a sufficient answer to the objection drawn from the perfection of God. It is no impeachment of Divine Love to let loose an enemy against us for our good, or to give us an opportunity to acquire merit, any more than it is to Divine Justice to permit an enemy to harass us as a punishment for our sins. Satanic temptations and invasions are sometimes permitted for the one purpose, and sometimes for the other, and in either case are perfectly compatible with the attributes of God."

"I think I can understand that," I remarked, "and I think also I can see in it a manifestation of Divine love. God, in permitting these vexations against the wicked, manifests his justice; but in permitting them against the good, he manifests his love, and turns the malice of Satan against himself. What Satan intends shall work our ruin, by the grace of God is made to work our higher perfection; and thus God overcomes Satan by educing good from evil."

"Undoubtedly," added Mr. Merton, "God often permits Satan to afflict the faithful, to prove them,—sometimes to humble them, to chastise their spiritual pride, and to become their occasion of rising to a purer and loftier virtue; and in such cases we may say he educes good from evil, and makes the malice of Satan redound to his own glory. In the cases where he permits Satan to harass by way of penalty, he equally makes the Satanic malice redound to his glory, for God's glory is no less interested, so to speak, in justice than in love. There is no discrepancy between the Divine attributes; and the manifestation of his justice is no less essential to his glory, or the good of his creatures, than the manifestation of his love or mercy. The beginning of love is the love of justice, equity, right."

"But be that as it may," said Jack, "I have heard it contended by theologians that Satan has been bound since the coming of Christ, and has no longer any power, since Christ triumphed over him on the cross, to besiege or to possess men, as it is supposed he had before."

"I am not answerable," replied Mr. Merton, "for what you may have heard theologians maintain. I concede that our Lord, on his part, triumphed over Satan on the cross; I also concede, that since the coming of our Lord, and the spread of Christianity, the power of Satan has been greatly curtailed; but I know no authority for saying that he does not continue to go about 'as a roaring lion, seeking whom he may devour,' or that he has not power still to besiege men, and literally take possession of them. The Church, whether Catholic or Protestant, has a form of exorcism, and continues to practise it. The faithful are daily winning victories over him, and if God gives them the grace of perseverance, they will finally overcome him, and obtain a triumph; but their warfare with him ceases not so long as they remain in the flesh. Satan, it is true, has no power to harm us against our deliberate consent, and it is far easier to resist him now, than it was before our Lord died on the cross, because grace is more abundant; but still he may besiege and actually possess the holiest of men, the most devoted followers of the Lord, at least so far as it is given to men to judge. He cannot harm us without our own fault; but he may vex, afflict, even possess us, without any blame on our part, as a man may become sick, or even insane, without any fault of his own.

"Out of the Christian society," continued Mr. Merton, "where there are wanting the means which Christians have to defend themselves against his approaches, and to drive him away, his power is, no doubt, far greater. Among Mahometans, and among the pagan tribes of Asia, Africa, and America, inhabiting a land which has, so to speak, never been baptized, or sprinkled with holy water, his power is still very great; and, if we may credit the well-attested reports of our missionaries, almost as great as ever. He recovers his power, too, in Christian nations in proportion as they recede from the faith and piety of the Gospel, and fall anew into heathenism."

"But there are some difficulties, under the point of view of jurisprudence, in the way of your doctrine of Satanic invasion," interposed Jack. "Suppose a man possessed by a devil kills another, or commits some act which the law regards as a crime, is the man guilty, and to be punished?"

"You are a lawyer," replied Mr. Merton, "and nothing is more natural than that you should ask that question. The difficulties you suggest, however, are no greater on the supposition of Satanic invasion than on any other theory. They are the same, whether we contend that the person is subjected by Satan or by mesmerism, by a primitive or elemental force of nature, or by what some manigraphs call madness without delirium, or instinctive insanity. The question turns on the fact whether the man is involuntarily and completely subjugated, or whether he retains the exercise of his free will; or, in other words, whether the actions are really his, or those of the power that oppresses or subjugates him. For myself, I think our courts are beginning to adopt a very dangerous doctrine with regard to insanity, and are admitting the plea of insanity where it ought not to be entertained. In an Eastern city, not long since, it was gravely contended by counsel, that a man must be held to be insane and irresponsible, because his crimes were so aggravated. Under this lies a dangerous principle, which, in its development, will lead to the conclusion that all great criminals are insane and irresponsible. But in regard to another class of cases, cases in which there obviously is no inebriety, ill health, or delirium, and yet in which the person seems to himself to be irresistibly urged by a foreign power, against his will, to the commission of horrible acts, I think the law, or the practice of the courts, is quite too severe. I take a case cited to my hand by a respectable French writer, that of a father who killed his young son. The father was an honest, temperate, and industrious man, of a mild and affectionate disposition, and it is clear that he loved his son with great tenderness.

"'The night in which I did the deed,' says the unhappy father, 'I was so agitated, that I trembled in my whole body.... I am unable to conceive how I could commit a crime so atrocious. I was so agitated, so troubled in my brain, and felt something within me so irresistible, that I was *obliged* to commit the deed. I was fasting. I was not sick; and I am wholly unable to explain how it was possible for me to do it. Twice before I had had the horrible inclination to kill my child. The first time was last winter, about six weeks before Easter. I was at work making a sledge, and my boy, as usual, was playing near me. In his playfulness, he climbed upon my back, and clasped me round the neck. My wife, thinking he would hinder me from working, called him away; but I loved him so much, that I patiently endured all his frolicsome tricks. I took him upon my knees to play with him, and in that very moment I thought I heard a voice within me, saying, 'You cannot help it. Your child must die, and you must kill him.' I was startled, seized with fear, my heart palpitated, and I instantly set him down, rushed out of the room, and went to the mill, where I stayed till nightfall, till my evil thought passed away.

"'The second time was one morning a few days before Easter. My wife was busy with the affairs of the house, and I was lying on the bed, with my child near me. He asked me for some bread, and I gave him a cake, which he eat with great pleasure. At that moment, as I was watching him with tender affection, I thought I heard again a voice within me, saying, in a low tone, 'You must kill him.' I shuddered at myself, experienced violent palpitations, and felt a heavy oppression within my breast. I instantly jumped from the bed, and ran out of the house. I began saying my prayers, went to the stable, and busied myself with various labors, and did all in my power to drive away the evil thoughts that beset me. I finally succeeded, but not till midday, in regaining the mastery of myself, and in recovering my tranquillity. In neither of these cases was I drunk, or had been for many weeks previous; nor was I at the third access, when I took the life of my child.'[6]

"Now here was a man who was not sick, who was not in liquor, who was not delirious, who was evidently a mild and loving father, and who yet, in consequence of an impression, killed his child, whom evidently he loved with all a father's fondness. This man the courts condemn as a horrid murderer."

"And why not?" said Jack. "It is evident his free will remained. Twice he resisted the temptation, and regained the mastery of himself; and nothing proves that he might not have done so the third time, if he had done his best."

"It is possible," replied Mr. Merton, "and therefore I do not say the man was absolutely innocent. But we see he did struggle against the evil thought, and twice successfully; and he yielded even at last only from an impression, all but irresistible at the moment, and therefore he cannot be said to have had the full possession of his freedom. In proportion as his power of external resistance was diminished by the impression, or the mysterious influence that acted on him, was diminished his responsibility. He who yields only to a powerful temptation, is less guilty than he who does the same deed under only a slight or feeble temptation. The courts should take cognizance of the strength of the impression under which the man acts, and take into the account the more or less resistance that was possible. If the man succumbs only after a long and severe struggle, that should go to mitigate his guilt.

"Dr. Cazeauvielh relates the case of a woman who attempted to kill her infant sleeping in the cradle. 'I am,' said she to the doctor, 'the most miserable of beings. Never was anybody like me. The other day I approached the cradle, and I looked upon my darling. Fearing I should do him harm, I went away to the house of my neighbor. Then, in spite of myself, I returned, for *something* seemed to push me. I went near my infant, and attempted to choke it with my hands, but my legs failed me, and I became senseless.' This woman, Dr. Cazeauvielh tells us, loved her relations and her child, and her intellectual faculties were not injured. It is true he regards her as insane; but how can there be insanity, with the full possession of the intellectual faculties? She struggled against the *something* that pushed her, and had a horror of the crime; the law ought, therefore, to treat her with indulgence, yet it does not, because there really is here no delirium. In the middle ages, which you regard as so barbarous and cruel, she would not have been held responsible, because her act would have been explained as the result of a foreign power, which for the time being overcame her resistance, and pushed her to do that for which she had a natural horror.

"Yet a difference should no doubt be made between cases like these, where the unhappy person commits a deed for which he has a natural horror, and against which he struggles, and those in which the criminal, so to speak, has a natural relish for his crime, delights, and persists in it. Take the case of Gilles Garnier, which occupied the attention of all France in the reign of Louis the Thirteenth. 'This man-wolf,' (*loup-garou,*) says Bodin, 'carried away a girl from ten to twelve years of age, killed her with his hands and teeth, and eat the flesh from her thighs and arms. Some time afterwards he strangled a boy ten years old, and eat his flesh. Still later he killed another boy, from twelve to thirteen, with the intention of eating him, but was prevented.' He was arrested, convicted, and burnt alive. There was here no insanity; the horrid deeds were all avowed with the minutest circumstances, the intention was express, and the crime was repeated and persisted in. I cannot regard this monster as innocent, for I cannot discover that he resisted or struggled against the diabolical impulse.

"Take the case of Leger, a recent case, related by Dr. Cazeauvielh, from the monster's own confessions. He lived in a cave, and had an unnatural craving to feed on human flesh. One day he perceived a little girl, ran to her, passed a handkerchief around her body, threw her upon his back, plunged into the woods and hastened to his cave, where he killed and buried her. Arrested three days after, he immediately told his name, where he lived, and said that having received a blow on his head, he had left his country and his family. In his prison he related how he had lived in caverns in the rocks. 'Wretch,' said the physician to him, 'you have eaten the heart of this little girl. Confess the truth.' He then answered in trembling, 'Yes, I did so, but not all at once.' After that he sought no longer to conceal his crimes, and with great coolness and indifference related a long series of horrible deeds which he had committed. He revealed them, even to the minutest particulars; he produced the proofs, and pointed out to the court the place of the crime, and the manner in which it had been consummated. The judge had no need to question him, for he himself disclosed all of his own accord. On the trial, his features wore a mild and placid aspect. He seemed quite unconcerned and insensible, except his face assumed an air of gayety and satisfaction during the reading of the indictment. After about half an hour's deliberation, the court rejected the plea of insanity, and declared him guilty of homicide, with premeditation and lying in wait. He heard his sentence with the same placid indifference, and was executed a few days after. This seems to me to prove that the middle ages were not more severe than we are to-day."

"But Leger," said Dr. Corning, "was evidently a madman. Georget is right in saying that he was a madman, because none but a madman would say that he had been led to commit murder by a blind and *irresistible* will."

"That might do to say, if we were certain of the truth of the materialistic doctrines taught at Paris some forty or fifty years ago, but which are now generally rejected. Dr. Cazeauvielh, however, concedes that persons of this description, without being deprived by their madness of free will, are yet carried away, driven onward by an idea, by something indefinable, which is precisely what theologians mean by obsession. The court decided correctly, I think, in rejecting the plea of insanity in the case of the monster Leger, and in condemning him to death, though evidently under Satanic influence when he committed his horrible and disgusting crimes—crimes which recall the Ghouls of the Arabian Nights—because there was no struggle of the human person against the invading spirit.

"Satan can by Divine permission enter our bodies, compel, as it were, the human person to stand aside, and use our organs himself, and do whatever he pleases with them; but he cannot annihilate the human person, or take from the soul free will. Always is it in the power of the possessed to resist, morally and effectually, the evil intentions of the devil. The possessed retains his own consciousness, his own intellectual and moral faculties unimpaired, and never confounds himself with the spirit that possesses him. Always, then, does he retain the power of internal protest and struggle. Wherever this power is exercised, and there is clearly a struggle, there is no responsibility attaching to him, whatever the crimes the body, through the possession of the devil, is made to commit. But it may often happen that this power to protest is not exercised, and the possessed yields his moral assent to the crimes committed by the demon that possesses him. He then becomes a partaker of their guilt. Wherever it is clear that he has not internally resisted, that he has not struggled against the demon, and protested against his iniquity, the law should punish him for the crimes as severely as if there had been no possession at all. The error of modern jurisprudence is that, not recognizing the fact of possession, it punishes alike both classes, or it lets off both under the plea of insanity. In the latter case justice becomes too lax, and the greater the criminal, the more enormous his crime, the less likely is he to be punished; in the former case justice is too severe, and persons really innocent, and meritorious even, are condemned as the basest of criminals. The law in the middle ages, or before the wonderful progress of intelligence and humanity in modern times, distinguished between the two classes, and knew how to acquit the innocent and to punish the guilty. Now the tendency is either to acquit or to condemn both indiscriminately."

Dr. Corning and Mr. Merton, after this, revived their former discussion of the question of insanity; but as nothing was really added on either side to what had been previously said, I do not think it necessary to record their conversation. For myself, it seemed to me that the question between the theory which explains the phenomena by insanity, and that which explains them by Satanic invasion, is of immense practical importance. When the old doctrine was rejected, the law became excessively severe, and humanity was shocked. Philosophers and philanthropists sought to mitigate it by asserting the doctrine of necessity, of materialism, of the inherent goodness of the soul, and by ascribing all misdeeds to external influences, to the action of nature, society, government, &c. In other words, they sought to mitigate the law by denying all moral turpitude.

But latterly the older doctrine of spiritualism, as opposed to materialism, and of freedom as opposed to necessity, has revived, and the old severity of the law must return, unless some new way can be discovered of escaping it. This new way is the plea of insanity. The tendency now is to make insanity a plea for every crime of some little magnitude. Our lunatic hospitals are crowded; new ones are constructed, and no inconsiderable portion of our population are likely to become their inmates. Physicians, carried away by their false science and mistaken humanity, discard all the old criteria of lunacy, and the courts, following them, will soon find that all persons brought before them for trial are insane and irresponsible. The guilty will go unwhipt of justice, because no guilt will be recognized. If the phenomena in question are to be explained by insanity, I do not see what crime it will not cover.

The subject deserves serious consideration. For my part, I cannot recognize insanity where the person evidently retains his intellectual powers underanged or unimpaired, where he retains the faculty of reasoning and judging correctly, however he may be driven by foreign influences to this or that crime. When he tells me that he was obliged by *something* to do this or that, and that when he did it, it seemed to him that it was not he, but some power impelling him, I raise no question of insanity, but simply, as Merton suggests we should, the question of internal resistance, and measure him by the greater or less energy and persistence of that internal resistance.

---

[6] *Pneumatalogie des Esprits*, p. 186 *et seq.*

CHAPTER XXIV.

LEFT IN THE LURCH.

Though I remained an invalid, there were times when I revived, and almost flattered myself that I might yet, in spite of the prognostications of my physician, recover. I was still comparatively young, and I did not precisely like the thought of dying. The simple pain of dying did not affright me; nor had I much reluctance to leave the world, where there was little that had any charm for me. But I could not help sending now and then uneasy glances beyond the tomb. There might be a spirit-world beyond, and death might not after all extinguish the life of the soul. I might, perhaps, live in that unknown world, retain my personal identity, and distinct consciousness and memory. I might, too, at least I could not say it was impossible, be punished there for my sins in this world, and be condemned to have for my companions those very devils whose acquaintance I had so assiduously cultivated here. That might not be pleasant. Indeed, I began to have many painful reflections, and to ask myself if I had not been all my life making a fool of myself. I had been promised great things, but what had I obtained?

"Your experience, my dear friend," said Mr. Merton, "I doubt not, proves the truth of the old saying, the devil always, sooner or later, leaves his followers in the lurch. You remember, probably, I called the morning after my introduction to you, to give you and Priscilla a warning as to what awaited you. You were then too elated, too full of hope, to listen to any thing I could say; at least, so it seemed to me at the time."

"Yet you were mistaken. The few words you said interested me much, and I wished at the time to hear more."

"Alas! it is one of the miseries of the world, that the wicked are much more active for mischief, than the virtuous are for good. Would to God that the followers of Christ had a tithe of the industry and energy of the followers of Satan. If I had been more earnest, more ready to sacrifice my own ease and my own pride, perhaps——. But that is idle. You will, I presume, readily concede now that you were then laboring under a delusion, and indulged hopes which have not been realized?"

"Undoubtedly."

"So it is. Satan never keeps his promises."

"I wish you to explain," said Jack, who that moment entered the room,—"I wish you to explain how it is, if Satan is as powerful, and does as many marvellous things as you pretend, that they who give themselves up soul and body to him, always fail at last. Your mighty sorcerers and magicians always find their master failing them when it comes to the pinch. Ninety-nine times the devil enables the sorcerer to open the prison doors, to become invisible to the sight or impervious to the sword of his enemies, to overwhelm them, or to escape them by flying away through the keyhole; but the hundredth time fails him, and leaves him to be captured, to confess his crimes, and to be burnt alive. According to all accounts, your witches are the most miserable old hags one ever meets—wretched old crones, living in the most abject poverty, and hardly able to procure the food necessary to keep soul and body together. The devil never comes when wanted, never makes his appearance before competent and credible witnesses. He performs his wonders in the dark; and when one would really prove the fact of his presence, he is away, and nobody can get a glimpse of him."

"And what else," replied Mr. Merton, "should be expected of the devil? And yet I would not treat your objection lightly, for it is one which has at times raised doubts in my own mind, and it makes me rather sceptical as to most of the tales of witchcraft, ghosts, and hobgoblins I hear or read of. But you should bear in mind that the devils are capricious as well as malicious, or rather, their malice itself is full of caprice. The devil, in all his invasions, seeks only to get himself worshipped, and to ruin souls. When he has made a soul his slave, made sure of its destruction in hell, his end is answered. He is a liar from the beginning, and the father of lies. He is the inveterate enemy of truth, and if he sometimes tells it, it is because compelled by a higher power; or if now and then, of his own accord, it is only because it serves his purpose of deception better than falsehood. If he sometimes keeps his promises, and seems to do the best he can for his slaves, it is for the same reason. Then, again, he is not omnipotent, he is not the supreme Lord; and however powerful he may be, there is One mightier than he, who can thwart him when he pleases. He can, as I often say, go only the length of his chain. It may comport with the purposes of God to suffer him to do many marvellous deeds, but never to suffer him to do them so uniformly or in such a manner that his victims shall not be able to detect the impostor, and know, if they will, that it is a foul and lying spirit they follow. Satan's delight is in deceiving, and he delights as much in deceiving those already his slaves, as those he would make such; and God so orders it, that his deceptions shall be discoverable by all not wilfully blind.

"The devil is called the prince of this world, but he is not its absolute lord. He can even here do only what he is, for the purposes of love or justice, permitted to do. It may turn out, then, that he is forbidden to come to the assistance of his servants in the nick of time, even when he himself is disposed to do so. He may raise the storm, but there is One asleep in the bark, who can at any instant awake, and say to the winds and the waves, Peace, be still. It is not fitting that Satan should be able to keep his promises in the great majority of cases to the last, for that would leave too little chance of detecting his delusions, and would confirm his worship. His failures prove his malice, and also that his power is not his own, therefore that he is not God. They serve, too, as punishments to his dupes, for it is fitting that they who, through evil inclination and undue love of the world or of pleasure, trust to him, should ultimately fail in the very goods promised.

"The principles of God's providence are always and everywhere the same, and there is a close analogy between the natural and the supernatural. God has given to the universe its law. He has placed before man a real, substantial, and desirable good; but he has made this good attainable only in one way, by obedience to his law, which is not an arbitrary law, but a law founded in his own eternal reason, in his own infinite, eternal, and immutable justice. He who attempts to attain his good, his beatitude, by any other means, invariably and inevitably fails. It is as our Lord said,—'I am the door;' and 'he that entereth not by the door, but climbeth up another way, the same is a thief and a robber.' Whoever seeks entrance into the fold of happiness by another than the God-appointed way, whatever that way may be, is predoomed to disappointment. All experience proves it. The departure by the ancient Gentiles from the patriarchal or primitive religion, led to the confusion of their understandings, and to the adoption and practice of the grossest and most abominable superstitions—the extreme of moral or spiritual misery. The man who seeks happiness, even in this life, from acquiring or possessing riches and honor, always fails, even when he apparently succeeds. The most miserable of men are they who make pleasure their sole pursuit. The reason is, that beatitude is not promised to those pursuits, lies not on their plane, and is not attainable by following them. He who attempts to attain it in any of those ways is no wiser than those philosophers of Laputa who sought to extract sunbeams from cucumbers. It is only in accordance with the same principle, that they who seek worldly felicity, by consorting with devils, should in like manner be disappointed."

"All that is very wise, and would do very well for a sermon," said Jack. "It may, for aught I know, be very true. I have no knowledge on the subject, and no acquaintance with the devil or his angels. But I wish you would tell me how it happens that the witnesses to these marvellous phenomena are seldom if ever men of real science, well known, and of name in the scientific world?"

"I thought you were one of those who would not admit authority even in matters of faith, and yet you demand authority in matters of science," replied Mr. Merton, in a tone slightly sarcastic. "You would have the French Academy, for instance, in science what Rome claims to be in religion, and admit a historical fact or a scientific conclusion only on academic authority."

"But you know," replied Jack, "that scientific commissions appointed to investigate and report on particular cases in France, never succeed in getting a sight of those marvellous facts which are so readily exhibited to others. Is not this a suspicious circumstance?"

"The devils, again," continued Mr. Merton, "may not choose to exhibit their superhuman powers before your scientific commissions. It might be against their interest. He is sure of the commissioners as long as he can keep them in their scepticism; but were he to suffer them to escape it, he might lose them. Compelled to acknowledge the existence of Satan, they might go further and acknowledge that of Christ, and become Christians, and labor to harmonize science with faith. Even God himself may choose to let them remain in their scepticism as a just punishment of their intellectual pride, their indocility, and their preferring their own darkness to his light. They take pleasure in sin, and he gives them up to their own delusions, and permits them to believe a lie, that they may be damned, as they deserve, for their sins. The malice, the cunning, the astuteness, the caprice of the devils, the prepossessions of the scientific, and the purposes of God are amply sufficient to account for the fact that these commissions never succeed in witnessing the preternatural or superhuman phenomena said to be witnessed by others."

"But how am I," asked Jack, "to believe that a poor old crone, who is half dying of starvation, is in league with the devil? Why does she not make use of her power to procure decent clothing and maintenance?"

"The devil is by no means a trustworthy or a kind and generous friend. He is a philanthropist, and never relieves the suffering under his nose, or cares for that of individuals."

"I have read," Jack went on, "a great many witch stories, and descriptions of witch feasts, and I cannot discover what there is in them to attach these hell-cats to their alleged orgies. I came across, yesterday, an account of the witches' sabbath. I can conceive nothing more absurd, ridiculous, or rather disgusting. The acquaintances of the devil generally represent him as respectable at least for his intellect, and many insist that he is a gentleman. But if all accounts are true, he is very low and vulgar in his tastes, has very little sense of dignity, and is in fact a very shabby fellow. In these orgies he appears, it is said, sometimes in the form of a big negro, more generally under the form of a black ram with immense horns, and in that form is very indecently kissed and worshipped by Mesdames the witches. We know from Tam O'Shanter that on these occasions there is much fiddling and dancing, but I cannot conceive how there can be much pleasure. The whole scene is fitted only to turn one's stomach."

"There is no doubt of that," replied Mr. Merton. "The devil and his worshippers certainly cut a very sorry figure in these nocturnal orgies, as they are represented; but I am not certain that that should be regarded as good ground of scepticism. I never understood that the devil was a *clean* spirit, and I should naturally expect some degree of filthiness in his worshippers. You must know something of the sins or moral diseases of mankind. Has it not sometimes occurred to you that some apparently very respectable people,—people who go well dressed and wear clean linen,—under the influence of their passions, acting out their natures, cut, to an impartial spectator, about as sorry a figure as Master Leonard and his witches? In the eyes of Infinite Holiness, I am inclined to think there is much that passes in refined and cultivated society that does not appear at all more clean and respectable than do these nocturnal orgies in yours. I do not vouch for the correctness of the popular descriptions of these orgies, but they are in accordance with the well known principles of depraved nature. The indulgence of any of our morbid passions degrades us; and in following our lusts, there is no beastliness which is not for the moment charming to us. How much more, then, when to our natural passions, rendered morbid by indulgence, is added the superhuman influence of unclean spirits! The sensualist lives constantly in a state as disgusting as ever the nocturnal orgies of witches were represented to be. It is the law of all vice to descend, and consequently, the more intimate we are with the devil, only the more rapid and deep is our descent. The moral of the witches' orgies is true, whether the particular descriptions be or not. He who takes the devil for God, must expect to have hell for his heaven."

"The academicians are right," I remarked, "in telling us that the whole of the alleged *diablerie* is all a delusion or an imposition."

"Not precisely in their sense, however," interrupted Mr. Merton. "The whole is unquestionably a delusion, a sheer imposture, but of the devil, not always of man. The devil promises according to the respective inclinations of his servants—to some riches and honors, to some sensual pleasures, to others power, dominion over men, and the secrets of nature. I doubt not that he knows more than men, but he can never be relied on, for he so mingles his lies with the truth, that we cannot separate the one from the other."

"That is true," I remarked; "and those secrets he promises we never gain. We grow proud, we assume airs, we feel that we are making marvellous discoveries; we talk large, use big swelling words, and seem to penetrate the secret of the universe; but we have only clutched at the air, and when we open our hand, it is empty. We had made no advance, we had found no vein of knowledge; and when the spell was broken, we found ourselves weaker and more ignorant than ever. The fairy gold was chips and stubble. The palace of wisdom we saw before us, and in which we proposed to live with the Sultan's fair daughter, disappears, carries her away in it, and leaves us only empty space. I well remember some of my early aspirations. I thought I was illumined by a more than natural light. The clouds rolled back before my searching glance; the darkness disappeared; there was no dread Unknown to confront me; I rose to the empyrean; I was all intelligence; I looked, as a lady of my acquaintance expressed it, 'into the very abyss of Being.' Yet it was all illusion—a devilish illusion—and my understanding was all the time darkened, and my eyes closed to the plainest and most obvious truths before me."

"It was a deception practised upon you—a deception practised alike upon all who would attain to a forbidden knowledge, or to knowledge by ways not permitted by the Supreme Intelligence—upon the Neoplatonists, the Gnostics, the Transcendentalists, and false mystics of every age," added Mr. Merton. "The light we hail in those forbidden ways or aspirations, is the light which we see when our eyes are shut. It is a preternatural hallucination, and he who follows it is sure not only to go astray, but to fall into the greatest absurdities, and to utter the most ridiculous nonsense."

"The same principle," I added, "is true with regard to the promised power over men. These Satanic revolutions, and the terrible doings of our revolutionary Berserkirs, all prove failures in the end. Cromwell supplants Hampden, and Napoleon Lafayette. The devil always leaves us in the lurch."

"This fact should be borne in mind," added Mr. Merton, "and if so, might save the world from much superstition. The superstition is not in believing in the reality of demonic invasions, or in believing that the devil sometimes exhibits a superhuman power, tells us, in dreams, visions, necromancy, or other forms of divination, facts of which we were ignorant; but in practising these forms, in confiding in the communications, and in seeking to avail ourselves of the power displayed. No reliance can ever be placed upon them, for supposing the demonic presence real, we have still only a lying spirit on which to depend. The dream of yesternight has come true, that of to-night will prove false. The *medium* you consulted the other day foretold correctly what was to happen; to-day her familiar spirit is a lying spirit, and her tale is false in all its parts. The predictions of the fortune-teller last year have been fulfilled; his predictions of to-day are a tissue of lies. If Ahab goes up to battle, he shall not die; yet is shot by a bow drawn at a venture. To trust in these things is gross superstition, and tends only to degrade, to render immoral, weak, timid, and miserable. The way of wisdom is to let them alone, turn your back on them, and never suffer your mind or imagination to run on them."

"It is worthy of remark, that the men who declaim the most against superstition are unbelievers in Christianity, and who, under pretext of making war on superstition, attack religion itself. And yet the Church has always forbidden all superstitious practices, and she commands her children to have no dealings with the devil, to forbear all resort to fortune-tellers or divination, and to pay no attention to dreams, omens, &c. Of course all such things are wrong, are sin, are treason against God; but they are also, and because treason against God, and a dealing with the enemy, unwise and degrading. There is no saying to what depths he may fall who gives way to them, or the misery and wretchedness he may bring upon himself, and even upon those dear to him. I could, were I disposed, draw proofs enough from my own experience, while I was a prey to the superstitions still so rife in our country; but I will not trouble you with them. But of this be sure, that you will never root out that superstition by denying the existence and influence of demons. The remedy is in religious faith, in cultivating a firm trust in God, in obedience to his commands,—and in the firm persuasion that all dealings with devils is unlawful, and that all regard paid to signs, dreams, and omens is superstitious and sinful, and, what will weigh perhaps still more with our age, wholly unprofitable. No good can come from seeking knowledge by forbidden paths, and much evil is sure to come."

"I am glad," said Jack, "that Mr. Merton has the grace to admit so much. It would have been a blessed thing for me, if I had been taught to regard mesmerism as unlawful; better still, if it had never been recommended to me as a legitimate science. I do not believe in Satanic invasions; but I do believe little good comes from departing from the old ways, and attempting to be wiser than our fathers were."

CHAPTER XXV.

CONCLUSIONS.

Our conversations were continued, but they threw no additional light on the main subject of our investigations, and I may well dispense myself from the labor of recording them. I found my early suspicion confirmed, and finally adopted Mr. Merton's conclusion, that the class of phenomena which had for several years occupied my attention, and to which, according to the spiritists themselves, the recent spirit-manifestations belong, are real, are facts which actually take place, and are, under certain relations and to a certain extent, superhuman in their origin and character. As these phenomena cannot be ascribed to God or to good angels, they must be ascribed to Satan, to evil spirits, the enemies of God and man.

I am well aware that this conclusion will be received by my brother savans with great derision, and that they will look upon me as having lost my wits. Even many who are not savans, who are sincere and firm believers in Christianity, and who, in a general way, admit the fact of Satanic invasion, will laugh at the supposition that the phenomena of spirit-rapping, table-turning, &c., are any thing more than very bungling pieces of humbuggery and sleight-of-hand. Be it so. Their good or bad opinion, their esteem or contempt, is of very little importance to me, who have not many days to live, and who have so soon to face another and a far different Judge. He who fears God, cannot fear man. My conclusion has not been hastily adopted, and it is, as far as I can see, the only conclusion to which a Christian philosopher can come.

Mr. Cotton had preserved, what so many have lost, the Christian tradition as to evil spirits, and was right in the main. His error was in ascribing *all* the phenomena exhibited by the practice of mesmerism to the devil and his angels. Mesmerism, though abnormal, is to a certain extent susceptible of a satisfactory explanation on natural principles. Man, as Mr. Merton, after the elder Görres, maintained, has a twofold development, the one normal, in which he rises to spiritual freedom by union with God, the other abnormal, in which he descends to spiritual slavery by descending to union with created nature. In the former he tends continually to escape from the fatalism of nature, and to ascend to the pure and serene atmosphere of spiritual freedom, in which the spirit becomes supreme over the body. In the latter he follows the laws of fatal or unfree nature, loses his spiritual dominion, becomes, or tends to become, subject in his soul to his body, while the body falls under the operation of the general forces of necessary nature, and responds fatally, or without freedom, to the pulses of the external universe.

In the ascending development, by the aid of grace and good angels, the man, the Christian mystic, like St. Catharine, St. Theresa, or St. Bernardine of Sienna, and so many others of the saints of the Church, rises to spiritual freedom, and even to a certain extent, liberates the body from the fatalism of nature. The body itself seems to enter into the freedom of the spirit, and, through the free soul informing it, to be able to resist the action of necessary or unfree nature, as the vital principle enables the living body to resist and overcome the action of chemical affinity. The body is as it were spiritualized, not absolutely indeed, but partially, as if in anticipation of the resurrection, or rather, as pointing to a resurrection and its glorious transformation hereafter. It is baptized, participates, if I may so say, in the sanctifying grace infused into the soul, becomes pure, and even when the soul leaves it, emits a fragrant odor.[7]

In the descending development, that is, in the abnormal development, in which we turn our backs on our Maker, who is at once our Original and End, our Creator and our Supreme Good, and tend in the direction from him, our soul lets go its mastery, and our body falls under the dominion of unfree nature, enters into the series of its laws, and is exposed to all its necessary and invincible forces. We become not merely sensual, but, in some sense, physical men, and act under and with the great physical agents of the universe. We become feeble and strong as the lightning whose bolt rends the oak, and is turned aside by a silken thread. Now to this abnormal development, mesmerism, in my judgment, belongs; and therefore, though abnormal, it is not necessarily preternatural. It belongs not to healthy but unhealthy nature, and its phenomena are never exhibited except in a subject naturally or artificially diseased. I have never known a person of vigorous constitution and robust health mesmerized. The experiments of Baron Reichenbach were all made on persons in ill health, for the most part on patients under medical treatment. The seeress of Provost was sickly, and suffering from an incurable malady; and it may be asserted as a general rule, that no one is a *subject* of mesmerism whose constitution, especially the nervous constitution, is in its normal state.

I have no doubt that many of the phenomena regarded by the vulgar as the effect of Satanic invasion, are to be explained by reference to this abnormal development, without the supposition of any direct agency of evil spirits. The precise limits of the power of this abnormal development we do not know, and therefore we are always to be exceedingly slow to assume the direct invasion of the devil to explain this or that extraordinary phenomenon, as Mr. Merton has already explained. The error of Mr. Cotton was in not distinguishing between abnormal phenomena artificially produced, and the phenomena of real demonic presence. He asked too much of us, and we gave him nothing. He failed to command from us the respect he deserved, and I am sorry for it. He was a worthy man in his way, and far less superstitious, and far more philosophical than those who thought it a mark of their superiority to ridicule him. But he is gone, and has in his own denomination left few behind who are worthy to step into his shoes.

Nevertheless, it would be wrong to infer, from the fact that the proper mesmeric phenomena are explicable on natural principles, that the practice of mesmerism is lawful or not dangerous. It is an artificial disease, and injurious to the physical constitution. It moreover facilitates the Satanic invasion. Satan has no creative power, and can operate only on a nature created to his hands, and in accordance with conditions of which he has not the sovereign control. Ordinarily, he can invade our bodies only as they are in an abnormal state, and by availing himself of some natural force, it may be some fluid, or some invisible and imponderable agent like electricity, or what Baron Reichenbach calls od, and Mesmer animal magnetism, and the older magnetists called spirit of the world. The practice of mesmerism brings into play this force, and thus gives occasion to the devil, or exposes us to his malice and invasions.

But, though it is unwise, as well as unscientific, to ascribe to Satan what is explicable on natural principles, the contrary error is the one which in our times is the most necessary to be guarded against. Nothing is more unphilosophical than to treat the dark facts of human history as unreal, or to attempt to explain them all without resort to demonic influence. Many of the facts recorded, no doubt, never took place. Many were the result of fraud, imposture, jugglery, and many are explicable by reference to the abnormal development of human nature; but after making all reasonable deductions for these, there remains a residuum, as Mr. Merton has said, which it is as absurd to attempt to explain without the action of evil spirits, as to explain the light of day without the sun, or the existence and preservation of the universe without God. Not otherwise can you ever succeed in explaining the introduction, establishment, persistence, and power of the various cruel, filthy, and revolting superstitions of the ancient heathen world, or of pagan nations in modern times. No genuine philosopher will attempt to explain them on natural principles alone.

They reveal a more than human power, and we have no alternative but to ascribe them either to God or to the devil. We cannot ascribe them to God, for they were too foul and filthy, too deleterious in their effects, too debasing and enslaving in their influence, to be ascribed to a good source. They were, then, from Satan, operating upon man's morbid nature, and permitted by Infinite Justice as a deserved punishment upon the Gentiles for their hatred of truth, and their apostasy from the primitive religion. Men left to themselves, to human nature alone, however low they might be prone to descend, never could descend so low as to worship wood and stone, four-footed beasts, and creeping things. To do this needs Satanic delusion.

The same must be said of Mahometanism. The old theory, which made Mahomet an out-and-out impostor, who said, deliberately, "with malice aforethought," "Go to now, let us make a new religion and impose it upon the world," no man, accustomed to philosophize, can for a moment entertain. No man ever yet went to work deliberately to devise and impose a false religion, or if any one ever did, he never succeeded. He who founds a new religion is never an impostor in his own eyes. He works "in a sad sincerity," and imposes on himself before imposing on others. Mahomet evidently believed in himself, in the sanctity of his own mission, and worked from an earnest conviction, not from simple craft or calculation. I am pleased to find the author of that admirable poem, *Mohammed, a Tragedy in Five Acts*, a work of rare sagacity and true poetic genius, rejecting the old theory of downright imposture. The estimable author maintains that he was sincere in part, and in part insincere. He was sincere in his assertion of the unity of God, and in his hostility to idolatry, but insincere in the assertion of his prophetic mission. I am not, however, satisfied with this. I do not deny that men may be half sincere, and half knavish, or that they be sincere and earnest as to the end, and wholly unscrupulous as to the means. But in nothing was Mahomet more sincere than in his belief in his own mission, and in the supernatural origin of the Koran. Never, without that conviction, could he have inspired his followers with it, or have himself persevered for so many years, amid the ill success and discouragements that he experienced. His gratitude, evidently unfeigned, to Cadijah, his first consort, and to Medina, which received him on his flight from Mecca, cherished to the last moment of his life, proves that he believed in his own mission.

The same thing is proved by his open vice and profligacy after his success. A man conscious that he is playing a part, that he has a character to sustain, that he is acting the prophet, would have been more circumspect, more wary in the indulgence of his lusts, and affected a life of more rigid asceticism. He would have been on his guard against scandalizing his followers, and would never have dared insert in his Koran those scandalous provisions which specially exempt him from obedience to the laws which he professed, by Divine authority, to impose upon his followers. Imposture can never afford to abandon itself openly to the empire of the passions. Heretics are usually more careful than the orthodox in regard to appearances. They usually affect great purity of life, a decorous exterior, and a grave and sanctimonious face and tone. Hypocrisy is austere, maintains in its look and tone an awful gravity, and never relaxes in public. It is only innocence that dares be light and frolicsome, and yield to its varying impulses. Nobody is so shocked with the imaginary impurities of Convents and Nunneries as your debauched old sinners, steeped in corruption, and the miserable slaves of their own morbid passions and prurient imagination.

What deceives the excellent and gifted author of the Tragedy, is the fact that so far as Mahomet asserted the unity of God against the polytheism of the unconverted Arabs, and opposed idolatry, he was on the side of truth and religion, and consequently was so far opposed to Satan. He thinks that thus far he could not have been under the influence of an evil spirit. Has he forgotten the demon of Socrates? Has he forgotten that the devil can disguise himself as an angel of light? Paganism, in its old form, was doomed. Christianity had silenced the oracles and driven the devils back to hell. How was the devil to reëstablish his worship on earth, and carry on his war against the son of God? Evidently only by changing his tactics, and turning the truth into a lie. There is nothing to hinder us from believing that Satan himself taught Mahomet the unity of God, and inspired him with horror of the prevailing forms of idolatry. The strong keeps the house, as our Lord says, till a stronger binds him and enters into possession. The devil would expel polytheism and the grosser forms of idolatry, no longer in harmony with the spirit of the times, that he might make the last state worse than the first; and whoever has studied history knows that Mahometanism has proved a far more formidable enemy to Christianity than was the paganism braved by the Apostles. The truths of the Koran are introduced only to sanction its errors, and its moral precepts, many of which are good, only to give countenance to its immorality, to its Satanic abominations.

Mahomet in his life was subject to what we call in these days the mesmeric trance, as was Socrates. He would often be suddenly arrested, fall prostrate upon the earth, and in this attitude and in these trances he professed to receive his revelations. Here are evidently the mesmeric phenomena which in some form always accompany the presence and invasion of demons. Mr. Miles has introduced these, and described them with great spirit, truth, and propriety, in the opening scene of his tragedy. The time is the night of Al Kadir, the place is the Cave of Hara, three miles from Mecca, where Mahomet was accustomed to resort and spend much time alone. Mahomet is seen prostrate upon the slope of a rock, resembling a rude pedestal, his face concealed by his turban. He is visited by Cadijah, his affectionate and beloved wife. To her he seems asleep.

She calls him, she approaches him, she embraces him, and tries to awaken him. All in vain. Finding her efforts fruitless, she exclaims,

> "Alas, this is not sleep! Some evil spirit
> O'ershadows thee."

When finally the vision departs, and Mahomet awakes, he breaks out,

> "Gone! gone! celestial messenger,
> Angel of light!
> . . . .
> . . . . . Yes—'twas there—'twas there
> The angel stood, in more than mortal splendor,
> Before my dazzled vision!—I have heard thee,
> Ambassador from Allah to my soul,
> Have heard and will obey."

To the question of Cadijah, "What mystery is this?" he answers,

> "Ah! the tremendous recollection bursts
> So vividly upon me, that my tongue
> Grows cold and speechless. I was here alone,
> Expecting thee, when, suddenly, I heard
> My name pronounced, with voice more musical
> Than Peri warbling in my ear.
> Ravish'd, I turned, and saw upon that rock,
> Resplendent hovering there, an angel form;
> I knew 'twas Gabriel, Allah's messenger.
> Celestial glories compassed him around;
> Arched o'er his splendid head, his glistening wings
> Shed light, and musk, and melody. No more
> I saw—no more my mortal eye could bear.
> *Prone on my face I fell*, and, from the dust,
> Besought him quench his superhuman radiance.
> 'Look up,' he said; I stole a trembling glance;
> And then, a beauteous youth, he stood and smiled.
> Then, as his ruby lips unclosed, I heard—'Go
> teach what mortals know not yet,—THERE IS
> NO GOD BUT ONE—MOHAMMED IS HIS PROPHET!'
> E'en as he spoke, his mantling glories burst
> With such transporting brightness, that, o'erawed,
> I sunk in dizzy trance, which still might thrall
> My inmost soul, had not those impious names,
> Breathing of hell, dispelled it."[8]

Here are presented, very clearly, the phenomena which precede or accompany the demonic approach and invasion. When the false god took possession of Balaam, he threw him to the earth; and it was in a sort of somnambulic state that he prophesied, or rather that the demon in him was compelled, against his will, to bless instead of cursing Israel, and to prophesy his glory. "There is no God but one," in the sense intended by Mahomet, and understood by his followers, is by no means a truth, for in that sense, it denies not merely polytheism, but was intended more especially to deny the Christian doctrine of the Trinity. The Koran repeatedly so explains it, and therefore the unity of God, as taught by the false prophet, is not a truth but a lie, and the Mahometans worship not the true God, but a false god, as do all who deny that God is at once three distinct persons in one Divine Essence or Being.

Nothing is less philosophical than the tendency in modern times, especially since the time of Voltaire, to explain great effects by petty causes, as the peace of Utrecht by Mrs. Masham's spilling a little water on the Duchess of Marlborough's dress. The stream cannot rise higher than the fountain, or the effect exceed the cause. A little fire can kindle a great matter, but that little fire is the occasion, not the cause of the widespread conflagration. Nothing more surely indicates a narrow, superficial, and unphilosophical spirit than the attempt, as is the case with most writers, to explain the origin, progress, and power of Mahometanism by the fanaticism, the cunning, the craft, or the superior genius and ability of Mahomet, even though we suppose him aided by a Jew and a Nestorian monk. There were fraud, craft, trickery, and all the means of imposition employed; yet never can they suffice alone to account for the terrible phenomena of Islamism, which, for twelve hundred years has waged battle with the cross, and possessed itself of the fairest regions of the globe. Whoever studies it calmly and profoundly must come to the conclusion that there has been at work in it a more than human power, and that, if not, as the Moslems believe, from God, it must be from the devil.

Do not ascribe so much to mere human power, wisdom, craft, fraud, dexterity, or skill. These are far feebler than it is customary in our days to regard them. In general men are duped themselves before they undertake to dupe others. Never yet was there a noted heresiarch who did not believe in his own heresy, and hence there is no instance on record of a real heresiarch, the originator and founder of a new heresy, being reclaimed to the orthodox faith, unless we except the doubtful case of Berengarius. I have never been able to sympathize with those Catholic writers who would persuade us that the Protestant Reformation originated in petty jealousies and rivalries between the Dominican and Augustinian monks. That view is too narrow and superficial; nor can we ascribe it to the pride, the vanity, and the ambition, or the intelligence, the virtue, the wisdom, and the sanctity of the monk Luther. Luther was a man terribly in earnest, a genuine man, and no sham, as Carlyle would say; and so were all the prominent chiefs in that terrible movement of the sixteenth century. The cool, subtle, dark, persevering Calvin, the fiery, energetic, and ferocious John Knox and their compeers were no petty tricksters, no *dilettanti*, no shrewd calculating hypocrites. They were terribly in earnest; they believed in themselves; they believed in the spirit that moved them, that spoke in their words, and struck in their blows against the old Papal edifice. It is nonsense to repeat, age after age, that the denial by the Holy See of the divorce solicited by Henry the Eighth, caused the separation of England from Catholic unity. That wily and lustful monarch, who must live in history as the "wife-slayer," found in that denial only an occasion of withdrawing his kingdom from its spiritual subjection to Rome, and of uniting in the crown the pontifical with the royal authority. Whoever looks beneath the surface of things, whoever studies, in a truly philosophical spirit, that fearful Protestant movement, must recognize in it a superhuman power, and say that either the finger of God, or the hand of the devil is here, and that its chiefs must have been inspired by the Holy Ghost, or driven onward by infuriated demons.

So, it seems to me, we must reason with regard to Cromwell and the stern old Puritans, fierce and terrible as the old Berserkirs from the North. There was something superhuman in the English rebellion and revolution of the seventeenth century; and if Cromwell and his party were not specially moved by the Holy Spirit, as they believed, they must have been animated and driven on by the old Norse demon. So also of the old French Revolution, and of all those terrible convulsions which have ruined nations and shaken the world. Men are indeed in them, with their wisdom and their folly, their beliefs and their doubts, their virtues and their vices, but there is more in them than these. There is in them the fierce conflict of invisible powers, ever renewing and carrying on that fierce and unrelenting war which Lucifer and his rebel host dared wage against the Most High, and which must continue till time be no more. All history, if we did but understand it, is little else but the history of the conflict between these invisible powers; and till we learn this fact, in vain shall we pride ourselves on our philosophies of History.

Carlyle has well exposed the shallow philosophy and absurd theories of our popular historians. Would he had himself gone deeper, and recognized the demonic and also the providential element in history, and not have attempted to explain its philosophy on human nature alone. Your Odins, Thors, Socrateses, Mahomets, Cromwells, Bonapartes, are not simply exponents of true, living, energetic manhood, and owe not their success, or their place in history to their clear perception and their instinctive adherence to the laws of true and genuine nature, as Carlyle would have us believe. The nature he bids us worship is the devil, the dark, subterranean Demon, that seizes us, blinds our eyes, and carries us onward, whither we know not, and by a power which we are not. It is the demon of the storm, the whirlwind, and the tempest, the volcano and the earthquake, and the Carlylean heroes are energumenes, Berserkirs, who spread devastation around them, who quaff the blood of their enemies, from human skulls, in the orgies of Valhalla, and leave as their monuments the ruins of nations. Carlyle has himself been touched with a German devil, and received a slight manipulation from the old Norse demon. But he has done well to say, "No sham can live;" he might have added, No sham is or can be productive. It is not by petty passions and petty tricks that nations are shaken to their centre, and fearful revolutions, which change the face of the world, are effected. Only what is real is, and only what is, can do. Under all the heavings and tossings of nature, there is a reality of some sort; and only by means of that reality can you explain the historical phenomena that arrest your attention.

I have just been reading, in order to relieve my weariness, Sir Walter Scott's *Woodstock*, not surely one of his best, but one of his most serious novels, in which he has endeavored to be something of the philosopher, as well as the unrivalled romancer. Poor man! wizard of the north, as he has been called, his magician's wand fails him here. How was he, with the shallow philosophy of the eighteenth century, to explain such a phenomenon as Cromwell and his Major Generals, those furious Berserkirs, true descendants of the old Vikings of the North? To say that Oliver and the Independents were mere long-faced, psalm-singing hypocrites, moved only by the ordinary motives and passions of human beings, is a libel on history. Long-faced, sanctimonious, and long-winded, famous for their dark cloaks and steeple-crowned hats, their psalm-singing, their Biblical phraseology, their speaking through the nose, and turning up the white of the eye, they certainly were; but whoso supposes they were so by virtue of subtle, calculating hypocrisy, knows them not. Whatever else Cromwell and the Puritans were, they were no hypocrites; their manners, their dress, and address, however objectionable we may choose to regard them, were not affected to cloak conscious vice or iniquity, or to deceive either their friends or their enemies. Never were men more serious, more deeply in earnest; and it was in obedience to what they held to be the voice of God that they preached, fasted, sung psalms, prayed, and—kept their powder dry. It was not by their snivel, their nasal twang, their Biblical phraseology, nor by an affectation of piety and dependence on the Lord, nor by any form of hypocrisy or cant, that they made mincemeat of the drinking, swearing rakehell, but brave and loyal cavaliers at Marston Moor, Edgehill, and Worcester. A chorus of spirits, black or white, joined in their psalm-singing, and invisible powers sped their balls to the hearts of their enemies, and gave force to the well-aimed strokes of their swords.

Certainly the hand of Providence in the affairs of nations is not to be denied, and certain it is that God visits nations in mercy and in judgment. A sound theology, an enlightened piety sees the providence of God in the growth of the infant colony, in the prosperity of states, and the revolutions and fall of empires. But he works by ministries; and the most terrible exhibitions of his wrath, the most fearful of his judgments are those in which he lets loose the demons, and permits a people to fall under their power. These demons work their own will, but are at the same time the executors of his vengeance—of his justice. The good, even in the greatest national calamities, are never injured, for nothing but sin ever injures; but the wicked are punished. They had chosen the devil for their master, and it is fitting that he whom they had falsely worshipped as God, who is no God, should be made the instrument of their punishment. The national sins of England were great; her kings had betrayed their trust—had led the people into error, and forgotten what they owed to the King of kings and Lord of lords. The Lord had a controversy with them, and he permitted the old Puritans to triumph over them; and whether they did so by simple human strength, or by the willing assistance of evil spirits, inflaming them with a preternatural courage, and driving them on by a preternatural fury, the principle is one and the same. So also of France, in her terrible revolution of 1789, and of Europe in 1848.

I read with sorrow the puny attempts of the author of *Woodstock* to explain away, as mere jugglery or trickery, the strange phenomena which disturbed the sequestrators of the Royal Lodge. He would, on the strength of an anonymous pamphlet, explain them as a trick played off upon the parliamentary commissioners by Dr. Rochecliff, Albert, Tompkins, Joceline, and Phebe. It may have been so; but the machinery he supposes is clearly inadequate to explain all the mysterious phenomena he acknowledges. The trick could hardly have failed, if trick there was, to be detected either by Colonel Everard or the Commissioners. But even, if his explanation of that particular case is to be accepted, or if a thousand instances are to be referred to trickery, it says nothing as to the general fact of demonic vexations and invasions. As Christians, we know that we are constantly beset by evil spirits, and the mysterious occurrences at the Royal Lodge of Woodstock, even if real, are only a step beyond ordinary Satanic temptations, as possession is only a further extension of obsession.

If much harm is done by superstition, perhaps even more is done by the denial of all demonic influence and invasion, and the attempt to explain all the so-called Satanic phenomena on natural principles. It generates a sceptical turn of mind, and the rationalism resorted to will in the end be turned against the supernatural facts of religion, and the same process which is adopted to explain away the Satanic prodigies, will be made use of to explain away the miracles of the Old and New Testaments. In fact it has been so done, and we have seen grave commentators laboring, as they believed, to explain these very miracles on natural principles; thus reducing Christianity from its high character of a supernatural religion to a system of mere naturalism, at best a simple human philosophy, perhaps inferior to many other systems. Jefferson, writing to Priestley, speaks, as he supposes, very well of our Lord, but disputes his merits as a philosopher, and says, in substance, "Jesus was a spiritualist, I am a materialist." How many men in our days regard themselves as very commendable Christians because they recognize the beauty and worth of certain moral precepts of the Gospel, precepts which are only the universal dictates of reason, and recognized by the common sense of all nations—heathen as well as Christian! Thomas Paine was more honest, for though he could say Jesus taught very pure morals, which have never been excelled, he refused to call himself a Christian. I have met many a professed minister of the Gospel who would find Tom Paine's creed, meagre as it was, too big for him: "I believe in one God and no more, and I hope for happiness beyond this life. I believe that religious duties consist in justice and mercy, and endeavoring to make our fellow-creatures happy." The Gospel, as it is preached by some "godly" ministers in New England, is too meagre to have satisfied a Rousseau, or even a Voltaire.

In the case of the Spiritists of our own times, much harm is done by telling them the spirit-manifestations are all humbuggery, imagination, fraud, or trickery. These people know that it is not so. They know that they are not knaves, that they practise no trickery, and have no wish to deceive or be deceived. They are not conscious of any dishonest intentions, and they have no reason to think that they are less intelligent or less sharp-sighted than they who abuse them as impostors, or ridicule them as dupes. The worst way in the world to convert a man from his errors is to begin by abusing him, and denying what he knows to be true. Except in the teachings of God, or what is the same thing, the teachings of men appointed, instructed, and supernaturally assisted by him to teach, we never find unmixed truth, for to err is human; and on the other hand, we never find pure, unmixed falsehood. Unmixed falsehood is universal negation, and no negation is possible but by an affirmation. Error is the misapplication of the true. These Spiritists are deceived, are deluded, I grant, for they are the sport of a lying and deceiving spirit; but they are not deceived or deluded as to the phenomena to which they testify, nor, as a general thing, do they wish to deceive others. Among them there may be knaves and fools, there may be quacks and impostors, but I have no reason to suppose that the mass of them are not as intelligent and as honest as the common run of men, as the world goes. Their error is in their explication of the phenomena, not in asserting the reality of the phenomena; and to begin by telling them that no such phenomena have ever occurred, that the spirit-manifestations are all humbug, is, to say the least, a very unwise proceeding. If you are a minister of religion, by doing so you are only playing into the hands of the devil, for you outrage the natural sense of justice and truth which these people still retain, and dispose them in turn to look upon religion itself, as held by the Christian Church, as a humbug.

I have known many apparently sincere and pious persons driven to apostasy by the scepticism with regard to the phenomena they have themselves seen. The very worst way in the world to deliver ourselves or others from the power of Satan, is to deny his existence. Resist the devil, and he will flee from you; laugh at him, if you will, and he will hie himself back to hell, for he cannot endure contempt; but deny his existence, persuade yourselves that there exists no devil, and he in turn will laugh at you, and take quiet possession of you. Oppose the Spiritists we certainly should, but not where they are strong and we are weak. The true way is to concede the facts, concede all that they really and honestly observe, concede even their mysterious and superhuman character, and then explain to them their principle and origin, and show them that they proceed not from good angels, even when apparently they are pure and unobjectionable, but from the enemies of Christ, from Satan and his angels carrying on, with devilish malice, their never-ending war against Heaven.

Such at least are the conclusions which I have been forced in my own mind to adopt, and such, it seems to me, all must adopt who study the question in the light of Christian theology. I am at least honest in these conclusions, and, though I may err now, as I have so often erred before, yet I am not more likely to err than others. Err indeed I may, but, if I must err at all, I would rather err on the side of superstition, than on the side of scepticism and irreligion.

* * * *

. I do not forget here, nor do I intend to assert any thing against the doctrine of the Holy Council of Trent, that concupiscence remains after baptism, for the combat, or that the *fomes* of sin remain, and that as long as one lives there is the possibility of sin. The body, in this life, is never wholly liberated and restored to its integral state; but that it is liberated in some measure, and that it in the saints, (in some saints at least,) in a degree participates, even this side the grave, in the freedom of the soul, I think is undeniable.

[7]*Mohammed*, a Tragedy in Five Acts. By George H. Miles. Boston, 1850, pp. 1-6.

CHAPTER XXVI.

CONVERSION.

My story, like my life, draws to its close. The change which my religious views have undergone has been more than once hinted. On religion, as on most other subjects, I no longer think or feel as I did in the day when I fancied I possessed more than human science, and wielded a more than human power.

I grew up without any decided religious doctrines, though inclining to what was called Liberal Christianity, that is, a Christianity kept up with the times, and conformed to the ever-changing spirit of the age. I was not an avowed unbeliever; I was not an open scoffer; I even thought it well to pay a decent external respect to religion, to attend church when convenient, and to patronize the Gospel, providing it was not preached with too much earnestness and devotedness, and not promulgated as a law which must govern all my thoughts, words, and deeds, but was proposed simply as a speculation, as a theory, or as an opinion, which I was at liberty to accept, modify, or reject, as seemed to me good.

Before my mesmeric experiments and acquaintance with Priscilla, I was a sort of Rationalist, accepting Christianity in name, and explaining its miracles and mysteries on purely natural principles. Afterwards, after my philanthropic schemes had miscarried, my worship of humanity as God had proved a failure, and my belief in progress had expired in the crucible of experience, I fell into a sort of despair, and would fain have persuaded myself that I believed in nothing. If I did not absolutely deny God, my belief in him became so obscured by the mists of my speculations and the corruptions of my heart, that I was in reality no better than an atheist. The devil was a bugbear invented by the priests, and men were mere motes in the sunbeam. I have already described the state into which I fell—a state from which I would risk my life to save my bitterest enemy.

Prior to the absolute crushing of all my hopes, which followed my having finished all the work I had marked out for myself to do, and found it nought, I regarded myself as a Free-Thinker, because I had either allowed myself to think, or had made myself acquainted with the thoughts of others, against religion. My freedom and independence of mind were in denying, not in believing. I was not free to think in favor of religion, nor sufficiently independent to believe Christianity, and labor in earnest to serve God and save my own soul. To have done so would have been sheer superstition, would have been sinking myself to the level of the vulgar, and to have exposed myself to the gibes and sneers of my scientific associates.

Nevertheless, my unbelief, my scepticism, and my radicalism, were a sort of violence done to my own better feelings and graver judgment. They never came natural to me, and I am sure I was never cut out for a philanthropist or a world-reformer. There was always something in the views and practices of my associates that disgusted me, and often was I obliged to hold my nose when they were discussed, as it is said Satan does when he encounters a confirmed sensualist. I had no natural relish for "the Newness," and when at worst retained a secret reverence for the past, and dwelt with pleasure on the time-hallowed, over which for ages had flowed the stream of human affection, human joy, and human sorrow. I stood in awe before the shadow of the hoary Eld, and wished always to find myself bound by indissoluble ties to what had gone before me, as well as to what might come after me. Half in spite, and half under the charm of Priscilla, I embraced philanthropy, but not inwardly, for her sophistry never for a moment deceived me. Never was there a moment when I did not see through the philanthropists, radicals, and revolutionists with whom I associated, or when with a breath I could not have swept away their cobweb theories; never for a moment was I deceived as to the actual character of the devilish movements I myself set on foot.

It may be thought strange, such being the fact, that I could or would have played the part I did. It might be enough to say Satan had power over me; but I associated with the prophets of "the Newness," and led on the movement, partly because I did not know what else to do, and partly because I could not endure absolute idleness. I saw indeed the destructive character of my movements, but I cherished a hope that by making things worse, I should prepare the way for making them better. You must demolish, I said, the old edifice, and clear away its rubbish, before you can erect a new, a more beautiful, or a more convenient structure on its site. I accepted, after a manner, the opinions and theories of the Neologists, not because they satisfied me, but because I knew not what else to accept; and, though not true, they might conduct me to truth. The road to the temple of Purity runs through the Bower of Bliss, the path to heaven crosses the devil's territory, and error is the prodrome of truth. Such were the maxims I adopted, not indeed because I believed them, but because they were convenient, and because I saw not otherwise how to justify myself, or solve the problem of experience. I adhered to my philanthropy, infidelity, and radicalism, not because I loved or believed them, but because I saw nothing true in the principles and reasonings I was accustomed to hear opposed to them. The religious and conservative people I knew, and I supposed them the most enlightened and the least irrational of their class, seemed to believe and retain either too much or too little. On one side they seemed to accept and act on the principles which I and my party professed, and on the other to insist on conclusions which could be logically obtained only from a contradictory set of principles, and which they with one voice condemned as false, mischievous, and leading only to superstition, idolatry, and spiritual thraldom. Their denials struck me as too sweeping for their affirmations, and their affirmations as quite too broad for their denials. I found myself in the unpleasant predicament, either of divinizing humanity, or of embracing a religion which they held to be worse than the rankest infidelity.

For a time, while I was in good health, while I possessed and wielded a more than human power, and had not yet exhausted the world in which I did believe, or despaired of recasting it after my own image, I got along without much difficulty; but when I no longer saw any object in life, when there was from my own point of view no longer any work for me to do, and I was thrown back on my own failing godship, and left to devour my own heart, I became wretched, more wretched than I can express. The blow which prostrated me, and the disease which it developed, and brought me to handgrips with Death, changed the current of my thoughts, but unhappily only to render them for the time still more painful. "You know, O Socrates," says Cephalus in Plato's *Republic*, "that when a man thinks that he is drawing near to death, certain things, as to which he had previously been very tranquil, awaken in his bosom anxiety and alarm. What has been told him of hell and the punishment of the wicked, the stories at which he had formerly laughed or mocked, now fill his soul with trouble. He fears that they may prove true. Enfeebled by age, or brought nearer to the frightful abodes, he seems to perceive them with greater clearness and force, and is therefore disturbed by doubts and apprehensions. He reviews his past life, and seeks what evil he may have done. If he finds, on examination, that his life has been iniquitous, he awakes often in the night, agitated and shuddering, as a child, with sudden terrors, trembles and lives in fearful expectation;" or, as I may add with St. Paul, "a certain fearful looking for of judgment and fiery indignation." As I found myself on my dying bed, things began to wear to me a very different aspect from what they did when I was in the heyday of youth, in the full flow of my animal spirits, or filled with the vain and delusive hope of subjecting all nature to my will. The lessons which I had heard in my childhood, and which I had ridiculed or forgotten, came back with startling power; and in my lonely reflections I was forced to ask what, if that which they tell us of death and judgment, of heaven and hell, the rewards of the good and the punishment of the wicked, should turn out to be true?

My trouble, my anxiety, and my alarm increased in proportion as Mr. Merton forced upon me, by his conversations, the full conviction that I had really been dealing with devils, that Satan is really a personal existence, and that I had made a covenant with him, and had acted under his influence. My rationalism had led me to question his personal existence, and to attempt to explain the demonic phenomena without the supposition of his interposition. Denying Satan, I had denied Christ; and being now forced to recognize Satan, I was forced to confess Christ, and all the Christian mysteries. By the same process by which I had explained away the demonic phenomena, I had explained away the miracles and the supernatural character of Christianity. By that same process of reasoning by which Mr. Merton compelled me to admit the false miracles, the lying signs and wonders of Satan, I was forced to admit the true miracles, therefore the Divine commission, and therefore the Divinity of Christ, because Christ claimed to be the Son of God.

Here is, I apprehend, the principal source of that difficulty which so many people find in admitting the reality of the demonic phenomena. They cannot admit Satan and his works, without admitting Christ and redemption, purchased with his own blood on the cross,—in a word, without admitting all the Christian mysteries and dogmas,—Christianity itself, and that not as an opinion, not as a speculation, but as the law of God for conscience. Most men have, at least, a dim perception of this fact; and as they do not like to admit Christianity in a Christian sense, they will not suffer themselves to believe that there is any thing Satanic in the dark phenomena of human history. For, whatever may be the professions we hear, whatever the apparent zeal displayed in the cause of a bastard Christianity, our age is an unbelieving age, and hates, I may say, with a perfect hatred, Christ and his Church. The age is blind to the perception of Christian truth, but sharp-sighted to whatever is requisite to prevent that truth from making its way to the heart. It sees very clearly what it must concede, if it accepts Mr. Merton's doctrine; and therefore, with all its energy and astuteness, it insists on explaining the demonic phenomena on natural principles, or on denying them outright.

But detached from the world by experience of its hollowness, and by my mortal illness, I became less disposed to resist the grace of God, and in some measure prepared to listen with candor to Mr. Merton's reasoning. I very soon became convinced that I had really fallen into the error of calling good evil, and evil good. I had really substituted Satan for God, and in doing so had committed the precise error the Christian clergy had always laid to my charge. I saw that they had been right in advocating what I called, with Priscilla, the system of repression, and I wrong in advocating the contrary system. I saw that, as a reasonable man, I must abandon the whole order of ideas which I had cherished in my Satanic pride and lust, and embrace that order of ideas which I had hitherto rejected as false and mischievous. There was no room for compromise. I must say decidedly either "Good Lord" or "Good Devil," and as I could no longer say the latter, I must say the former.

Many people, knowing my order of thinking when I was well and in the world, may blame a change so complete and so universal; but only because they are people of confused, incomplete, and disjointed thought, whose views are always dim, obscure, and incoherent, and who can never understand the operations of a mind that reduces all its views to their fundamental principle, to a clear, well-defined, and self-coherent whole, so that any change at all must be change of principle, and involve an entire change of system. Philosophical and logical minds may err, but in their premises, not in their conclusions from them. No question with them is ever a question of detail, and none ever turns on a collateral issue. If they start from infidel premises, they will come to the conclusion that Satan is God, and adjust their theory of the universe accordingly. If they assume, as their point of departure, that liberty is in the absence of all restraint, and that liberty in this sense is good, they must come to the conclusion so earnestly insisted upon by my instructress Priscilla, and of course reject that whole order of ideas which asserts the need of law, the utility of government, or the necessity of restraint. That, in doing so, they go against common sense, they are as well aware as are their opponents; but that fact cannot move them, for the legitimate conclusion from it, if their premises are right, is that so-called common sense is wrong, and needs to be corrected. If the common opinions, doctrines, or judgments of mankind are against them, they are indemnified by finding a common feeling, a secret but real feeling, of all men in their favor; for the very fact that restraint is necessary, proves that perverse nature demands, when left to itself, universal liberty or unbounded license. They have but to adopt the doctrine of the innate purity and sanctity of nature, to call this natural feeling a pure and holy instinct, and bid us follow nature, in order to make out their complete logical justification. They are simply consequent, to use a logical term; and their opponents, who accept their premises but deny their conclusions, are inconsequent.

The common run of men, who oppose this class of thinkers and speculators, not by a complete and coherent system constructed on the principle of law and authority, and who are constantly saying Good Lord and Good Devil, Good Devil and Good Lord, trying forever to conciliate both at the same time, and endeavoring with all their might to serve both God and Mammon, which He who "spake as never man spake" declares to be impossible, whenever they are hard pushed, cry out against them as logic-choppers, hair-splitters, narrow-minded system-mongers, and represent them as wanting in broad and comprehensive views, in liberal and generous feelings, as mere theorists, destitute of plain, practical common sense. What is really a merit in them, is denounced as folly or crime, and the whole pack,

"Tray, Blanche, Sweetheart, little dogs and all,"

are let loose against them. This is wrong. Either our feeling, our sensitive and affective nature, is to be made subordinate and subservient to our reason, or our reason is to be subordinated and made subservient to feeling. To attempt to maintain them as two equal, coördinate, and mutually independent powers, after the manner of the Gallicans in relation to Church and State, is only to prepare the way for internal anarchy and disorder. The fool makes reason subservient to his feelings, emotions, affections, or passions, and as to his proper manhood, lives as a slave; the wise man subjects these to his reason, that is, to understanding and will, and lives, moves, and acts as a freeman.

Now I had one of those minds which reduce their views to system, or to their fundamental principle. My starting-point, my fundamental principle was false, and therefore my whole system or theory of the universe was false. This once discovered, I necessarily embraced the opposing principle, and as necessarily embraced it in all its legitimate consequences. I never was so constituted as to be able to strike a balance between truth and falsehood, or to accept a principle and deny its consequences. In matters of practice, I can understand, where no principle is sacrificed, what are called compromises, and I have never needed to be told that true prudence usually forbids us to push matters to extremes. When we act, we must consider the practicable, and the expedient, as far as principle leaves us any discretionary power; but in asserting principles, in the question between truth and falsehood, right and wrong, I have always felt it necessary to be on one side or the other. It ought not therefore to be considered strange that, forced by Mr. Merton and my own serious reflections to deny that Satan is God, I should swing round to the other extreme, and assert that God is God; or that, starting from this bold proposition as a first principle, I should adjust, or endeavor to adjust my whole order of thought to it. I am aware that my having done so will, with the mass of my countrymen, bring reproach upon my memory, and induce some who may cherish a regard for me to attempt to apologize for my want of inconsistency and incoherency; but, happily, the praises or the censures of men cannot affect me any longer, and I shall soon be where they cannot reach me.

Brought back to an intellectual conviction of the truth of Christianity, my trouble increased; for if Christianity be true, it is not simply the revelation of a truth to be believed, but also of a truth to be practised—of a law to be obeyed. I had not obeyed that law; I had deliberately, systematically violated all its precepts for years, and had taught others to do the same. I had fallen under its condemnation, and had incurred its severest penalties. The prospect that now opened before me was not pleasing. There was a vision of blackness and despair. The judgment I derided, the heaven I had scorned, the hell I had braved or treated as a fiction, were all realities. I must soon appear before my Judge, loaded with crimes and sins innumerable, and of the blackest dye. It was impossible to imagine one more wicked or guilty than myself. I could plead nothing in excuse or extenuation of my guilt. I had proved myself the enemy of my race, a foul-mouthed and black-hearted rebel against God, my sovereign, who had done nothing to me but load me with benefits. It was no pleasant thought. I had consorted with devils. I had chosen them for my associates, and what more fitting than that I should be left to my own choice, to reap the fruits of my own doings, and be doomed to dwell eternally with them in hell? It was what I deserved, what immaculate Justice might well inflict. The thought was not to be endured.

I had made a covenant with death. I had entered into an agreement with hell, and had by a solemn pact given myself to the devil, and who had ever heard that such a one had ever received grace to repent? Had I not blasphemed the Holy Ghost, committed the unpardonable sin? My accomplice had been rescued, it was true, but she had been less guilty than I. She had been deceived, seduced by the wiles of the serpent, and struggled to break the meshes he had cast around her as soon as she fully understood their real character. Guilty she certainly had been, but there was some limit to her guilt. I can hardly say that I was deceived. From the first I suspected the truth, and when I remained blind, I remained so wilfully. I had acted deliberately;—not from the strength of feeling, or the heat of passion, but coolly, from calculation, with full assent. There was a great difference between us. What hope, then, remained for me?

The world will laugh at me for all this, and wag their heads at the mighty magician starting back with fear of death and dread of hell. The world has no faith. If it can make sure of this life, it thinks we may jump, as Macbeth proposed, that which is to come. But the world is nothing to me now, and I am not moved by its mockeries. I am not ashamed to own my fears. I fear not dying. I fear what may come after death. I fear the last judgment. I fear hell. I fear being condemned to dwell forever with the damned. The salvation of my soul to me now is the great, the all-absorbing question—the question of questions.

Mr. Merton continued to visit me, and to unfold to me the scheme of Christian Redemption, and assured me that, if I willed it, there was salvation even for me, for Christ had died for all, had made ample satisfaction on the cross for the sins of the whole world, and that great as my sins were, they were surpassed by the Divine Mercy. He instructed me in what I had to believe, and in what I had to do. The baptismal waters were poured over me, and I was confirmed by the Holy Chrism, and I hope that my pact with Satan is broken, and my soul delivered. But I know not whether it be so or not; I know not whether I deserve love or hatred. I still fear and tremble, but will not despair. I am trying, as far as in my power, to undo the wrong I have done, and have dictated with that view these my confessions, which will see the light as soon as may be after I am no more.

All are kind to me. My friends, those who have known me in my pride and wickedness, strange to say, do not desert me; and those I love best are constantly near me, and do all they can to relieve my pain, and to strengthen my good resolutions. Priscilla is not unfrequently my nurse, and James is most kind and affectionate to me. If human aid or sympathy could avail me, I should have nothing to fear. But here I lie waiting my departure. How it will fare with me hereafter, God only knows. His will be done.

My story is told. My confessions, as far as I can make them to the public, are made. Let no man see in me an example to be followed, or regard me otherwise than as a miserable wretch who, in manhood and health, abused all God's gifts, and has nothing to relieve his character from utter detestation but a late death-bed repentance. My life can serve as a beacon; let it so serve. Yet I beg all whom I have wronged to forgive me, for I would, as far as possible, die in peace with all the world. I have nothing to forgive, for I have received no wrongs. I have done wrong to the world, but I have suffered no wrong from it. I cannot ask that my memory should be cherished, for it deserves only to be execrated. Yet is it pleasant to feel that there are some who, bad as I have been, still love me, and will drop a tear of sincere grief over my lifeless remains. There are, too, some who, from the abundance of their charity, will, as they pass by my final resting-place, breathe the prayer, so consoling to the living at least,—"May his soul rest in peace." After all, good is greater than evil, and love stronger than hell.

www.ingramcontent.com/pod-product-compliance
Lightning Source LLC
Chambersburg PA
CBHW011717240626
47153CB00009B/2899